In this work of fiction, the characters, places and events are either the product of the author's imagination or they are used entirely fictitiously. Any resemblance to any living person is purely coincidental and completely unintentional.

oOo

If you enjoy this story please take a moment to review it accordingly on Amazon and other sites.

Other books by John Pye

Pray To The Devils (Book Number 2 in the Brenan and Scott Series)

Cathedral of Lies – DI Doug Taylor Book 1.

Field of Lies – DI Doug Taylor Book2.

Guardian of Lies – DI Doug Taylor Book 3.

The Nick of Time – a humorous account of John Pye's service with Staffordshire police.

The Vampire of The Villas – a short story and the author's own true account of the death of a man who believed in vampires.

Acknowledgements

I would like to thank the following people for helping with this book:

Professor Dame Sue Black, DBE FRSE FRCP FRAI, leading forensic anthropologist and director of the Centre for Anatomy and Human Identification.

Sue Carney, MPhil, BSc(Hons), MCSFS, ChFP (Biology), chartered forensic practitioner and consultant forensic scientist

Julia Bell, 'The DNA Detective' from BBC's *Who Do You Think You Are*, BBC Radio 4's *Inside Science*, ITV's *Long Lost Family* and other DNA/genealogy based mystery and science programmes.

Professor Lorenzo Meseguer Luján, University of Salamanca (Spain) and cellist at City of Birmingham Symphony Orchestra.

Phil Lee, MA, PGCHPE, FHEA, Detective Chief Inspector and Senior Investigating Officer, Staffordshire Police (retired) and currently senior lecturer at Staffordshire University Institute of Policing, School of Law, Policing and Forensics.

Kevin McNulty, friend, detailer and editor.

Nick Tucker, Staffordshire Police (retired), friend, advisor and editor.

Andy Maxfield, Staffordshire Police (retired; police procedure).

Bridie North, Anatomical Pathology Technologist, Stoke Royal Hospital Mortuary.

Alan Faulkner, Staffordshire Police Firearms Dept (retired).

Gladys Pye, soulmate, wife, inspirer and encourager.

WHERE THE SILENT SCREAMS ARE LOUDEST

JOHN PYE

Chapter 1

Hanley, Stoke-on-Trent
Monday 15th April 2019

A FADING ECHO. A scream's fading echo, lingered somewhere in a dark, unseen corner.

Was that his imagination? Was it a scream? There could be no one down here... Could there?

The lift's door slid shut behind his single step forward. The diminishing rumble as it climbed away to its more usual destinations left him in the blackness of a vast lofty basement. It was a kind of blackness that could almost be touched – a blackness that makes the pulse race, and pushes even the soundest of minds towards panic.

Half a dozen inadequate fluorescent tubes flickered resentfully into life as his searching fingers stumbled upon the switch. A hesitant sigh of relief, a smidgen of composure restored.

Detective Constable Ed Stanier made a reluctant start at the job he'd been given. The slow crunching of his leather-soled shoes on the gritty concrete floor hinted at his uncertainty, his unease. The poor lighting didn't help. No windows down here, just row after row of ceiling-high wooden-racked shelving.

Even with the strip lights, the word gloomy still fitted. The torch in Stanier's right hand was a must, its beam playing back and forth over the regimented lines of dust-covered box files and brown paper evidence sacks.

He came to a halt to scrutinise the slip of paper in his left hand against a name which had been dedicated to one entire section of shelving: JACQUELINE MCGOVERN – MURDER. The thick marker-pen wording had been dulled by the years. He shook his head. He wasn't looking for a murder case, although that outcome seemed probable.

He moved on, now more familiar with the surroundings. He'd

been down here before but not often. He'd seen some terrible things during his life as a copper but there was something about this place that unnerved him.

Grief, pain, cruelty and horror filled these boxes on an unimaginable scale. Of course, everything was available on computer hard drives and memory sticks, but this was where he'd find the original signed statements and printed reports. This was where the gory SOCO photographs were kept; where the knives, the guns and poison bottles were stored; where victim's blood-stained clothing and plaster casts from crime scenes lived.

The pace of Stanier's footsteps picked up as he spotted a separate section of shelving: darker, dustier, visited even less than the other contents of the room. He had his bearings now. He knew where he should be looking. These were the serious cold case files, the unsolved murders, the unexplained hit and run road deaths, the missing people who never made it back home.

This was where the secrets were, where the ghosts lingered; this was where the incomplete jigsaws waited to be finished; this was where the silent screams were loudest.

Stanier's torch beam flickered across a case he remembered: *OPERATION SANDSTONE,* a triple murder enquiry. The inch-high victim's names were stencilled along the top bay: *Jennifer McQueen, Susan Hemmings, Erica Asquith.* Three names, three prostitutes, one case. Four double rows of five-metre-long shelving. A spate of DNA-connected murders. Unsolved serial killings going back up to fourteen years.

The detective found himself doing more head shaking as the countless long days and nights came back to him. The enquiry had been sent down here after three years of intensive investigation. The book was never closed on these cases. They were all dug out and reviewed occasionally but the gaps in between would get longer as the years passed and the layers of dust deepened.

The beam of light finally landed on what, by the size of it, was a pretty insignificant matter. Three box files, a ring binder and a brown paper exhibit sack. The name: *Poppy Hunt* was scrawled, freehand across the front. The additional words: *Missing Person* followed the name.

Within one minute Stanier was nervously heading back towards the lift, boxes piled under chin, evidence sack under arm. He'd be glad to be out of the place.

"Traffic Office" was the architect's proposed function for the police station's largest top floor room. That was when the place first opened back in 1965. It had served its purpose well as a busy central hub for the area's patrol car cops until the entire branch succumbed to government cutbacks in the early 2000s. The last occupants left behind a time capsule of dusty office furniture, broken chairs and faded yellow post-it notes. All had since moved on to pastures new, or retired. The spectre of closure and eventual demolition of the entire building now loomed on the horizon.

A mysterious phone call from CID supremo, Detective Chief Superintendent Geoff Brown the day before had put Detective Sergeant Yvette Brenan on notice that her routine was being disrupted yet again. His instructions to acquire a lockable, out-of-the-way office and trusted partner were the only detail he was prepared to give at that stage. Brenan's two conditions: 'Daylight and desk please, sir,' were easy to agree to.

'Yes, Eve, get whatever you need.'

The ridiculously oversized and shabby room was the only one available with functioning phone lines and Internet connections and so, by default, had become Brenan's new base. Nothing more than a stamped door number, *410,* now identified it. The original, handsome copper nameplate, with its stylish white sixties enamel lettering – *Traffic Office* – had mysteriously disappeared leaving four screw holes and a rectangle of dull, years-old, mismatching paint. No doubt, it now served as a nostalgic keepsake for some former patrol car driver.

The bank of wooden-framed hopper windows running the entire length of the room certainly fitted one of Brenan's stipulations, irrespective of the fact that the views afforded were nothing more inspiring than the police garage down below and the equally depressing horizon above. Her old brown wooden desk in the CID office had seen her through many long enquiries and was her other specified requirement. This, in spite of the fact that the room contained half a dozen abandoned green metal relics, some still with blotters in place and working biros in drawers.

The two red-faced, gasping detectives who had carted Brenan's desk into the lift from floor one and heaved it along the corridor were understandably inquisitive.

'What's going on, Sarge? What case you working?'

Brenan's glower and shake of the head spelled out the only answer they would get as clearly as if she'd said, *You should know better than that.*

Even if Brenan had been of a mind to tell them, she couldn't. DCS Brown's nine o'clock follow-up call that morning had merely drip-fed the intrigue enough to send Stanier down to the basement to retrieve the Poppy Hunt file. Ostensibly, it was looking like some sort of cold case review. But why the continuing secrecy?

The Poppy Hunt case had been reviewed as a matter of course just eighteen months before. That short gap, to Brenan's way of thinking, made this sudden cloak and dagger set-up all the more peculiar and even her own DCI did not yet know what was going on.

Ed Stanier was always going to be Brenan's first choice of oppo on any enquiry. They'd worked as a team on dozens of cases. The pair enjoyed a good working relationship. They were colleagues, trusted friends and mates. Stanier was old school and still preferred his suit and tie for normal working days. His comment of, 'Scruffy bugger,' was frequently said with sufficient volume to be overheard when one of his modern-day, long hair and jeans counterparts came within range.

A couple of inches short of six feet, stockily built, and with a routinely stern expression, Stanier looked every day of his forty-five years. His full head of neatly clipped hair was copy paper white, although his own description leaned towards silver/grey. No one could attest to its original colouring and even ancient course group photographs tended to suggest it had always been so. In police circles, particularly CID circles, Stanier was a rarity. The quietly spoken, veteran detective was a dedicated family man. His marriage to nursing sister Val had survived twenty-three years without a hiccup whilst those around him had succumbed to separation, divorce and remarriage on an epic scale. He'd never shown an interest in promotion and intentionally avoided taking the necessary examinations, but was acclaimed throughout the division as an expert on criminal law. His discreet advice to a senior officer or two, when a heat of the moment decision was about to be made, had saved the day on many occasions.

To be fair, DCS Brown's phone call had gone as far as describing the job as: '…a cold case review with a difference.' He'd paused before adding: 'possibly', and paused yet again to add: 'If the information's correct, Eve, then you'll understand the reasons for the mystery. Find out if there's any mileage in it. If there is, we'll be into a whole different ball game.'

Chapter 2

BRENAN EMPLOYED THE muscle of two gangling, acne-etched police cadets to shift the broken furniture to a far corner and salvaged a less-than-rickety desk for Stanier

The room seemed to have missed out on at least one round of redecoration since its closure and this added to its less than uplifting feel. The large-sized Rafa Nadal calendar she pinned against the grubby backdrop was a small attempt to add some colour. The two "working desks" were pushed into a corner against a radiator and close to the window. Other comforts included a small table supporting a kettle, mugs and tea caddy. A coat stand and waste-paper bin supplemented the corner oasis. Any number of metal and plastic stacking chairs were available from the three ceiling-high piles, as long as potential sitters were comfortable with the garish shade of red.

Brenan was at her desk, eyes fixed on laptop and note-making, as Stanier pushed the door open with a foot and struggled in. He placed the files down alongside her desk.

'That's all there is on it, Sarge.' The mood of the moment determined whether Stanier should refer to Brenan as "Sarge" or "Eve". When there were bosses about it was definitely "Sarge". He gave his nose a rub with the back of an index-finger as he spoke. 'It's all a bit dusty. I remember the case vaguely. It's got to be over ten years ago?'

Brenan's honey blonde ponytail bobbed as she looked up from her computer monitor. The colour was her latest attempt to cover the natural mousey brown which had recently allowed a few grey hairs to surface. The smile she gave Stanier offset the slight hardness present in her features. Strangely, it was that sculpted bone structure, that harsh, determined look which made her attractive; it forced men to take a second look.

She was no pushover. The two-inch scar on her left cheek had diminished as much as it ever would. It was a thin, pink, hardly noticeable reminder of the injuries she'd suffered four years before, arresting a fifteen stone off-licence robber on her way home after a long shift. The purchase of her nightly bottle of Shiraz had coincided with Sean Cafferty's blundering, drug-fuelled and axe-wielding attempt at a hold-up. The gormless thug would remember that night regretfully with every brushing of what remained of his teeth.

A double-crack of cartilage against bone issued from somewhere in Brenan's thirty-eight-year-old frame as she stood to her full five feet eight inches and stretched. She pushed a balled fist into her lower back and straightened up. Her smile evidenced the fact her own teeth had remained intact, white and perfect.

'Yes, eleven years more like. It was 2008. Summer, I think.'

Stanier lifted one of the stacking chairs down and settled opposite Brenan as she took the folder from the top of the pile and eased back into her own seat.

'So… Dead or alive?' Stanier said. 'I'm assuming she's turned up somewhere, so which of the two is it going to be after all this time. It's too soon for another standard review already.'

'Don't know myself yet, Ed. Must be something a bit different about this one, though, as we're expecting a visit from someone about DNA. That's pretty much all I do know.'

'Forensics on a Misper case? Does sound like a body then.' Stanier's puzzlement was showing on his forehead.

'Yes, my thoughts too. But…' Brenan looked directly at Stanier as she spoke. 'But this is not Forensics. It's a visit from a private individual. It could be a crank or some kind of headline-grabber. We won't know until we start talking.' She patted a hand down onto the folder. 'And, until then, this stays in here between you and me. This girl's parents are still out there,' she added as she opened the folder and ran a finger along the first few lines of typed detail. 'Probably still living at 27, Meerham Gardens on the Birchfield estate. Probably keeping her room ready and waiting for her to come home – even after eleven years. If there is something going on with this case after all this time, we may have to speak to them, and we'll need to know everything before we do that.'

Stanier gave a nod. 'So when do we get to see this DNA guy?'

'DNA *girl*,' Brenan corrected, and pointed at her monitor. 'Madeleine Scott. All I know is that she's some kind of self-professed private eye DNA investigator. When the DCS gave me the few crumbs he's allowed me, I imagined she was a busybody, a know-all trying to make a name for herself. I've done a few Internet searches and the jury's still out on that one. It's pretty easy to fake a plausible-sounding background on here.' She tilted her head towards the computer. 'But, if some of this stuff is real, then she's had some interesting success.' She patted the files. 'But never on police cases, always on genealogy-based mysteries.'

The three box files, ring binder and exhibit sack Stanier had found held nothing in comparison to the usual paperwork generated on a murder case, but they were all packed and bulging. There was a lot to go through. 'We need to get ourselves briefed on this case before *Ms* Scott gets here.' Her emphasis on the "Ms" was deliberate. 'It wouldn't look well for her to have the upper hand, whatever her game is. It's half eleven now and she hopes to be here for two.' Brenan selected a wad of paperwork and left Stanier to help himself.

The Missing Persons form itself was a standard one and had altered little in its format during the eleven years since fourteen-year-old Poppy Elizabeth Hunt disappeared off the face of the earth after school on Wednesday 11th June 2008. The form covered all the usual details and catered for numerous scenarios and eventualities, even though, nine times out of ten, the person would turn up within hours of the report being made.

Some of the questions must have seemed peculiar and unnecessary to a fretting mum or dad who just wished the policeman would get up off his fat arse and go looking. Wanting to know which dentist and doctor the child was registered with and things like a National Health Service number would appear pointless. The terrible fact was that, if the worst did eventually come to the worst, a dental chart could often prove the identity of a disfigured or decomposed corpse, and a doctor or hospital may be able to give other identifying features – maybe even DNA.

Immense steps forward in DNA had continued to benefit criminal investigation, medical study, and even genealogy, on levels which a few years before would have been impossible to comprehend. It was now considered a vital part of a missing person enquiry to be able to access the person's DNA profile.

Both of Poppy's parents had given a DNA sample to the police at the time of her disappearance, and these could have been used to compare with the DNA from a corpse should a body or skeleton ever be found. But, during the last case review, eighteen months before, the original exhibits were re-examined. The reviewing case officers went back over the initial scenes of crime work. It had all been undertaken meticulously and done with the thought in mind that future technological advancements might still tease out important clues which were then out of reach. Consequently, the girl's pink Wisdom toothbrush had been carefully bagged and stored away by SOCO back in 2008. The reviewers sent it for re-evaluation and, even with the passage of nine years, it quickly produced a result. It meant that Poppy's own full DNA fingerprint could be uploaded onto the Missing Persons Bureau data base. It might have seemed a belt and braces move but there was another reason. It discreetly manoeuvred around the problems that could have arisen if Poppy had been fathered by someone other than the man who believed he was her dad.

Everything had been processed and stored digitally from the beginning. The police HOLMES computer system (Home Office Large Major Enquiry System) had been operational for many years before Poppy went missing. It was a fact, though, that the original paper files Brenan and Stanier were going through were easier and quicker to access for an impromptu appraisal.

In any missing person enquiry, a recent photograph would be vital. Poppy's school photo was still pinned to the top left-hand corner of the form. The pin holding the three-inch square colour picture had rusted slightly and created two minuscule brown blemishes on the still-glossy surface. The girl, black blazer with the red badge of Birchfield High, white shirt and red tie, looked back at the camera, eyes wide and cheeks restraining that lovely smile from breaking into a full-blown, hand-covering-mouth giggle. She looked all of her innocent fourteen years and three months, but not a day more.

Stanier and Brenan soaked up the detail as they read through, seeing a familiar pattern of events unfolding. *Worried parents telephoning to say their daughter had not arrived home. The fact they had already called the school and spoken to her friends – the ones whose homes she would often visit.*

Vivid imagery formed of the customary police approach to what usually had a happy ending. *Parents sitting tightly together on the sofa; pensive expressions; mum close to tears; uniformed bobby opposite, folder of papers on knee, concerned face but with the stock reassurances: 'Don't worry yourselves. We get a couple of these every week. She'll be at a mate's house or doing something she's forgotten to tell you about.'*

By eleven o'clock that night, the stakes had been upped several notches. Police dogs were combing the local park. The police helicopter spent an hour noisily hovering back and forth, powerful search light and heat-seeking cameras probing the school grounds and the park.

A bigger hunt got underway the next day as the urgency increased and the dreadful possibilities became more real – police officers in overalls beating their way with sticks through the park's bracken and roadside bushes. Posters appeared compiled from that same school photo – red banner across the top: *MISSING PERSON* and the words, *Help Bring Poppy Hunt Home.* Neighbours helped the police by tacking the notices to trees and billboards and dishing them out for display in shops. The local newspaper featured a two-page spread including a half page taken up by her photograph.

The microscope focused onto the parents: their own background, their friends, their interests and personal lives. It was clear from the beginning, though, that the Hunts – dad and mum, David and Laura, and seventeen-year-old sister Katie – each played their part in a loving, hard-working, clean-living, well-balanced family. The fact they had to endure an in-depth police search of their house was a terrible, but necessary, part of police procedure.

Copies of everything were neatly filed in the boxes. A DVD was included, covering recordings of the TV news reports and the Crimewatch programme which reconstructed events leading to the girl's disappearance. A tear-jerking interview with the parents formed part of the filmed records. A more recent DVD covered a Crimewatch update which went hand in glove with the last police review. A computer hard drive was tucked into the box containing the entire HOLMES backup.

At exactly one o'clock, Stanier's stomach grumblings notified him that his day-in, day-out staple lunchtime diet of inch-thick peanut butter sandwiches was calling him. The documents the pair had managed to read through gave them enough to make only a brief assessment, but they'd got the drift.

'Seem to have covered all bases from what I can see,' Stanier said, rising and grabbing his butty box.

'Looks that way,' Brenan hoisted her shoulder bag into position and picked up her own foil-wrapped prawn salad bap.

Chapter 3

FIVE FEET ELEVEN inches, auburn haired, bony. Madeleine Scott presented her business card at the public enquiry desk at half past two. With briefcase held against knees of skinny-fit denim jeans she smiled through the security glass. The hair was scraped into a tight bun. It gave an unrestricted view of how the arms of her overly large, black-framed glasses clung precariously to her ears. The three-inch high heels could well have been made from the same red leather as the Cubitt briefcase.

Five feet two inches, balding, plump. Enquiry office clerk Stan led Scott through the security door to the lift and then upwards to the top floor. Each of Scott's pointed-toe strides appeared a match for two of Stan's.

The two detectives rose to their feet as the woman, complete with dangling "Visitor" lanyard, was shown in. She looked around, eyes wide and mouth slightly open in bewilderment at the large, dilapidated space. Their own impassive expressions included fixed eye contact and a single nod apiece. None of this was rehearsed but might as well have been. It was one of those police traits done almost by instinct. It was difficult for them to hide their automatic cynicism of Scott. She was a non-police person, apparently claiming to know more than they did about a serious police matter. Brenan was wary but knew an open mind was a must. She spoke first, outstretching her right hand in greeting, 'Miss Scott, I'm Detective Sergeant Brenan.' She glanced at her colleague. 'This is DC Stanier.'

Stanier's handshake preceded his open-hand gesture towards the spare stacking chair at the desk end. 'Nice to meet you,' he said out of good manners, although he was unsure of his own honesty. Scott perched her wiry frame on the edge of the seat, briefcase on her lap.

'I see you've looked me up,' she bowed her head to where her own name lingered in the Google search bar of Brenan's screen. 'I have no qualifications in DNA research or crime detection. My own field for the past seven years has been in genealogy – researching family trees for private clients in the main. Something which, although I say it myself, I know my way around pretty well. I've been involved with the DNA side of genealogy since the private firms first started in this field.' She gave a long sigh before getting into her explanation. The metaphor *walking on eggshells* was firmly in her mind. 'Before I begin to explain my interest in the Poppy Hunt case, can I talk you through my understanding of the police DNA system and how my field can overlap.'

'Be our guest,' Brenan said, her tone neutral.

'As you know,' Scott gave a nervous cough, 'much better than I do, the National DNA Database, used by the police – the NDNAD – stores DNA fingerprints, profiles, call them what you will. It holds both the DNA of criminals and that recovered from crime scenes. It matches them up and hopefully spits out the name and mugshot of the offender you're looking for. That's if their DNA is already on file from a previous arrest of course.'

Brenan required no lectures on these points. She was trying hard not to be rattled by this outsider. She reluctantly forced herself to accept that Scott needed to state certain facts to elaborate on what she had to say, whatever that was going to be.

Scott continued, 'Family tree research has been one of the world's most popular hobbies for a long time now. Some of the private firms specialising in genealogy have expanded their business by getting into DNA research. They use it as a tool to trace distant family members and other heritage links.'

Brenan's expression showed a hint of uncertainty. She knew a little of this but had nothing more than a layman's understanding. Stanier's look suggested similar.

'These private firms,' Scott went on, 'make particular use of what is called *familial* DNA searching. They can compare a sample sent in by a person wanting to find distant relatives with all the others on their database and quickly find everyone who may be related. It doesn't matter how small the link is, the computer will spot it and from the amount of DNA shared between the two can even suggest what the relationship may be. They've quickly developed huge databases, far bigger than any of the national ones used by police forces. That's because their participants are willing contributors wanting to track down distant relatives.

'The UK's NDNAD, the world's largest national site, currently holds over seven million profiles of convicted criminals and people awaiting trial. The genealogy sites are much bigger. AncestryDNA, for instance, has almost twenty million people.'

Brenan's face flickered some surprise at this huge difference.

Scott continued. 'The genealogy firms' speciality of tracing distant relatives through *familial* DNA searching is effective and enormously popular.' She had put emphasis on her two uses of the word "familial". She was treading carefully. She needed to be sure the two detectives were up to speed with the term and how different the searching methods were between the NDNAD and the genealogy sites. The last thing she wanted to do was come over as a smart arse.

Brenan's arms-folded, back-upright posture had, so far, created a rather stand-offish atmosphere. She relaxed her shoulders, placed her hands down on her knees and offered a nod of understanding. It was clear that Scott was working hard not to step on toes. The tension needed easing. She leaned forward across the desk, placed a hand to her chest and managed a genuine smile. 'I'm Yvette… Eve, if that's okay, and this is Ed.'

'Great, I'm Mad.'

Brenan's quick sideways glance at Stanier lasted a millisecond before the penny dropped. Her tight-lipped smile morphed into a grin. 'Madeleine… Mad. Coffee?'

Scott's eyebrows raised above her glasses at the offer. 'Please. That M6 was the usual bastard.'

Brenan put the coffees together and invited Scott to help herself to milk and sugar. She leaned back into her chair with her own mug clasped beneath her chin and pondered the genealogist's words for a few seconds. *Yes, she'd heard of familial DNA checks and knew the police system was capable of something similar.*

'We can only get access to familial checks in the most serious of cases,' she said. 'It's not often allowed as it can be expensive in terms of manpower. Familial DNA searches, from a police perspective, are where the offender is *not* on the database. It concerns looking further afield, trying to trace any blood relatives from the crime scene stain he's left behind who *are* listed on the NDNAD. People who might be related to him. We'd then have to use detective work to try and find our suspect by interviewing those blood relatives who *do* show up on file. We'd be asking them if they could point the finger at one of their own relatives. If they couldn't, or refused, we might even find ourselves involved in family tree research.'

Scott nodded. 'Yes, as I understand it, the police database is really designed to find only *positive* matches, to find a person with a DNA profile which is exactly the same as a crime scene stain.' She looked at Brenan as she gave her own examples of how the police system worked. 'DNA in a rape case from semen would be a good example, or maybe from skin cells in a glove left behind at a crime. The NDNAD is constantly comparing those crime scene stains with the profiles of people already on record, and with the profiles of newcomers to the database and new crime scene stains appearing on the database.'

Brenan's nods of agreement throughout seemed to endorse Scott's grasp of the police system.

Stanier leaned forward to interrupt. 'Fascinating, but I'm wondering where our missing girl Poppy Hunt comes into this.'

'Okay. I'm getting to it, but bear with me.'

Stanier reluctantly sat back in his chair, allowing her to carry on.

'The police national database calibrates its DNA samples into a couple of lines of numbers and letters. That resulting string of characters is common to one person alone – a sort of registration plate, if you like.' She shrugged. 'Okay, so identical twins do have the same code, but research has even come up with ways to disseminate between those now. The reality is that the odds of two random people having the same DNA code are billions to one against.'

The detectives felt as though they'd not learned anything

particularly new yet. They exchanged a glance with each other both trying hard to keep their impatience under control whilst also respecting Scott's need to compare the police system with the genealogy ones. They watched as she flicked up the catches on her briefcase and extracted a batch of paperwork and a Dell laptop. She withdrew an eight-inch glossy photograph from her papers, placed it face-up and slid it across to the desk's centre. It was an enlarged copy of the same Poppy Hunt picture they were already familiar with.

She resumed her explanation. 'The DNA profiles of missing persons in the UK are stored on a separate database. It's yet another acronym, the MPDD – or Missing Persons DNA Database runs alongside the NDNAD. You both know only too well that the most common use of *that* DNA fingerprint would *usually* only ever arise if Poppy's body turned up somewhere to prove it was her.'

Brenan gave a solemn nod at Scott's all-too-true words as the genealogist continued. 'DNA is processed and calibrated differently on the genealogical sites than the methods used on the NDNAD. Unlike the police, those publicly available genealogy sites are not looking for *identical* matches. They're looking for *partial* matches, for DNA shares, for blood relatives. More often than not, these will be people completely unknown to the family tree researcher who's sent in his or her own sample. The results, though, *will* be people *definitely* related to them somehow or other. Firms like AncestryDNA can search and compare the DNA profiles as each new participant sends in a sample. They can hunt down even the vaguest of family ties. The tiniest DNA share often provides a remote connection to a distant and, until then, unknown relative.'

Scott glanced from Brenan to Stanier and back a couple of times, checking that they were still with her. Their single nod apiece suggested they were keeping up and encouraged her to plough on. 'As you've already said, the NDNAD *can* carry out familial searches in serious crimes where the offender is not on file. The thing is, though, with the limited numbers on the NDNAD there may be no strong matches at all. There could be hundreds of minutely associated people. A complex enquiry into each slightly connected person would be hugely expensive and could even involve in-depth family tree work. Okay, if you were lucky and there was a strong match, it would show at the top of the list. It could give a good starting point for enquiries to find your suspect. It could be a parent or a child, which may be fairly easy for detectives to work back from to find the person they're after, but it's rarely going to be easy.

'The publicly available sites have developed algorithms within their systems designed specifically to find even the tiniest of DNA shares *and* to suggest what each relationship might be. The NDNAD doesn't have these algorithms and it doesn't have the huge numbers to work with. Its success with familial searches is limited.'

Scott took a second photograph from her papers, but placed it face-down alongside Poppy's picture. She made no reference to it and continued with her explanation. 'When I'm working on a family tree for someone where a DNA profile has been submitted, I'll quickly get back indications of distant relatives from the genealogy firm. More often than not, the person who's sent in the sample will already have attached an online family tree they've started to build. I can use this to move the research along as most of the hard work will already have been done for me. Strong connections to other DNA submissions can show up quickly, depending on the strength of the DNA share.' She wrinkled her nose. 'I frequently get ones showing only a tiny percentage – maybe a distant cousin. The actual connection may go back centuries to, perhaps, a six, seven or eight times great grandparent.'

She turned over the second photograph and adjusted it to line up perfectly with Poppy's.

The photographs were the same size but the second showed a young child of, perhaps, eight or nine. The striking thing, though, was that it was the same face. It *was* Poppy Hunt. A younger version. But the clothing and hair style showed it was a boy.

Brenan's and Stanier's eyes drifted up from the photograph and met in a silent, open-mouthed stare.

Chapter 4

THE PHOTOGRAPH SHOWED the child had not yet embarked on the divergent path following puberty where the features and body would morph unmistakably into a male. It was also clear that, regardless of whatever changes the future might bring, those facial characteristics were, and always would be, uncannily on parallel lines to Poppy Hunt.

'Christ,' Stanier said. '*That* is weird. I mean, it could be her. When was this taken?'

'Two months ago.' Scott's finger pressed down onto the boy's photograph. 'He's coming up to eight now. Jason Fitzgerald. He's at Wardlow Primary School in Stafford – bright little lad.'

Brenan and Stanier waited in silence for Scott to deliver more.

'A new teacher started at Wardlow three months ago,' Scott said as she pulled more paperwork from her briefcase and cast her eyes over it. 'Mrs Anita Greaves. She's twenty-five and transferred from Birchfield Primary School following her marriage and house move over to the Stafford area.'

The mention of Birchfield was the first signal of a real connection. Poppy's school had been Birchfield High and, before that, Birchfield Primary. She lived on the Birchfield estate. Brenan shuffled her chair closer to the table as Scott went on.

'Mrs Greaves had been a pupil herself at both Birchfield Primary and Birchfield High before doing a degree at Nottingham University. She lived on the Birchfield estate just fifty yards from Poppy.'

Scott looked up at Brenan. 'She was Poppy's best mate. They were inseparable. They sat next to each other at school and even holidayed along with parents a few times.'

'Annie Shephard,' Stanier said, recalling the girl's name from his quick scan of the paperwork.

'Exactly,' said Scott. 'We have a lot to thank Mrs Greaves for. Her powers of observation and tenacity in bringing this to notice are the reasons we're here talking about this. Annie knew there was something more to it. Poppy's disappearance hit her hard as a child and never left her. She was intrigued by the similarities and couldn't leave it alone.'

Scott had the detectives' attention now. 'The teacher spoke with the boy's parents. She told them of Jason's similarity to her old school mate but initially held back the fact Poppy had been missing for eleven years. The parents added more intrigue when they divulged that they'd fostered Jason soon after his birth and then adopted him.' Scott took a long pause. 'He was a foundling. Abandoned when he was just a few days' old.' She pulled an A4 photocopy from the bundle and handed it to Brenan. 'They had the newspaper cuttings and all the information.'

Brenan held one hand against her mouth, forehead wrinkling as she took in the details of the old newspaper cutting with its black and white, inch-high heading: *Newborn Boy Abandoned on Housing Estate.*

Blue biro handwriting headed the page: *Sentinel Newspaper, Saturday 12th February 2011.*

A photo showed a tiny baby wrapped in a towel, white hospital skull cap pulled down above chubby sleeping face, nasogastric tube taped to nose.

'So where *was* he found?' Stanier said.

Scott's wide-eyed tilt of the head forewarned of another surprise. 'On the doorstep of Birchfield Medical Centre, less than a quarter of a mile from Poppy's home.'

A tragic story was emerging as the minds of the two detectives raced ahead with theories. The doppelgänger mystery and the geographical connections were still not really providing a positive link to the missing girl, though.

'They've not told the boy about his background yet,' Scott said. 'Social Services provided them with as much of his history as was known. It's left to the adoptive parents to decide when to tell the child and I guess it must be a nightmare decision to make.'

Both Stanier and Brenan folded their arms and silently pondered the possibilities. Scott evidently had more up her sleeve.

'The adoptive parents had an unusually clear-minded approach to the situation. They understood that at some point in the future Jason may want to trace his true family. Mrs Greave – Annie – knew a bit about family tree investigation as her husband has been researching his own for a couple of years. He suggested a DNA test on the boy through one of the publicly available firms and they agreed. It was just a spit sample. Annie realised that someone who could quickly unravel the mysteries of a family tree would be useful, hence my involvement.'

She took a sip at her coffee. 'I arranged a meeting with the parents and Social Services on the best way forward. I was firm on the issue of confidentiality. It was vital that nothing should leak out, but also – and more importantly – that Jason's rights, even as an eight-year-old, should be considered. At that stage we were still looking at nothing more solid than a little boy having a striking likeness to a girl who'd gone missing eleven years ago.'

Brenan shot a glance at Stanier as the intrigue grew.

'So,' Scott continued, 'the parents and Social Services were happy for me to handle the matters. Jason's sample was sent off with me named as the investigating genealogist.'

Scott opened the lid of her laptop and switched on as she spoke. 'The results came back via email within ten days.' Her computer was soon displaying a page with a logo for an independent genealogy research firm: *Geneaus DNA*. Various graphics and different sections filled the screen. A thick grey band headed the page and, within it, a string of white letters spelled out: *Hello, J.F. (page managed by Madeleine Scott).*

No explanation was needed – "J.F" was clearly Jason Fitzgerald.

A small cameo profile of a head with short, cropped hair and shaded in blue gave the clue that J.F was male. A column to the left was headed: *Ethnicity Estimate*. A pie-chart gave suggestions on Jason's distant, mostly English, origins.

A central column was headed: *DNA Matches*. A number of small photographs had been inserted below this. These were individual family tree enthusiasts whose files had been automatically linked as distant blood relatives. A short line of text read: *Two hundred and thirty-seven 1st to 8th cousins traced.*

Brenan was surprised at the number. Scott noticed. 'Yes, two hundred and thirty-seven may seem a lot but actually it's about average. Not a bad thing – less for me to try and work through.' She then hovered the cursor over the button marked: *View All DNA Matches.* She clicked and a different screen heading appeared: *J.F's DNA Matches.*

'Obviously we're always confined by the parameters of who's actually decided to investigate their own history or family connections, *and* sent off a DNA sample. Believe me, the numbers are huge and often the relatives can be so remote that even contemplating joining up the dots brings on nightmares.' She scrolled the page up until she reached the beginning of the actual list. Line after line, two hundred and thirty-seven different names.

A cameo profile commenced each entry, blue ones like Jason's, and pink and pony-tailed outlines for females. One or two had even been substituted with a tiny .jpg photograph inserted by the DNA donor. A forename and surname followed each photo or cameo, although some people had opted for the anonymous route and supplied initials or a nickname in the same manner as Scott had done for Jason.

'The list starts with the strongest connections to Jason and works down to the weakest. We all have an equal fifty-fifty share of DNA with our parents, but that reduces with every step forward to grandchildren or backward to grandparents. It weakens further when you go out sideways to aunts, uncles and cousins.'

'So I'm gathering,' Stanier said, 'that the bigger the percentage of DNA share the relative has, the closer the relationship is?'

'Exactly that,' Scott said. 'An easy to follow example would be a child. As I said, a child shares fifty percent of his or her DNA with the father and fifty percent with the mother. Twenty-five percent of that DNA would therefore be shared with each grandparent and so on down the line. When you start to work out further afield into aunties and uncles who would be perhaps sisters or brothers of your parents it diminishes further and further still within their own children who would be your cousins, but the link is still there and still traceable.'

Scott hovered the cursor over the first name in the list. It was a pink profile and showed the name Barbara Spruce. 'This lady is the closest relation to Jason who has submitted DNA, no doubt in an effort to help with her own family tree. She shows as being a possible first to second cousin to Jason. That word "cousin" is a generalised term at this point and the computer arrives at this through the specific amount of DNA shared between the two subjects.'

She gave the detectives an inquisitive stare. She knew she'd been bombarding them with complex facts and here were a few more. 'So, the DNA share is measured in a value called centimorgans. We all have about 6,800 centimorgans, so you'd share around 3,400 with each parent. This lady shares a mere 253 centimorgans with Jason and the computer works that out, in these generalised terms, to possibly be a first to second cousin. The genealogy computers are pretty clever with these relationship possibilities but, in the more distant ones, there can be an overlap, hence the description "first to second". In point of fact, it can go even further to predict more accurate relationships. She clicked her mouse again and now the prediction suggested that Barbara Spruce was in fact a first cousin once removed.

Brenan and Stanier had been trying to keep up as they trawled the confused ideas they had in their own minds. Without a large sheet of paper and a free half hour it seemed daunting. They were now convinced, though, that Scott really knew what she was talking about.

Scott took the last sip from her now-cold coffee and got back into her stride. 'I've spent the past few days involved with emails and, more recently, telephone calls to Australia. I've been in touch with Barbara Spruce.' The pause she left was not intentionally for effect but it had one. 'She is thirty-seven, a dance teacher, and lives in Melbourne.'

Brenan and Stanier looked on, amazed at the lengths the woman had gone to.

'My conversation with Barbara has revealed the following.' She stabbed the keyboard again and yet another screen appeared. It showed a small and simplified section of a family tree. The name Barbara Spruce occupied the bottom with her maiden name given as Davey. A black line led upwards to the name of her mother, Mrs Beverley Davey. Beverley's maiden name showed as Trickett.

Brenan blinked. 'Wow! Trickett. That's Poppy's mum's maiden name.' She found her eyes drifting back to the two photos.

'Correct,' Scott said. 'Beverley Davey is Poppy's mum's elder sister. Her daughter, Barbara, married and emigrated several years ago and it is her who shows as being Jason's blood relative.'

Scott pushed herself back into her chair and exhaled as she prepared the bombshell she was about to deliver. 'The relationship suggested by the computer that Barbara Spruce is Jason's first cousin once removed fits entirely with my theory.'

'Which is…?' Brenan's words petered out as the pieces of a three-dimensional jigsaw started to slot together in her mind.

'That Jason Fitzgerald is Poppy Hunt's son.'

Brenan swallowed hard as gears and cogs slammed into place inside her mind and the full implications meshed. 'So Poppy had a baby eight years ago. Three years *after* she disappeared off the face of the Earth.'

Scott gave two solemn head nods. 'That's what it's beginning to look like. She would have been seventeen.'

'She's still alive.' Stanier phrased the words as a statement, a sort of a hopeful remark rather than a question.

'Well, if I'm right, she certainly was eight years ago.' Scott's voice had become hushed. 'But eight years is a long time.'

Brenan got to her feet and stared out at the horizon. The summit of the old Hanley Deep colliery slag heap loomed like a volcano, high above a building line of 1960s tower blocks. Attempts at grassing and foresting its surface had made patchy progress over the years. A sole surviving pottery kiln stood defiantly, seventy years since its last firing. The bottle-shaped brickwork shoulders and neck had become a nursery for self-set bushes and brambles.

The scene evoked reminders of the area's vanished industrial past. It also prefaced the social decline now poisoning the area more than any toxic spoil tip or smoke-belching pottery factory could ever do. A fleeting memory came back to Brenan of how she and the other kids used to hurtle down the steep sides of the loose slag heap on discarded pieces of tin – blackened faces, squeals of delight.

The memory was gone as quickly as it came. 'She's out there somewhere,' Brenan said, eyes fixed. 'Someone's holding her.'

Chapter 5

Day 2 Tuesday 16th April

'FUCKIN' HELL, EVE!'

The words were those of Detective Chief Inspector Dominic Forrest. It was the following morning and Forrest was seated in his second floor office. His wall clock showed sixteen minutes past nine. The fifteen minutes he'd taken to read through Brenan's report had been silent. The one stray minute of time had been taken up by the unlocking of his door, the removing of his coat and the settling down into his chair. The frown he made as he'd fumbled for his key came with some irritation at being ambushed by the two detectives waiting outside his office. What could be this important?

Forrest was a good looking, broad-shouldered and dark-haired six-footer. To Brenan's way of thinking, in recent years, he had lost his direction and drive in favour of the promotion ladder. He'd been a good cop and a no-nonsense thief taker in his early years, but some of that obsession with the job had led to separation and ultimately divorce. Since then the nickname "Forrest Grump" seemed to fit him well. There was no pleasing this man. Brenan's usual mistrusting scepticism of everyone categorised him as "uncompromising and petulant". To her mind, his budget cutting and political correctness had become priorities that soared high above actual crime detection.

Forrest's career strategy since then had taken him quickly through the ranks in his fifteen years of service. Conversely, the disregard of such matters by Brenan had halted her own twenty-one-year career at detective sergeant.

The report, still open at its last page on Forrest's blotter, was the reason Brenan had worked through until nine o'clock the night before without claiming the due four hours' overtime. It meticulously detailed the entire sequence of events and went on to draw possible comparisons with two infamous Austrian crimes and a Californian case where young girls had been kidnapped and held in captivity for years. Regular rape, the resulting children, and the treatment of those children at the hands of the offender made Brenan's account both thought-provoking and chilling in equal measure. She had, in her usual, inimitable way, managed to hammer home in grand and sickening style every vile scenario possible. The bit was firmly between her teeth and no amount of political correctness or sycophantic ladder-climbing by bosses would stand in her way. She was determined to find out what had happened to Poppy Hunt and to bring the person responsible to justice. Most importantly, if Poppy *was* still alive, she *would* find her.

After reading the four and a half pages there would be few senior officers, Police and Crime Commissioners or higher politicians who would dare to gamble their jobs with budget cutting on this one. Brenan knew the meticulous writing-up of the entire sequence of events, along with the hours of Google research she had spent on like cases, was the only way to circumvent attempts by Forrest or other top brass to stall the enquiry.

'Fuckin' hell, Eve!' Forrest repeated with a slight increase in volume. 'Even *I've* been kept in the dark on this up until now.' His shake of the head was a restrained show of displeasure that Detective Chief Superintendent Brown had kept his cards so close to his chest. Perhaps even more annoying was the fact that, apart from Brown – and probably the Deputy Chief Constable – the two people entrusted with the details were about as junior in rank to him as was possible.

Forrest stole a sideways glance at Brenan. Her reputation frequently preceded her. That temper was renowned throughout the county and her crime clear-up rate was the stuff of legends. Oddly, these were traits that could hold a person back in the modern police force – or police service, as Forrest had now taken to calling it.

'So, DCS Brown knows you're letting me in on the secret now then?' Forrest asked with a degree of sarcasm.

'Yes, boss,' Brenan responded, holding back a smile but managing to inject her own sarcasm. 'I spoke to him as soon as Miss Scott left last night.'

Forrest stared at the paperwork. 'Without question, if the child is proved conclusively to be Poppy's this will develop into a major enquiry sooner or later.'

Brenan grimaced. 'If the child is hers, and if she really is still alive, then a word in the wrong place could create a media explosion – TV, newspapers... If the story got out, it could panic the offender into drastic action. It could sound the death knell for Poppy.'

Forrest nodded more than his uncompromising temperament would usually allow. He'd quickly identified that one wrong move on this could be a career-stopper for him too. 'Okay, what's your next step?'

Brenan looked at Stanier. This was his cue. He was the legal man.

'We need to be certain, without any doubts,' the detective began, 'any doubts whatsoever, that Jason is Poppy's child, and we need to begin the evidence chain. We must start from day one as we mean to go on, and with the thought in mind that we *will* get this bastard in court eventually. That means all this new evidence must pass through our own accredited experts. It must all be logged, exhibit-labelled and statemented.'

Forrest had hardly started to come to terms with what the case entailed but this pair were already thinking about a court file.

Brenan took the lead again. 'The only way to properly compare Poppy's DNA is for our lab to get hold of Jason's sample.' She dug into her pocket. The polythene exhibit bag she pulled out contained something familiar to Forrest: a plastic DNA swab container.

'Madeleine has been thinking ahead from the beginning on this.' Brenan dangled the item. 'She's saved us a lot of time by having the forethought to take a buccal swab from Jason, along with the spit sample she used for the genealogy site. This can go straight off to the lab today. It can be compared to Poppy's Missing Person Database file and the boffins should quickly be able to establish if, indeed, Jason is her son.'

Stanier leaned forward in his chair. 'And that will be the first in our chain of evidence.'

Forrest pressed a finger to his lips. 'If you get it off to the lab, I'll make a request for a rapid result.'

'Cheers, boss.' Brenan gave a small cough and handed over a second report. 'This one covers the detail for that lab work on the swab, but you'll see that I've also gone to some lengths to ask for additional work on it.'

A vertical crease appeared between Forrest's eyes. He had a distinct feeling that he was not going to like this.

'Madeleine has pointed out that Jason's DNA sample will contain fifty percent of his mother's DNA, and that will make it a fairly simple job for the lab to compare it with Poppy's and so prove that she is the mother. Equally it could disprove that.' Brenan left a long pause. 'Madeleine also points out that Jason's sample will contain fifty percent of his father's DNA.'

The comment hit Forrest like a bombshell. He sat forward in his chair immediately understanding what Brenan was getting at.

She continued. 'We need to trawl the NDNAD to see if Jason's father is in there. If he is, we could crack this entire case within days. If Poppy really is still alive, this could lead us straight to her.' Brenan paused. 'This kind of search is technically a familial search.'

This last point upstaged Forrest. Budget figures had now entered the equation. He blew out loudly. 'Familial searches on the NDNAD are a real rarity. They cost an absolute fortune. We'd have to present the case in detail to the FINDS Strategy Board.' Forrest loved his acronyms and wanted to regain a little kudos after what he considered a rebuff by DCS Brown. 'Forensic Information Database Strategy Board,' he expounded. 'We won't be able to do anything without their say-so if we're after a familial search.'

Brenan lifted her left hand slightly from the desk top and showed a flattened palm to Forrest. It was her attempt at a diplomatic "slow down and listen" to her senior officer – diplomacy was never her strong suit. 'Yes, boss, you're right,' she said, attempting to dilute the apparent disrespect. 'Madeleine has explained the difficulties with familial DNA searches on our system. It *can* be done, but it doesn't automatically produce the detailed results the public genealogy sites do. It often leads to hundreds of possible hits all requiring family tree research which may or may not lead to an offender. That's why it's expensive and time consuming. However –' she inched forward – 'if our lab were to instigate a familial search using Jason's DNA profile as a crime scene stain, but looking for nothing other than a full fifty percent paternal-only match, it could be game over in a day or so. Yes, it would technically be a familial search, but with the slimmest of search parameters. So, no hundreds of possible relations, no massive amounts of detective work. If his dad is hiding inside the NDNAD we've got him and maybe Poppy as well.'

Forrest held his breath as his mind caught up. This could put the finishing tape in sight even before the starting pistol fired.

Clearly Brenan had done her own research. 'Sir, I think you'll find I've covered everything in that second report. You'll see it includes a plea to the FINDS Board to carry out a familial search on Jason's sample, but only for a fifty percent paternal match. Absolutely nothing more. They can't fail to approve it. The Chief Constable or the Deputy could email this straight through to FINDS. Every hour could be vital.'

Forrest reddened. He could feel himself being undermined so much he was in danger of the floor swallowing him up. But, if this went tits-up, any delaying tactics on his part could be dangerous to his future. As for saving face on the issue of his diminished authority… His smile returned and the redness paled.

'Okay. I'll get straight on to DCS Brown and see if we can get the Dep to shunt it off to the FINDS Board with a follow-up phone call.'

'Thanks, boss.' Brenan's hesitation and small cough gave Forrest a distinct feeling of *déjà vu.*

'You'll see in the second report that I've also made reference to Miss Scott and how valuable her work has been. We'd never have found any of this out had it not been for her. My additional request is that she, Miss Scott, is allowed to work alongside us – in the short term at least.'

Forrest screwed up his face so much it reminded Brenan of her neighbour's pug, but she ploughed on.

'Madeleine remains in charge of Jason's genealogy investigations. Whilst we can't use those details or resources in any criminal investigation, Madeleine is still legally able to research the boy's ancestors. If the NDNAD search for his father fails – if he has no criminal record – then Madeleine believes she could possibly find links to him through family tree work.'

Forrest slumped back in his chair. 'Asking a lot there, Eve.'

'She's on our side, sir, Brenan said. 'She wants nothing out of this. Maybe a few expenses would be fair, though.' This point was added as though it was already a done deal.

Forrest looked down at his desk. 'She'd have to be checked. Background, pre-convictions, all of that before they even think about letting her work further with us. But I agree, it sounds like sense. I'd need a detailed report.'

'It's all in there, sir.' Her eyes landed on the report Forrest was holding. 'She's single, aged thirty-six and got her own apartment in Milton Keynes. University degree in English Language and English Lit, studied law and gained an LLB through Open University, applied to join West Mids Police a few years back but failed on the eyesight. Has run her own business as a consultant genealogist for seven years and trades under the name *WhoRU*. No pre-cons unless you're going to count a speed camera ticket six months ago.'

Forrest made an intentionally over-the-top stunned face. 'Bloody hell, Eve! What time did you get to bed last night? I suppose you're going to hand me a list of everyone who knows about this now, or have I finally caught you out on that one?'

Brenan smirked and handed the typed A4 across the desk. 'That includes Social Services people, adoptive parents, Australian relatives, schoolmate and police personnel right up to you, me and Ed.'

Forrest ran his eyes down the list. 'Fourteen and counting. If we do get positive proof that the boy is Poppy's, it won't be long before we have to tell the parents what's going on.'

Forrest was left punch drunk and pondering how to go about the vitally important steps that had been laid at his door.

Brenan and Stanier made it back to the fourth floor by quarter past ten. Stanier's first job involved another journey down to his least favourite place, the basement. He arrived in the gloom filled with dread and with the hairs on the back of his neck ready to prick up at a moment's notice. His task was a difficult one. He wasn't really sure where to start looking for a file on a foundling baby. It was not a category to crop up every day and there was little doubt that, whoever had filed it, had the same dilemma. The main index book helped little. "Abandoned", "Foundling" and "Baby" produced nothing. The seasoned detective tuned into his twenty-five years of police jargon, legal definitions and cop's mentality. He started to leaf through from the beginning until he stopped at the heading: *Children and Young Persons Act (UNSOLVED).*

The sub-heading had not required much imagination: *Baby Jason.*

Stanier's echoing stroll landed him at the unsolved section within moments. He waved his torch across the numbered bay and quickly homed in on the meagre assemblage: two box files and one paper exhibit sack. All bore a handwritten thick blue marker-pen title: C & YP BABY JASON 11th Feb 2011.

Now, back at the lift, he stood in the gloom awaiting its trundling arrival. He took one last edgy look back over his shoulder as he placed the consignment inside – he was keen to be out of this place. The pressure of his fumbling thumb on the basement's light switch returned the vast space to its coal-mine blackness. The noise that came as the door closed jolted his eyes into an angled sideways stare. He could almost have convinced himself that the small metal-on-metal shriek was something more sinister – but that would have been daft.

Stanier dumped the consignment down alongside Brenan's desk. 'I bloody hate it down there. Next time go yourself.'

Brenan looked up from her computer screen. Her rolled eyes accompanied a grin. 'Hopefully there won't be a next time – not on this case anyway. Let's take a look at the exhibits.'

Stanier cleared his own desk and removed the contents of the exhibit sack. Each item was sealed in separate transparent plastic bags of different sizes. Printed lettering and dotted lines took up one whole side of each bag to cater for the required detail, including the description of the item, officer seizing, and time and date. The dotted lines had been filled in with handwritten permanent marker. A separate list showed names, times and dates to account for every removal and examination. Page and paragraph numbers were given to the documentation in the box files so reference could be made, and the result or progress of examinations.

One eighteen-inch square bag was marked with a general title: *SOCO (Fingerprints and Tapings).* It contained a multitude of individually numbered bags collected and recorded by the scenes of crime officer. The term SOCO or Scenes of Crime Officer had changed title during the eight years since Baby Jason appeared outside Birchfield Medical Centre. They were now known as Crime Scene Investigators, or CSI. Advances in forensic science constantly made this aspect of police work more complex, but the general role of the position remained unaltered. The two detectives had worked under both regimes but frequently drifted back to the more commonly known title of SOCO. The smaller bags contained dozens of different fingerprints and adhesive-taped particle specimens taken from the Medical Centre door's woodwork, glass and handrail poles. These sixty-two exhibits had not been sent in for forensic examination. No one could have known what the investigation would turn into and in reality, such a painstaking and hugely expensive undertaking, would be unlikely to reveal anything connected to the child anyway. The medical centre had always been a busy place and these dabs and fibres were all probably connected to the regular ins and outs of staff and patients. It was doubtful that whoever abandoned the baby ventured any further than the top of the steps.

Stanier went for a chronological approach. They didn't need to read the label to work out the contents of the next bag. Even through the fogged-by-the-years plastic, there was no doubting it was a large shoebox. The sides pictured a snazzy-looking, red, white and black training shoe with the *Adidas* logo. One end had been cut down both seams and folded flat. The paperboy finding the child had described in his statement how the box had been used to hold the baby and towels. No doubt the cutaway section was to allow extra space for the tiny mite's legs.

The item was marked as "Exhibit JJL1" after the initials of paperboy, Jason Joey Lewis. The detectives would not remove the exhibits from the bags. Only forensic scientists would do that.

The next bag had been given the exhibit label JJL2 and contained a hand towel. Its original white now a shade of stained grey. Another bag marked as JJL3 contained similar, whilst a fourth bag held a tiny baby grow, along with a minuscule white vest. This bag had been removed from the baby at the hospital by Dr Abdul Raheem and given the label AR1.

The colour scheme of the baby grow, pink with darker pink elephants, prompted Brenan's remark, 'Not from a friend or relative then.'

Stanier was up to speed with her thinking straight away. 'Yes, wrong colour – should've been blue.'

'Yes. Hand-me-downs or car boot sale.' Brenan was holding the bag to the light and manipulating the contents to try to look at the label. 'Looks too big for a new-born anyway.' A jiggle of the bag worked the collar into position. 'Hmm, British Home Stores. Little Birdie range.' Another shuffle of the contents revealed more. 'Size six to nine months.'

Stanier pushed out his bottom lip. 'Hardly little birdie clothes for a new-born. The doctor's statement taken on the day weighed Jason in at five pounds two ounces which, going by my own kids, was pretty tiny. That baby grow would have swamped the little blighter.'

Another bag contained more of the SOCO's exhibits. A cautionary notice had been added to one label: *Warning – Biohazard.* The description explained: *Pages from book used as nappy liner.*

Brenan placed her elbows on the table, hands covering face and gave a long sigh. Thoughts of the young girl, alone and with no help or comfort, trying her best for the child overwhelmed her. 'Poppy, you poor bastard. What have you been through?' She turned to Stanier. 'We'll send every damn thing through to forensics, Ed. Forrest will blow his top, but what the hell. Put a note on the big bag of dabs and fibres to soften the blow on that little lot. The SOCO did a good job on the day but it's pretty unlikely any of it will take things forward. A bag of red herrings, so no urgency.' She sat back upright to compose herself. 'Is that it? It's not much.'

'That's it,' Stanier said. 'A DVD and backup flash drive covering all the typed documents and statements, along with downloads of the *Sentinel* and *Midlands Today* coverage.'

'Any thoughts yet?'

'Well, the shoebox and clothing were featured in the *Sentinel*, but zilch came from that. We're looking at a whole new ballgame now, so I'm not going to criticise the fact some stuff never went to the lab. The towels and book pages could get us somewhere though, even after all this time. They could even turn up Poppy's DNA – or someone else's.' Stanier held the bag containing the shoebox and turned it over in his hands. 'Covered in fingerprint dust from the SOCO attempts. But the report says that nothing other than a few of the paperboy's dabs were recovered. Forensics may turn up something new with their latest techniques. I think a pretty detailed enquiry was made into the shoebox at the time, but I'd like to have a good look to see if we can get any further.'

Brenan's look showed her agreement. 'Yes, same with the baby grow. We have to remember that we haven't even got a positive ID on it actually being Poppy yet.'

Stanier's side-to-side loll of the head showed his feelings. Madeleine Scott's theories suggested there was not much doubt, but he was experienced enough to know anything was possible.

They spent the next hour and a half on Internet research and telephone calls. Brenan on the baby grow, Stanier on the shoebox.

"Sorry, can't say," had to be their polite explanation if someone asked the reason for their enquiry. As half past one arrived Brenan folded down her laptop lid. 'Fancy a bite of lunch in the salubrious realm of the Birchfield estate?'

'If we must,' Stanier said as he logged off and stood to his feet.'

Chapter 6

BRENAN TOOK THE wheel of her Ford Fiesta for the journey, pointing the car through the midday traffic and out of town. Forrest's surprisingly generous agreement to mileage allowance for them both dispensed with the problems of vehicle availability from the depleted CID transport pool. The weather forecaster's prophecy of an unusually hot week for mid-April was proving right so far.

Shirtsleeves above elbows, and jacket left in the car was Stanier's attempt at looking non-police as they climbed the steps to the *Bottom Knocker* pub. The tongue-in-cheek title was derived from a now-redundant pottery industry skill – a saggar maker's bottom knocker. The renaming of the 1960s hostelry had come with its refurbishment a few years ago. It did nothing to improve its previous reputation.

Brenan's own attempt at a "casual bite to eat" whilst passing through was equally inept. Her white blouse, black slacks and black shoulder bag were fine for most occasions. A lunchtime visit to the *Bottom Knocker* was not most occasions, though. Since its refurb, the pub had become more of an evening sports venue. Huge TV screens took up every wall, a different match on each. The lack of football on this particular lunchtime, along with the meagre show of other customers, offered no respite from the potentially seizure-inducing flicker of several differently-tuned stations. The accompanying boom of some completely at odds music added to the discomfort. A sign suggesting hot or cold food could be purchased from 10 a.m. until 9 p.m. was worth a test, if only visually.

The landlord, a six foot two Mohican-haired, muscle-bound gorilla, watched their entry with a slow and calculating stare from his place behind the bar. He appeared to have been drafted in more for his thuggish looks than his potential competency and pleasant welcoming demeanour. An intertwined mass of tattoos climbed from his inches-wide wrists and disappeared via massive steroid-pumped biceps into the close-to-tearing short sleeves of an FCUK T-shirt.

A twitch of recognition briefly softened the hard man guise as Nicholas Mazewski took in the blonde ponytail and searing glare he received from Brenan. This was the detective who, a few months earlier, had threatened to take Mazewski's pub licence, rip it into bits and set fire to it. Her threat included the promise to do it on the porcelain lid of the gents' toilet cistern, which was then in regular use as a cocaine cutting and dealing block by the pub's numerous dealers and users.

The warning was acted upon swiftly by Mazewski, irrespective of the fact the withdrawal of such facilities cost him two hundred quid a week in back pocket money. The pub was by no means free from the diseases of crime and drugs, but was decidedly better. The fact the pea-brained landlord had since turned into something of an informant for Brenan set the standard with this type of openly loud-mouthed but privately weak individual.

Mazewski checked the other customers to ensure no one would witness his pretence at a smile. 'Sergeant Brenan,' he offered.

'Mr Mazewski,' Brenan returned. 'Got some food on?'

'Of course – and five stars on the hygiene.'

Mazewski's voice never seemed to match his physique. It was a good octave too high. Brenan put it down to the steroids. It was the reason she referred to him as "SD" in any informant activities. Only she knew it stood for "Small Dick". Mazewski's wish to prove Brenan wrong would always remain a wish.

'Sarnies for me please, Nick. Ham salad on brown and a half lager top. How about you, Ed?'

'Same,' Stanier said. 'And a pint of bitter shandy.'

Mazewski jotted the food order onto a pad and nodded a sullen-looking girl over from further down the bar.

Waiting for the girl to move out of earshot, he started to pull the drinks. 'So, what's to do?' He knew this was more than a routine police visit.

'You've been here, what, two years now, Nick?' Brenan said. 'That's pretty good going in your trade these days. Last bloke only lasted six weeks.'

'Just over eighteen months,' Mazewski replied.

'Crooks, thugs, druggies, scroungers, con men… Oh, and women – mustn't be sexist these days.'

Mazewski looked on, understanding that Brenan's list was an inventory of the greater part of his clientele. His mouth shaped into an inverted "U". His raised shoulders added a casual: *So what?* 'We get a lot of decent people in as well, Eve, and you know that's a fact.'

Brenan wasn't disagreeing. 'But what about pervs ? Sex offenders, child molesters?'

'No fucking hiding place, Eve, and you know that too. If the police want any help with that kinda thing, they'll get it in spades from the whole community. And I mean everyone. So what is this? A heads up for some fucking weirdo we've got in our midst, who needs a bit of vigilante persuasion to move on?'

'No, nothing like that and I don't go along with vigilante stuff anyway. Might be something or nothing. I wanted to know that we can rely on a bit of help if needed.'

The *Bottom Knocker*'s sandwiches were surprisingly good and the trio parted company with curt smiles. Stanier had remained his usual quiet self. "I'll speak when the time's right," was his normal response when questioned on his reticence.

The pair had another four pubs and a working men's club to cultivate in a similar manner to the *Bottom Knocker.* They were premises inside the Birchfield estate or close to it, and all were different in relation to the type of clientele they attracted and standards they kept. Brenan had only pencilled in one more for today, though, and that would be a swift visit to *The Southwood Inn.*

The *Southwood* lay on the outskirts of the estate and was regarded as a "nice little boozer" by most who visited. Over the years the pub had become known as the "*Sythe*" – a take on the pronunciation of the word "South" in a strong Potteries accent. It was also a regular out-of-town haunt for both off-and on-duty cops. The main reason being the fact that the landlord, John Eardley, was himself a retired detective sergeant. Eardley's three decades of police service had ended nine years ago. A good conduct medal and four commendations, along with a twice broken nose and other lasting injuries were reminders of his time on the force. Being old-school, he was a good man to have behind you in any rough house and a stalwart supporter of the police with eyes ever open for wrongdoers.

Eardley was behind the bar polishing glasses and replacing them on shelves as Brenan and Stanier made their entrance. His broad smile greeted them. He was a big man, six feet two inches and still looking as though he could handle himself. A thin covering of silver hair topped a round and slightly florid face. A blood pressure check-up might be a worthwhile consideration in the near future.

'Well, well, well,' Eardley said, his smile morphing into a big grin. 'Could have done with you two last night. Had a couple of scrotes in trying to use my toilets as a bloody drug den. Soon sent 'em packing. Pretty sure they were two of Nick Mazewski's former clientele from the *Bottom Knocker*.'

'I'm sure you managed, John,' Stanier said.

'I did that, Ed, I certainly did that. Anyway, what's to do? Experience tells me that DC Stanier and Cadet Brenan only team up when there's a big job on?' Eardley's joking reference to Brenan referred to her rank when he first met her – a fresh-faced police cadet making tea in the CID office.

Brenan gave a derisory shake of the head. She was used to Eardley's humour and this particular greeting was always a sure-fire bet. 'Something might be afoot, John,' she said. 'Don't be offended that we can't give you the story on it but, as we start digging, some gossip is bound to start bouncing around.'

'No problems, Eve, I'll help out any way I can, and you know that.'

A half beer each and a twenty-minute natter on old times brought the visit to a close. The necessary inclusion of Nick Mazewski in the gossip had injected some humour. The old chestnut of his belief that his pub was haunted and how he hated changing barrels on his own flew in the face of his hard man persona. It had been a standing joke for some time. The pair headed out to the car park.

Brenan unlocked the car. 'Not given anything away there, Ed?

'No, not at all,' Stanier climbed aboard, 'but, if and when the public do get hold of this, it could give us dozens more eyes and ears. Never asked how you'd gone on with the baby grow.'

'Early days yet,' Brenan replied as she pulled out onto the road and started the journey back into town. 'The Little Birdie range was produced for British Home Stores from May 2006 until October 2008, so getting on for two and a half years. Last stock was held in stores until December 2008. Any remaining stock had the labels removed and was sold as a job lot to a private enterprise.'

'Barcode?' Stanier quizzed.

Brenan was used to Stanier's economy with words. 'Yes, the stock number in the barcode proved it was delivered to the Hanley store in June 2007. They restocked in August that year. That doesn't mean for certain it was sold between those dates as there could've been stock left over. An actual date of sale is impossible. The BHS stores closed down in 2016 and there's nothing left of individual shop records. It's a sketchy possible starting point but we could be working along the lines of it being purchased from Hanley between June and September 2007.'

Stanier clasped his hands to his face in mock fear as Brenan braked to avoid a blue Micra on a death wish. 'Knob,' was Brenan's opinion on the lady's driving skills before she was back into her explanation. 'And, even then, we're still going from the label suggesting the child was born six to nine months before that four-month window. Vague to say the least. Could have been a big or a small child for its age.'

Stanier worked back on his fingers. 'But, taking the label to its extreme, the garment was purchased for a nine-month-old child. So, nine months before June 2007, when the stock arrived at Hanley, would give a first possible birth date of September 2006.' He looked up as he mentally calculated the second part. 'The last date it could have been purchased for a nine-month-old, or for any age was August 2007 when the stock was replaced. Go back the full nine months for a maximum age of the child would give us… What?'

Brenan had followed his line of thinking and jumped ahead a calculation. 'Perhaps November, December-ish 2006. So we *might* – and it's a big might – be looking for someone who had a baby girl between maybe, September 2006 and December 2006.'

Stanier gave his head a scratch. 'All we can say is that it was purchased locally for a baby girl.' His pause indicated more uncertainty. 'Born between those dates would make her around thirteen now.'

Brenan stared at the road ahead as she pondered the extreme possibilities of tracking down the original owner of the baby grow, and how far forward it would take them even if they did. 'Everything so far seems to have happened inside the Birchfield estate. So it's a lot of ifs and maybes but, if it was purchased legitimately from the store as a gift, then there could be some mileage in it. How about a chat with the Registrar's office? It's a long-shot but maybe we can track down the births of girls born to addresses on the estate who would now be thirteen.'

Stanier pursed his lips. 'Nothing ventured, nothing gained.'

They'd made it back to the police station's top floor corridor before Stanier got chance to explain his work on the shoebox. Brenan fumbled in her bag for keys as they approached the office door. The phone was ringing out. Two missed calls on her mobile had been drowned out by the town centre traffic and the chances were that it was the same caller – Madeleine Scott.

'Hi, Eve, been trying you for a while,' Scott said. 'I wondered if you'd any update yet.'

'Sorry, Mad, we made our case to DCI Forrest this morning and can only hope he's not going to sit on it. I think we should get a decision through pretty quickly on whether you can stay on the case or not. It'd be a pretty unusual step, but I think I've done enough to convince Forrest at least. As for the business on how the FINDS board are going to play the familial search, well, we'll have to keep our fingers crossed.'

Scott's voice came back through the earpiece. 'Okay. I'm carrying on regardless anyway. I'm researching the blood relatives who've shown up on Jason's *Geneaus DNA* file. You'll remember that the closest relative, the second cousin, produced the link to Poppy. Now, I know we're hoping to get the go-ahead for the familial search on the NDNAD to nail the father, but that's a really slim chance. It'll only work out if he's on file for previous offences. So I'm ploughing on researching in the meantime. I've only got another other two hundred and thirty-six to work on.' There was a sardonic edge to her voice.

'The big snag though,' she continued, 'is that I can't differentiate between Poppy's relatives and the father's relatives. It makes it damned hard work. You see, any time I spend working on a relative from Poppy's side is completely wasted. But I won't know whose side the person is from until I'm well into the research on each individual. My only interest lies with relations of the father. Unfortunately, working with what I have, there's no way to differentiate between the blood relatives on Jason's DNA file. I could spend hours researching and building a family tree from one individual, only to then discover it's a relative of Poppy's.'

Brenan narrowed her eyes and gave the telephone handset a wary stare 'So, you just said, "working with what I have". I'm getting to know you a bit better now, Madeleine, and that seems to indicate there's a way around this?'

A muffled snigger preceded Scott's answer. 'Yes, the time will come, and pretty soon I think, when we have to involve Poppy's parents in all of this. If I could input their DNA onto the genealogy site – if they'd agree to that and let me run both their files as manager, like I am with Jason's – I could compare their DNA matches to those which show as Jason's DNA blood relatives. I could then strike out the ones that are duplicated in Jason's hits. That way, I'd be able to discount all of Poppy's relatives from her own parent's sides and just work on those connected to Jason's father. It could cut down the workload massively.'

Chapter 7

Day 3 Wednesday 17th April

BRENAN AND STANIER were back in the office by half past eight the next morning. There was no news from DCI Forrest, so they were concentrating on their original lines of research.

Brenan switched on her laptop and turned to Stanier. 'How's it going with the shoebox?'

Stanier flipped back a few pages of the A4 pad in front of him. 'It was for a pair of Adidas Crazy 8 trainers. Colour was red, black and white, as shown on the side of the box. They're actually described as "Kobe Bryant Basketball Shoes". Kobe Bryant was an American basketball superstar. The size given on the box is US 10.5.'

Stanier gave Brenan a stare as he gave more detail. 'Now you learn something every day. The US size their shoes the same way as we do, imperial rather than the European method. Having said that, the Yanks shoe sizes for men are all a full size larger than the UK ones. So, what would be a ten and a half for them would be a nine and a half for us. It's even dafter for women – two sizes different. Anyway, the barcode is almost totally destroyed and tells us nothing.' He gave a frustrated sigh. 'It seems that this particular model of shoe was only ever produced at the Adidas factory in Indonesia specifically for the American market. They were a very expensive shoe and only available on sale from October 2010 until January 2012. It may sound daft but, if these actual trainers still exist and are in good nick, they'd be a collector's item and worth a few quid. But who'd want a pair of second-hand stinking trainers? I'm sure I don't know.'

'So those dates must limit the numbers then?'

'Exactly,' Stanier said. 'So more work there. If you look at the picture on the box, they're very distinctive.'

Brenan was thoughtful for a few seconds. 'See if you can

download some decent images of the particular model and colour of shoe. Maybe do a bit of in-depth research on the trainer itself, the tread pattern and laces perhaps.'

An elevenses coffee was followed up with another trip out to the Birchfield estate. Passing visits to the *Hollytree* and the *Miners Arms* pubs continued the campaign to foster public support should the need arise. The tactic was slowly getting faces clocked and names known.

The pair arrived back at base by half two and met Forrest in the police station foyer.

'Ah! Been after you two. Come on up to my office.'

Stanier caught Brenan's eye. Was this good news or bad?

'Close the door, Ed,' Forrest said as he dragged out his chair. 'Take a seat, both of you.' He unlocked a drawer and pulled out a sheaf of paperwork, placing it down onto his blotter. He stared at Brenan. 'Your report, Eve – or should I say reports – have caused quite a stir. The FINDS Strategy Board convened a special meeting at lunchtime on this.' Forrest handed the paperwork across the desk. Brenan shuffled her chair forward, allowing Stanier to move his own seat in sideways for a head-craning squint at the text.

The document, a photocopy, carried the logo and initials of the *National Police Chiefs' Council* in the top left. A coat of arms and the title *Home Office* sat in the right corner whilst a central heading read: *FIND Strategy Board.*

A sub-heading read: *Emergency Meeting: Missing person – Poppy Elizabeth Hunt (Staffordshire Police).*

An *In Attendance* list catalogued those present along with the organisations represented. It included two VIPs from the *Home Office Forensic Information Databases Service (FINDS),* a representative from the *Information Commissioner's Office*, a double-barrelled name held the impressive title of *Commissioner of the Retention and use of Biometric Material.* More attendees included designations such as *Forensic Science Regulator* and chair of the *Biometric and Forensics Ethics Group*. The Chief Constable of Dorset was named as the chair of the actual meeting. It was an impressive and powerful line-up.

Brenan speed-read through the necessary bumf of minutes and apologies, homing in on several references to her own name and to the "detailed accounts", as her reports were described. She turned four more pages without taking in a word until she spotted a heading and a five-paragraph proclamation.

Decision:

The Board has examined the proposals made in the police report by Det/Sgt Brenan which were supported through her chain of command up to and including Staffordshire's Chief Constable Mark Adderley.

The STR encoded DNA profile resulting from the buccal cheek swab taken from Jason Fitzgerald (given DoB 07.02.2011) by witness Miss Madeleine Scott with consent and in presence of adoptive parents is to be treated as a crime scene stain.

A subjective analysis of this crime scene stain will be carried out against the MPDD profile of Poppy Elizabeth Hunt (Dob 02.03.1994) in an effort to establish if the said Jason Fitzgerald is the son of Miss Hunt.

A familial DNA search against this crime scene stain is also hereby authorised against all male files held on NDNAD. The search will be restricted to fifty percent "father" only match.

These actions will begin this day (Wednesday 17th April 2019).

Brenan's wide-eyed expression showed her astonishment at the success. 'So we've got it. Hopefully, undeniable proof that Jason is Poppy's son, and a familial search for the father. If he's on record, we've got him.'

Brenan gave Forrest a hard stare. 'Does good news come in threes?'

'It seems so,' Forrest replied. 'Yes, you've got a green light for Madeleine to work along with you. To be reviewed weekly, but try to keep some kind of control over the expenses.'

CID were often accused by other police departments of not requiring much of an excuse to throw a party. It was certainly true that the cracking of a case, or at least a major breakthrough, would, without question, lead to a "do", to coin a police phrase. The bigger the development would usually increase the magnitude of the "do" in numbers attending, length of time spanned *and* in the volume of alcohol consumed. Even the smallest step forward could signal an advance upon the most preferred watering hole. It was also true to say that a demoralising failure or merely a simple end-of-the-day debrief could equally provide the excuse for a "swift one".

The good news certainly did merit the seventy-yard walk to the police station's nearest pub, the *Smithfield.* A glass of Shiraz for Brenan and a pint of Falstaff for Stanier made for a pleasant wind-down and a mull over progress so far.

Scott's shout of, '*Yes!*' down the phone at Brenan's news demonstrated her enthusiasm to continue "helping the police with their enquiries". Her pledge to be with them the next day to make a start compounded her eagerness. This time she would use the train rather than the stressful M6.

Chapter 8

Day 4 Thursday 18th April

BRENAN AND STANIER were waiting on Platform Two of Stoke-on-Trent's Victorian railway station the next morning. The Virgin Trains Class 390 Pendolino rumbled heavily in and halted with the merest squeak of brakes. The rapid clunking of several doors preceded the leisurely disembarkation of a handful of passengers and was followed by the hurried boarding of thirty or forty. At 09:50, the train was two minutes late and quick to get on its way for the onward journey to Manchester Piccadilly.

Stanier eyed Madeleine Scott at the far end of the platform: stylish red-belted raincoat, high heels, small suitcase and pensive expression. A look of relief washed over her as she spotted her two-person welcoming committee.

They were back at the nick within twenty minutes, Scott eager to explain the suitcase. 'I've booked in at the Premier Inn. It's only a five-minute walk from here. Just one night, but I wanted to see how things were panning out before getting back.' She looked at Brenan. 'So we got it then?'

Brenan struggled to keep her smile in check. She pushed the FINDS Strategy Board paperwork across the desk to her.

Brenan, Stanier and Madeleine Scott took the lift down to Forrest's second floor office as midday approached. Forrest seemed intrigued with Scott's in-depth knowledge on the workings of genealogy and DNA research. He kept to his best behaviour, giving eager nods as each specific was explained. He leaned forward extending his hand towards Scott. 'So I guess this is welcome to the team, Madeleine.' He turned to Brenan. 'We must keep Jason's adoptive parents completely in the loop on all of this.'

'We're meeting them at Stafford, at their place.' Brenan checked her wristwatch. 'At four o'clock. The Social Services team first involved by Madeleine will also be there. We're hoping Poppy's schoolmate – Jason's teacher, Annie – will be there too.'

Forrest blinked at the rapidity with which Brenan had looked ahead and got wheels in motion.

She continued: 'It seems as though the adoptive parents, Mr and Mrs Fitzgerald, are keen to help. They know the full story and, if they stay onside with us, it's a done deal. Social Services tell me the adoptive parents have the final say. We've retrieved all the evidence from the baby Jason case as well.'

'Such as?' Forrest said.

'The baby grow, shoebox, towels and things.' She pulled two photocopied newspaper reports from her briefcase and pushed them across the desk. The first was from the original article dated Saturday 12th February 2011, a day after the baby had been found. The second was from the following Monday, the 14th. The heading for this later story read: *Abandoned Baby – Police Need Your Help.*

A photograph showed the two small hand towels and the shoebox. The text explained the request:

Staffordshire Police are seeking the help of the public in identifying the mother of the new-born baby boy found on the steps of Birchfield Medical Centre three days ago. The baby, named by staff at the centre as Jason, after the paperboy who found him, was wearing the baby grow shown in the picture. He had been wrapped in one of the towels and placed in the shoebox, also pictured. Detective Inspector Alec Shaw of Hanley CID said: 'We are concerned for the well-being of the mother, who is likely to need medical attention. Evidently some tragic situation has caused her to leave her baby and it is vital that we find her. Someone may recognise these items or even have an idea about the mother's identity.'

An inset photograph of the baby from the original newspaper article preceded a phone number and contact details.

'We've recovered the typed file. Not a massive amount, and it's all on one flash drive. There are quite a few hard copy printouts, statements and whatnot. The SOCO did a good job on the day and, all things considered, a pretty good investigation was carried out. But nothing seems to have come from it. It was, after all eight years ago. We weren't as hot with IT and CCTV leads as we are now, so nothing on that front. We have to accept that no one could've known what this was going to grow into.'

Forrest's expression showed his understanding. 'Lucky we'd still got the towels, shoebox and things,' he said.

'Yes. It all went up to the hospital in the ambulance, along with the baby, before any police arrived. The SOCO man chased it up and recovered it from Social Services, who'd taken the kiddie into care later that afternoon. The baby grow, towels and shoebox did go to the lab but nothing of any value came from the examinations apart from a couple of prints off the shoebox.'

Forrest's expression remained impassive. 'And I'm gathering there was no match on file?'

'No, nothing,' Brenan said. 'But, as you know, prints and DNA of Mispers are held on a separate database now. Poppy's prints were lifted from her bedroom soon after she went missing. The abandoned baby case stayed properly live for about six months before being wound down. That case has not been reviewed and I guess that sort of case never would be. It was probably viewed as a sad situation where the mother couldn't support the child. It was filed. I've resubmitted everything to forensics for full analysis… shoebox, towels… all the SOCO exhibits. Yes, I know nothing was found first time around and we're another eight years behind on this, but there's been a lot of technological progress since then. If archaeologists can scrape DNA from King Richard's bones after five hundred years, then it's worth a shot.'

Madeleine Scott had remained a quiet observer on what would normally be a confidential police conversation, but Brenan's comment about King Richard brought her close to a snigger.

Forrest spotted the reaction. 'See what I have to put up with, Madeleine.' He looked back at Brenan. 'You really tightened the net by narrowing your request down to just the father and it certainly clinched the deal to get that familial search authorised. There were only thirteen familial searches done for the entire UK last year. Get

Ed to fast track the Baby Jason exhibits to forensic before you set off to Stafford. I'll request a rapid result.'

Scott chose her moment carefully. She needed to ask a favour and felt that just now Brenan and Forrest were working as harmoniously as they ever would. She began with an explanation about the *Geneaus DNA* spit sample and its paperwork. She'd planned ahead and brought two kits along with her. 'I was telling you, Eve, how samples from Poppy's parents would help me with the research.' She made an apologetic face; she knew she was lumbering Brenan with a job that would tug at the heartstrings. 'You're going to have to tell them what's been going on sooner or later. If you can get their spit samples I'll send them off to my Geneaus DNA account and try to get them fast-tracked.' She looked from Brenan to Forrest and back. 'It really could save weeks or even months.'

Forrest caught Brenan's stare as Scott explained what she needed. It took him back to the days of his own hands-on involvement with the public not so many years before. He'd had many heart-breaking meetings with families and knew the balance between distress and hysteria was always waiting to be tipped by one wrongly chosen word or peculiar request. 'See what you can do, Eve.'

The trio got to their feet to leave. 'Nice to meet you Madeleine,' Forrest said easing into a bent-knees stance. 'And thanks Ed,' he added. Forrest didn't need to spell it out to Brenan that he wanted a private word with her.

As the door closed behind Stanier and Scott, Forrest's dip of the head invited Brenan to retake her seat. Her suspicion that she was in for some kind of dressing down couldn't have been more incorrect.

'We've known each other a long time Eve, worked a lot of jobs together over the years and yes I know my nickname… I know some of the jokes that get banded about – "Forrest… can't see the wood for trees.'

Brenan's expression was impassive, puzzled at where this was leading.

'It's easy to forget why you joined this job when you get on the promotion ladder,' Forrest continued. 'I was up most of the night going through this.' He patted a hand down onto Brenan's progress report. 'If this girl is still alive there's only us in this world who can find her. Forrest Grump just left the building.'

Brenan, Stanier and Scott were ten minutes late for their four o'clock appointment. They found the Fitzgeralds' four-bedroomed detached tucked away in a corner of the Doxey Farm Estate half a mile from Stafford centre.

With its neatly-trimmed front lawn and newly-planted cherry blossom tree, 16 Garthfield Crescent appeared to be a pleasant family home. A Volkswagen Passat sat on the drive, in front of a separate garage. A view through to a decent sized rear garden showed a kid's swing and a covered-over circular trampoline. The iron basketball hoop fitted against the side of the house gave notice that at least one elder child might also live here in addition to young Jason.

The BMW parked kerbside suggested that Social Services were already taking up seats in the lounge. A yellow Toyota Aygo was parked in the driveway behind the Passat. Scott sat forward in her rear seat and pointed at the car. 'Annie's car. Glad she's made it – be good for you to both meet her.'

Stanier pulled his own Audi in behind the BMW, aware that the plethora of cars and visitors might well draw unwanted attention to the Fitzgerald household. The trio climbed out, briefcase apiece, mobiles in pockets.

Thomas Fitzgerald opened the front door as they approached the house. Social workers Lloyd Anderson and Miriam Lawton were sitting around a coffee table in the lounge. The two got to their feet for a round of introductions and first-name terms were quickly agreed on. Lloyd, an athletic-looking, well-groomed black man broke the ice. 'Good to meet you and, before we start, we're here to help in any way possible.' His colleague, Miriam, was a little cooler. Her smile was forced, and an ingrained distrust of the police hovered around her. She was sceptical of their sincerity. Jason's welfare and rights were her priorities.

Patricia Fitzgerald appeared from the kitchen and was followed into the room by schoolteacher Anita Greaves.

'Cuppa tea?' Pat asked. 'Never known a bobby turn one down.' Her offer was made with the trace of Northern Irish accent which still remained, even after twenty-two years living in Staffordshire.

'Please,' both detectives responded.

'Coffee for me please, Pat,' Scott requested. 'Decaf if you've got it.'

Another round of introductions followed and, with Anita's help, the drinks were sorted.

'Jason's over at his school friend's house for tea,' Pat Fitzgerald added. 'And his brother, Eamon, is busy upstairs with homework.'

It was important to Brenan and Stanier to know the entire family set-up. It was the usual way with a detective: poke noses into everyone's business, no matter how insignificant or unconnected it might be.

Pat Fitzgerald saved Brenan from the embarrassment of seemingly unnecessary questions. 'Eamon is fifteen,' she said. 'He's our son, our flesh and blood. I couldn't have any more children, so we adopted. Of course, we knew Jason's story from the off. It's been a heart-rending decision trying to decide when we should actually tell him he'd been abandoned. We've only got around to it since this affair came to light. He seems to be taking it well, but who knows?'

Brenan started things off. Her idea was to get everybody to explain their own part in sequence, a timeline of events. Stanier, armed with a calendar and A4 notepad, threw in questions on times and dates in preparation for the witness statements which would be needed from everyone. As the stories were related and moved towards the present day, Scott reiterated her genealogy work which had positively pointed at Poppy being Jason's mother. Brenan explained the ongoing forensic work which would unquestionably prove this as fact. There was no hushed silence; the entire group had already drawn this conclusion.

Brenan caught the eye of Miriam Lawton as she summed up. 'So, we know for a fact that Poppy was alive three years after she went missing. It's my belief, and probably that of everyone in this room, that she was kidnapped and imprisoned somewhere, probably right under our noses. Used for sex – raped – and has given birth to at least one child. We've discussed similar cases abroad. The only thing to be grateful for, so far, is that, for some reason, Jason was spared and has the chance of a normal, happy life.'

The despondency level peaked as Brenan added more. 'The paramount rule that we must all share is secrecy. I don't doubt that, if the investigation continues for any length of time, the media will get an inkling of something going on. The offender must be considered to be violent. If Poppy *is* still alive and something spooks him, he might try to dispose of the evidence. By that, I mean Poppy.'

The comment brought total silence.

'The more people who get to know about this,' Brenan reinforced, 'and the longer it drags on, the more the danger increases that there will be a leak.' Brenan's solemn glance at each face emphasised the importance of her words.

'It's only right that Poppy's parents are made aware of what's happening as soon as possible,' she paused. 'It's vital that *we* deliver that news as soon as we have DNA confirmation. We don't want it being leaked. Now we've got this far, that's our next objective but, again, the numbers of people who know will also increase. Even something as simple as the number of visitors here today might get nosy neighbours interested.'

Miriam Lawton's eyes remained fixed on Brenan throughout the secrecy warning. The furrows of mistrust and worry on her forehead had smoothed. Brenan was certainly determined to get to the bottom of this mystery. It was clear the detective was a no-nonsense and caring professional. It was also clear the welfare of Jason and Poppy, if she was still alive, were her overriding priorities.

Lawton shuffled forward in her chair. 'To be clear about the reasons for our involvement in all of this –' she bobbed her head over at the Fitzgeralds – 'Tom and Pat, as the adoptive parents, are in the driving seat on any of the decisions and agreements for samples and evidence connected to Jason. If Jason had still been in the care of the local authority, the decisions would have been ours. Having heard and seen everything that's gone on I'd like to think we would've acted in the same way.' Lloyd Anderson gave a supporting nod.

'We can only advise,' Lawton continued. 'And, even then, only if we're asked to. Poppy's situation is unknown, but the efforts and aims of the detectives are centred on finding her, if indeed she's still alive. We must remember that Jason, the child of this monster, could also be at risk himself if something is leaked. We really don't know what we're dealing with.'

Brenan gave an exaggerated nod at Lawton's remarks. She was right. They weren't just protecting Poppy.

It was ten past seven and threatening rain as Stanier pulled his Audi in outside the police station. There had been no news from Forrest on a result from forensics.

To have abandoned Scott to her hotel room for the rest of the evening, after all she had done, would have been less than charitable. Nevertheless, Stanier turned down Brenan's idea of a curry and drink. 'No, make it a girl's night out,' was his escape route. He knew Brenan was up for some hair-down time. This enquiry had the potential to make the jump to light speed any time soon and he needed some home-time with the wife and kids while the going was good. Brenan, being an avowed life-long single woman, was unaffected by such problems. They would drop their gear off at the nick before heading out for a night on the town.

'Go steady on the ale,' Stanier jokingly yelled, as the two doors were banged shut. The pair, briefcases above heads and unbuttoned raincoats billowing, never heard the advice. They were already in mid-dash for the police station's entrance, fighting against a sudden rain-laced gust.

Chapter 9

Day 5 Friday 19th April

BRENAN'S NO-SHOW the next morning at nine o'clock did not surprise Stanier. He successfully deflected DCI Forrest's phone call with some experienced flannel. 'Yes, her coat's here, sir, so she's knocking about somewhere. I'll get her to call you when she reappears.'

Stanier's unsympathetic head shake would be the only greeting Brenan was likely to get when her ashen phizog finally peered around the office door. Her colleague's noisy exhalation emphasised the performance he made of looking up at the wall clock. It was twenty-five past nine. 'Forrest was after you,' he said, as she slumped into a chair. 'But I covered. Coffee? Paracetamol?'

Brenan pressed a hand against her forehead and made her own noisy exhalation. 'Both please, Ed.'

More strong coffee helped to drag Brenan back into the land of the living by ten o'clock. She got to her feet, straightened up and took in a lungful of air. 'God, that woman likes her vodka! Good job she's heading back today.' She made another loud exhalation, the tail-end of which became a snigger. 'We had a bloody good laugh, though.'

Forrest, keen for an update on yesterday's Stafford meeting was about to try Brenan's office again. The rather meekly-knuckled rap on his door prompted him to replace the receiver. It was far removed from Brenan's usual forceful introduction, but the DCI was none the wiser. He did, though, notice her rather pallid look. 'You okay, Eve? You look a bit tired.'

'Yes thanks, boss. Didn't sleep too well.'

Brenan managed her update with the assistance of a Nespresso from Forrest's machine, but dearly wished the cup could have been three times the size.

'Has Madeleine gone back now?' Forrest asked, as the summary was concluded.

A squint at her watch through the still-banging headache prompted a falsely bright voice to chirp her reply. 'Yes. Ed picked her up from the hotel. Train was due out at ten to eleven, so she'll be on her way.'

After a slow wander back along the corridor and the lift journey upwards, Brenan settled back into her office chair, intent on another round of paracetamol and coffee. She was ten minutes into more Internet research when the desk phone rang. It was Forrest.

'You'd better get down here double quick.'

She took the stairs – painful with a headache, but quicker.

'Close the door, pull up a chair,' Forrest said. 'You are *not* going to believe this.' He pushed a handful of emailed paperwork across. She took in the heading on the form: *National DNA Database*. Brenan was familiar with the form. She looked up from it to stare at Forrest. 'A result already?' She thought of young Jason's DNA comparison with Poppy's. Her mouth fell open, hangover temporarily forgotten. Forrest was clearly agitated. He'd read the paperwork three times since the email pinged in his inbox. 'Yes, we've got a result. And, when the scientists realised what they were looking at, it delivered such a bombshell they pulled all the stops out.'

Brenan wasn't expecting Forrest's display of astonishment. It seemed a sure-fire bet the result would show Jason was Poppy's son. It was more of a formality than anything else. She gave him a puzzled stare. 'So, we've proved Poppy is the mother…?' Her words faltered.

Forrest shook his head but answered in the affirmative. 'Yes, we've done that all right, but it doesn't stop there.'

A thought came to Brenan. 'So,' she said slowly as her eyes tried to mop up some legible detail from the blurry wording on the report, 'you're telling me –' her face brightened – 'that the familial test showed the father *is* on record?'

Forrest's brow furrowed. Brenan was usually quick on the uptake. 'Yes, Eve, he's on record alright. But we still don't know who he is.'

Brenan clasped a hand to her throbbing forehead and wished Forrest would spit it out. 'Are you saying we know who he is?'

Forrest lifted his hands, palms upward. 'No, no! We don't know who he is.' He pushed himself back into his seat. 'But we know what he's done.'

Brenan looked blankly back before starting to mutter the obvious. 'Kidnapped Popp…' Her words petered out as she grasped Forrest's meaning. 'He's done *more*? His DNA is on file for something else?'

Forrest's nods were now full-scale neck exercises. 'You bet your fucking life he has. This bastard has more secrets than we could ever have believed.' He pointed at the report. 'Skip through to page seven.'

The three names jumped out and hit Brenan between the eyes before the page was completely turned: Jennifer McQueen, Susan Hemmings, Erica Asquith – *Operation Sandstone*. The DNA connected unsolved prostitute murders that had remained a stain on the murder detection rate of Staffordshire Police for fourteen years.

Back in her office and alone, Brenan poured yet another coffee and attempted to come to terms with what the forensic results really meant. She felt dazed. The world had just changed. Three cold-case murders and a potentially live kidnapping/rape case was massive in any chief constable's book. This was destined to be a huge, full-scale investigation with all available manpower thrown at it. Warming her hands on the hot mug, she stared out at the bleak slag heap horizon. Depressing, yes, but thought-provoking too. Poppy's plight was always the main element of this investigation. The words, "If she is still alive" had become a rider to every mention of her name. Those words, though, reinforced the alternative that she might already be dead. Keeping the enquiry small, intimate and secret was, without doubt, the best way to protect Poppy from harm by her captor if, indeed, she was still alive.

Brenan's grimace at the foul taste still lingering in her mouth from too much alcohol fitted the moment. That bad taste would have been there even without last night's vodka. Anger was building inside her as each nip of caffeine eased her mind back to its normal clarity. If this enquiry was to be rubber-stamped by HQ for the manpower, support staff, vehicles, technology and a budget in keeping with its magnitude, the secret would be out within days. Brenan was back on her feet and bounding down the stairs two at a time.

Forrest's alarmed face as she burst into his office quickly turned to anger. The phone was pressed to his ear and the caller, Detective Chief Superintendent Brown, was plainly unaware of the intrusion. Forrest's eyes doubled in size and roundness as he tried to keep his voice and comments on an even keel with his boss. 'Righto, sir, I'll get that arranged.' His furious glare and violent sideways head lunge at the door, spelled out two words as if they had been shouted through a megaphone: *GET OUT!*

The indistinct metallic rattle from Forrest's phone told her the Chief Super was still in full flow, giving directives to Forrest, suggesting a working model for such a vast enquiry, determining which divisions could supply detectives, a suitable Major Incident Room (MIR), a senior investigating officer.

Brenan stood her ground. Worse than that, she stepped inside, pushed the door closed and shook her head with venom equal to Forrest's. She mimed the word, 'No,' with exaggerated facial movements.

'Sorry, sir. Excuse me for a moment.' Forrest clamped his hand tightly over the receiver and levelled a glowering look at Brenan. 'What in God's name do you think you're doing? This had better be bloody good!'

'Sorry, boss, sorry.'

Brenan had massively overstepped the mark and she knew it, but was not stopping now. Her arms were spread wide. 'Just give me some time,' she pleaded. 'We keep using the phrase "if Poppy is still alive". Isn't that what this is really all about? Those other girls are all dead. We know that. They died fourteen years ago. Yes, we've got to find the bastard who did that, the same bastard who's done whatever he's done to Poppy. But, if she *is* still alive, *is* still being held prisoner, we could be signing her death warrant by going flat out on this. It's the main feature since this all started a few days ago. A full enquiry with teams of coppers swamping the Birchfield and everything that goes along with that kind of high-powered, full-on investigation. The secret will be out in no time.' She went silent, hands falling to her sides, voice petering out. 'Just give me some time.'

'Apologies, Chief Superintendent. Something's cropped up. Can I ring you back?'

Detective Chief Superintendent Brown was renowned for his quick temper but had stayed strangely quiet throughout Forrest's return phone call. Brenan's proposal of a continuing secret investigation on a small scale was surprisingly *not* dismissed out of hand. In fact, a fly on the wall during that call would have seen a quizzical smile form on Brown's lips. His murmured comment of, 'She's right,' was spoken after he'd put the phone down, but he still wanted a face-to-face chat.

Brenan and Forrest managed the journey in forty minutes, a near-silent forty minutes at that. Brenan's single attempt to smooth Forrest's ruffled feathers was made as he pulled his car in through the gateway of the characterless modern brick pile which now served as police HQ. 'Sorry, boss, I can't get Poppy out of my mind and if she is still ali…'

Forrest cut in. 'Okay, forget it. Let's see what he says.'

Forrest continued to feel undermined as he and Brenan sat facing Brown across his modern, light oak desk. The collection of family photos and the "Mister Happy" coffee mug added some humanity and even humour to the frequently stressed out CID chief. Forrest, though, had taken a crumb of comfort from the fact that the Detective Chief Super had actually wanted this discussion at all. He clearly wasn't accepting Brenan's proposal unconditionally. In fact, the theory that Poppy Hunt was most likely already dead seemed to be pointing to a thumbs down. 'There's been nothing to suggest she's still alive for eight years now,' he said.

Maybe that forty-minute journey had given him too much

thinking time.

Brenan's response was impudent: 'Until Jason came along, there was no evidence she was alive during the first three years she was missing either. We've still no evidence she's dead. Just give me more time, boss.'

Brenan's brazen words received an icy glare from Brown, but a slight twitch at the corner of his mouth gave away the grin that was being restrained. 'Is there anything more you'd like, Eve?' he replied sarcastically. 'Anything else that might take us further away from policy and managing serious crimes?'

Brenan could think of a few things but decided to keep her mouth shut for once.

Brown decreed that Brenan and Stanier *could* continue as they were for two weeks. They were to supply daily updates to him via Forrest. When the two weeks were gone, with or without any progress, the enquiry would change direction completely. It would centre decisively on a full-scale triple murder investigation and on the arrest of the offender.

The return journey was as quiet as the outward one had been. It was already seven o'clock as they pulled in at the side of the nick. Brenan offered Forrest an olive branch. 'Fancy a swift one, boss?'

Stanier had already booked off duty, so it was the two of them sitting opposite each other at one of the small iron-legged tables in the bar of the *Smithfield*. Brenan opened up the conversation. 'Sorry, boss. Can't seem to help myself. I have to plunge in with both feet. I was well out of order bursting in on you.'

'Who am I to disagree with that?' Forrest said. 'Anyway, it's done now, but you've set yourself a task. You've got some great leads and some good potential with your ideas on the baby grow and trainers. But, Christ, Eve, they're both shoe-leather jobs. You need detectives on the ground asking questions, knocking on doors making phone calls. You and Ed can't do it all on your own. I told you I'm fully behind you on this but it doesn't seem to have sunk in.'

Brenan made a solemn face, took a deep breath and sighed the words: 'Two weeks.'

Chapter 10

Day 6 Saturday 20th April

COPPERS, BY NATURE, are nosy buggers. Consequently, Brenan and Stanier had to endure a near constant barrage of questions from colleagues. Faces continually peered around the door as they tried to get on with their work. Friendly attempts to glean information on what was going on in room 410 were relentless, but were all politely rebuffed.

Brenan did well to smooth talk a joiner into an eight o'clock turn out on a Saturday morning. It was half past nine by the time the man finished off screwing and plugging a large whiteboard along one of the room's walls. He'd already fixed the digital door lock and Brenan was hoping this would play its part in stopping unwanted guests.

The workman gathered his tools, thanked Brenan for the brew, and disappeared into the corridor. She waited for the door to close before positioning the two small photographs of Poppy and Jason in the centre of the huge board. She stood back, arms folded, eyes glued, and became thoughtful. She'd watched such boards on other major investigations slowly fill like a colony of bacteria on a Petri dish. New faces would take up their own places, along with names. Vehicles, addresses, events and dates would all start to compete for space. More and more connecting arrows and coloured lines would join one feature to another until everything centred on one staring face.

She'd also been party to the exact opposite: no new leads, no new faces, no connecting arrows, until the bitter pill of defeat had to be swallowed, and the case made its way down to the basement.

'Penny for 'em?'

The words were Stanier's as he entered, clutching a scrap of paper with the – as yet to be remembered – door code. He looked at the number. 'Don't worry, I'll eat this.'

Brenan's smile was laced with humorous sarcasm. 'You know where you've got to go today, don't you?'

Stanier's eyes drifted towards the ceiling. 'I can't possibly cart all the *Operation Sandstone* stuff up here.'

'Just bring the log books and forensic reports for the time being. I know we can access it all up here on HOLMES, but I'd like to see some of that original paperwork.' She sat back down and spread the latest forensic report on the Baby Jason exhibits out on her desk. The previous look she'd taken at the document had been brief. She now needed to concentrate on the detail. The pressure was already on, though, and DCS Brown had reminded her that she must tell Poppy's parents everything that had come to light before something was leaked to them. It was a priority Brenan did not relish addressing. The Detective Chief Superintendent had stipulated, though, that no detail should be released concerning the *Operation Sandstone* murders. That aspect was to remain top secret and would only cause the Hunts even more anguish.

Brenan was frustrated by the thought of the different tasks they needed to get to grips with. 'Tell you what, Ed. Leave the basement until tomorrow.'

Stanier made a big sigh and acted out flicking sweat from his brow. In reality, though, seasoned detective or not, he was less than keen to go down there again.

Brenan smirked at Stanier's display and tried to put the idea of the forthcoming meeting with the Hunts to the back of her mind. She rubbed the back of her neck as she concentrated on the details of the forensic report. It was the scientist's comments on one issue which jolted her mind fully into focus. The description of how two pages from an old book had been used as a makeshift nappy liner. It augmented the pitiful situation the then seventeen-year-old Poppy had been in. The attempts the young girl had made to keep the baby clean with nothing more than a piece of torn towel and the pages of a book. A small tear formed in a corner of Brenan's eye.

Stanier, sitting opposite and working on his own research,

pretended not to notice as his colleague surreptitiously dabbed to prevent the tear from gliding down her cheek.

The poorly photocopied prints of the pages puzzled her. She went through the forensic report on this aspect, soaking up the scientist's detailed description and findings. Sitting back in her chair, she studied the ceiling, trying to fix her mind on something that wasn't quite right. She was missing something. A small detail didn't quite fit.

The thought continued as they took the fifteen-minute drive out of town to the Hunt's. It was rather like waking from a vivid dream with the memory completely blanked, never quite able to capture the theme. She couldn't pin it down.

The Birchfield estate: a sprawling 1950s development two miles east of Stoke centre. Four thousand five hundred houses across eight hundred acres. This council-managed social housing plan, in its day, had been the largest such project in Europe. The *Right to Buy* scheme of the 1980s led to many of the properties being purchased by their tenants. The idea of self-ownership had, in many parts, lifted the area, although some chunks remained firmly in the grip of criminals, drug dealers and social outcasts. A lack of maintenance, a jacked-up scrap car on the drive or perhaps just an untidy garden often underlined this.

Meerham Gardens, on the other hand, was a decent enough spot. Thirty-two semis, now all privately owned, with mostly tidy gardens and a mix of friendly and caring neighbours.

The last time the Hunts had heard from the police had been eighteen months ago when a review team paid them a courtesy visit. The officer's attempts to reassure the parents that their daughter had not been forgotten brought the whole heart-rending, emotional upheaval back to life. This latest meeting, arranged by telephone the day before, vaguely suggested a similar sort of appraisal of the situation. Laura Hunt's near-to-tears voice had implied she wasn't taken in by the charade and feared dreadful news.

Brenan's push at the white plastic doorbell of number 27 produced an "Avon Calling" chime from somewhere inside. Her own nervous shuffle of the shoulders was in sync with Stanier's adjustment of his tie-knot as a blurred figure appeared on the other side of the opaque door glass.

David Hunt's prompt response hinted that he had been waiting. Of course he had. The intentional few seconds between doorbell chime and opening up had been performed as an attempt at calm normality. It was never going to work. Normality had left this house eleven years ago.

Brenan and Stanier had not met the Hunts before and, until the revelation that sparked this reinvestigation, had never played any part in the case. David Hunt was wordless as Brenan held her warrant card forward and made the introductions. The sadness in the eyes of the forty-nine-year-old insurance assessor had been intensified by a sleepless night induced by this impending visit. The suggestion of another review into the case didn't quite hold water with David or his wife. They had come to know how the police worked over the past eleven years and something was different about this.

A pensive and equally drained Laura Hunt stood, hands clasped at waist level, in the lounge as David led the way through. Poppy's sister, Katie, now twenty-eight and married, stood alongside her mum, left arm draped around her shoulders and showing unmistakable signs in her facial features of those strong Hunt family genes. Katie's husband and five-year-old daughter had stayed at home on police advice. A mantle shelf and sideboard with variously sized framed family photos held more reminders of how happy, carefree and ordinary things used to be at 27, Meerham Gardens.

'Please take a seat.' David Hunt's sweeping hand movement suggested the sofa.

'Tea? Coffee?' Mrs Hunt asked. The slight tremor in her voice evidenced the stress and concern brought on by the possibility that the worst of news was about to be delivered. It was pretty clear to the two detectives that the Hunts had debated the reasons for this visit and feared they were about to be told a body had been found.

The five sat around a coffee table, steaming mugs on coasters. Father, mother and sister watched as Eve Brenan laid a wad of paperwork from her briefcase face down. She'd spotted the worry and quickly wanted to put minds at ease, but knew the truth was unlikely to bring much comfort. Leaning forward, she quickly dispelled any thoughts that they had found a body.

'Firstly, I have no news to offer on Poppy's whereabouts.'

The looks remained impassive. No news was not necessarily good news. 'I do have an unexpected development to discuss.' She turned over the photograph of Poppy and followed up quickly with the one of Jason. Laura Hunt's hand went to her mouth. She picked up Jason's photograph, chest heaving rapidly and close to hyperventilating. 'What is this? Who is this? What does it mean?'

The mother's intuition and maternal instincts instantly latched onto the reality of the situation a country-mile before Brenan had expected her to. The detective realised her plan to carefully guide the Hunts through this emotional cataclysm had been quickly thwarted.

David Hunt's eyes grew steadily wider. The incredible likeness and the fact a police officer investigating his daughter's disappearance was pointing this out made it a whole lot more than a coincidence.

Brenan had no option but to get straight to the point. 'DNA has proved that this young man is Poppy's son. He's eight years old.'

David Hunt took the boy's picture from his wife and stared. A crazy-paving of confusion took over his forehead. His wife stood up, small white hands clenched tightly into fists, eyes wide and fixed on the wall. Her mind had dragged the scant detail together in seconds and assembled the same scenario the detectives had pondered for the past two days. Her response seemed close to hysteria as she shouted at the wall.

'I always believed she was still alive!' The woman visibly shuddered as she delivered her verdict. 'She's being held prisoner somewhere. Someone's got her.'

It was four o'clock when Brenan and Stanier arrived back at the police station. They'd grabbed a cheese bap and a shandy at the *Sythe*. Forrest's office was their next port of call.

The DCI, dark jacket draped on chair back and white shirt sleeves rolled to elbows, sat back and listened carefully. 'You've impressed on them the importance of keeping the lid on all of this?

'Yes,' Brenan replied. 'We've outlined the possible scenarios as discreetly as we could.'

'To be frank, sir,' Stanier interjected, 'they were in front of us most of time. They're both extremely well-read on the Fritzl and Natascha Kampusch cases in Austria, along with the more recent Jaycee Dugard case in California.'

'Difficult day,' Forrest sympathised.

Brenan's blink implied that the remark was an understatement.

'Okay,' Forrest said. 'Anything new?'

'Possibly.' She drew the word out, adding a philosophical shrug of the shoulders. 'There is something of interest in the latest forensic report.'

On cue, Stanier extracted the paperwork from his briefcase as Brenan continued. 'You see, up until now, neither hide nor hair has been seen of Poppy's schoolbag or contents. She had the bag with her when she left school, but it was never found.'

Forrest knew this. He shuffled closer to the desk as Stanier pushed the forensic report across to him with a finger against a line of text.

Brenan's eyes were on the document as she gave more. 'How this has come to be overlooked, I don't know, but the biohazard exhibit NH 25 was described by the SOCO as: *Two pages of a book used as a nappy liner.* The lab has now identified those pages in more detail as being…' She read out the line of text: *Two torn pages (four sides in total) of the preface from a book by Arnold Bennett.*' She looked up momentarily. 'Now, they've recognised that fact quite easily by virtue of the author's name appearing on the fourth side at the end of the preface.'

Forrest folded his arms and sat back in his chair. 'Okay. Interesting, but what's been missed by the earlier enquiry?'

Brenan gave Forrest a meaningful stare. 'The soiled home-made nappy liners never even went to the lab. Now, that's not particularly surprising because the incident was being treated as an abandoned baby rather than the child kidnapping it's become. It was, after all, just a couple of pretty unpleasant messy pages torn from an old book which never in a million years could take the enquiry forward.'

Forrest ping-ponged his gaze between Brenan and Stanier hoping for something ground-breaking.

Stanier explained more. 'Poppy was reading Arnold Bennett at school when she went missing. Now, a possible inventory of her schoolbag was researched, and it was considered a sure-fire bet that, amongst other things, there would have been a copy of Bennett's book *The Card* in there. Her parents both stated this in their original statements and went on to explain how much she was loving reading that particular book.'

Forrest cast a sceptical eye. 'So, you're thinking that those two pages are the first connection that's been made to Poppy's missing bag?'

'It possibly is, sir,' Stanier said. 'We all know that Bennett remains Stoke-on-Trent's most famous author, but I can't see too many school kids nowadays being avid fans of him. Even eleven years ago, Poppy was probably a bit of a one-off. I read *The Card* at school myself and love his books, but I'm thinking they're more interesting to adults than fourteen-year-olds.'

'I love Bennett's work too,' Brenan said. 'It might be a bit out of the league of a typical fourteen-year-old but, having said that, I think I read *The Card* myself at about the same age. Odd how she's managed to keep that copy for those three years of captivity before Jason was born, though.'

Forrest anchored his attention onto Brenan, unsure if this new discovery meant much to the case. 'Okay, I'll update DCS Brown on today's progress, but it doesn't seem a lot yet, and the clock's ticking remember.'

As the two of them stepped out of the lift on the top floor, Stanier commented on an amusing piece of history from his teenage days. 'That was my bloody nickname at school you know. All Arnold Bennett's fault.'

Brenan smiled thinly, not knowing what to expect.

'Yes, we were reading *The Card* at school, so I'm guessing now that it must have part of the curriculum back then. If you remember, the story was all about a young chap in Stoke-on-Trent named Edward Henry Machin. He was known about town by the nickname "Denry". It was all down to a sort of Stokie dropping of the aitches.'

Brenan grinned, now beginning to recall some features of the story. 'So the letter D at the end of Edward took the place of the letter H, making Denry. And your middle name is…?'

Stanier hung his head. 'Henry.'

Brenan started to giggle but then stopped in her tracks, still several yards short of the office door. She stared at her feet, her mind suddenly elsewhere. Stanier's tale had been the trigger she'd needed to unravel the earlier mental conflict.

'The book wasn't *The Card*. Those pages are from another Arnold Bennett book. I'd forgotten the storyline of *The Card*, but you've brought it back.'

They were soon on the A34 heading south and intent on obtaining inside information into the workings of the mind of the fourteen-year-old Poppy Hunt. Teacher Anita Greave, Poppy's old school mate, was one of the few people up to speed with the story and able to give good information on school life at Birchfield High back in 2008. She probably knew more than Poppy's parents on this subject, and seemed less susceptible to the emotions which, understandably, affected the Hunts.

Brenan's quick Internet search before setting off seemed to point at another Bennett story, *The Old Wives' Tale,* as being the book from which the pages had been torn.

The thing was, at this stage, Brenan herself had simply no idea how the issue could possibly impact on the case. The knotted feeling in her gut, though, was telling her something crucial hinged on it.

Annie's yellow Toyota Aygo was strikingly obvious to the two detectives as they pulled onto the rear car park of the *Wayfarer* pub just outside the town of Little Stoneleigh. The meeting spot was a good halfway house between Stoke and Stafford and ideal for their quick chat.

It was approaching six o'clock as the trio entered the spacious lounge of the "open all day" country pub-cum-restaurant. Three coffees and an alcove table gave them the essential privacy they needed.

Brenan explained the anomaly to Annie and at the same time indicated her own uncertainty about its significance.

'Well, I can tell you for a fact that our class was definitely reading *The Card* when Poppy went missing. The two of us talked about the story quite a bit. Sometimes we'd do homework together at one another's house.' Annie smiled at the memory. 'Poppy was way in front of me on English Lit. She virtually ate books. I remember how much she loved it and how keen she was to read more of Bennett's work. She'd already got through another of his and used to rave about how good it was. Some of the witty lines and descriptions were hilarious and Pop would sometimes use them herself in a jokey way...' Annie halted mid-sentence. 'Gosh! "Pop"! Where did that come from? I haven't referred to her as "Pop" since she went.'

Brenan arched an eyebrow. 'Could that other book have been *The Old Wives' Tale*?'

Annie stared into the middle distance. 'No, definitely not. I only got around to reading *The Old Wives' Tale* myself a couple of years ago. It's a simply huge book. No, we only did *The Card* at school.' She was thoughtful again before a smile crossed her lips. 'Colossal bigness,' she said, still staring into nowhere.

Brenan and Stanier exchanged a puzzled glance.

'Colossal bigness. That was one of Bennett's funny lines that Pop used to use. It was from the other book she'd read.' A smirk engulfed the schoolteacher's face as the childhood memory was captured. 'Kids can be horrible. I should know. If we were in town together or walking home from school and we spotted someone overweight or tall she'd whisper, "colossal bigness" to me and we'd be doubled up.' She dabbed a tear from the corner of an eye with a tissue. The salty droplet was a mix of both emotion and humour. She then casually threw in the title of the book. 'It was called *A Great Man.*'

Chapter 11

Day 7 and Day 8 Sunday and Monday

SUNDAY PRESENTED A dilemma: to work or not to work. Sundays were always good days for catching witnesses at home and frequently turned up trumps with an early house call on a wanted villain. The downside of working on the accepted day of rest was that hardly any businesses or other organisations were available to help the police with their enquiries. Brenan was annoyed at wasting a whole day from her two-week deadline but felt it would not take them any further. They took the Sunday off.

They were both back in the office for eight o'clock on the Monday morning, pooling ideas and getting on with telephone and Internet enquiries. Stanier concentrated on the shoebox and baby grow whilst Brenan dug more deeply into the new Arnold Bennett book theory.

Hanley's library was the area's major public book-lending facility. By chance, the building lay in the same broad, edge-of-town road as the police station. In fact, the huge five-storey monolith sat right next door and was constructed in that same sixties modernist style. Brenan's walk from one front door to another took one minute and landed her inside the high-ceilinged spacious foyer five minutes after nine o'clock.

With her warrant card shown and her request for the undivided attention of a suitably knowledgeable staff member, she found herself with chief librarian Miss Lisa Dix.

'Nice to meet you, sergeant,' the librarian said, as their handshake parted. 'What can we do for you?'

Brenan made apologies for giving away nothing on the actual case she was looking into and explained that the matter was highly confidential.

Dix was nonplussed. 'I understand. Fire away.'

Brenan got straight to the issue. 'It all seems to concern Arnold Bennett books.'

'Okay,' Dix said, and headed off into the main ground floor area. 'Follow me.'

They stopped at the end of one of the dozens of bookshelves. The initial letter "B" gave a clue to how things were organised.

Dix stood back from the rows of books and gave a sideways waft of the hand at a particular selection. 'These are the Bennett books we currently have in stock. There are other branches around the city who may have a different selection. If a particular book is requested and isn't on our shelves, we can usually locate a copy and get it sent here for lending. Other than that, we'd have to buy a copy in.'

Brenan ran her eyes along the four feet length of shelving dedicated to Bennett's work. She unfurled the photocopies of the book pages she'd brought with her and handed them over. The print was barely legible. 'I believe this book preface comes from a copy of the Arnold Bennett book, *The Old Wives' Tale.'*

Dix browsed the semi legible print, its readability made even more difficult through the photocopying process. 'Well, I'm sure you're right on that. From what I can tell, the text is certainly talking about that book and, of course, Bennett's name appears on the last of the pages, indicating that it's a preface done by him. You're in luck with this. One of my staff is a leading light in the Arnold Bennett Society. If anyone can tell all there is to know about Bennett books, he can.' With that, Dix half-turned and called into the open doorway of a nearby office. 'Brian, can I borrow your brain for a moment?'

Brian appeared from the doorway, early fifties, wide-eyed, ruddy-faced, overweight and balding. His brown cord trousers were held tightly and high above his waist by a mismatching light grey belt. The flap of his off-white shirt hung partly out. His features were a picture of eager helpfulness. 'If I can find it,' he jokingly answered to the brain question.

'Oh, yes,' Brian commented as he looked at the text. "Definitely the preface from *The Old Wives' Tale*, and from a fairly early copy.' He stooped towards the section of Bennett books on the shelf and dragged out a new-looking plastic-coated copy of *The Old Wives' Tale*. It bore an image of two attractive ladies in Victorian style dress.

'This is the version we now have in stock. It's published by Penguin nowadays, whereas your much earlier copy would have been by Hodder and Stoughton.'

'So, how old then?'

Brian wobbled his head from side to side to show his uncertainty. 'Difficult without seeing and feeling the actual paper. Different text layout.' He pointed at the first line. 'Indent on the first paragraph. Don't do that even in a preface nowadays.' He quickly thumbed through the pages of the new copy to find its own version of the preface and pointed out the difference. 'See. No indent. Other, more modern style clues as well.' His finger moved down the page of the new book. 'Single speech marks, see? Double speech marks in your old copy.'

'So, how old then?' Brenan repeated the unanswered question.

'Latest… 1920. Maybe even a bit earlier.' Brian ran his hand along the line of Bennett books. 'Funny you should be interested in Bennett's books, I was just reordering some copies. We're always losing them.'

'How come?' Brenan said, interest picking up.

Miss Dix nodded her head toward her colleague. 'What Brian really means is someone keeps nicking them.'

Brian gave an elongated blink. 'Yes, we do get quite a few books stolen, and lots of audio books, but rarely novels and not usually these earlier authors. Someone has been very keen on Bennett for quite some time and must have a pretty reasonable collection by now.'

Back in the far corner of room 410, Stanier, feet up on desk edge, looked across at Brenan. She had given him part of the library update. He took a sip from his coffee mug. 'So, *brainstorming* time then.' His emphasis on the word accompanied a sarcastic sneer at his own use of what he would term as "Boss Chat".

Brenan was likewise, feet-up and coffee sipping. 'Brainstorming it is then, Ed. We know Poppy was mad on Bennett books. We know she'd read –' her finger moved down a page of scribble – '*A Great Man*, and we know she was reading and almost certainly had a copy of *The Card* with her when she went missing.'

Stanier replaced his mug on the desk top and folded his arms. '*And* we know she's had an old copy of *The Old Wives' Tale* from somewhere.' He gave Brenan a sideways glance. 'Knowing the way your mind works, *you,* or rather *we*, are both wondering if she's getting supplied with Bennett books and maybe others by the kidnapper to keep her happy.'

'It's a theory worth looking into. It could be a massive time-wasting red herring, but we'll see how far we can take it. See if it leads anywhere. I've gone through the whole rigmarole with the library people. Bennett produced sixty-four books, twelve plays, the libretto for an opera, not to mention dozens of articles for magazines and newspapers.'

Stanier was impressed at the diverse knowledge Brenan had picked up during her two hours at the library.

'My Arnold Bennett expert, Brian, has explained that quite a few of the sixty-four are about self-help and management, so how about we stick to the fiction?'

'Agreed,' Stanier said.

Brenan looked down at her notes. 'The library has kept computerised records and used scanned barcodes for many years now. These go back beyond the time when Poppy went missing, although, to get access to the earlier ones, they'd have to retrieve old hard drives. There are several libraries dotted around the city. That includes the larger town branches and the smaller ones in housing estates.'

Stanier pulled his feet off the desk and sat forward. 'Birchfield Estate!'

'Yes. Great minds…?' Brenan offered. 'It's a "four and a half days a week" branch in the Birchfield Neighbourhood Centre on Houlston Drive.' She looked down at her scribble. 'Been open since

2007. All the City libraries are linked. Brian tells me there wasn't much call for the lending of Bennett's books from the Birchfield branch, so they only keep a few in stock. Special requests to lend unavailable copies have always been extremely rare but – and here's the rub – theft of the few Bennett books kept there has been noticeably high. It's a decent-sized library but confined to one large room. The Bennett copies they had in took a pounding between early 2009 and 2015. I'm going to take a trip up there.

'Anything new on the baby grow?'

Stanier leafed through a stapled-together three-page document on his desk. 'Yes. The Registrar's office emailed me back. They were concerned that some of the detail we're after may fall under data protection. I've explained that, under our circumstances – that's to say, investigating a serious crime – we'd be exempt under the Data Protection Act. They wanted to get back to me after consulting their solicitors, but I know I'm right on that one.'

Brenan's single slow blink accompanied a glimmer of a smile. 'I'd always have a tenner on it when it involves your legal knowledge, Ed.'

Stanier's own slow blink was a pretence at nonchalance. 'Yes, we should get the full results through for Tuesday. So, in view of the baby grow being pink we're only looking for baby girls. They've already told me that 537 baby girls were registered as being born to mothers living in the Stoke-on-Trent area between 1st September and 31st December 2006. Apart from a handful of home births, and a few unexpected arrivals here and there, all these were born at the Stoke Maternity Hospital. So, we're waiting on the names and addresses of the mothers within the postcode areas for the Birchfield estate. That's the thing they've become twitchy about, data protection. We can widen our search out to cover the rest of Stoke-on-Trent. We could take in the Staffordshire Moorlands and Newcastle-Under-Lyme areas if we get nowhere.' Stanier looked frustrated. 'But that'll be a massive job.'

Brenan agreed. 'Let's see if we strike lucky close to home first.'

'As for the shoebox,' Stanier continued, 'we're struggling. Only a couple of local outlets possibly had this model in stock, Horne Sports in Hanley and the JD Sports outlets. So, that could be Hanley, Longton or Burslem. None of them have any existing records going back to around October 2010 through to January 2012, when the trainers might have been in stock.'

Brenan went quiet for a moment. 'So,' she began, 'we may only be left with the hope that someone remembers the snazzy-looking trainers. Pretty bloody doubtful after all this time.'

'Seems that way,' Stanier agreed. 'The other thing is that they're described as "Basketball Shoes". I did look into that aspect but, again, don't hold much hope. The suppliers all seem to be of the opinion that, in the main, the trainers would probably have been bought specifically because of their look rather than for someone wanting to play basketball. Couple that with the fact that the game isn't that popular in the UK and it makes tracking down the shoes nigh on impossible. There are basketball teams and a national league in this country although the closest to Stoke is a team calling themselves *Cheshire Phoenix* at Ellesmere Port.'

'Okay,' Brenan said. 'We'll keep our powder dry on that aspect. Did you manage to get any more detail on the actual trainers?'

'Yep,' Stanier replied. He rummaged in his in-tray and pulled out an A4 sheet. 'Adidas sent me through this photo of the tread pattern.' He pushed it across to Brenan. The design was uniquely fashioned into a cartoon style puddle of water with cross-hatching in the centre.

'That *is* peculiar, not something you'd forget, although the chances are that, after eight years or more, these shoes no longer exist…' Brenan was cut short by the desk telephone. She picked up.

It was Forrest. 'You'd better get down here.'

Forrest was at his desk, a full day's worth of reports untouched in his in-tray and an expression somewhere between anger, frustration and humiliation, if there was such a place. To his left, slouched in a chair, elbows on arm rests and sausage fingers laced across beer-gut was someone neither Brenan nor Stanier had seen in a few years, Detective Chief Inspector Ray Perkins.

Perkins' small pig eyes cruised Brenan's figure for a full wordless fifteen seconds before he slowly swivelled to Stanier. 'Afternoon, Ed,' he drawled, completely ignoring Brenan. Misogyny, sexism and chauvinism seeped in equal measure from every pore of his blue-jowled, thickly eye-browed face. 'Long time no see.'

There was no love lost between Perkins and anyone else in the room. Stanier's blink as he turned away from Perkins to Forrest showed this fact in spades. 'Afternoon, Chief Inspector,' he said, although it was not possible to establish which chief inspector he was being respectful to.

Forrest attempted to empty the room of air with his deep breath as the pair took seats in front of his desk. His fist-to-mouth cough preceded some apprehensive and faltering dialogue. 'I know that you've both met DCI Perkins from when he served as DI here…'

Brenan's cold stare at Perkins implied the sentiment, "How could we forget?"

'Mr Perkins is now working for the National Crime Agency.'

Perkins purposefully leaned inwards and curtly took over the introduction. 'A little organisation you may not yet have bumped into out here in the sticks, the Regional Organised Crime Unit. We do all love our little police acronyms, so ROCU is another one for your list.' Perkins' unblinking stare was riveted onto Brenan's eyes as he attempted to stamp his authority on this investigation with the finesse of a pneumatic road drill. He pushed himself into the backrest again and re-laced his fat digits over his stomach 'Covering the entire West Midlands, as we do, we particularly investigate, amongst other serious crimes, *missing persons.*' Perkins increased his volume for the last two words but did not stop there. '*Child rescue,*' was his next, almost shouted, phrase. His volume reduced, but was still above normal as he continued. 'Our Serious Crimes Analysis Section looks into the emergence of serial killers and serial rapists. We have specially trained staff.' Perkins cocked his head to one side, eyes menacingly wide and with a condescending smirk curling the edges of his lips. 'Am I ringing any bells?'

Brenan returned the stare with enough contempt to relegate Perkins from the league. 'My enquiry and the way in which it is being handled has been sanctioned by the force Detective Chief Super. I was not aware that the NCA even had any knowledge of this. It has been agreed that Poppy Hunt's safety could well lie with the confidentiality of this case, and how it's handled.'

It would have been etiquette at the finish of this explanation for Brenan to have added the word "sir", but she did not.

'You can't make up your own fuckin' rules, Brenan, and even the DCS has to toe the line with this. Not my words, before you think about telling tales. This has come from the NCA Director General.' Perkins casually brushed a piece of non-existent lint from a trouser leg. 'You see, Brenan, your lucky break on Friday, with young Jason's familial hit pointing towards a serial killer, set all sorts of alarm bells off in my office. Serial killers are my field, remember?'

Brenan stared blankly back at Perkins and then moved her gaze over to Forrest. She was unsure where this was going.

'In fact, Sergeant Brenan, you might even say that your actions inspired my next move.' Perkins had assumed a sickly smile. 'Fact is, I have now identified Jason's father. The three times *Sandstone* prossie murderer and kidnapper of Poppy… what's-her-name?'

Brenan's chin dropped fractionally creating a half-inch gap between her lips. She took a second to compose herself and to think things through. 'My God! He's on file? You're saying he's on file after all. We can still work together on this. Maybe we can track him down, keep obs and still keep it quiet until we know if Poppy's alive and find out where she is.'

'Well that's a lot of ifs and maybes, Brenan, but don't forget who's running this show, *and* who found out who this bastard is. I remember you and your impetuous actions only too bloody well. My only thought on your possible ongoing involvement is that we might – and it is a *might* – benefit from a local female officer, in case the girl *is* still alive.'

Brenan's anger was barely in control at Perkins' sexist remarks. Her eyes flashed a laser stare as an incisor bit down hard enough to draw blood inside her lip.

Madeleine Scott stepped from the shower of her Milton Keynes apartment as the phone started ringing. She blindly fumbled for her glasses with one hand whilst the other snatched at the towel.

It was a full half minute before she'd got her act together, steamed specs on nose and soapy ear hardly dry enough for the phone. After another five minutes she'd started to get the full drift of what Brenan was telling her. 'So, how come the complete change around then?' she said into the receiver. 'I mean, you've already been told by the lab that there's no match on file for Jason's father.' She paused, thinking it through. 'If he'd been on record, he would have been matched to the three murders within twenty-four hours of actually going on. They simply don't make mistakes like that.'

'I know,' Brenan's voice came back. 'Exactly my thoughts, but I never had chance to voice that point. I was as good as chucked out of the office and, anyway, I didn't want to jeopardise our chances of still having some input.'

'So am I still on the case?' Scott asked.

'It was never mentioned, and I specifically didn't bring it up. As far as I'm concerned, our department is directed from HQ and no one there has told me any different, so we stick to plan A.'

'You say they've already got an address for the offender?'

'Oh, yes! Perkins made a big play of that, but he won't divulge any details yet. He says they're planning a few days' surveillance to see if it gives any clues as to whether Poppy might still be alive, and then it'll be a visit from an armed response team and the door will go in.'

'I'm worried,' Scott said. 'This is the last thing we needed. Look I haven't phoned you as I've been up to my neck researching the offender's profile through Geneaus DNA. I've got some interesting stuff but, if they've already nailed him, I can't see it being any use.'

'You fancy coming up?' Brenan said.

'I'll get sorted and jump straight in the car.'

Brenan and Stanier resolved to carry on with their own enquiries, in spite of Perkins' takeover. A snatched ten private minutes with Forrest had not disallowed this idea and they were not going to make a point of telling Perkins anyway. It was clear Forrest felt uneasy about the situation, angry even that he had been side-lined yet again. If he'd had his own way, Brenan would have continued for the full two weeks as originally decided.

Brenan filled the afternoon with a visit to the Birchfield branch library and a more detailed study of the book thefts. Stanier, back at the office, updated the whiteboard with the photographs of the three murdered women from the *Operation Sandstone* case. He knew the entire investigation was set to balloon in size now Perkins had appeared. There seemed little point in going further than those additional three photos. Perkins was confident his potential target was not only the *Sandstone* murderer but also Poppy's kidnapper and rapist.

Stanier slumped back into a chair and gazed at the whiteboard, his mind racing forward as he pictured Perkins' premature arrest of the murderer – the glory, the credit, the slaps on the back. Stanier knew only too well that, even after the fourteen uneventful years since the *Sandstone* murders that the arrest of the offender would only be the beginning. A huge major enquiry team under a Senior Investigating Officer would pull all the strings together. CSI, Forensics, detectives and CPS solicitors would spend months preparing a watertight court case and Perkins would slip away from the graft to bask in the glory.

Stanier chewed at his biro for a while as Poppy's photograph caught his eye, drilling into his mind. The urgency of the whole situation was now growing exponentially, doubling in size with every second of Perkins' narcissistic approach.

Madeleine Scott booked into the Hanley Premier Inn at quarter past six that evening. She dumped her suitcase on the bed of her first-floor room, trotted down the stairs and out to the car park where Brenan was waiting in her Ford Fiesta. They made it to *The Southwood Inn* by half past.

John Eardley gave Brenan a wide-eyed smile from his spot behind the bar. 'Twice in a week, Cadet Brenan! The *Sythe* is honoured – or could it be that something is hotting up down in the Birchfield?'

Eardley's par-for-the-course humour drew a derisory eye roll from

Brenan. The *Southwood* was filling quickly with early doors diners eager to get to grips with the highly regarded food menu. Steak and kidney pudding and chips for Brenan hit the spot, as did the lasagne for Scott.

Brenan's well-meant idea of staying with a half lager all night was never going to work. Her decision to leave the car and take a taxi back was made before the evening was half an hour old. A lengthy and gloomy discussion took place over the food with a full update on the events and the unsavoury history attached to DCI Ray Perkins.

It was several drinks and several hours later before Eardley was able to call "last orders" and settle in at their table. He wiped a handkerchief across his sweating brow and pulled his chair in close. 'I've done my bit for today. I'm leaving the staff to the mopping-up operations.'

If there was one person on the Birchfield that Brenan could trust it was Eardley. The retired detective still had his finger very much on the pulse. He'd never lost his copper's mentality and insight. Brenan would not be telling him the full story – not yet anyway – but enough to let him know there was some police infighting going on which was definitely not in the public interest.

The pub's door bolts were slid into place behind the noisy but well-behaved last group to leave before Brenan mentioned the name "Perkins". It was enough to strengthen Eardley's resolve to help out. The fact that Perkins was now a DCI on the high profile NCA and a top-ranking officer in the Regional Organised Crime Unit's Viper Squad increased the scarlet hue of the licensee's cheeks.

'That bastard! How the hell has he landed a job like that in today's supposedly lily-white, incorruptible police force. He was a bloody dinosaur before T-Rex hatched, and that's without mentioning the sexist bullying side of the corrupt, empire-building toe rag.'

Scott sat back in her chair, struggling to keep a fit of giggles in check. 'You don't like him then?'

Eardley's introduction to Scott had come much earlier in the evening. Brenan's trust of Scott was good enough for him. He continued with his angry disbelief on Perkins' prominent position.

'I'll keep my eyes and ears open for sure. You seem pretty certain it'll concern an operation somewhere on the estate.' The comment had not really been posed as a question, but it stopped Brenan in her tracks. She knew nothing about the identity of the man Perkins had earmarked as Poppy's kidnapper and a triple murderer. Brenan's earlier attempts to get more from Forrest had delivered nothing, but he did seem sincere when he'd said, 'You know as much as me, Eve.'

The drinking session came to a halt at one o'clock as headlights lit the car park. Their taxi had arrived.

Chapter 12

Day 9 Tuesday 23rd April

SALLY SATNAV GUIDED Scott to Brenan's apartment in nearby Newcastle-Under-Lyme for half past seven the next morning. Brenan's Fiesta had spent the night on *The Southwood Inn* car park. She was relieved to see its alloy wheels were still in place as Scott drew up alongside.

Their arrival at the police station's top floor office just before eight was soon followed by the kettle's hollow background roar. Brenan's head was surprisingly clear given last night's pub lock-in, but the coffee was welcome.

The clicking of the digital door lock heralded Stanier's arrival, but Eardley's parting comment from last night had been bugging Brenan. Stanier didn't even get chance to manage his usual, 'Mornin',' before Brenan was voicing concerns. 'Ed, we don't even know if Perkins' suspect does live on the estate. He could be anywhere.'

'Good morning, Constable Stanier,' the detective said out loud to himself. His grin at Scott was accompanied by a shake of the head at his partner's customary brusque greeting.

He went straight into a reply. 'Yes, same thing crossed my mind. It's possible the suspect doesn't live on the estate. Clearly, Perkins is trying to stop us interfering with what he's going to call "his collar". He's hoping to lock this bloke up, rescue Poppy and save the world all at the same time. He'll be keeping schtum on all the detail until the last moment.' Stanier folded his arms and stared at the whiteboard. 'He's already told us he's planning a raid, so he must have a team with him and they must have their own vehicles and comms. If his offender wasn't living somewhere on our patch, he wouldn't have even bothered with us, so it's got to be somewhere nearby. If he's really planning a few days obs before kicking the door in, it's going to take some finesse and careful planning.'

'Not something Perky's known for,' said Brenan. 'What *you* got planned for today, Ed?'

'Badger the Registrar for those new-born baby details and see if I can get to the bottom the baby grow side of things. I've got an appointment up there at half ten. I'm not going to drop everything because Perky's turned up.' He gave Brenan a hard stare. 'So what *are* we hoping to do now he's muscled in?

Brenan scowled. 'We all think there's a chance that Poppy is still alive, right?'

The nodding heads all around signalled full agreement as Brenan gave her take on the situation. 'I've seen what a blundering bully Perkins is before. He's going to get plenty of glory if he clears up the three cold case serial killings. Yes, resolving those killings is hugely important, and who knows what else this bastard has done? But Perkins isn't playing this right. Poppy is not on his list of priorities. He didn't even know her surname yesterday. We need to find out where his team are keeping obs, where this pad is that he thinks the suspect is living. It's possible that, if we can do that, we could still pull off a rescue or influence Perkins before this all goes pear-shaped and she gets killed.'

Scott was standing at the window, checking out the gloomy view across the city as she listened. She was becoming quite attuned to some of the police jargon and favoured phrases used by her new colleagues. She managed a smile at Brenan's apt "pear-shaped".

'I still can't get over how he's suddenly identified the father,' she said. 'It must be DNA for him to be so certain. I mean, you've not got prints on anything. How could the lab have missed him being on file against the three murders in the first place?' She shook her head. 'Not to mention the most recent full DNA sequence from the baby Jason exhibits, which again tied him into the three murders and Poppy's kidnap.' She turned back into the room. 'So, has the murderer, by some miracle, only just gone on the NDNAD in the last few days? I bloody well doubt the chances of that. How the hell could they miss him not once, but four times?'

Brenan's mobile phone ringtone cut into the conversation. She glanced at the screen: *John Eardley*. 'Hi, John.'

Eardley's voice was muffled and much lower than his usual boisterous pitch. 'Got a couple of gents in here having a full English. Jeans, trainers, big guys, Brummy accents. Parked a grey Beamer outside. Certainly look like undercover Old Bill to my well-trained eye. Not local, though. Not with that accent, and not with a BMW.'

'Thanks, John,' Brenan responded, almost feeling the need to whisper herself. 'Make sure your CCTV is on and try to get the car number.'

'Already sorted on both counts, Eve. Speak later.'

Scott and Brenan were in no rush to bump into any of Perkins' team and especially not Perkins himself. They left their trip out to the *Southwood* until eleven o'clock. A debate on the situation continued during the journey. 'So, if the two guys who've been in for breakfast are ROCU cops, it looks as though the suspect *is* actually on the estate or nearby,' Brenan said.

A quick recce of the pub car park showed no BMW. Whoever the men were, they had gone. Brenan parked the Fiesta in a side street and they took an alley through to the pub.

'All clear?' she asked, as Eardley met them on the pub steps.

'Yes. Went about fifteen minutes ago. Come on through to the office and take a look at the CCTV. You need to keep your heads down anyway. It wouldn't do to have Perkins arrive for his own full English and spot you.'

A large monitor took up some of the desk space in a tiny, cluttered side room which Eardley used as an office. It showed an eight-way split screen with different views both inside and outside the pub. Eardley shuffled the mouse back and forth to catch the required time field before expanding a camera view covering the pub's lounge to full screen. The colour picture showed part of the bar from the back and the entrance door. The time frame in the bottom right hand showed eleven minutes past ten as the door swung open and two hefty, but fit looking, young men strolled in and up to the bar.

'No sound, John?' Brenan quizzed.

'No, didn't bother with that option. But, like I said, definitely both Brummies.'

'Freeze it there,' Brenan said, as one face came closer to the camera. 'Yes. I remember him. He was a DC at Bromsgrove. I was on a surveillance course with him only last year. Decent guy. Not his fault he's now got Perkins for a boss.'

Eardley swapped screens to show the car park and a shot of the BMW as it pulled in at the side of the pub. He slid a torn half page of note paper across the desktop to Brenan. 'Can't see it too well on the camera but that's it, for what good it'll do you.'

'Can't you run a computer check on it to be sure?' Scott said.

'No, no,' Brenan said. 'It'll be blocked on the PNC so it won't tell us anything, but it'd also flag up that a police officer had carried out a check. It wouldn't take thirty seconds to establish the ID of who'd done it. Perky would know we were watching him, and we'd be in serious trouble for misuse of the PNC as well.' Brenan turned to Eardley. 'Every chance he might come in here John, if they're close by. I'm guessing he'll remember you.'

'He won't forget me. Last time we spoke was about twelve years ago when he was a DS. I had him by the throat in the CID office. I'll keep my head down if he shows up.'

Brenan and Scott cruised some of the estate streets in the area of the *Southwood* for twenty minutes. It was a pretty half-hearted stab at spotting the NCA observations team. The last thing Brenan wanted was to alert Perkins' people to the possibility someone was watching them.

They only had one prominent clue at the moment – the BMW that had visited Eardley's pub. The National Crime Agency and Regional Organised Crime Units were, for the main part, a professional bunch with expensive resources. They had a mix of everyday vehicles at their disposal to blend in with the background. They would normally work alongside local police, but it was clear in this case that Perkins had contrived to officially allow his team anonymity and to work as a separate entity. Such a procedure was only normally used in cases involving police corruption.

To Brenan, Perkins was manipulating the rules for his own ends. Getting a collar for the three *Operation Sandstone* murders could push him up the ladder to Detective Chief Super in double-quick time. The more than healthy pension attached to that rank was desirable in any retiree's book. Adding the kidnapping, rape and murder of Poppy Hunt to the charge sheet could stud Perkins' prospects with diamonds. The possibility that Poppy might still be alive and, if so, desperately in need of ultra-careful handling by the police, was a millstone likely to impede Perkins' expectation of a quick and efficient operation. If she really *was* alive, and happened to be saved into the bargain, he'd be expecting kudos equal to the bestowing of a Victoria Cross.

Brenan placed Poppy at the top of her list and would use every trick in her book to find where Perkins' suspect lived. If she had to break rules, she would. Her years of police work and the many hours she'd spent on observations herself might help her mission but the vast estate with its thousands of houses was not going to give up the secret easily.

They trawled a few hotel car parks on the way back to the police station, hoping to spot the BMW. It was likely the team would have taken several rooms somewhere nearby, but nothing was leaping out as a clue.

They were almost back at the police station when Brenan's phone kicked into life. She pulled over and checked the screen, cursing herself for never getting around to setting up blue tooth for hands free. The screen read *DICK SMALL.* Scott caught a glimpse of the name as Brenan pressed the answer button. Her furrowed brow gave way to a snigger. She was becoming tuned in to Brenan's sarcastic humour.

'Nick!' Brenan said into the phone.

'Hi, Eve,' the voice responded. 'Still not sure what you're interested in, but been hearing a bit of gossip.'

'We'll be with you in fifteen minutes.'

Only ten minutes had passed when Brenan pulled in kerbside and walked across to the *Bottom Knocker.* The short journey had been time enough to update Scott on the world of licensee Nicholas Mazewski.

The large, roughly tarmacked car park was relatively empty. The few regular lunchtime punters had mostly finished their cheap and cheerful chicken curry or fish, chips and peas and made their way back home. A handful of die-hard beer drinkers were the only remaining customers until the later football matches.

Brenan nodded at Mazewski behind the bar. 'Nick,' she said.

'Sergeant Brenan,' Mazewski responded, tattooed bulging arms folded across steroid-pumped pectorals.

Scott struggled to keep her eyebrows in check as the unexpectedly high pitch of the big man's voice attempted to drag them skywards.

Mazewski pulled the ordered two halves of shandy and did his best at a smile as Brenan introduced Scott as a colleague.

'So, what's to do, Nick?' Brenan asked as they settled onto high bar stools, sufficiently distant from the prying ears of the few remaining punters.

Mazewski leaned slowly across the woodwork, eyes swivelling and head turning with sufficient secrecy to attract attention from miles around. 'Something might be going on in Devonish Crescent. Arthur Mills came in last night. He's a pensioner, but he's got a bit of form – years back, mind. He lives there and mentioned in passing that he'd seen some suspicious looking characters in the street and a couple of motors that didn't fit in. He said it'd been going on for a couple of nights now.' Mazewski leaned in even closer. 'Now I don't know what it is that you're interested in, Eve, cuz you've not told me the full story. What I do know is that Devonish Crescent backs onto Malbon Square, where Barclays Bank is.' Mazewski's focus swapped from Brenan to Scott and back. 'Now I know that don't fit with your interest in pervs and child molesters, but it sounds like something you should know about.'

Brenan and Scott walked back to the car. Brenan was strangely quiet as she settled into the driving seat. This latest news sounded interesting to Scott and she'd expected the DS to be enthusiastic.

Eventually Brenan spoke. 'So bloody frustrating. This could well be Perkins' team but time's running out. If this really is where the suspect lives, they're not going to hang about for long. Once they've eyeballed him and are sure he's living there, they'll be ready to move in. The only thing that could hold Perkins back is him covering himself against later criticisms over Poppy.' She tilted her head backwards and stared at the car's roof lining. 'I can see the observation logs now, full of entries and orders from Perkins. "No sightings of Poppy. No suggestion she was in the building or where she might be." God! I wish we could do a quick recce. A drive through would be good, but it'd blow us out straight away. If this is a ROCU team they'll be PNC-ing every car and videoing everybody going near.'

Scott's wide eyes narrowed down to slits. 'Nobody knows me.'

Brenan turned in her seat. 'No, Mad, it'd never work. You're not surveillance or undercover trained, and I'd get shot if anyone found out I'd let you do that.'

Scott stared out fixedly through the windscreen. 'Methinks you might get shot anyway.' Her sideways glance was as conspiratorial as a wink.

Chapter 13

THE PLAN TOOK ten minutes to engineer. The trip to the local Lidl store and the short journey to Malbon Square added another fifteen.

Scott emerged on foot into Devonish Crescent from the alley leading back to the corner of Barclays Bank. With its sweeping curve of thirty-eight time-worn semis, the residential street she now looked out onto was one of the Birchfield's less than half-decent localities. Several abandoned wheelie bins, each with a giant painted house number, competed with parked cars for pavement space. An arsenal of satellite dishes stared skywards. Overgrown privet hedges rubbed shoulders with variously designed and differently-coloured panel fencing to enclose a mix of both tidy and unkempt gardens. Glancing left and then right, she consumed the information on offer, hoping her untrained but razor-sharp mind might pick up something unusual.

Her belted black raincoat and jeans were not strikingly noticeable. The high heels though, were not particularly well thought out for a woman traipsing door-to-door to deliver Lidl flyers. The bundle she'd tucked under her arm during her thirty second visit to the store would be more than enough.

The alleyway transported her into the street almost mid-way on the even-number side. She turned right, swallowed hard and then pushed open the gate of number eighteen. Behind her glasses, Scott's eyes narrowed as she headed down the path, flyer in hand. The fluttering butterflies in her stomach increased their wing beats exponentially as a thought came to her. If this hunch was right, she was probably being watched, videoed and talked about from somewhere close by. To make this look authentic, she could not miss any of the houses.

The high-definition image of the back of Scott's head enlarged to fill the laptop screen before panning back out and moving downwards to hover over her backside. 'New visitor on the block,' a male voice said over a radio.

'Keep it professional boys,' a female voice responded. 'No arses or tits.'

'Sorry, Sarge,' came the reply, as the camera moved back up to the head.

'What we got?'

'Newcomer visiting number eighteen, Sarge. Delivering post or something.'

'Okay, keep an eye on her.'

Scott's butterflies morphed into thrashing pigeons. It was fortunate she could not hear the police conversations and as she delivered her third flyer as the commentary started again.

'Managed to zero right in, Sarge. She's delivering Lidl flyers, so no problem. Looks like she's going to do the entire crescent. She'll be here for a while.'

Ostensibly, the delivery lady got on with her mundane and stress-free job. The truth of the matter, though, was that Scott's nerves were jangling off the scale. It was as she exited the last gate and crossed to make a start on the other side that those nerves went into overdrive. Then she spotted the BMW.

The car number matched with the one visiting the *Southwood* and the two hulking figures in the front seats were unquestionably also the same men seen on CCTV. Scott considered Brenan's outlined predictions of what she should look out for if a house in Devonish Crescent really was a target, and the location of Perkins' OP, or observations point. Here was a definite clue that they had got it right. The short course on Police Obs that Brenan had given Scott during the dash to Lidl had made clear what she should be looking out for.

Scott could feel the two BMW men watching her as she crossed the road. She carelessly thumbed through her flyers, apparently oblivious to the world around her as she stuck to Brenan's golden rule: no eye contact.

Two neighbours were chatting over the low wicket fence

separating their gardens at Scott's next port of call. 'Hello, love, you've picked a funny time for that,' one lady said.

Scott managed a passable gormless face that didn't really fit with the shoes. 'Pays the bills,' she replied, and felt buoyed up by the act. Her confidence was growing.

After a few more houses, she realised she'd got her wits about her and concentrated more calmly on the surroundings. There was a vehicle, half on the pavement, outside most of the houses. The two *For Sale* signs and the one *To Let* she spotted seemed to pulsate as if they were neon adverts.

Scott's rapid mind registered the estate agents names on the boards and quickly discounted one of the *For Sale* signs with its *View By Appointment* addition. The fact that a family complete with dog were still in residence was the deciding factor. She slowed her delivery pace as she got closer to one of the *To Let* houses and even casually checked her mobile phone as a cover for a couple of covert snapshots of the scene.

It was the gangling, pimply youth tinkering with his motorcycle in another garden who really captured Scott's attention. His surly, 'O'reight,' came with a strong Potteries accent in reply to her chirpy, 'Hello,' as she headed, arm outstretched, for the letterbox. The young man's eyes only fleetingly ventured up from the oil-drenched gearbox innards he was working on before returning to his work. It was enough for Scott, though. The brief glimpse she did catch riveted her eyes on the number plate of the lad's motorcycle.

'That dozy cow's in the target's garden now. She's dropped her flyers; there's stuff every bloody where.' A couple of laughing voices could additionally be heard behind the police officer's commentary.

Scott's down-on-haunches stance as she collected her flyers from the ground provided opportunity for a surreptitious look at the "empty" *To Let* house opposite. A glint of reflected light behind an upstairs window pane suggested a three-inch glass circle further back into the room and Scott's imaginative brain quickly concluded it was a camera lens.

The unheard-by-Scott police commentary continued. 'Ha-ha! You should see this! It's bloody hilarious! She's got the target's son running round the garden now, collecting her flyers up and his hands are that filthy it'll all end up in the bin.'

It didn't all end up in the bin. Scott diligently managed to complete Devonish Crescent in her quest to inform residents of Lidl's latest bargains.

Back in Brenan's car, Scott blurted out her recall of the motorcycle's registration plate. She needed to get it off her chest before she forgot it. 'Jesus, I could do with a drink,' her trembling voice added as she sat back to relate the full story.

'So what made you concentrate on that property as being the OP?' Brenan finally got chance to ask.

'Well, there was the BMW, large as life. There was no panel van or similar which you said was a possibility and, as the other option was an empty house, it looked likely.' She closed her eyes momentarily and sucked in a lungful of air. The calming effect as she exhaled better placed her to explain the best bit. 'I don't think that I've merely located the OP.' She blinked at her sudden spontaneous use of police jargon. 'I think I've identified the target's house. I think it's number twenty-three. But there's more.'

Brenan's cagey frown showed her hesitancy about accepting Scott's theory without proof and she was keen to know what the dramatic, "But there's more," comment meant. 'Explain.'

'It was that lad on the drive with his motorbike,' she nodded down at the registration number scribbled on Brenan's pad. 'His features. The hair and eye colouring, the skin tone, the bone structure.'

Brenan looked sideways from the driving seat at Scott, puzzled by these apparently grabbed-from-thin-air sentences.

Scott started again. 'Young Jason Fitzgerald has certain definite and noticeable facial similarities to his mother. We've all seen that in the photographs. He also shares his DNA fifty-fifty with his father and, almost certainly if we could see his father, we'd possibly notice similarities to him in Jason. The lad on the drive of number twenty-three with the motorbike… Everything about him hit me like a ton of bricks. It was as though I was looking at the family album. Those additional features in Jason that he gets from his father, we don't even notice because we've never seen his father. We've got nothing to compare him to. As soon as I saw that lad, I was convinced I was looking at Jason's half-brother.' Scott gulped in another breath. 'Perkins may have got it right. His father may indeed be your man, may really be Poppy's kidnapper.'

Chapter 14

HALF AN HOUR later, the pair were back in Room 410 and huddled over a laptop. Stanier, fresh back from the Registrar's, was keen to hear what had happened. Scott had done well under the pressure to remember the motorcycle plate. Brenan quickly established that she'd got it right when a PNC check came back to the owner: Kevin Patrick Powell, 23, Devonish Crescent, Birchfield. A check on the Driver and Vehicle Licensing Agency brought young Powell's details on screen immediately. He was nineteen and did indeed live at number 23. With no other vehicle number easily available to draw on for more family names, Brenan logged into the council's online electoral register for the house.

It was no surprise when 23, Devonish Crescent was revealed as the Powell family home. The details were sparse: three family members who were of voting age. It was possible though that there were other younger members of the family also living there, but the short list seemed to spell out: father, mother and son.

Brenan stared long and hard at that first name on the list, Mr Mark Timothy Powell. It didn't take much working out to come to the conclusion that this was Kevin's dad.

Mrs Sarah Pauline Powell showed on the second line, and would be Mark's wife and, no doubt, Kevin's mum.

The third and last person listed at the address predictably showed as Mr Kevin Patrick Powell, a match for the PNC owner of the motorbike. This was the sullen, oil-stained young man who had reluctantly helped Scott pick up her leaflets.

Brenan's eyes moved back up and fixed upon the name of the as-yet-unseen Mark Timothy Powell. 'So this must be Perkins' target,' she said. 'The guy he's earmarked as a serial murderer, kidnapper and rapist. The man who could still be holding Poppy Hunt prisoner!'

Brenan next tried a PNC check for a criminal record on Mark

Timothy Powell. She input a nominal, wide age range of between thirty-five and sixty-five but closed the search parameters in with North Staffs post codes. She hit the send button. The result came back within seconds: *NO MATCHES*.

Brenan pulled a dumbfounded face. This was not what she'd expected. If Perkins' evidence really was strong enough to identify Mark Powell and justify such a big obs operation, then surely there'd be a criminal record and everything that comes with it. She opened the fields wider by adding even more years and increasing the area. A few Mark Powells and several Timothy Powells came back connected to the Midlands with criminal records, but still no Mark Timothy Powell. A national search did throw back two people with an exact match on the name but, frustratingly, the ages were wildly out, both mere teenagers so far too young. Brenan lightly thumped the side of a fist down onto the desktop. 'We're going to need a date of birth to be sure, but it's looking like the Mark Timothy Powell from 23, Devonish Crescent has no police record.'

'Could the name be false?' Scott asked.

Brenan dipped her head forward. 'Yes, anything's possible. Certainly, Perkins seems sure of his facts and he's no doubt done all this digging. He might have already untangled this mess. We'll try for a driving licence registered to him at Devonish Crescent.' She rattled out the required detail and gave the "Send" key a frustrated stab.

'Bingo!' Brenan said, with more surprise than elation. Mark Timothy Powell of 23, Devonish Crescent, Birchfield now had his own page on Brenan's screen. It also gave his driver number which supplied a date of birth putting him at 45 years of age. Frustratingly, though, he didn't have a photo ID driving licence, just one of the old-fashioned green paper ones.

'Damn it!' Brenan said. 'No photo and no endorsements, not even as much as a speeding fine!' She added more keystrokes and input a fresh criminal record search with the all-important date of birth.

The *NO MATCH* response which flashed onto the screen took the wind out of her sails. 'He's got no bloody record at all under any version of that name. So what the hell has Perkins turned up?' She swivelled in her chair to face Scott. 'Mad, I don't like to suggest this, but is it possible that you've eyeballed the wrong house, wrong family. Maybe even been a bit too imaginative on the location of the police OP?'

'No, Eve, no. That little grease monkey in the garden is Jason's half-brother – I'm sure of it.' She paused. 'That makes his dad a dangerous individual. How about a criminal record check on the lad?'

Brenan swivelled back to the screen. The full name, along with that driving licence date of birth, immediately registered a hit. Young Kevin was not a bad lad but had got himself in trouble with the law for a couple of fairly minor pieces of naughtiness. He had taken a motor bike without the owner's consent twelve months earlier and had been caught in a stolen car with some mates.

Kevin had not suffered any harsh punishment but had hopefully learned his lesson. It was a lesson, though, that generated him a Criminal Records Office number. The fact that his prints and DNA were also registered, along with a mugshot was to be expected.

Brenan and Scott looked at each other. Time was running out. They had no clue when Perkins was planning to hit the address, but it wouldn't be long. Scott was certain she'd hit the jackpot with the right family even though it was nothing more than a hunch. Kevin's criminal record didn't take the theory any further forward, but his National Database DNA profile could provide the answer.

Brenan knew it was a simple job for the NDNAD to compare Kevin's profile with the crime scene profile left behind by the serial killer fourteen years ago. It would not be a complex, wide-reaching and expensive familial search, but a check of one sample against another to see if there was the fifty percent match of father and son.

She was straight on the phone and the answer came much quicker than expected. 'But you already have this detail,' the scientist said. 'This was the positive result picked up from the full familial search carried out by the VIPER Regional Organised Crime Unit for…' There was a pause whilst a computer screen was read.'…DCI Perkins. So, yes, Kevin Patrick Powell shows a full fifty percent share with the *Operation Sandstone* profiles. Very definitely a son.'

'Okay so now we know for sure,' Brenan said as she replaced the receiver. 'But the chances are pretty high that Perkins will now find out that we've been snooping.'

'Almost certainly,' Stanier said. 'What I can't get my head around is why did our initial search on the system using Jason's DNA as a crime scene stain only threw up connections to the Sandstone murderer? Why didn't it turn up Kevin Powell as well?'

Scott's voice was flat. 'Because the computer does as it's told. We asked for nothing less than a full fifty percent familial result, a paternal only test, and that's what we got – his father. Kevin is Jason's half-brother and, as such, they only have a twenty-five percent DNA share. It was never going to pick up the connection unless we widened the parameters. Anyway, we know we've got the right family, but we've still got nothing on the chief suspect. How about the Registrar's office, Ed? It would be nice to know when the Powells were married.'

'I know exactly who to telephone on that,' Stanier said. 'The Registrar's deputy has promised me all the details on names and addresses for our baby grow enquiries and is happy to provide any data on this case now.'

Brenan gave Stanier the nod to give it a try and turned back to Scott for more inspiration. They all knew time was running out.

'Let's try an ordinary Google search on Powell senior and see if anything turns up,' Scott suggested.

Brenan's computer keys were clacking before the sentence was finished. The simple check produced the most unexpected surprises of the day. The local Sentinel newspaper yielded no less than six hits over the last five years. The first one was a published letter to the editor from "Birchfield resident, Mr Mark Powell". Powell's gripe centred on vehicles parking dangerously on pavements on the estate. A similar letter complained about "boy racers" and the need for more speed humps. Again the author was a Mark Powell.

The name Mark Powell appeared in another three articles or letters, all in the same vein and always only identified as Mark Powell, a Birchfield resident. A fourth one, though, published a month before, was a Sentinel reporter's article and included a photograph. Half a dozen adults and some children were pictured sheltering under umbrellas outside the entrance to Birchfield High School. The ear to ear grins of the rain-sodden group sat beneath a headline boasting: *School's Excellent Ofsted Rating.*

The three investigators clustered around the screen. The newspaper's wording briefly explained the praiseworthy achievements which had brought about the award. It also gave names to people in the photo whose efforts had helped the success: Headmaster, David Barnes, local councillor Peter Tucker, community Governor Mrs Pat Burton, staff governor Julie Morrell and parent governor Mark Powell were all named. It was not the best of photographs. The adult standing far right was no doubt Powell, but a shared umbrella and a gangling fifth former in front dogged any chance of detail.

Brenan gave a slow head shake. 'Not a lot of help. We're stuck with half a name and no address.' She pointed at the screen. 'Is this school governor, named Mark Powell, actually Mark Timothy Powell of Devonish Crescent? Chances are, yes, but we're still not certain.'

Stanier straightened up and stood back from the desk. 'Well, obviously Kevin left school some time ago. If Mark Powell is still listed as a Parent Governor, then there must be a younger child who still attends the school.' He dragged out a chair and squeezed in alongside Brenan. 'Check the school website. I'm a school Governor myself. The schools have to publish the names of the Governors, so it will likely give his full name but there'll still be no address.' He paused, then clarified: 'Data protection.'

A few more seconds were spent rattling at the keyboard and in no time the school website and its list of governors appeared. Brenan hovered the cursor over the name Mark Powell and tapped her index-finger down. The full screen which opened was dedicated to Parent Governor, Mark Timothy Powell. No address was included but the full name matched – a pretty singular permutation, at least for the Birchfield estate. The three pairs of eyes moved down in sync and locked onto the quarter page, head and shoulders photograph of Powell and stared silently. A fair haired, chubby-faced, well-groomed and smartly dressed mid-forties man smiled at the camera.

Scott broke the silence. 'That's *not* Jason's dad – and, I'm sorry to say, it's not Kevin's dad either.' Brenan saw anger in her eyes. 'So it can't be the *Operation Sandstone* murderer either.'

Brenan's forehead puckered. 'So what the hell's going on here? What's Perkins' game? This has to be the Mark Powell from Devonish Crescent.'

Scott turned away from the screen to the blank wall and stared. 'Perkins is jumping the gun. There's evidence here, yes, and maybe even some kind of pointer showing us where Poppy's kidnapper, the *Operation Sandstone* murderer is, but the answers don't lie with Mark Powell. His features are entirely incompatible with both boys. I'll stake my reputation on it.'

The internal phone on Brenan's desk cut Scott's theories short. It was DCI Forrest. 'Eve, thought it only fair that you should know this. Our Firearms Unit have just been mobilised for a job on the Birchfield estate to assist the ROCU VIPER team with a search warrant and an imminent arrest. DCI Perkins is given as the SIO. It's got to be the Poppy Hunt and *Sandstone* job.'

Brenan cut in. 'The Powell family, Devonish Crescent, right?'

There was a slight pause from Forrest's end of the phone. 'Yes but how the hell…? Where've you had that from?'

'You've got to stop it, sir. He's got his facts wrong. The Powells are going to need our help and sympathy and they could help us find Poppy. Booting the door in and locking up Mark Powell is the last thing we need.'

'Too late, Eve, they'll be going in right now.'

Chapter 15

THE FRONT DOOR of 23, Devonish Crescent crashed inwards on first contact with the police *Door Enforcer* ram. The bright red paint of the sixteen-kilo lump of iron was in stark contrast both with the white plastic of the door and the black combat gear of the human bulk wielding it. The ease with which the muscular, balaclava-faced and riot-helmeted figure carried out the act showed a degree of experience in matters of door wrecking. His then graceful sidestep looked wildly out of context, but was done to allow the immediate stampede over the threshold which followed. The door handle had hardly smashed into the hall wall before the equally black-clad and muscle-bound gang were inside and yelling, assault rifles pointing forward.

The shouted chorus of "ARMED POLICE PUT YOUR HANDS IN THE AIR!" had the desired effect: it numbed minds, it stopped people in their tracks. Except for fourteen-year-old Rebecca Powell. The overload of terror, confusion and violence was more than enough to trigger a devastating epileptic seizure. Rebecca's last attack had been over six months ago and was brought on by a vicious dog fight in the street. This was worse.

There were few things capable of turning the tables on the concrete-hard will and in-bred technical training regimes of police firearms team members, but here was something new. The slightly built schoolgirl had instantaneously slumped unconscious to the floor, half-in, half-out of the dining room and hallway, head and shoulders on parquet block and legs on tufted Wilton. Her foaming mouth, thrashing limbs and convulsing chest signified a serious and genuinely life-threatening condition. The police sergeant threw down his door smasher, tore off his riot helmet and balaclava to expose the anguished face of a father of a teenage girl himself. Rebecca was soon lying on a police blanket in the recovery position on the pavement, swathed in a uniform overcoat with said sergeant tenderly brushing her blonde locks from pallid cheeks. An ambulance was on its way.

Firearms team leader Inspector Wayne Ford ushered a confused, tearful and handcuffed Mark Powell through the gate and towards the open door of a waiting police car. Powell gave DCI Ray Perkins, clearly the man in charge, an anguished look. The angry glare Ford aimed at Perkins was the one which really spoke volumes, though. If Ford had been given an opportunity to speak to Perkins at that point it would have been by way of a series of questions and expletives along the following lines: "What the fucking hell have you brought us to? Have you done no background on this job? Did you not know that there was a sick child? Why were we even needed here?" They were all questions Ford would ensure were asked in writing before the day was out.

Mark Powell's shaky voice made a plea towards Perkins as a statutory police hand pressed down on his scalp, urging him into the police car. 'Whatever is this about? What have we done?'

Perkins tried to retain his stonewall countenance, but things didn't seem right. No sign of Poppy and, on the face of it, a caring Powell family to boot. The "Rebecca" event looked likely to be problematic too.

Mr Powell's shout to his equally handcuffed and shaken son Kevin, who was being led to another car, augmented his own confusion over the whole affair. 'Kevin, is this some of your doing? What do you know about this?'

The young man's tear-stained face cracked into even more misery at his dad's suggestion of blame. 'No, Dad! I've done nowt!'

The desperate thump-thump of handcuffed Powell senior's head against the door glass joined with his muted shouting voice as the door was closed. 'What have you done with Beccy? Where is she? Has she got her medication? Call an ambulance!'

Brenan's race to Devonish Crescent was made all the quicker on account of the Incident Response Vehicle which was about to pull off the police forecourt. The flagged-down driver had a *Blues and Twos* high-speed journey underway before she and Scott had buckled up. It was enough for him to read the urgency in Detective Sergeant Brenan's eyes to understand that her initial shouted order of 'BIRCHFIELD ESTATE! STEP ON IT!' involved a serious incident.

The police car's blaring klaxon joined forces with that of the ambulance as the two vehicles entered Devonish Crescent within seconds of each other. Scott's brief glimpse of the unconscious Rebecca as she was stretchered into the back of the ambulance caused her own sigh of anguish. The tightly tucked-in NHS blanket permitted nothing more than a view of the young girl's pale skin and blonde hair. She digested those scant physical details and knew that her theory was looking even more likely. Perkins had made a big mistake.

Brenan set herself on a beeline for Perkins. The police car's door was left hanging open. She confronted the DCI on the pavement and closed right up face-to-face. 'You fucking idiot! What have you done?!'

'You're on a charge, Brenan. You don't speak to me like that! And what the hell do you think you're doing entering into a firearms operation without permission?'

'There was no need for any of this. You've probably destroyed any progress we've made.' She leant forward, closer to Perkins ear. She still hoped to keep Poppy's name secret from the wider public. 'You may have signed Poppy's death warrant.'

'Back off, Brenan. I'll sort you out back at the nick. In the meantime, make yourself useful. The wife is still inside. I want her cuffing and taking in. We're going to start taking this place to pieces bit by bit until we get to the bottom of everything the Powells have been up to. We could be looking at another Fred and Rose West here.'

Brenan sneered at Perkins. She had a lot more venom in store for him, but the opportunity presented by contact with Mrs Powell was worth the torment of keeping her powder dry for a while.

The firearms team beat a hasty retreat, Inspector Ford formulating the words for a damning report on Perkins before he even exited Devonish Crescent.

Brenan found Sarah Powell sitting dazed and visibly trembling in the lounge. 'Okay, Hazel,' she said quietly to the uniformed policewoman who had been placed on guard, 'I'll take over.' She settled onto the sofa and put an arm around the woman's shoulders. 'Let's go up to hospital and see how your daughter is.' Handcuffs were never a consideration.

Ed Stanier pulled into the crescent as close to the Powell house as the police barrier tape allowed. Brenan was exiting the garden gate, her right arm supporting Sarah Powell. Stanier's waving hand was a welcome sight; Brenan needed to get Mrs Powell away from here as quickly as possible. Fortunately, Perkins had been distracted with other details of his botched operation. Scott caught up and jumped into the front seat.

Brenan did her best to calm the near-hysterical woman during the journey. Sarah Powell's jumble of questions illustrated her own mystification on the police raid. 'Is it something our Kevin has done? He's a good lad really. I thought he'd learned his lesson after that stolen car thing.'

'No, it's nothing to do with Kevin, Mrs Powell,' Brenan said, although she knew that wasn't exactly correct.

'Why have they taken him off then? And Mark. Handcuffs on both of them. I saw it.'

'Procedure,' Brenan said, lost for a decent explanation. 'Let's get up to the hospital and see how your daughter is before we do anything else.'

'Oh God, Beccy!' Sarah Powell's voice melted into sobs.

Rebecca Powell was to be admitted to a ward for observation, at least overnight. She was responding well to treatment and a bed was being arranged. Her mother took up a chair alongside her in a private cubicle and Brenan happily left the pair for a few quiet moments together.

With her mobile switched to silent, Brenan followed Stanier and Scott out through the main entrance of the Accident and Emergency unit into the chilly air. The near constant calls and text messages from Perkins and now Forrest were well down her list of priorities and she'd no intentions of answering. The three chose a spot away from the ears of the inevitable cluster of smokers.

Scott was the first to speak. 'You've worked out what's going on?'

Both detectives gave half-hearted nods. They'd drawn their own conclusions. Brenan summarised her understanding: 'From the bits I've picked up, Sarah Powell is Kevin's mother. His father, we know for a fact, is not only the *Operation Sandstone* murderer, he's also Jason's father. That's all proved by DNA and that makes him Poppy's kidnapper into the bargain.' She hesitated. 'But he ain't Mark Powell.'

'That's my theory in a nutshell,' Scott said. 'I don't know how these things work in police investigations, but I'll put money on this. Our good friend DCI Perkins has obtained the authority for a full familial DNA search using the crime scene profile recovered from the *Sandstone* murders and the baby Jason exhibits. A fifty percent share match – as Kevin would be to his biological father – would quickly be linked to the criminal record of Kevin Powell, proving without doubt that he *is* the son of the murderer. Now, Perkins may or may not have made more enquiries, but my hunch is that the one thing he didn't do was get Mark Powell's DNA checked. There could be a number of things he's done to back up his theory, but surely the most important thing would be to check Mark's profile against the crime scene profile. I don't think he's done that, because I don't think Mark is actually Kevin's biological father.'

Stanier was keen to add to the story. 'My results came back from the Registrar's.' He pulled a crumpled page of scribble from a pocket and flattened it out. 'They were able to tell me that Mark Timothy Powell married Sarah Pauline O'Leary on Saturday 3rd July 1999 at St Stephen's Church on the Birchfield estate. They further told me that on Sunday 2nd April 2000, the then Mrs Sarah Pauline Powell gave birth to a baby boy at the City General Maternity Hospital. The birth was correctly registered at the Stoke-on-Trent Registrar's a few days later. The child was christened Kevin Patrick Powell. Both Sarah and Mark Powell are registered as the parents.'

Scott and Brenan listened silently to Stanier's detailed account, but Brenan's eyes remained closed as she concentrated on the detail. 'So,' she said. 'They married on 3rd July 1999 at St Stephen's; a church wedding, not a rush job. And Sarah gave birth on 2nd April 2000.' She was suddenly eyes-wide and pressing at the keys of her mobile. The calculator app provided an answer on-screen to her question and she was quickly into an explanation. 'Kevin was born thirty-nine weeks after the marriage. Taking the gestation period as the accepted forty weeks, that was a pretty close call. Nothing wrong in that, but Kevin must have been conceived close to the wedding date. In fact, probably a week or so either way.' She turned and gave Scott a long hard stare. 'You're convinced that Mark is not Kevin's dad, right?'

'Right.'

'Explain fully so we're all understanding,'

'Explain fully?' Scott would have laughed at that request had it not been for the seriousness of the situation. 'I'll try the shortened version,' she started. 'Like I said at the start of all this, I'm no expert, but I've been working with this kind of thing for a few years now. You get a feel for it. It's something we all have in us to some degree. A bit like how amazing it was that Annie, Poppy's schoolmate, could spot the similarities in the eight-year-old Jason to Poppy, eleven years later and thirty miles from home. I spotted the same kind of facial similarities in Kevin. Not to Poppy, but to the male features in Jason – similarities he's taken from his father. It's classic genetics. Children get half their DNA from their mother and half from the father. Some genes are dominant. Genes don't blend; genetic inheritance follows rules. We inherit things like our height, skin colour, hair colour, eye colour and general build from our parents and, in turn, they've inherited the same things from their own parents. So we can often have similarities to grandparents and further back. So much is inherited and tends to manifest itself in offspring, not so much because of environment, but because of inherited DNA. Even the way we act and react to other people. Our interests, how extrovert we are, how talkative we are, it's all inherited. Young Jason was a bright and talkative lad, something he seems to have inherited from Poppy.

I only got to meet Kevin for a few moments, but he was quite the opposite. He may have inherited that from his mum or his dad, but Mark Powell seems a gregarious man, wanting to be involved in debate and social problems. Kevin came over as introvert – quiet, hard work really. And, from the photos we saw, Mark was nothing much like Kevin: wrong hair colour, wrong build, wrong eye colour and a good few inches taller than Mark. I only got to see a glimpse of Beccy as she went into the ambulance, but there seemed to be some of Mark's genes there. The only way to be sure is a DNA test.'

'Something Perkins should have done either officially or by stealth before he crashed in and destroyed a family.' Stanier said.

'Exactly,' Brenan agreed.

'Of course, you're right,' Stanier said. 'But you can see where the bonehead went wrong. He carried out the same Registrar enquiries that I did. He seems to have convinced himself that the closeness of the marriage to the date of conception was a good enough call to suggest that the newlyweds had produced Kevin. Yes, Kevin's DNA had already proved he was the son of Poppy's kidnapper and no doubt Perkins would have followed up with a DNA test on Mark, fully expecting it to show him as the kidnapper, murderer and rapist.' Stanier's mouth tightened as though experiencing a bitter taste. 'Easy to say after the event, I know, but it was always bad practice not to establish the DNA match first. A good surveillance, a bit of following, would have got the necessary for the lab. A glass from the pub, a hair comb from work, something from inside his car. Not necessarily legal but better than this crock of shit.'

Brenan had gone into serious head shaking mode. 'God, how I wished I'd pressed the FINDS board for a full familial search on Jason's DNA. It would have hit on Kevin as his half-brother straight away and we'd have sorted all this out before Perkins poked his nose in. Big mistake,' she said. 'Fucking big mistake. Things could have been so bloody different.'

'Don't beat yourself up on that score, Eve,' Stanier said. 'Chances are it would have been refused.'

Brenan's downturned lips momentarily pinched upwards at

Stanier's support. 'Time for a chat with Sarah,' she said. 'She's got some explaining to do, and I've a feeling this is going to be pretty emotional. I'd rather leave it a while, but there's a nasty chance we'll be interrupted by Perkins sooner or later.'

With the help of the hospital staff, Brenan and Scott acquired the use of a spare consulting room. Stanier was happy to concede that this was women's work and went out to the car park to keep an eye open for Perkins.

Brenan sat next to Sarah Powell and started to carefully walk her through chosen parts of the story so far. The woman was now composed but had become withdrawn and quiet. The three *Operation Sandstone* murders were discussed, but Poppy Hunt and Jason Fitzgerald were not.

'I remember the murders,' Sarah said. 'One was a girl from the estate. Terrible things.' She looked Brenan straight in the eyes, forehead lined with puzzlement. 'How can this involve our family? We've been happily married nearly twenty years now. Just that spot of trouble with Kevin, but he's only nineteen himself. He couldn't have… He'd not long been born when that started. Please tell me all of it.'

Brenan placed her hand on top of Sarah's. This was going to be tricky but there seemed no easy way. 'You know when Kevin was in trouble with the police – the motorbike and the stolen car?'

'Yes,' Sarah said, but her quizzical expression declared incomprehension of any connection to the police raid.

'Kevin, by law, had to supply a sample of his DNA for the national database.' Brenan's words seemed to hang in the air waiting for Sarah to feed them into her brain and analyse.

Her impassive expression changed as if an electric chair switch had been thrown. A twenty-year-old secret was now digging upwards, clawing its way to the surface, breaking free to tell the world, just as she'd feared it always would do for every minute of every day of those two decades. Her story came out then. It came out in sobs, in bouts of hyperventilation. It came in screams, but it all came out.

Chapter 16

IT WAS HALF past eight when Brenan arrived at the top of the four stone steps to Hanley Police Station. The April sun had already set over a gloomy, wet Stoke-on-Trent. She shook the rain from her umbrella and stepped into the foyer. Civilian enquiry office clerk, Stan, looked on, arms folded, from behind the high-topped counter. 'Everybody's been after you, Sarge. There's some gaffer from NCA going ape.' The man covered his mouth with a hand as if to take her into his confidence. 'I think he's a bit pissed actually, Sarge.'

Brenan's, 'Thank you,' was stopped dead in its tracks by Perkins' bullish entry from the right-hand doorway, which led down to the interview rooms. A wave of beer fumes preceded his slurred staccato sentence. 'Serious trouble, Brenan!'

Brenan levelled a cold stare at him. 'I think we can both agree on that, Chief Inspector, but *you* not me.'

'Right, that does it!' A cloud of spittle accompanied Perkins' elevated voice. The on-looking EOC downed his biro and stared over. DCI Forrest entered stage left just as Perkins stepped aggressively into Brenan's personal space. 'Ray! Cool it. Let's discuss this upstairs in my office.'

Perkins turned on Forrest, but pointed his finger back at Brenan. 'This piece of shit has seriously undermined an NCA coordinated operation, probably one of the most serious investigations in years. She actually disobeyed my orders to take a prisoner – a prisoner suspected of conspiring to pervert the course of justice in a triple murder case.'

Forrest took a step closer to Perkins and quietly said: 'Ray, let's talk about this upstairs.' His blink at the alcohol fumes was accompanied by a face screwed with revulsion. 'You've had too much to drink, Ray. Now, upstairs please.'

'This stupid tart,' Perkins said, finger still pointing, 'has seriously undermined my authority.'

Forrest took a breath of fresh air before closing up to Perkins' ear. 'Get fucking used to it, Ray. I did.' He then turned and headed back to the stairs.

Forrest closed his office door firmly and walked around to his seat. Perkins had already slumped into a chair uninvited. Brenan made straight for the hopper-style window, unhooked the catch and pointedly hinged the panel flat down onto the sill. The fresh, but chill, damp evening air flooded in.

'I'm not covering for you on this, Ray.' Forrest said. 'The more I've heard, the bigger the cock-up this whole operation seems to be.' He waved a two-page report at Perkins. 'FU inspector is livid. He says there's no way in the world this should've been a firearms job.'

Perkins sat forward in his chair, hands on armrests, eyes wide. 'The threat was there, if we were to believe the theories – theories wholly supported by Sergeant Brenan here.' He waved a dismissive hand towards Brenan. 'There was every chance the missing girl... What's her name? Hunter? Every chance she might be being held at the property or nearby.' Perkins coughed and cleared his throat to give himself more thinking time. 'A quick and unannounced entry into the house was vital. The girl might have been there, knife or gun against her head. There was potential for a hostage situation, a desperate kidnapper. *And* he had a shotgun certificate!'

Forrest stared across at Perkins. There was no sharp intake of breath. Forrest selected another report from his desk and held it out to Perkins. '*Had* being the operative word, Ray. Past tense. He surrendered it three years ago, and you knew that. The records show that you had one of your team check it.'

Perkins coloured up more intensely than the standard drunken hue. 'These people don't play by the rules,' he said. 'The fact that he's had one shows he'd got access. I wasn't going to put my men's safety in jeopardy by even considering that a vicious bastard like that is going to play by the rules.'

Brenan pulled out a chair at the desk end and sat. 'I've not met Mark Powell yet, and I don't think you have, but the bits I've seen don't even come anywhere near placing him in the category of "vicious bastard".'

Perkins sat back into his chair, shaking his head as though disgusted with the whole affair. 'Anyone who rapes and murders three women – minimum! – is a vicious bastard in my book.' He sat forward again and glared at Forrest. 'She,' he said, finger pointing, 'shouldn't even be in here. This is a discussion between senior officers.'

Forrest ignored the remark. He swivelled to meet Brenan's eyes, giving her the opening.

Brenan took the signal. 'Mark Timothy Powell has no criminal record. Not under that name anyway. From my enquiries he looks like a hard-working and caring family man with a social conscience.'

Perkins snapped back. 'It's easy with hindsight to criticise, Brenan. My enquiries point squarely at him being the *Sandstone* triple killer and therefore also Poppy Hunter's abductor and rapist – probably her murderer as well. As for the firearms job, I'll never put my men at risk. Belt and braces every time.'

Brenan slowly shook her head and stared right through Perkins. If she'd spoken one word it would have been "pathetic". Instead, she opted for a whole sentence. 'You've got the wrong man, Chief Inspector, and the sooner you think about releasing him from custody the better. And the girl's name is Hunt, Poppy Hunt.'

A flush of anger rose from Perkins' collar, overtaking his pulsating jawbone. 'I have positive proof. DNA. I've got the right man, Brenan, and you're in deep water on several counts.'

Forrest used both arms to make a separating gesture across the desk between the pair. 'Enough! Sergeant Brenan, you'd better explain your theories. If we've got an innocent man in the cells, that's something that needs serious attention.'

'Two innocent men, actually, sir. He's got the son locked up as well. Some nonsense about attempting to pervert the course of justice.' Brenan turned to Perkins. 'If you're so sure of your evidence, perhaps you could enlighten us.'

'Kevin Powell has a record,' Perkins snapped back. 'His DNA

profile is on the national database. His father is now proven to be the kidnapper, murderer and probably a whole lot more.'

'Nobody's going to disagree with that, Chief Inspector. You're absolutely right.'

Forrest screwed up his forehead at Brenan's comment until enlightenment settled him back into his chair. 'Eve, are you saying Mark Powell isn't Kevin's father?'

Brenan closed her eyes and gave a single nod.

Forrest's mouth fell open a fraction. He swivelled back and set Perkins with a furious stare. 'Ray, please don't tell me that you've not checked Mark Powell's DNA.'

'Okay, so we haven't yet got the DNA profile of Mark Powell, but it's a done deal. We know it's him. Time was of the essence. The girl's life was in danger. A covert operation to get hold of Mark Powell's DNA could have taken weeks. We hadn't got that time. We need to start grilling him immediately to find out where or what he's done with Huntley, or whatever her name is.'

Brenan stood, folded her arms, and rested her back against the wall. 'You're suddenly showing a lot of interest in *Poppy Hunt*, Mr Perkins.' Her delivery of the girl's name was almost shouted.

'Sergeant Brenan… Enough,' Forrest said. 'You *will* show respect for Mr Perkins' rank.'

'Sorry, sir. But I'm worried that this operation has seriously jeopardised our chances of finding Poppy alive. I've had the benefit of Madeleine Scott's expertise on this. She has several sound reasons for believing that Mark is not Kevin's father. So much so that we briefly interviewed Mrs Powell at the hospital. It was an emotional and revealing episode which has, in my opinion, increased the gravity of this enquiry even more.'

'So now we're taking advice from civilians, are we?' Perkins attempted to scoff, but his face was paling by the second.

Brenan ignored the remark. Her dour expression would have taken any seriousness meter into the red zone had such a device been invented. She continued: 'Sarah Powell says that, twenty years ago, in the week before she and Mark were married, she went out on a hen night with her mates in Hanley. They had a curry, visited a few pubs and ended up at *Regimes* nightclub. She was drunk and got separated from her friends. She remembers climbing into a vehicle she thought was a taxi and telling the driver her address on the Birchfield. A lot of what happened is still a blank. She must have dozed off. When she woke up, the driver was in the back with her trying to rape her. She fought him violently. He badly knocked her about – punches, slaps, pulling her hair. He threatened to kill her. The next thing she remembers is finding herself alone in a wooded area. It was still dark. She'd been raped.'

Brenan gave Perkins a look of disgust, but he preferred to stare at his shoes. She handed some paperwork over to Forrest. 'There's a lot more to come out yet and, yes, I know we're twenty years behind on this, but I've still followed the current rape guidelines. Sarah is up at the hospital with her daughter. She's going to stay overnight. If what she's saying is correct – and there's absolutely no reason to disbelieve her – this job just got even more serious. I'm worried for Sarah's welfare. It may sound unbelievable, but she's kept this a secret even from her husband for twenty years.'

'Yes, actually, Sergeant, it does sound unbelievable,' Perkins interjected, hoping to redeem some authority. He got to his feet, turned on his heel and left.

Brenan closed her eyes for a long second, relieved at Perkins' departure. She held Forrest's gaze. 'The woman is on the edge of a breakdown and, unless this is dealt with sensitively and with a great deal of understanding, she could easily become suicidal.'

Forrest sucked in a giant lungful of air. 'What a fucking mess!'

'Agreed,' Brenan said, hoping that Perkins' departure would allow the return of some common sense. 'Madeleine Scott has offered to stay the night with Sarah and, before you say it, yes, I know she's not a police officer, not trained in these things but she's got a better feel for this than a good many I can think of.' Her eyes went toward the door. Perkins had left a lingering smell of alcohol behind. 'She got on well with Sarah and offered to do it as a friend would.'

'Who am I to intervene, Eve? Anyway, seems like a good idea.

Back to basics, though, and, as you've said, we're twenty years behind on the rape so there's no forensics to back it up apart from Kevin's DNA.' He scratched his head as soon as he'd said it. 'God above! The poor sod. He knows nothing about it. How the hell can we proceed along these lines?'

'I think we should deal with it as it comes out, boss. We must be guided by how Sarah wants to play it. I've spoken with the Sexual Advice Referral Centre at Grange Park. They'll have the video suite ready for us anytime we want it. I've suggested tomorrow sometime, but it'll depend on how Sarah feels about it all. If she wants to make a witness statement, I've got one of our senior female detectives awaiting a mobile call and ready to step in at any time. Even if Sarah doesn't want this part of things to go to court, there could still be something, some tiny detail that she may remember which could point us in the right direction.'

Forrest gave the sigh of a man with a lot of troubles on his shoulders. 'Looks like being a long night. We've still got two innocent men in custody and a whole raft of potential complaints hovering. Not to mention the Powells' house with no front door.' Forrest cupped his chin in a palm and rested the elbow on the desk. 'This has torn the enquiry wide open, Eve, you know that, don't you?'

'Yes. My two weeks finished early. It'll have to be a full-blown investigation.'

'We'll use the office you've already got as an MIR. It's massive, so it should work as a Major Incident Room. I'll put some detectives' names in the hat and push the list through to HQ for approval. If you and Ed can start getting the necessary done tomorrow morning, we can hope to be ready for our first briefing in the afternoon.'

Chapter 17

Day 10 Wednesday 24th April

LAST NIGHT'S RAIN was now a memory, evidenced by a few scattered puddles on the police station car park. It was Wednesday morning and half past eight as Stanier took the lift up to the fourth floor. He keyed in the digital lock number to Room 410 and stepped inside. He was surprised to see Brenan standing on a chair attempting to fit a battery-operated wall clock into position.

'What you up to? I'd have done that.'

'Done now,' Brenan said, hopping down and checking for alignment. 'Briefing's a goer for two o'clock,' she said. 'Detective Chief Super and the big guns'll be here. IT boffins from HQ and BT are coming in for ten to get computer and phone hook ups done. Reckon we'll need a few more chairs eventually, and some tables.' She looked over at the far end of the room where the piles of broken chairs, desks and other rubbish had been dumped. 'I've got a skip arriving on the front anytime now, so we could do with a couple of cadets if there are any about.'

Forrest had worked until two in the morning. Of the eighteen detective constables he had requested from neighbouring CID offices, most were well thought of, dependable, experienced and resourceful. Consequently they would be begrudgingly released by their own detective inspectors who feared that divisional detection rates would plummet. All had previously been involved in major enquiries. The additional overtime pay would serve to ease the pain of the unsociable and long hours away from home, if only slightly.

Two detective sergeants had also been assigned, along with six HOLMES computer operators from the uniform branch. The instruction had been given: *be there.* No explanations were offered, but everyone was reminded of their obligations under the Official

Secrets Act. It seemed a little heavy-handed but spelled out the importance being attached to confidentiality.

Forrest was already in his office. He knew how things worked, knew it was important to keep in with the NCA, but Perkins was in trouble and looking at disciplinary proceedings. Forrest planned to keep the Regional Organised Crime Unit informed. Further surveillance operations were likely if a suspect was identified and it was vital the secret was kept watertight. ROCU were, after all, the recognised experts on surveillance, regardless of Perkins' cock-up.

By half past eleven, Room 410 was a hive of industry. Stanier temporarily removed the scant few photos from the whiteboard whilst the civilian IT and BT engineers went about their jobs. The rubbish at the far end of the room had been cleared and the skip on the front of the nick filled. The lorry collecting it jostled for position with the HQ Purchasing Department box van unloading desks. The room's grubby paintwork would remain, but the strip lights had been cleaned and one flickering tube replaced. The computer terminals had been installed and HOLMES 2 was up and running.

Forrest found Brenan and Stanier in the canteen at half past twelve. They both bore a few grubby marks to face and forearms – evidence of their recent labours. Their hurried early lunch was now just crumbs on plates, although a second round of tea had arrived.

'Well done, you pair,' Forrest said. 'We're on target for the briefing.' He looked around the canteen and received several nods from familiar faces. 'I see there's quite a few here early.'

'Yes, boss,' Brenan said. 'We're getting organised, but we're short on vehicles, so it'll have to be mileage allowance with everyone using their own cars.'

Forrest puffed out his cheeks at the thought of the skyrocketing expense. 'What's the latest on Sarah and Rebecca Powell? And Madeleine? She's not still up there?'

'No. She texted me. She got back to the hotel at half three this morning.' Brenan was unsure if Forrest would go along with the next idea. 'Look, I know this is all unorthodox, but I've invited her to the briefing.'

'Well, Eve, you won't know it yet, but I've been appointed SIO and it sounds like a good idea to me.'

A feeble 'Oh?' was the best response the stunned Brenan could manage. Forrest was really stepping up to the plate. 'Great,' she added, still not quite believing what she'd just heard. 'And, as for Rebecca, she's doing okay. She's likely to be discharged later this afternoon. Her Mum's tired out and emotional. I don't know how this is going to turn out. It could destroy the family.'

A police cadet appeared. 'Sergeant Brenan,' the lad said. 'There's – ' he looked down at the crumple of paper in his hand – 'a Mrs Sarah Powell at the front desk asking for you.'

Five minutes later Brenan pensively took up a seat across the table from Sarah Powell. The stark, echoing confines of Interview Room 3 were not, to Brenan's mind, conducive to the modern thinking on how to best attend to the needs of a rape victim. The fact that the attack took place twenty years ago was unlikely to make much difference in the black and white world of a Professional Standards investigator. There was no tape recorder and no one else present, just the two women and two mugs of coffee.

Sarah Powell's face was a roadmap of mental and physical exhaustion. The events of yesterday had scooped up every living second of that tortured twenty years and demolished her frail house of cards. The birth of daughter Rebecca had rekindled some happiness in between the insomnia and nightmares, but living with her secret and the lies it created had been an unending battle.

Brenan said nothing. It was important that Sarah made her own beginning. It took two whole minutes of head-in-hands silence, eyes fixed on the table top, before three large tears trickled down her cheeks and dripped noiselessly onto the green Formica.

'Now that it's come to this,' she started, 'I need to tell my story. God, how I wished I'd told it all those years ago! It's made things so much worse now. Mark's a good man. He loves me. He'll understand, he'll come to terms with it, he'll stick by me – but it'll hurt him. It'll hurt him that I could never tell him. It's Kevin I worry about more than anything. He's always been a lost soul. Almost as though he knew something.' Sarah pulled a well-used handkerchief from the wrist of her cardigan and dabbed her tears. 'I guess I'd be stupid not to think that both of them haven't had thoughts over the years. There've been many times when an off-the-cuff remark has been made by family or friends about where Kevin gets his looks and ways from.'

Efforts to hold back more tears came in the form of deep breaths and hands pressed to face. Brenan's hand-across-table touch of fingertips implied that she could take all day if she needed to. 'All I'd ever wanted,' Sarah continued, 'was Mark. We were the original childhood sweethearts. It was just a week before we were to be married. I came to my senses in the dark, in some forest in the middle of nowhere, and I realised what had happened. I wanted to kill myself. I thought Mark wouldn't want me any more and that I'd lost everything. I was quite knocked about, bruised and a few cuts. My neck was hurting; I think he'd tried to strangle me. Stupidly, I started to wonder if I could get away with not telling anyone and maybe the marriage could go ahead. Maybe I could forget all about it. I'd got a black eye. I thought my biggest problem was making up a story about that. How wrong I was. I knew that, if I was going to go down that route, there was no way I could report it to the police.

'It was about half past three when I got myself together. I found my bag and shoes in the grass; the only things I was short of were my pants. I was surrounded by trees and bushes and, of course, it was dark, but I could see occasional car headlights down below me – a road. I stumbled out from the bushes onto a trackway. That was when I realised it was Park Hills, only about a mile from the estate. There's a golf course and a country club out there, lots of pull-ins and little car parks. The sort of place where courting couples go, but it was too late and there was no one about. I saw the lights from cars a couple of times and knew it must be the road leading from Birchfield towards Coalvale estate.

'I started making my way down the track. I'd told my parents I might be stopping over with Denise. She was a workmate and I sometimes did stop at hers, so I knew they wouldn't be wondering where I was. Denise had her own flat at Dixon Court, near the town centre. I couldn't go home, not in the state I was in and at that time. I wouldn't have been able to hide it from my parents.

'I hadn't got a mobile back then and, when I reached the road, I'd made my mind up that I would confide in Denise. I thought she'd understand, and she'd got a car. I had to walk almost into the estate to find a phone box. I only saw a couple of cars, but I knew that how I looked would make people realise there was something wrong. So I kept in the shadows and prayed there were no police cars about.' Sarah's head was shaking. 'God, how I now wish there had been. It took Denise ages to answer my call and I guess she was still suffering from the effects of the hen night. I stayed in the phone box until she turned up. I'd told her nothing in the phone call; I wasn't able to. I'd asked her to get to me straight away. She wanted to take me to hospital and get the police involved when she saw me and heard what had happened, but I became hysterical and she agreed to take me back to her place.'

Sarah's tears flowed as though a tap had been turned. She bent forward, both hands clasped to her face and rocking in her chair. Brenan touched her elbow in an affectionate show of support.

A full minute passed before she was able to add the poignant ending. 'Then Denise said it: "What if you're pregnant?"'

Chapter 18

BRENAN GOT BACK to Room 410 in good time for the two o'clock meeting. There were several early arrivals – well-known faces, experienced plain clothes officers who knew there were never enough seats to go around. The conversation grew in volume as numbers increased and standing became the only option. Handshakes were shared with old friends and conjecture flowed freely as to what this was all about.

A rumble of dragged chairs drowned out the chatter as the room stood in respect for the line of senior officers who now filed in and took their places at an improvised top table. Brenan, Stanier and Madeleine Scott were included in this line-up. Top table positions for them and the inclusion of Scott, a civilian, was a divergence from the norm. Forrest was increasingly showing himself to be someone happy to take a common-sense approach if it was likely to get the best result.

CID top boss Detective Chief Superintendent Geoff Brown tapped his water glass hard against the table top. It immediately achieved the silent attention of the room. 'Ladies, gents… Serious matters to discuss. I'll say this once only: you will have noticed the lack of information on offer regarding this investigation, and I hope you all understand exactly how *life or death* this secrecy could be.' Brown's emphasis on the words was extreme. He went further: 'It's important that absolutely nothing is discussed with anyone outside of this team without the express permission of your SIO, DCI Forrest.' He turned to Forrest and then continued. 'Anyone found to have breached these important guidelines will be looking for a new job.'

Forrest took Brown's introduction as his invitation to start with an outline and quickly got into a satisfactory summary of the background to Poppy's disappearance. He soon turned his head to Eve Brenan, who sat on the edge of the line-up. 'Acting Detective

Inspector Brenan will play a pivotal role in this enquiry. She and DC Stanier have already uncovered some interesting features.'

Brenan's forehead went into serious wrinkle-mode. Forrest had got her rank mixed up. She was, after all, just a detective sergeant.

Forrest ploughed on. 'I'm also introducing you to Madeleine Scott.' His hand now gestured toward Scott. 'Miss Scott is not a police officer. She is an expert genealogist with a good knowledge of DNA, who has already proven to be of the greatest assistance to this enquiry.'

A low muttering passed around the room as a wave of scepticism drifted between chairs. The difficulty coppers have with accepting non-police personnel into the family reared its head again. Forrest took a sideways look at Brown, hoping this small show of disharmony would quickly peter out. He then turned to Brenan. 'Eve, if you can explain what has come through from forensics.'

Brenan's forehead still showed some puzzlement on the issue of her current rank, and part of her was wondering if Forrest had been keeping secrets from her. She shook away the surprise and went straight into a no-punches-pulled explanation about Poppy's school mate Annie, her foundling son Jason Fitzgerald and the DNA connection. She got to her feet part way through and stuck the photographs of Poppy and Jason back onto the whiteboard. She then placed a third photograph above Poppy's. 'This, for what it's worth, is a computer-generated image of what Poppy may now look like. I've seen this programme used before and must say it's usually pretty accurate.' The girl's main features endured, but subtle changes to the chin, nose and mouth successfully applied the years and turned the face into that of a young woman.

'Have we got any other identifying features or jewellery she may have been able to keep?' a voice asked.

'Inch long scar, left knee, from hockey,' Brenan said. 'No other marks, deformities or injuries. Only jewellery is a small silver ring, right hand, third finger. It has a poppy design embossed around the circumference and the inscription inside "To Poppy from Nan 2006".'

Brenan then went into an explanation of Scott's work and the magnitude of her findings so far. A sea of cynical eyes locked onto the genealogist as their blinkered principles were reconsidered. A blush rose from Scott's neck. The phrase, *you could have heard a pin drop*, understated the silence.

A few low-voiced expletives tumbled around as people began to grasp the fact that Poppy had secretly given birth some three years after her disappearance. The awful possibilities were now understood by the entire room and the reasons for the secrecy dawned.

One of the front row detectives threw in a question. 'What will we be telling the parents, boss? We'll need to know. There's almost certainly going to be occasions when we'll have contact.'

Forrest stared at the asker. 'I don't want anyone making contact with the family without the express permission of Sergeant… Acting Inspector Brenan,' he corrected. 'I accept that, in the real world, that's not always going to be easy, but DC Stanier and Inspector Brenan have already created a bond of trust. They will work as the liaison between the family until maybe someone else is appointed.'

Brenan cocked her head in puzzlement. Forrest had actually corrected himself over the rank issue. There was definitely something going on. She also took note that Forrest, for a change, did seem to be talking a good deal of sense.

Forrest continued. 'The parents are now fully in the loop on this part of the enquiry. The importance of them, the family, also keeping everything confidential is vital. If Poppy is still alive, still being held prisoner, and her captor realises we're on to him… Well, it could prompt him to dispose of the evidence – her. *That* is our greatest fear.' Forrest allowed the murmurs which were passing around the room to quieten before adding more on this aspect. 'We need to identify the kidnapper and positively locate Poppy before making any moves to arrest him. If she *is* still alive and being held nearby after all these years, then it's a bloody good hiding place. If we lock him up before we've located her, and he goes "no comment" we're stuffed, and she's dead.' The DCI allowed his words to sink in. He gazed around at the grim but determined faces hanging on to his every word. 'So we've got to identify him, find him and follow him until he leads us to her.'

'Just sayin', boss…' The comment this time came from the third row. DC Charlie Sawyer was old school. He could be pretty brusque at times, but was known for getting results. 'Yes, just saying. What if Poppy –' he looked down at the scribble on his notepad – 'who is now aged twenty-five, has actually been making her own decisions for the past few years. Perhaps she's got misguided reasons for not going back to her parents – Stockholm syndrome even?'

Mutterings of derision floated around the room.

Sawyer banged the flat of a palm down onto his clipboard. He raised his voice. 'It's got to be considered. We can't bury our heads in the sand.'

DCS Brown interrupted. 'Okay, ladies, gents! Charlie makes a serious point and, yes, it's something that has been considered. The Stockholm syndrome Charlie mentions is an issue, or rather *could* be an issue we have to consider. For those of you who don't know, this is where hostages develop a psychological alliance with their captor as a survival strategy. Certainly, Poppy *was* kept alive by her captor for three years and if she's still alive then it's a possibility.' Brown cleared his throat and relaxed back in his chair, face even more solemn. 'As you've already realised, this case is probably up there with the most serious that anyone in this room has been involved with. What you are now going to hear takes it up even more notches.' He levelled his eyesight at Brenan. 'Eve.'

Brenan pinned another three photographs onto the whiteboard and felt tipped names under each. They were names which brought back memories to some of the older detectives. Brenan's bracketed words *Operation Sandstone* tied the three together. Her explanation of the positive DNA connection to these three serial rape/murder cases of prostitutes, and to Jason Fitzgerald, sparked an outbreak of under-the-breath swearing throughout the room.

Just when the room thought this could not get any worse, Brenan blue-tacked yet another photograph onto the board. It was the mugshot of young Kevin Powell taken from his rather inconsequential criminal record file. Brenan's felt tip squeaked some more as she included a square for the lad's mother and etched in the name *Sarah Powell.* Brenan gave commentary as she worked. 'If we count our three murder victims and then include Poppy, our kidnap/rape victim, as number four, then this lady –' she pointed to Sarah Powell's name – 'should be considered as our fifth victim. But, in point of fact,' Brenan went on, 'from a chronological point of view, Sarah Powell may be our *first* victim.' She then moved on to Kevin's mugshot. 'This young chap is also now proven by DNA to be the son of our wanted man. Conceived, it seems through a violent rape.' Total silence now enveloped the room as Brenan related the Powells' full story.

Brenan placed the felt tip down on a desk top. She was confident her outline had struck the right chord. The sombre mood and grave expressions confirmed her belief. If the room could have spoken as one, the sentence would likely have been: *"We'll nail this bastard if it's the last thing we do".*

She moved on. 'Sarah Powell is, at this moment, at the Sexual Advice Referral Centre at Grange Park. She's doing her best to get through a comprehensive witness statement with DC Vicky Potts. I've already had a summary of Sarah's story and it is horrendous.' Turning back to the whiteboard Brenan wrote out a date beneath the Sarah Powell square: *Sat 26th/Sun 27th June 1999.*

She continued. 'Sarah believes that *this* is the date of the attack, and without doubt, after midnight, so officially that makes it the early hours of the Sunday. That weekend is arrived at by back-calculation from her wedding date, which was the Saturday of the following weekend – the 3rd July 1999. It seems that the offender *did* attempt manual strangulation. Fortunately, he failed. Sadly, though, he got much better at it.'

Without looking back at the board, Brenan landed a pointing finger directly in the centre of the whiteboard's crime scene close-up of prostitute victim Jennifer McQueen. 'Our first murder victim.'

She kept the digit in place whilst watching her audience. 'Plenty of determination there.'

The gruesome image showed the woman's neck horribly distorted. Two clearly made out thumb marks were gouged into the throat. Brenan, still eyes-forward, directed her finger as if under remote control until it came to rest between the pictures of Susan Hemmings and Erica Asquith.

'Different again now,' she added. 'Ruthlessly determined and seemingly planned murders.'

Her description needed no further development. The photographs spelled it all out. These were ligature strangulations rather than manual. The possessed level of violence was made clear by occasional hints of a blue nylon rope so grievously tightened as to become almost concealed by distended throat flesh. Both victims had suffered an identical end with a tightening implement remaining looped into the rope at the back of the neck – a car wheel brace for Hemmings, a mechanic's socket extension bar for Asquith. The subsequent winding had squeezed the very life from the women. The mince of unrecognisable goo that had been bone and cartilage proved difficult for even a pathologist to recognise as human.

Brenan clasped her hands together down at waist level. 'Now, to get back to Sarah's case. I've explained about her fateful hen party at *Regimes* nightclub. The place ceased to exist about fifteen years ago. The offender may or may not have been a legitimate taxi driver. We don't know, and so both the *Regimes* angle, and the possible taxi idea is something different teams will be allocated. Both of these aspects could hold clues but, after twenty years, it's going to be difficult. Another team will be allocated the job of researching what was going on in the world when this was happening and, in particular, in Stoke-on-Trent around the all-important dates. These could act as memory joggers for potential witnesses. We hope to identify the location of the attack. The chances of any evidence after so long are miniscule but, if we don't look, we'll never know. It'll be down to Sarah and what she can remember. If she's up to it, I'm hoping to get her up to Park Hills tomorrow for a look around, but it'll be bloody stressful for her.'

Brenan looked over at DCs Wendy Bailey and Rob Kent. 'Wendy,

Rob, you're teamed up and will be tracking down Sarah's old workmate, Denise. A detailed statement please. She might not be easy to track down as Sarah hasn't heard of her for over twelve years.'

Brenan took a long pause. 'Sarah Powell may be our best hope at getting a lead on the offender and a route through to Poppy Hunt.' She turned to meet DCS Brown's stare, indicating she was done.

'Thank you, Inspector Brenan,' Brown said. He'd been impressed with her performance and now was making a point over the rank thing. It could well be that she might need that extra bit of authority in the coming days, weeks or months as pressures built and tempers frayed. 'Okay, we need an operation title and, as usual, it's an *ad hoc* word from the dictionary with no connection to the matter in hand.' He looked down at his notepad at the agreed word and signalled Brenan to do the honours.

Brenan, marker pen in hand, reached to the top of the whiteboard. The squeal as the felt-tip pressed against the surface was not as eye-screwing as chalk on blackboard but the pungent benzene smell was picked up by those nearby. When she'd finished, two words stood out along the top edge: *OPERATION DENOTE.*

'Thank you, Inspector,' Brown said. 'And *Operation Denote* is the only information you will divulge to anyone inside or outside of the job. If you get pressured on the subject by any colleagues of whatever rank, refer them to me or your SIO, Mr Forrest.'

'Time to deal with some of the mundane elements,' Brown added and handed over to Forrest to discuss expenses, teams, mobile phone numbers, mileage sheets and the like. A detective sergeant was awarded the flamboyant sounding title of "Action Man" and would have the role of issuing specific lines of enquiry to particular teams.

'All of the old ground has to be gone over,' Brown said when Forrest had finished. 'Every original witness concerned in the three murders must be tracked down and re-interviewed. The missing person enquiry for Poppy and the abandoned baby case for Jason are going back under the microscope. An entirely new investigation into the rape of Sarah Powell will be part of *Operation Denote.'* He gave a shake of the head. 'With a twenty-year delay that's not going to easy.

It would have surprised Brenan if she'd got to know, but Forrest had actually pleaded with DCS Brown to be put in charge. He'd got all the qualifications and had sailed through the necessary SIO courses since his promotion to inspector. He'd even completed a few stints in the role on domestic murders. But this was different, this was a high category, high profile, investigation which seemed to be growing with each day.

If Brown had stuck to the letter of the SIO's manual then the case should really have been handed to a detective superintendent – minimum – but he didn't. He stuck with his hunch, twisted the facts a little, crossed his fingers and gave the job to Forrest. The case had inspired the true cop inside Forrest, the cop that had not been seen for some time, and he wanted to crack the case.

As a consequence his life had just changed significantly. SIO in charge of *Operation Denote* was going to be more than a full-time job. His comfortable second floor office had already been taken over by a temporary DCI from another division. The shabby square box he'd inherited was two doors down from 410 and was another of the condemned fourth floor's forgotten rooms.

Brenan eyed Forrest as he was seeing the Detective Chief Super through the door. She hung back until Brown was well out of earshot. 'Boss, I'm not complaining but what's this acting DI business?'

'Yes. Sorry. I didn't get chance to discuss it with you before the briefing. We need a DI and you're already clued up on this one. The DCS was happy to rubber stamp it for me.'

'Fine by me, boss,' Brenan said, aware that the title was not likely to increase her already monumental work load, but would increase her pay scale a little.

Forrest took the chance to further discuss some of the enquiry lines that had been put into place. 'So, we've got a team working full time on possible places where Poppy could be being held. The best theories seem to be that it's somewhere not too far from her home.'

He gave her a solemn look as he continued. 'Weight is certainly added to that theory by the fact that the Medical Centre was chosen as the place to leave baby Jason.'

Brenan cut in. 'Well, that does fit, yes, but remember we're talking eight years ago. She could have been moved since then.'

Stanier was standing nearby and the conversation wasn't private. He hated having to repeat the unsavoury point which was being avoided. 'Or she might be dead.'

Forrest's lips tightened. The entire team accepted this possibility but, as yet, that's all it was – a possibility. He continued with his original theme. 'The length of time she's been held, even the three years before Jason was born, would tend to indicate somewhere secure enough to totally prevent outsiders catching a glimpse or getting suspicious of goings-on.' He paused. 'Maybe even somewhere with additional hidden living accommodation.'

Brenan and Stanier had been theorising on such issues and quickly agreed. 'Yes,' Brenan said. 'It would fit with what we know about most other well-known cases. Some kind of purpose-built or converted basement or cellar seems likely. That was how Fritzl did it. Soundproofed or deep enough to stop sound escaping.'

'Could put our offender in for having some building experience maybe,' Forrest speculated.

Stanier agreed, but could see complications. 'Toilets and drainage might be a problem, though. The depth alone might put it out of conventional connection to sewers. I can't imagine any of the houses included in the original build for the Birchfield estate would've had basements included in the plans.' He considered his own hypothesis for a moment and then added: 'The estate was built in the early fifties, mostly semi-detached houses. There were a couple of apartment blocks which included shops and other community facilities at ground level, and I guess some of those could have had purpose-built basements. I'll suggest an action for the Planning Department to be contacted regarding any below-ground-level constructions in the original plans.'

Forrest said: 'Charlie Sawyer has it in his sights to work with

Severn Trent on any peculiar drainage issues. I'm thinking things which may have come to light by accident, perhaps through an unauthorised development breaking into existing sewerage or services. And yes, Ed, before you say it, we all know it's unlikely this bastard will have applied to the Planning Department or Severn Trent for permission or help to build his prison, but something might tie in with a *legal* development. Get Charlie to take on the Planning Department side of things too.'

Brenan gave Forrest a hard stare. He was surprising her. Maybe, just maybe, she'd been wrong about him. 'All this has got to be looked at, and somewhere along the line it could throw up something, but it's bloody slow. The biggest lead we've got is Jason.'

Forrest's face showed his accord. 'Agreed, but we've got a big enough team now to get on with these other jobs while you and Ed continue with your current lines. If Madeleine is still happy to work with us on the genealogy and as manager of the DNA sites she's already with, we've got a good chance of making progress.'

Scott had been listening and gave an eager nod at Forrest. She was more than keen. Brenan walked over to her and plonked herself on the corner of her desk as Forrest disappeared into the corridor. 'So you're okay to carry on?'

'Too right, *Inspector*.' Her infectious grin prompted a certain crinkling around Brenan's eyes. 'So what do I call you now?' Scott asked. 'Inspector? Boss? Maybe even guv, like they do in police programmes on the telly.'

Brenan's crinkles morphed into a grin. 'I'm Eve to you, Madeleine. I guess you'll get used to this police-speak, jargon, call it what you like. So, a DI is known to the troops as, "boss". Same goes for the DCI. Confusing, I know. Couple that with the fact that either will sometimes be called "sir", or "ma'am" in my case. Depends on how sticky or difficult the conversation is going. "Guv" or "governor" doesn't even come into it here. That's just in London and the Met. You'll drop into it if we're going to see this through 'til the end.'

It was after four o'clock before the teams turned out and headed for their cars, action forms and witness statements clipped into hardback folders, laptops stuffed into briefcases. It had been a late start and a long-winded first briefing. It was unlikely anyone would achieve much until tomorrow. The few short hours left for brainwaves and clue finding were unlikely to strike gold today. There did, though, exist a determination to find Poppy Hunt after eleven years of captivity and to safely deliver her home – if she was still alive.

Chapter 19

Day 11 Thursday 25th April

THE NEXT MORNING was the first real day of the now fully operational *Denote* enquiry. The eight o'clock briefing was similar in make up to that of the previous afternoon, save for the absence of DCS Brown. It was going to take a little time before the machinery started to operate efficiently. Updates following last night's scant few hours were limited in number and importance, but everyone now had direction and a well-formed perception of their individual tasks.

Charlie Sawyer was always keen to offer input but frequently stated the obvious. 'We should be looking at other Misper cases,' he started. 'This guy has been operating for some time. His rape and attempted murder of Sarah Powell twenty years ago might well have been his first offence.' Sawyer's shrug displayed the uncertainty about this. 'He certainly progressed when he started his manic eighteen months of prostitute murders six years after that. So he upped his game, but then he seems to go quiet for a few years before he kidnaps and rapes Poppy.' Sawyer looked genuinely uncertain. 'Could there be other unsolved Misper cases, other unsolved murders elsewhere which might fit in with those missing years?'

Forrest was quick with his response. 'Thanks, Charlie, and, yes, the Misper Bureau are providing us with possibilities. As for nearby cases which could fit – young females, long term missing – there are a few. A seventeen-year-old girl went missing from Birmingham City Centre in 2011. A twelve-year-old girl from Shrewsbury is another and that was about 2013. A fifteen-year-old girl from Nottingham back in 2009. There are another eight cases within a seventy-mile radius which are not dissimilar, but nothing really close. We've got a team looking at the ones I've mentioned, and liaising with the different forces. We can't afford to get tunnel vision, but our man does seem at home in North Staffs.'

'Other foundling baby cases might be worthy of a look,' chimed the voice of DC Dennis Rawlins. 'If there are any around the relevant dates, a DNA test would prove a connection straight off.'

Brenan accepted the idea was sound, but not without complications. 'We need to tackle it, but we only discovered Jason through good fortune. Tracking down foundling babies from twenty years ago, or even recently, is not easy. We most certainly won't have DNA until we actually know the child's identity. It's doubtful that police forces have any records other than, perhaps, an initial small file like we had in the abandoned Jason case. We'd be hanging our hopes on Social Services coming up with the goods and all the data protection regulations which would bog us down, but it certainly needs to be looked at.'

By half past nine, most of the two-man detective teams ventured off to make a start. Several would need to get telephone and computer enquiries out of the way before making physical contact with potential sources. Normally this would be done from any available telephone or any vacant chair in the building, but the secrecy concerns created yet more problems. Three of the ten phone lines dedicated to the team had been wired into other semi-derelict rooms on the same floor of the doomed building, along with two new computer terminals. These rooms would be busy on most mornings after a briefing.

Madeleine Scott was busy at her laptop in the main office. Brenan studied the complicated screen of names from behind as she shuffled an arm into a mackintosh. The sky was gloomy, and rain was possible. 'Bloody hell, Mad, have you got any hope with all that?'

Scott swivelled in her chair and spread her arms out wide, palms upward. 'Like you said about the crime scene yesterday, "if we don't look, we'll never know". I must admit, though, I've never been faced with trying to track down a single person from so many tenuous threads.'

Scott's words were a little ironic as the crime scene had now been identified and that was where Brenan and Stanier were off to. Sarah

Powell's emotional early morning drive to Park Hills with DC Vicky Potts had pin-pointed the spot with a degree of certainty driven by twenty years of nightmares.

The woman's forty-five-minute emotional hike through shrubbery, bushes and winding stony tracks had culminated in Sarah's trembling outstretched arm and quavering utterance of: 'There!'

After the two-decade gap, the white paper zip-up forensic suits handed out to Brenan and Stanier seemed a little over the top. No one was holding any breath on finding anything from the original crime, but it was protocol, and there'd always be some know-all wanting to make a name for themselves after the event. The fact remained that the entire location had not been disturbed by building or other human interference in ages. It was a protected beauty spot, and not even managed by the council. The shrubs and grasses, the swathes of bramble and great walls of dog rose had grown, died off and regrown over those twenty years since the attack. Generations of foxes, badgers, rats, mice and birds had eked out a living and procreated.

The experts were busily going about their jobs as though the attack had taken place yesterday. Gathered-up items, whether likely to be connected or not, seemed too numerous to list. But listed they were, and labelled, and photographed, and bagged. The ground cover was being taken right back to the bare earth by a team of overall-clad constables under the watchful eye of the CSI manager. Strimmers and black bin liners were employed to help the task.

Brenan and Stanier stayed for an hour. Enough to get a feel of the place, enough to see that the job was being done properly, enough to understand that the area, with its numerous concealed pull-ins, was still, as Sarah Powell had described, "a place for courting couples". The dozens of used contraceptives found added weight to this and furthered speculation that it could be a place used by prostitutes.

'I want every condom you find sending off to the lab,' Brenan said to CSI manager George Stodford before she left. 'DNA tests on the contents. Not a witch hunt for the here and now,' she emphasised. 'And there's no way I'm expecting to find any evidence from twenty years ago, but no stone unturned – literally.' Stodford gazed solidly at Brenan throughout her directive. He made no comment, but his expression implied the sentence: *Eve, this is me you're talking to!*

Stanier's phone pinged up an email as they got back to the car. It was a reply from the Registrar about his baby grow enquiries. 'Wow!' he said, adjusting his reading glasses. 'You remember they told me 537 baby girls were born in the Stoke-on-Trent area during the last four months of 2006.' He caught Brenan's eye. 'Those were our *best bet* dates for the actual birth of the baby grow's first owner. They've itemised the mothers into post code batches.' He dragged the list up with a finger and then pinched the screen outwards to enlarge. 'Seventeen addresses on the Birchfield estate.' He turned to Brenan again. 'They've got to be our best chance. Let's go door knocking.'

With their phones now loaded with WhatsApp photos of the baby grow and towels the pair headed directly out to the Birchfield. A "heads or tails" decision furnished Brenan with the car for her eight more widely-spaced addresses, while Stanier's nine houses were all within an easy walk and close to the Medical Centre.

The blank expressions worn by some of the residents were to be expected; it was a long time ago and these were peculiar questions for the police to be asking: *I understand a baby girl was born to a mother at this address about thirteen years ago. Does the same family still live here? Do you recognise this baby grow?*

It was no surprise to discover that three of the families had moved on and there was no one in at another two. It *was* a surprise to Eve Brenan, though, when Ed Stanier rang her mobile phone to say nothing more than: 'Bingo! Meet me at 17, Bromley Court.'

Stanier had sunk his backside into a two-seater sofa at the address and was nursing a mug of tea by the time Brenan pulled up outside. Her own brew was quickly produced as Stanier got the introductions out of the way. He explained that householder, Mrs Shirley Rowlands, was the mother of Daisy, now twelve, who had been born at the what was then called, City General Maternity Hospital.

'Oh yes, it's mine,' she said. 'Or rather, our Daisy's. Like I was telling Mr Stanier, my sister bought it. Daisy was a big baby, nine pounds two, and a quick grower. She was in and out of baby clothes almost before you'd unwrapped them.'

'So Daisy's birthdate then?' Brenan asked.

'The 16th December 2006. She'll be thirteen this year.'

'So, how can you be sure the one in the photo is the same one?' Brenan asked. There was some scepticism on her face.

'Well, *I* can't, but I presumed that, with you coming around here, you'd satisfied yourselves that it was. I mean, I can't believe that you've gone to all this trouble after so long. It was such a trifling thing. Damned annoying at the time, though, what with all my stuff going as well. That was why I reported it, but it was years ago.'

Brenan gave a Stanier a confounded look, hoping that he was a little further into the story and had a better understanding. He was and he did.

'It was stolen from the washing line along with quite a few items belonging to Mrs Rowlands,' Stanier explained.

'I see,' Brenan said. 'So when was this?'

'Oh a good few years after Daisy was born. My sister had just had a little girl and so I looked some things out for her. It had been in a drawer for ages but was still like new. I washed it and hung it out.' Mrs Rowlands looked to the ceiling for inspiration as she tried to calculate a rough date. 'Beth… that's my sister's little girl, was born on the 2nd February 2011. I intended giving her the baby grow along with some other presents when she was out of hospital and settled. Obviously, it would have been on the big side for a new-born, but it would have come in eventually.' Rowlands stopped mid-sentence and gave Brenan a puzzled look. 'Lot of trouble to go to after all these years, for a few bits of second hand clothing.'

Brenan gave away no clues. Her smile urged the lady to complete the story.

'I forgot about the washing and left it out overnight. The next morning my husband discovered someone had broken into the shed and then I realised they'd also helped themselves to stuff off the washing line. Taken two of my bras, three or four pairs of panties, my best jeans, two blouses and my cardigan. Oh, and the baby grow and two hand towels.'

'And you reported the theft to the police?'

'Well, yes, that's why I was thinking you knew. I wouldn't have bothered, but my husband's drill had been pinched from the shed and then he said a couple of other sheds had been broken into in the street and tools pinched. The local bobby called around and took all the details. This was a good few years ago and the police used to want to know everything then.' Mrs Rowlands stuck out her bottom lip. 'Nowadays, they try to talk you out of it if you ring up to report something and, if they do appear, it'll be days later.'

Brenan exchanged a glance with Stanier. She accepted what the lady was saying was a sad fact. She unlocked her phone and opened up the WhatsApp pictures of two hand towels that had also been found with Jason.

Mrs Rowlands peered at the pictures. 'Well, yes, they look the same, but they were just white hand towels so I'd never be one hundred percent.' She became thoughtful for a moment. 'You know, I've remembered now that I actually forgot to tell the policeman about the baby grow. I was more concerned about my jeans and underwear. It wasn't until a few days later that I realised it'd been pinched too. I didn't think it was worth ringing to have him add that on. The policeman was thinking it was some kind of sex thing as to why my underwear had been pinched.' She became thoughtful again and gave Brenan a puzzled look. 'What's this all about? There's more to it than an eight-year-old petty theft and how have you got to know about the baby grow anyway if I never told the policeman that bit?'

Brenan could do no more than offer a pensive tilt of the head. She wanted to ask why Mrs Rowlands had not seen the Sentinel photographs with the baby grow, but that would have given away too much information.

'It was February, half term coming up as I remember,' said Mrs Rowlands. 'We were going away on holiday that Saturday. Now

February half-term is usually the second Saturday in February and so I guess it happened one night earlier on in that week.'

This timely piece of information provided Brenan with an answer. The Rowlands almost certainly got to hear the story of the abandoned baby but would never have seen the local newspaper report with and photographs as they had gone on holiday. They had no reason to connect the baby to their theft.

'So,' Stanier said as they set off back to the nick. 'It begins to look more and more likely that the offender *is*, or at least, *was* keeping Poppy somewhere on the estate. He's plainly a pretty accomplished petty thief. Garage and garden shed burglaries always used to be beer money or easy drugs money. Tools, bikes, kids' toys, all quickly offloaded at second hand shops or car boot sales. We've got enough to track down the old crime file now and maybe pick up a few more clues.'

Brenan agreed. 'Yes, it's also interesting that he's been stealing clothes for Poppy into the bargain. Books and now clothes. Almost as if he's looking after her!'

Chapter 20

STANIER FIRED UP his laptop as soon as they got back and logged into *Crime Management System 2 (CMS2).* It was a computer application that had served the force well for a long time. It provided instant access to current crimes and to those going back as far as twelve years.

When the name *Anthony John Rowlands* was typed into the injured party search column, along with Rowlands' date of birth, the crime reference number instantly popped up. The Rowlands family were indeed a rare breed. Their 2011 shed burglary and washing line theft was the only occasion they had been victims of crime whilst living on the Birchfield estate. It was not, however, the only crime the offender had devoted his talents to on that night of Tuesday 8th February. A total of four sheds and two garages around Bromley Court had been broken into. PC Frank Milton, who dealt with the outbreak had helpfully linked all the crime files as being down to the same offender.

PC Milton, a forty-seven-year-old veteran had been put out to grass following a serious assault whilst doing the job of local bobby out on the Birchfield estate a few years before. Brenan and Stanier tracked him down to where he now worked in the custody suite at Etruria, just a mile from Hanley nick.

Anyone working in the custody suite would not accord with the description "out to grass". It was a nerve-wracking, stressful job, but the nine to five regime arranged particularly for Milton suited his insomnia and headaches a lot better than earlies, noons and nights.

'What's this all about?' he said, as he settled his tired, gaunt frame into a chair across the table from Brenan and Stanier. They were in a side room at the custody suite. The manic shouting and swearing of an extremely violent and abusive prisoner resonated as a background murmur, even through the thick concrete cell walls. It was something to which the trio, through experience, were all oblivious.

Brenan explained the theft incident but held back from including the baby grow or venturing into any connection with abandoned baby Jason or missing Poppy Hunt.

Milton folded his arms, dark eyes blinking behind wire-rimmed spectacles, and trawled his memory banks. 'Blimey, that's going back but, yes, I do remember. We'd been having a spate of shed and garage break-ins. It'd been happening off and on for ages. I always recorded everything, but the DI kept moaning at me about his crime figures. He wanted me to cuff all the small crimes, you know… not record it.' Milton gave the detectives a stare. 'I had my own theory on that sort of thing. I always refused and used the argument that small things lead to bigger stuff. The thefts were spasmodic really, so no particular nights, but almost certainly down to the same offender. We set some obs up a few times, but with it being no set night of the week it was difficult. I suggested it needed about three weeks of solid obs with a couple of us in jeans and trainers lurking about in the shadows. We'd have caught the bastard, but the bosses wouldn't hear of it. "Too expensive," they said, so it carried on for ages and we never caught him.

'Tools and bikes were his main targets. The clothing theft was a bit out of context but definitely the same thief because the washing line was tied to the corner of the shed he'd nicked the drill from. At first, I presumed that part of it was an opportunist sort of thing. You know, with it being left out all night and him there pinching anyway. It crossed my mind he might be some sort of perv. The underwear, get my drift? The jeans and cardigan angle might have cancelled that idea out, though, so perhaps he was hoping to flog it all at car boot sales.'

Stanier took notes of PC Milton's ideas. 'Did you get anywhere at all? Any clues on the offender? We are going to need a witness statement from you on all this, Frank.'

'No problem, Ed,' Milton said, but had now trained a suspicious eye on the two detectives. 'What's this to do with? You're both working out of the old Traffic Office on this big hush-hush job, aren't you?' Milton didn't wait for an answer. He knew how things worked – he wouldn't get one. 'I had a few lines of enquiry, yes. I'd got some names in the frame. Lads on the estate but none of it came to anything. I'd be struggling to think who they were now after so long, but I'll get my thinking cap on.'

Brenan's eyes met Stanier's. They'd worked with each other long enough to achieve at least a smidgen of mind-reading skills. The decision was made. Milton would be taken into their confidence, at least on some of the issues.

Brenan lowered her voice to a confidential tone and leaned in across the table. 'This goes no further, Frank…' The clandestine performance was unnecessary, there was no one else present, but it did add gravity. She carefully watched Milton's expression as she enlightened him on the baby grow and hand towels – items which had not made the original crime report. Neither detective was surprised at the constable's reaction – he was one sharp cookie. He had been a good copper during his several years on the Birchfield.

'That abandoned baby, eh?'

Brenan gave a nod.

'Shit. If only the lady had got back in touch with me. I'd have made the connection straight off.' Milton looked at Stanier and then hard at Brenan. 'More to it though, Sarge. Lot more to it, eh? The abandoned baby side of things would have passed out of police hands long ago.'

'Shrewd man,' Stanier said, as they parked up. They were back at the police station.

'Yes,' Brenan agreed. 'We need to take a close look at Frank's crime reports for the other connected crimes and anything he's thinking might have been committed by the same offender. I wouldn't mind betting that PC Milton would enjoy joining the team for a while to gather it all together.'

It was half past three when Brenan and Stanier made it to the canteen for a late lunch break. They'd collected their sandwich boxes from the MIR and taken the opportunity to cajole Madeleine Scott to join them with her tuna and mayo on brown. The engrossing genealogy research must have side-lined her own hunger pangs.

The only thing canteen-like about the room were the tables, the chairs and the people eating. The metal roller-shuttered hatch separating the kitchen area had been in the down position for over two years. Cost-cutting had seen the back of the team of jolly lady staff with their constant banter and raucous smutty laughs. The plates of wholesome and, sometimes, tasty food they served up from breakfast through to late afternoon had been replaced by the contents of personal Tupperware boxes or bags of brought-in chips. The open side door to the kitchen area still gave access to a few abandoned amenities: kettles, toasters, cutlery and crockery. But teabags and the basics for other hot drinks were down to the individual.

The trio settled down to a hoped-for, but never-yet-achieved regulation forty-five-minute munching session and a useful catch-up.

'How are *you* doing?' Brenan asked of Scott after explaining their progress.

The genealogist took a tiny sip at her camomile tea. 'Slow but interesting. I'm still waiting for the return of Poppy's parents DNA results. I'll be able to extract her side of the hits from Jason's relatives then and concentrate on the ones that only come from his father.' She nibbled her sandwich and dabbed a tissue to her lips. 'I can't work up a lot of enthusiasm until I've done that, or I'll just be gambling. I've started work on some of the hits with possible North Staffs connections and there are some partial family trees which will expand to help, but they are equally as likely to be Poppy's relatives at the moment.'

Forrest peered around the door before the trio had managed twenty-five minutes. The hard stare he directed at Brenan indicated that lunchtime was over. 'Eve, the three of you, upstairs now… Please.' The "please" was an afterthought for Scott's benefit.

They hastily filed out. Forrest's demeanour and lengthened stride quickly led them up the staircase and to Room 410. A DS and four DCs, along with the six computer operators and the civilian Crime

Scene manager were variously sitting in chairs or perched, backsides on desk-ends. The rest of the team were still out on enquiries. The lack of keyboard clatter, the solemn stares and off-hook telephones implied that some serious news had been received.

The closed Venetian blinds, unfurled projection screen and whispering overhead projector indicated a film show. Brenan, Stanier and Scott took seats. Forrest gave the already securely closed door a hard testing press and then turned back into the room.

'A body has been found. At least, a skeleton has, at the spot identified by Sarah Powell as the rape location at Park Hills.' He swivelled towards the Crime Scene Manager George Stodford. 'Fill us in please, George.'

Stodford was a heavily built fifty-three-year-old. His turnip-head and muscular neck seemed more suited to a rugby forward than a Crime Scene Investigator. A coating of almost spray-on ginger hair covered the turnip from its receding hairline to its square-cut nape. More than a hint of grey around the edges. Of the two twinkling blue eyes set into the round and serious face, one in certain light, twinkled less than the other. It was glass, the reason why the former police inspector's promising career had been so cruelly and prematurely halted. A penknife-wielding sixteen-year-old's futile attempt to evade arrest for shoplifting had changed Stodford's life forever.

His subsequent degree in forensics and rise to prominence as a civilian CSI boss accorded the man acclaim and respect with colleagues old and new. His never-ruffled and never-hurried demeanour went hand in glove with that meticulous but singular eye for detail. His favourite words at the commencement of any investigation would rarely stray further than, 'maybe', 'possibly', or 'could be' – but resulting evidence in Crown Court following scientific analysis was rarely challenged.

Stodford had dispensed with his paper zip-up crime scene suit in favour of a white shirt, Longton Rugby Club tie and grey slacks. A smart dark blue blazer hung on a nearby chair back.

'We've recovered dozens of surface items,' he began, 'some possibly recently deposited, some maybe earlier. We've cut bracken and ground cover completely back in one area and got down to a bare topsoil – some turf, but not much due to lack of light preventing growth over the years.' Stodford cleared his throat. 'Now, the witness has described this area confidently as being where she was when she resumed consciousness. She states that, back then, twenty years ago, this patch was not as overgrown by brambles as it was when we started this morning. I decided to widen the perimeter by another six feet and, in doing so, quickly came across a number of human left hand bones beneath the top layers of debris.'

Comments of surprise rippled around the room as Stodford gave the signal for the lights to be dimmed. The projector's beam hit the screen to show the hacked-back and strimmed patch of ground in question.

Stodford's surgical-style, nitrile-gloved hands appeared on screen in vivid HD quality as they delicately teased loose soil from biscuit-coloured pencils of bone. The simultaneous audio part of the recording had, for the purposes of this briefing, been turned off, allowing the CSI man to voice-over. With a touch at his laptop screen he jogged the film forward to the next relevant part. A long femur, jutting from the black earth now filled the wall-mounted screen. Other small foot bones were then shown in a haphazard jumble with Stodford's smooth-haired painting-style brush delicately flicking away dirt.

'There was a lot of disarticulation and a wide scatter, particularly of the smaller bones. Animal scavenging maybe. I do not believe the body has been buried, but possibly pushed inside undergrowth.'

Total silence enveloped the room as the film was moved further on. A hip bone part of the pelvis now filled the screen. Its tan colouring showed starkly against the disturbed areas of fruitcake-rich soil. Stodford's brush had all but dusted its intricate rounded curves, notches, bends and folds clean of larger deposits and leaves. The brush was turned and held by the bristle-end to be used as a pointer by Stodford to identify certain features.

'Expert analysis may take some time to come through,' Stodford said. 'But that, and DNA tests will establish the sex and give a guide to the age. You can see now that I'm pointing out the developing wider sciatic notch on the pelvis, indicating that this is probably a female.'

Stodford moved further forward in time again, adding more comments as he found the section he wished to show. 'It's going to take some time to completely excavate the site. We already have a large tent over the main area. The Coroner has visited, and the pathologist is there now. We're getting a forensic anthropologist on the job as soon as we can. I'm going back up with DCI Forrest shortly.'

A human skull now filled the projection screen.

'The skull,' Stodford said, 'was found over ten feet from the main torso bones and you'll see that the entire mandible is missing, so no lower jaw, no lower teeth. It's a pretty big item, but we can't find it. Many of the teeth from the maxilla – the upper jaw – are missing. Two have been recovered nearby and appear to have dropped from their sockets along with the decomposition processes.' Stodford looked around the room at his audience. 'The separation of teeth from the sockets after death is more likely to happen in a younger person. What teeth do remain all appear to be in good condition. Again, this points towards a younger person.'

As the film stopped and the lights came back on, Brenan was caught in a fixed pose, left hand supporting chin, index-finger tapping against lips. She stared blankly at the table top. 'Any clothing, George?'

'Nothing yet,' Stodford said. 'Certainly no suggestion that the body was wearing clothing at all. Very unusual and therefore another reason to suspect foul play. There may be a stash of clothing yet to be found. We've a lot more to excavate, but it begins to look as though the body was naked.'

'What about jewellery? Rings, necklace?' Brenan's eyes were glued, unblinking on the same spot.

'Again, nothing yet, Eve.' We're dealing with just bones, remember? Not a scrap of flesh and all very disarticulated. We certainly haven't got anything like a complete skeleton so far.'

'What about hair? Any sign?' Still Brenan had not moved.

'No sign of the hair mass. It could have separated at any stage during later decomposition and probably during the animal scavenging. The head was a good distance from the torso. It may have been moved around the site by animals over several months. If it's there, we'll find it.' Stodford left a pause before adding more. 'That is, if there was a hair mass. People do strange things to conceal the identity of murder victims.'

Forrest caught Stodford's eye. 'How long to finish the job, George?'

'Couple of days perhaps. I want to be able to give the pathologist and anthropologist everything possible to work with. But we'll be up there for a long time before we close it down.'

'You both think it's her, don't you?' The words were Scott's. She had resumed her spot back in front of her laptop.

'Don't you?' Brenan threw the question back. Her expression was downbeat, downhearted.

Stanier was his usual wordless, staring-into-space, self. His only movement was the continual twisting of his wedding ring. He gave a long, single blink, eyes opening to focus on Scott before delivering one of his rare speeches. 'Too much of a coincidence, Mad, for this to be the work of someone else. Whoever has dumped that body – and that's what's happened: murdered elsewhere, stripped of all identifying clothing and dumped – has used that spot before. It's a good, safe place. He knows it. He's comfortable there. Whoever has dumped that body has to be the same person who raped Sarah Powell, and the same person who kidnapped and raped Poppy. That skeleton is one of his victims, and Poppy is – was – one of his victims.'

It was nearly half past five when Brenan and Stanier pulled up outside 7, Bromley Court, a few doors down from Mrs Rowlands' house. The two detectives had brought copies of PC Milton's paperwork along, which contained the other reported shed and garage burglaries from the same night as the baby grow theft.

Half-five, of a weekday, was a truly inconvenient time to be visiting the home of a working family but, nevertheless, a good time to catch people in. Garages and sheds at four homes had been burgled that night. The last two addresses they'd checked were "a negative", to use a police term as the theft victims had moved house since the incident and would take a little more tracking down.

A delicious smell of something beef-like met the detectives as home owner Stan Peake opened up. The apologies for calling at an inopportune moment were accepted after a brief and lacking-in-detail explanation of their reasons. 'That's okay,' Peake said, inviting the two inside.

Two teenage children were ushered out of the room as Mrs Peake emerged from the kitchen. 'Can you believe it, Linda? It's about that time when someone broke into the shed and pinched my bike.'

'Goodness,' Linda said. 'That is literally years ago. I didn't think the police were interested in things like that any more.'

The investigators caught each other's eye. The sorry state of local policing was being rubbed in today.

Stanier looked through the paperwork. 'I see that you thought that you actually saw the offender.'

'Well, that's right, although I didn't realise at the time. I woke up needing to use the bathroom and happened to look through the bedroom window. It was ten past three and there was this chap pushing a bike sneakily along the pavement in the direction of the main road. He'd got a little rucksack on his back. I thought at the time, "he's up to no good". But it wasn't until the next day I realised it was almost certainly my bloody bike he was pushing!'

Chapter 21

Day 12 Friday 26th April

FORREST OPENED THE next morning's briefing at eight o'clock and started with an update on the Park Hills crime scene. It was on his mind, that as a civilian, Madelaine Scott was not familiar with the regular use of police jargon which flowed so freely between detectives. 'The locus… or crime scene,' he falteringly added for Scott's benefit, 'has been guarded by uniforms overnight. We've got forensic specialists and CSI looking at another long day, although Mr Stodford has honoured us with his company for this briefing.'

Stodford gave an update on yesterday's findings. He was happy to field a few questions but was keen to get back as soon as he could.

'So, how long before we'll be looking at a cause of death – a PM and confirmation of ID?' DC Charlie Sawyer asked.

Stodford understood the enthusiasm for more news on this. 'Well, as we have nothing more than a skeleton, the examination will actually be a skeletal analysis rather than a post mortem. Our Home Office pathologist, Mr French, will be there alongside a forensic anthropologist, who will lead the analysis. Cause and date of death, along with identity confirmation, will be the main goals. Any bones likely to give answers will be sent to the lab. The most usual DNA-rich ones will hopefully provide us with a profile. Obviously, we're hoping for a dental ID, but the missing mandible and other teeth won't make that easy. The lab will prioritise the case but, even then, it could be several days before we get a DNA profile.'

After another ten minutes of explanation and questions Stodford shuffled his papers together and quietly left.

More updates came in the form of revamped old leads from the prostitute murders, work with the council on building issues for the cellars and basements, and some cross-border Misper enquiries.

It was a quarter past nine before Brenan managed to put in her two penn'orth on the baby grow theft and the associated shed and garage burglaries. 'So,' she said, after recounting Mr Peake's story, 'the bicycle the man was seen with was almost certainly Mr Peake's. Fact is, it was dark and the street lamps were not much help. In PC Milton's report, submitted the day after, Mr Peake describes this man as being around six feet two. He was slim, muscular, and wearing dark trousers or jeans with a bomber-type jacket, baseball cap and possibly short hair. Not much to go on now when we take into account that it was eight years ago. The striking feature, which *is* very much of interest is that, as he walked further away, he was slightly illuminated by one of the street lamps. Red trainers, noticeable red trainers which fits with the shoebox baby Jason was found in.' Brenan stalled for thinking time. 'After those eight years, it's understandably impossible for Mr Peake to add anything new. We're lucky PC Milton recorded the detail he did. Remember, back then, this was not the most serious of crimes.' Brenan turned her attention to the back row of chairs. 'Frank will be working with us for a while in an effort to dig out all those old garage and shed crime reports, which he always believed were down to the same offender, who we're now satisfied is our man.'

Milton, now conversant with the entire case, was sitting, folded arms, and cross-legged at the back of the room. He responded with a smile as several people turned to acknowledge his good work.

Brenan caught DCI Forrest's eye. Her next line had been agreed on. 'It's been decided,' she started, 'that we should give the offender a temporary name. A code name if you like. It'll make life a little easier for us all during various discussions and planned operations. At the moment, we're continually referring to him as the offender, the murderer or our man. This code name, again, stays strictly within the team.' She then turned to the whiteboard and drew a large central box in green marker and etched the murderer's new handle: *KOBE*.

Turning back to her audience, she said. 'Pronounced "Kobee" after the patron of the red Adidas trainers.'

Madeleine Scott sat quietly through the briefing, listening and digesting the information. She'd smiled with appreciation at Forrest's diplomatic police jargon pointer on the word "Locus" but with an English language degree already behind her was confident she'd have worked it out. Her slog through the genealogy work was yet to come up with anything interesting enough to pass on.

Forrest reaffirmed the importance of security. The botched raid on the Powell household had created a significant amount of press interest and Forrest had lost count of the number of favours he'd called in to keep the matter quiet. The issue had been referred to the Independent Police Complaints Commission. A certain DCI Perkins had been suspended from duty pending the outcome, but for the time being Poppy's name had been kept quiet.

The activity over at Park Hills, on the other hand, was not something that could be kept under wraps, and the press had leapt on it. Fortunately, no connections to any local cases had yet been made, but huge media interest was growing. A Sky News TV van, complete with camera team and roof-mounted satellite dish, had taken root in a lay-by on the main road close to police incident tape. The crew's drone was seen circling overhead for fifteen minutes. A police inspector's law lecture on drone-flying restrictions brought about its grounding. Nevertheless, it had been aloft long enough to capture images of the three large grey CSI tents and a plentiful supply of white-suited figures combing the area. An assumption on the type of investigation such police activity warranted did not require much imagination.

A cut and edited aerial clip was quickly prepared in the back of the van and would be ready for transmission come the scheduled ten o'clock morning broadcast. A "Breaking News" banner had already started to flow right-to-left along the bottom of the channel's bulletins: *Staffordshire Police carry out search of wooded area close to Stoke-on-Trent housing estate – sources say body found.*

Telephone calls were being made and, come that ten o'clock programme, there would likely be more than the banner's few words and the drone's pictures.

Forrest gave a frustrated snort. 'Our main reason for keeping such a tight ship has always been for Poppy's safety, but the chances are that this body is her. I will have to give a press release confirming that human remains have been found. But I won't be mentioning the name Poppy Hunt until I know for sure. If our offender is watching the news, he'll immediately know we've found one of his victims, but he won't know how this has come about and what connections we've made.' Forrest shuffled his papers together and finished off: 'He won't know that he's left a trail, albeit a bloody thin and winding one that has led us to that spot.' The DCI got to his feet. 'He's going to think the body has been discovered by chance. Let's keep it that way for the time being. This meeting's over.'

Brenan sidled over to PC Milton as the room emptied. The constable had secured himself a desk and laptop and arrived as instructed, in civvies. His smart dark suit made him look every inch an old school detective. He looked up over the top of his specs as Brenan offered a greeting. 'Nice to have you with us, Frank. You got a plan?'

'Well, it's a doddle to locate the old crimes through this CMS2. I've already got hold of a shedload – if you'll excuse the pun. I've dug out all the ones that seem to fit for the sub-division over a five-year span between 2007 and 2012. I've been going by postcode to cover just the Birchfield and the Burrow Hill estate, which is as near as dammit part of the Birchfield. I could cover the other housing estates in the sub-division after that and go back further if need be. I'll see how it pans out.'

'So, what have you been looking for?'

'I've been concentrating – ' Milton looked up at Brenan – 'to start with, anyway, on crimes classified as theft and burglary. I've minimised the list by not including house burglaries and, that way, I'll cover items nicked both from gardens and sheds or garages. I've included theft of bikes, which goes under a separate classification, to cover any misclassified ones.' Milton took another look at Brenan. 'A stolen bike from the garden would be classed as a stolen bike, but a bike stolen from a garage should be classed as a burglary. I didn't deal with all the incidents, remember, and some matters may well have been misconstrued as not being crimes. Peeping Tom reports, for instance. Often, stuff like that, particularly where someone disturbs the offender before he steals anything, tends to get batted off and not officially reported as the attempted crime it really was. I'm thinking a householder may have seen him through the window and phoned it in as something like that.'

Brenan gave Milton an approving pat on the back as she continued to read through the details on his screen. He seemed more than pleased about his temporary move and was tackling the job with enthusiasm. She settled into a chair alongside to take a closer look at what he'd been doing.

'I'm making a timeline for you,' the constable explained, 'with corresponding crime numbers for all the offences which could possibly be connected.' He scrolled his screen up a page. 'There are two particularly interesting ones here.' He clicked the cursor to open the files. 'They date back to November 2010 and were literally around the corner from Poppy's house.'

Forrest was keen to get back to his own office and clear some paperwork. He was stalled at the doorway by a HOLMES operator. The policewoman was holding a telephone with a hand clasped over the mouthpiece. 'It's Mrs Hunt. She's in a right state. She's seen the Sky news banner and put two and two together. Openly asked me if it's Poppy.' The room went silent as Forrest did his utmost at delivering a caring and sensitive reply which gave away nothing. His face was all apology as he replaced the phone and turned to Brenan. 'Sorry, Eve, you're going to have to get down there and do your best to calm her down. We don't know for sure this is Poppy, and we certainly don't want any mention of her name creeping out. Make sure none of the neighbours clock you as cops.'

Brenan's long sigh outlasted a rapid series of blinks. This wasn't going to be easy. She could not give out any opinions to Mr and Mrs Hunt, even though, in her heart, she felt that the skeleton was Poppy. It was vital to say nothing to confirm their worst suspicions without solid proof.

Chapter 22

IT WAS JUST before eleven when Brenan and Stanier arrived outside 27, Meerham Gardens. There was no need to knock; Laura Hunt's outline was visible through the frosted glass, hand waiting on handle.

'Tell me it's not her, Eve! Please, for God's sake, tell me it's not her!'

Brenan switched on her autopilot. 'We don't know what we're dealing with yet, Laura. It could be a few days before we have any ideas who it might be. You can't torture yourself like this.'

They were in the lounge now. David Hunt sat motionless in an armchair, three days of stubble and hollowed, red-rimmed eyes verifying the lack of sleep. The sight of Brenan and Stanier brought on another bout of nail biting, although there was already nothing left to bite.

Sky News on the TV began its eleven o'clock broadcast – bad timing for Brenan. Pictures of the lane leading from the main road up to Park Hills filled the screen, a police car, blue and white plastic police tape fluttering, two uniformed officers, hands behind backs, standing chatting. David Hunt suddenly came to life, snatching the TV remote and cranking up the volume. They'd already seen the banner and a lacking-in-detail ten o'clock transmission, but there was likely to be more content this time around. The screen changed to the aerial drone view: the tents, the CSI figures and then back to the police cars. An unseen newsreader's voice now came through loudly, mid-sentence, as the picture changed again to show the head and shoulders of a reporter standing roadside with trees and tall hedges behind.

"And we'll go over to Liz Silver, who is at the scene at Park Hills in Stoke-on-Trent. Liz, can you tell us any more about this incident?"

The reporter's shoulder-length dark hair was being tousled by a light breeze. She was holding a microphone at chin level and pressing her free hand against a hidden earpiece.

"Thank you, Adam," she started. "There has been a great deal of police activity here since yesterday afternoon. A wide area has been cordoned off and diversions set up. The Golf Club and Country Club, which are accessed by these lanes, have both closed their doors at the request of the police. Several Police Forensics vans have been seen visiting and leaving. I understand that confirmation has now come through from Detective Chief Inspector Dominic Forrest of the Stoke North police division that human remains have been discovered. Mr Forrest says the enquiry is at a very early stage and we should not speculate on what has happened here."

Silver turned to her left as the camera shot moved out a fraction to include a young lady standing next to her. 'Miss Theresa Knott works at the country club,' she said. 'Theresa, can you tell us what happened this morning?'

Knott, a heavily built young woman of perhaps twenty-three stared vacantly for a few seconds. She held a palm to her forehead, ostensibly to hold her hair in check but, more likely, to extend her thinking time. Copious layers of makeup gave the girl a dull and lifeless look which seemed to tally with reality. Her eyebrows were so thickly daubed as to look cartoonish. 'Er, yeah… Like I said, I come this mornin'… I do a bit of cleanin', and behind the bar at night… Anyway, the cops stopped me, said the club was shut…'

Brenan stepped over to the TV and flicked the power off. 'This doesn't help anyone, David,' she said. 'I promise to update you properly and fully as soon we know what this is about.'

She bit at her lip before making the decision to give the Hunts the latest information on Jason's baby grow and how it had originated from a washing line theft close to their own home. Her follow-up with the details of the other shed and garage break-ins was a strategy she hoped might divert the couple from the Park Hills drama. Maybe it could even prove useful in other ways.

David Hunt was back down in his chair, concentrating hard as Brenan explained the connections. 'I remember. I remember!' he said animatedly. 'Our garage was broken into one night as well. It was a couple of years after Poppy went.' He swivelled to meet Brenan's eyes. 'Could it be the same man?'

'Every chance,' Brenan said. 'What was taken?'

'Nothing,' Laura Hunt interrupted, as she recalled the incident. 'House a couple of doors down had some power tools nicked from their shed, though, I think. Oh, and a bike was stolen from next door.'

David fixed his vision firmly on the carpet, wishing he'd said nothing. Brenan spotted the anguish building in the man and knew that there was more. 'It could help, David. Whatever it is, it could help.'

David Hunt slowly shook his head as he began to explain. 'I didn't think anything *had* been taken at first.' He gave his wife another uneasy look. Her response was puzzlement. He'd been keeping something from her.

David edgily got back into the story. 'The side door of the garage had been forced. It was only a flimsy padlock so a screwdriver would have done the trick. I'd got some old drawers and boxes in there, paperwork and discarded kids' toys and whatnot. Stuff had been strewn about on the floor by the burglar and, at the time, I presumed it was somebody checking to see if there was anything worth pinching. Kids maybe. I never kept any power tools or valuable things in there.' David gave his wife a nervous glance. 'It was months later… I decided to look out some of Poppy's old school books and knick-knacks. They were things I'd put in the garage out of the way, ages before she went missing. I suddenly remembered them, and I wanted to take a look and maybe even store them in the house out of the damp.' David met Brenan's gaze full-on. 'They were gone. The particular items weren't there. I turned the place upside down. It wasn't until a few days later that it came to me that whoever had broken in must have taken them.'

'Was your garage break-in reported to the police originally?' Stanier asked.

David lifted his hands in resignation. 'No. Didn't seem worth it at the time. I didn't think anything had gone. After I realised someone had actually taken stuff, Poppy's stuff, I battled with myself for days. I was going through a bad time. I managed to shake myself out of it by being sensible, as I thought. There was no reason on this Earth for anyone to specifically want some of Poppy's things. She'd been missing for ages by then, so I tried to convince myself I was wrong and maybe it had been chucked away by me or Laura.' Another sheepish look was cast towards his wife. 'I'm sorry I never told you. I knew how it would upset you.'

Brenan produced the crime file copies Frank Milton had given her. 'We know about the incidents you've described: a stolen bike from next door and a drill from a shed a couple of houses up. It fits with what you've said. It happened on the night of Saturday 13th November, 2010. So, what was taken?' Brenan said.

'Some of her old books and music, from when she first started playing cello at school. A handful of photos. Nothing worth anything to anyone else.'

'The police were never updated on this then?' said Stanier.

Hunt's single blink confirmed that they were not.

'He's been nicking for her,' Stanier said, as they walked back to the car. 'Getting things that she needs and, by the looks of it, stuff by request. Pinching her old books and things for her from her own home.'

Brenan said nothing, just listened.

Their intention to drive straight back to the nick and update Forrest on the conversation was cancelled by a text message from Forrest himself: *Meet me up at Park Hills NOW.*

Stanier steered into the parking spot indicated by the uniformed constable and waited as details were jotted onto a clipboard. They had a fifty-yard trek up the stone-mottled track before they came to the main locus. A white-suited and face-masked CSI met them at a boundary marked by tree-to-tree lengths of black and yellow *Crime Scene Do Not Enter* tape.

Things had changed drastically since their last visit. The tape stretched away into a thicket of crowded trees and jostling brambles either side of the original pull-in where ground cover had been hacked down. Several distant, white-clad CSI figures wrestled with dog rose and self-set saplings inching their way onwards through impossible spaces to get the job done. Bright afternoon sunshine dappled the ground through gaps in the leaf canopy.

Forrest met them at the perimeter, unrecognisable at first in his crime scene gear. He pulled his mask to one side. 'Nearly done with cross-contamination risks,' he said. 'But best get suited up to be on the safe side.' He gestured over at a box of crime scene overalls.

It took a few minutes to awkwardly struggle into the suits and get comfortable. They then followed Forrest across the freshly-strimmed earth, sticking to the narrow corridor designated by a makeshift fence of iron poles and fluttering tape. Small red pennant-style flags dotted the earth where finds had been made. Some of these finds, still in place, were plain to see: a jutting femur, a radius and an ulna. One of the large tents covered the main locus; the pelvis and rib cage were in here, still being photographed and scrutinised.

A huddle of white figures could be seen further into the untouched undergrowth. Two of these were hacking and cutting to make access easier. 'Hi, Eve. Ed,' said George Stodford as they approached. 'Hand bones,' he said, pointing down at a patch of cleared earth. 'And a ring. Not good, from what Mr Forrest tells me.'

Brenan closed her eyes for a second, hoping against hope.

The bones, completely devoid of cartilage, flesh or skin, lay disarticulated, but still vaguely hand-shaped, in a lightly excavated one-foot square of moss-covered ground.

Another figure, Home Office forensic pathologist Timothy French, made himself known. 'Sergeant Brenan, Mr Stanier.' His Oxford educated tones resonated through the muffling effect of a paper face mask. 'This is the right hand. CSI have done well to find this as it was actually beneath the surface soil. The corresponding radius and ulna bones are in a different area of the locus.' His gloved finger pointed downwards. I concur with CSI's thoughts that the body was not buried and was probably just pushed into undergrowth.

This hand, though, as I say, was beneath the topsoil and is likely the work of a fox. They do tend to target hands and feet, quite often taking them away from the body and caching them by digging a shallow hole, just like this. It would explain the intact and correct positioning of the bones we have here. It seems likely that there was sufficient flesh and cartilage to keep all the bones in place. Subsequent decomposition through both bacterial and insect activity has completely eliminated all traces of flesh and cartilage, but not particularly disturbed the positioning.

'So, how have you managed to find it?'

'Metal detector sweep,' French said, dropping to his haunches and pointing to almost touch the bones. Brenan and Stanier copied the pose. 'Here,' the pathologist said. 'You can see a small silver coloured ring still fitted around the proximal phalange bone of the small finger. A significant find I believe?'

Brenan stared at the ring, narrowing her eyes at its tiny embossed floral motif, those wide petals so recognisable as a poppy. She wanted to throw up.

Chapter 23

Day 13 Saturday 27th April

THE SATURDAY MORNING briefing began with an update on the Park Hills situation. Forrest was keeping quiet about the ring for the time being. It had been removed in the late stages of yesterday's crime scene examination for evidence bagging. As if any more identification were necessary, the internal inscription from Poppy's grandmother was plain to see. He knew that, as soon as he released the detail to the rest of the team, he would also have to tell the parents. He desperately wanted a positive DNA match before any of that but, with the post-mortem not likely until Monday, he was feeling pushed into a corner.

Brenan kept a poker face throughout the briefing and concentrated her input on the outbuildings and garden thefts. It was a feature which drew interest from the team, particularly so when the break-in at the Hunt's garage was mentioned. Frank Milton listened intently. Of course he knew all about the other thefts but this one from the garage at the victim's home was news to him and it really got his attention. When Brenan went on to mention what had been taken, Milton's dropping jaw and ascending eyebrows could have won the "surprised face award". He kept his powder dry until Brenan finished up and then raised one timid finger. His manner was slightly indecisive, almost as though he was questioning his own logic. It was enough to catch Brenan's eye. 'Yes, Frank?'

'Might be nothing, Sarge – sorry, Inspector – but you mentioned cello music. A cello was stolen from Birchfield High. It was around the time of the shed and garden thefts. It was a weekend burglary and, with it being at the school, it would never have popped up in my trawl through sheds and garages. I actually made the initial visit to the school, took a statement and got SOCO out… CSI as you now call them. The paperwork would have made its way through to CID – well, it should have done! I don't think anything came of it. Pretty weird thing to pinch.'

Brenan's gaze fleetingly moved from PC Milton and landed on Forrest sitting next to her. 'Thanks, Frank,' she said. 'That might be interesting. Dig out the old file on it – everything you can find.'

When the briefing finished, Stanier pulled out a chair alongside Brenan. He'd got a large wad of copied crime files in his left hand which he plonked down in front of her. 'Frank was a bloody brilliant local bobby on the Birchfield. A mine of information, with a vast knowledge of the local crooks and idiots. He was forever clearing up minor crime on the scantest of detail.' He placed a hand on the paperwork. 'Take a look at that lot. It's what he's dug out so far on the petty thefts. Given the right resources, he might well have caught the offender in the act. There's twenty-seven similar minor crimes there. All in and around the Birchfield. This first lot covers the eighteen months prior to, and just after, Jason's birth.'

Milton now appeared alongside with more paperwork. 'That Birchfield High School burglary, Ed – the cello.' He placed several copied sheets down. 'It was on one of the discs I'd already got out. It's all there: witness statements, MO, SOCO report.'

Stanier eagerly started leafing through the report. 'Two years after Poppy went missing,' he said, directing his voice at Brenan but with eyes still on the paperwork. 'This type of job is usually down to schoolkids, but it's a bloody coincidence.' He turned a couple more pages and then suddenly stopped. 'Bloody hell! Take a look at this.'

Brenan was out of her seat and peering over Stanier's shoulder before he took his next breath. The A4 photocopy was a crime scene photo taken from beneath the school corridor window where the burglar had climbed in. It showed a clearly defined training shoe pattern. The mark was picked out in dried light brown mud against the dark green plastic floor covering. A few shards of broken glass also within the picture lay close to the print. A wooden twelve-inch ruler had been added by the photographer to give perspective.

Stanier's widening eyes remained fixed on Brenan, but his right hand magically delved into his in-tray and stumbled on the right document without their help. He placed the picture of the Adidas Crazy 8 trainer sole pattern down on the desk alongside the crime scene photo. It took no more than an urgent look in Forrest's direction and the word, 'Sir,' to encourage the DCI to join them.

The unique shoe pattern precluded any need for further conversation on the identity of the burglar, other than one word from Forrest: 'Kobe.'

Brenan gave Forrest a serious stare. 'We need some enquiries up at the school urgently on this. The fact that it's now a Saturday and eight years after the event isn't going to hold us up.'

Forrest nodded. 'You crack on with that. CSI are hoping to be done up at Park Hills this afternoon or tomorrow morning latest. We're definitely on course for a post-mortem some time Monday. I've told PC Milton to take a day off tomorrow; he's got some pre-planned family arrangements, but I can't see any days off for anyone else on the horizon.' Forrest paused. 'Madeleine excepted. She's explained to me how she's getting along, and I must say I'm impressed. She's taking the weekend off. She says she can get on with her genealogy research from home and has some catching up to do on other work. I've had funding agreed for her accommodation and travelling expenses from HQ already. The Deputy Chief Constable has pulled his face. Can you believe it?'

Brenan gave a wry smile. Yes, she could believe it. But what she couldn't quite comprehend was Forrest's refreshingly altered mind-set. He seemed to have transformed in less than two weeks from a budget-obsessed, career-fixated bureaucrat to the real cop that he was before the promotion ladder appeared.

Brenan and Stanier arrived at Birchfield High School at half past ten. The school gates were open despite it being a Saturday. The building's facilities were forever in demand for various out-of-hours activities. A morning Zumba class was in progress in the main hall, so Brenan knew the caretaker was somewhere to be found.

A middle-aged, overweight, blonde lady, clad in flab-hugging orange leotard, and late for her desperately-needed workout, came across the two detectives in a corridor and was able to direct them to school caretaker-cum-community officer, Hugh Banks.

Banks examined the detectives' warrant cards with a degree of suspicion. 'So what can I do for you?'

Stanier did the talking for a change. 'We're looking into an old crime, nothing special. No great value, but circumstances dictate that we need to speak to the teacher who was most involved. She may not even work here now.' Stanier rechecked the witness statement he was holding. 'Music teacher, Miss Phoebe Halton.'

It transpired that Miss Halton was still a "Miss" and still did several hours per week both at Birchfield High and a couple of other schools locally. Within forty-five minutes Brenan and Stanier were sipping tea in the lounge of her Newcastle-Under-Lyme detached home, courtesy of a telephone number from school records.

Distant but inspiring tones of Bach's Fugue in G Minor emanated from the piano keyboard in Miss Halton's music room as an unseen, but talented, private pupil prepared for the Grade 6 exam. The fifteen-minute delay came as a mind-soothing relief to the two police officers after a hectic and stressful few days.

'Gosh, the mystery of the missing cello,' the music teacher said, as her pupil departed and the reason for the detectives' visit was explained. 'That's simply yonks ago.'

The perilously thin early sixties woman relaxed back into a green winged arm chair and crossed one black leather-trousered leg over the other. An art-deco theme existed about both house and owner. A cigarette in a long Bakelite holder would not have been out of place.

Edging around their real interest in the case was not easy. Miss Halton was sharp although, in her profession, she may well have preferred the adjective "astute". 'Yes, I see. So it seems that your real concern lies within the identities of the students who were taking cello classes at Birchfield High at the time of the theft. It's an awfully long time ago to be putting such energy into what I can only imagine is a fairly minor crime in the usual scale of things.'

The detectives remained wordless.

'So, I gather that, perhaps, you have arrested the perpetrator and the clock is ticking, so to speak.' Miss Halton looked from one detective to the other. 'I trained as a lawyer before deciding on my passion for music as a profession.

'Hmm,' she mused at the continuing lack of detail. 'I got nowhere with that one, did I? Maybe we'd best put our cards on the table. It's Poppy, isn't it?'

Brenan was taken aback by the woman's speed of perception. Her impassive look momentarily slipped – the game was up. 'Yes, Miss Halton, it is, but how have you worked that out?'

'I had five youngsters at Birchfield who were doing cello back when Poppy went missing and, yes, Poppy was one of them. I teach both cello and piano, but cello is my real passion. I like to promote cello through the schools I teach at with the hope that, one day, I'll find a star.' She looked upward, as if to the heavens. 'I'm still looking. Most kids only take up cello as a bit of a fad and then get bored when the lads start showing an interest. Most of my school pupils seem to be girls. I've only ever had one lad at Birchfield, and he was clueless.'

Halton uncrossed her legs and sat forward in her chair. 'Poppy could well have turned into that star I was looking for. She was bloody good. She'd got potential and a real feel for the soul of the instrument. Tended to go off into the realms of popular music a bit, but that's not a bad thing.'

'So how did you know we were interested in Poppy?' Brenan said.

'I didn't really. You just told me, although, to be fair, Poppy's face kept coming to me every time the subject of that stolen cello cropped up over the years. Like it did when you first mentioned it.'

Even though Poppy's body had almost certainly been found, the policy of keeping tight-lipped remained in place and Brenan was loath to break it. 'There are reasons why we wish to keep the crux of our investigation secret for the time being. It partly concerns the welfare of Poppy's parents.'

Halton gave a nonchalant lift of the shoulders. 'I often wondered what happened to Poppy. I'll help however I can.'

Chapter 24

BRENAN AND STANIER arrived back before lunch. Stanier updated the HOLMES database on their latest findings, whilst Brenan tracked Forrest down to his office. He was keen to hear about the stolen cello. She pulled out a chair. 'No question in your mind then, Eve? Definitely down to Kobe? Wouldn't want a red herring at this stage.'

'Red herring in red trainers?' Brenan quipped. 'No, boss, not in my book. This was him alright. Poppy's sent him on an errand to collect the very instrument she'd been practising on at school.'

'How the hell has he managed to pull it off? A bloody cello is no small thing to sneak off into the night with.'

'Exactly,' Brenan agreed. 'Obviously using a vehicle. We've always thought he was living close by on the estate. The original idea was that he was walking or riding a stolen bike home.'

Forrest sat back in his chair. 'Not just any vehicle; a van more likely.'

Brenan shrugged, half agreeing. 'Frank Milton covered pretty well everything when the burglary was reported. It took place between around five on the evening of Saturday the 11th December 2010, when the caretaker locked the building and quarter past seven on the Monday morning. That was the thirteenth, when he opened up and found a broken window in a corridor.'

'So we're looking at the Saturday evening or anytime Sunday through to early Monday morning then,' Forrest concluded.

'Yes, and Frank has now also been able to pinpoint the theft of the music from the Hunt's garage as being on Saturday 13th November 2010. Even though Mr Hunt didn't report his own burglary, Frank has tied it up with the theft of power tools two doors away and a stolen bike from next door, which David Hunt mentioned. These *were* reported to the police. So the books and cello music were stolen a few weeks before the cello was stolen.'

'So, as well as his petty thefts to provide an income, he's been out on a shopping spree for Poppy. He's actually pinched some of her old stuff from her parents' garage, but doesn't seem inclined to take chances by breaking into the house. He's made do with what he could find in the garage.'

'That all fits and it might be the reason why he ended up having to steal the cello. Perhaps the music rekindled her interest in playing again. God only knows how it's turned out like this.'

'What about Miss Halton? Could she add anything to her original statement?'

'Actually, yes she has. She'd described the cello back in her statement when it was first pinched. It was nothing special, not of any particular value.' Brenan checked her notepad. 'A Celilio student cello – a starter kit. It included a soft carry-case and folding music stand. Not heavy, but quite bulky, and worth no more than £400. What Miss Halton was able to add didn't come to light until a couple of weeks after the theft. You see, the wrong bow had been taken by the burglar. Again, you learn something every day. The bow for a cello is actually quite short in length. Shorter than both a violin and a viola bow. You'd think, with it being the largest instrument, it would have been the biggest bow. Seems the burglar also thought that and went and took a violin bow.'

'And the police were not updated on that?' Forrest said.

'No.'

'What's been going on, Eve? Has Poppy managed to develop some kind of control, a bond with this bastard at some stage?'

'Well, Charlie Sawyer mentioned the possibility of Stockholm syndrome… a sort of relationship between captor and victim,' Brenan said. 'But this seems more like Poppy, the hostage, may have developed some kind of power over her captor.'

'Not a good enough power,' Forrest muttered. The thought of Poppy's silver ring was in his mind

'There is something to come from it, though,' Brenan said. 'I've not told Miss Halton anything like the full story yet, but she's a shrewd woman. She says that the cello could never be played with a violin bow. If someone really wanted to play it, they would have to get the correct type of bow from somewhere. She suggests that such single purchases would be unusual.' She paused. 'The real bow remains at the school to this day, so he never took the chance of returning to do a second burglary for it.'

Forrest stroked his chin between thumb and forefinger, accepting that the razor had not done a particularly good job that morning. 'So what are your thoughts?

'One of two things could have been going on. Either Poppy had developed some kind of hold over him, or he'd taken pity on her for a while.'

'We've yet to discover exactly what kind of fully-fledged monster this bastard is. He's raped and murdered three women, at least. And now it's looking like he's done the same to Poppy. The date of the cello theft – December – could even put it in line for having been an intended Christmas present!'

'Well, one thing's for sure,' she said, 'everything he's got for her, at least everything that we know about, he's stolen. Books from the library, clothes and baby grow from washing lines, music from the parents' garage and now the cello from school. All stolen. He never buys anything, so he never leaves a trail, or so he was thinking.'

'So,' Forrest questioned, 'if he did get her a cello bow, where did he get it from?'

'It would be another stepping stone in the right direction if we could find out. Miss Halton has given us plenty of possible outlets to purchase from. Several music shops in and around the city and then plenty of online sellers. Amazon, eBay and a few other music specialists. We'll need to start checking these to see if any keep records that far back, but I'm more inclined to think he'll have pinched one from somewhere.'

Brenan had been thinking about passing the cello bow enquiry on to another team. They'd already got more than enough to contend with, but the conversation inspired her into action. 'Fancy doing a bit on the bow, Ed?' she said, as they made their way to the canteen, sandwiches in hand.

'Might as well. Sunday tomorrow and we'll be limited on what we can do.'

There were three music shops in Hanley and one each in the nearby towns of Burslem and Newcastle. They decided to split, Brenan walking into the town to cover the three nearby ones, and Stanier taking the car to visit Newcastle and Burslem.

The line of questioning had been narrowed down to:

Do you supply cello bows without cellos?

Is there much call to purchase a single cello bow?

Do you keep records of such sales?

Have you ever had one stolen?

It was soon established that all the shops could supply single cello bows on request, but none kept them in stock. The sale of a cello was something of a rarity and only the area's biggest instrument dealer, Sherwood's of Hanley, regularly had one in stock and on display.

Roy Sherwood was a short, energetic man in his late sixties. Even with a working day at the shop almost completed, he still looked ready for a dinner date. He was dressed immaculately in dark suit, white shirt, turquoise tie and matching pocket handkerchief. The thinning hair seemed to have benefited from more than a tinge of *Just For Men*, and a sizeable dollop of gel.

'Yes,' Sherwood said to Brenan from his position behind the counter, 'we supply instruments to all the schools in the area. A cello would come as a kit with its bow and case and a few more bits and pieces. We normally only sell the student model but can get more expensive, higher quality ones if requested. As for a bow on its own…' He touched his fingers to his lips. '…very rare. We've only got two concert cellists on the books. These top musicians guard their instruments with their lives. It would be unusual for anyone to need a new bow. They would usually get it re-haired.' The man's face changed as enlightenment took over from uncertainty. 'Thinking about it, we *did* once supply one of the concert cellists with a couple of Dorfler Bows – expensive ones, cost him a packet. He was frantic to get them for a concert.' Sherwood's expression changed yet again as he recalled more. 'I remember now, it was Brian Bannister. Nice chap. Lives a few miles out of the city – Little Stoneleigh way, I think. He plays with the City of Birmingham Symphony Orchestra. He did a couple of Saturday morning displays in the shop for us. Years ago now, mind you. He was raising money for charity. He filled the place, so it was good for business as well.'

Now full of enthusiasm to help out, Sherwood about-turned and disappeared into the back office as his muted tones continued: 'Those two bows were the only ones we've ever sold separately from a cello and, as for your question about theft, no, definitely not. We've only ever had one single cello kit in at a time and that would always be a student set-up, with a bow and everything.'

The sound of metal filing cabinet drawers being opened and closed was heard as the shopkeeper wittered on. 'If someone had shoplifted the bow, we would have had to order another from the suppliers. We do get problems with shoplifting, same as all the shops do, but never a cello bow.'

Sherwood was soon back behind the counter and holding one of Mr Bannister's recent invoice copies. 'There we are: name, address and phone number.'

'So why did Mr Bannister need two new bows?' Brenan said, as she folded the paper into her handbag.

'Do you know, now that you've said it, I'm pretty damn sure he said his had been stolen. I don't think he told me the circumstances. It's such a long time ago.'

Brenan trekked back to the MIR to find that Stanier was already back from his own less fruitful enquiry. The tries at Bannister's home phone resulted in a disappointing voicemail recording: he was not in. 'Hmm,' Brenan said. 'From what Mr Sherwood said, he's in great demand. I guess Saturday evening concerts will be his main working day. Hopefully we'll catch him tomorrow.'

Chapter 25

Day 14 Sunday 28th April

SUNDAY, THE DAY of rest, arrived, although such a description didn't really fit this Sunday. The team would be working. Forrest, in keeping with normal major incident tradition, had allowed a one hour "lie-in" as he'd jokingly termed it. The daily briefing began at nine instead of the usual eight.

There had been no more revelations from Park Hills. 'We're hoping for a PM sometime tomorrow,' Forrest said.

DCs Wendy Bailey and Rob Kent had been tasked with finding Denise, Sarah Powell's old workmate, who she had turned to for help after the rape. They'd tracked her down to Middlesbrough where, now married with two children, she was working as a doctor's receptionist. 'Everything checked out, boss,' said Rob Kent. 'She was horrified when she heard exactly how things had turned out. She so wishes she could have persuaded Sarah to go to the police when it happened, but she wouldn't have it.'

There were more summaries from other teams concerning the reinvestigation of the years-old prostitute murders also down to Kobe. The entire HOLMES computer database for these earlier cases was now linked to all facets of the new crimes and leads.

'We've got a van cropping up in the *Sandstone* enquiry,' said one detective assigned to that side of the investigation. 'HOLMES dug out five sightings over the period of the three prostitute murders which could have been the same vehicle.' The man waggled a downwards facing palm as he spoke to emphasise the uncertainty. 'The sightings came in from working girls in the main and suggested the bloke being a kerb crawler. There was also an unconfirmed sighting of Jennifer McQueen, the first murder victim, getting into such a vehicle on the night she was murdered.'

Forrest responded. 'Yes, this has been looked at time and again, both on the original enquiry and on subsequent reviews. It was only ever a sketchy description of the van. It was possibly a white Ford Escort but, notwithstanding all manner of PNC attempts to narrow down the field, and literally hundreds of separate enquiries, nothing.'

The officer nodded. 'Yes, and obviously after so many years *that* van will be long gone now – scrapped – but we've got these links to the estate and the night time thefts. I know we're talking eight years ago when Jason was abandoned, but bikes, power tools, and now a cello. He must have had a van then as well.' The officer continued: 'If he's such a creature of habit, or maybe it even involves his employment, the chances are he may still have a similar vehicle, even if he's given up the petty theft.'

Forrest thanked the detective and then turned to Brenan. 'Get Frank Milton to look at the more recent petty thefts on the estate just to be sure Kobe's not still at it.' Brenan made a note as Forrest turned his attention to DC Charlie Sawyer. 'Charlie, you've been looking into the possibility of buildings on the estate which could have been used as a potential prison for Poppy.' Forrest cleared his throat. The detail about Poppy's ring was still secret to all but a chosen few and he had to be careful how he phrased his points. 'I know we're increasingly talking in the past tense and I'm as guilty as the next. We must remain optimistic. Almost certainly, Poppy was – is being held somewhere on the estate, and may still be. That place – house, basement, cellar or whatever – still exists somewhere. Charlie, anything to tell us?'

Sawyer's long sigh matched his weary appearance. 'Been going through countless building applications and plans, both old and new, with the local planning department. It's a huge task. Several large public buildings had basements built in with the original plans when the estate was constructed back in the fifties.' Sawyer referred to his notepad to explain. 'The two schools – that's the primary and high school – have large basement areas and there's even a small one at the nursery. The three churches were built at the same time and all have basements. There's the newly built Neighbourhood Centre with a large basement. The shops and Barclays Bank in Malbon Square, beneath the apartment blocks, again all have basements. A few privately owned properties have applied for planning permission over the years to excavate basements, but none have been approved due to building regulations.'

Brenan commented. 'I guess there's always going to be the odd rogue developer who just does it anyway.'

'Yes,' Sawyer replied. 'The planning officer said exactly that, and sometimes these things never come to light. I'm working my way through everything and physically examining the whole lot for signs of habitation. The Planning Department are working with me on it as a routine planning inspection. That way, I'm not really inclined to show my warrant card. If people want to think I'm a council official so be it.'

Brenan smiled at Charlie's useful twisting of the rules. She wondered how Forrest would deal with it.

Forrest's grin gave her the answer. 'Bit too much info, Charlie, but well done and keep us updated.'

The meeting was over by quarter to ten and Forrest was hoping for an hour's respite to clear some paperwork.

'We're off over to Little Stoneleigh to have a chat with Brian Bannister, the bow-less cellist,' Brenan said. 'Might be a red herring, but worth a look. Spoken to him on the phone and it turns out his bow was stolen from his car in Birmingham back in 2011. It seems unlikely to be connected, but he's not that far away. It's an unusual theft, so worth a look.'

The market town of Little Stoneleigh lay ten miles and twenty-five minutes from the city centre. Brian Bannister's eighteenth century, whitewashed, stone block cottage was to be found another two miles further away in the picturesque village of Oulford.

Huge oaks shadowed the property, the leaf canopy that was beginning to form darkening the golden thatch of its roof. Deeply inset red painted window frames disclosed the substantial thickness of the walls.

The crunch of tyres upon pebble drive alerted the owner to the arrival of his expected guests and he met them at the front door. 'Afternoon.' He extended a hand to Stanier who was first in line.

Brenan received a similar greeting and, after warrant cards were checked, the pair settled themselves in on high stools at their host's breakfast bar with mugs of Nespresso Lungo Forte apiece.

Bannister repeated the account he'd given by telephone of the theft of his cello bow, albeit in greater and more emotive detail.

'It was a Saturday. Nearly always a big concert on a Saturday. I'm Cello Section Leader with the CBSO – that's the City of Birmingham Symphony Orchestra.'

'That's like top dog then?' Stanier threw in.

Bannister smiled. 'Top dog? Not been called that before, but I suppose, metaphorically speaking, and strictly cello-wise, yes. There are eight of us at the moment. Should be ten, so we're recruiting now, if you know any good cellists.'

The detectives grinned at Bannister's joke. 'None I can think of at Hanley nick, Mr Bannister,' Stanier chuckled.

'Anyway, getting back to it,' Bannister said. Brenan noticed a hint of emotion had entered his playful humour. 'When this happened, I had the role of Tutti Cello and would be playing together with the orchestra rather than playing the solo passages. At present we have four Tutti Cello, three Sub-Principal Cello and me as section leader. The only good thing about the theft was that it happened after the concert and not before. But I had another venue on the Friday and was frantic to get a decent replacement bow quickly and try to get used to it. I'd got others, but hate them all. The main one that was stolen was a twenty-first birthday present from my parents, a Charles Peccatte make. It was valuable.' There was some emotion present in Bannister's expression. 'The Police over in Birmingham didn't seem too good at finding my bow, Inspector, so what brings you here from down the road in Hanley?'

'We'll tell you what we can, Mr Bannister,' Brenan said, 'but I'd like you to explain what happened first.'

'We'd had a big concert at Symphony Hall in Birmingham; a full house. Over two thousand two hundred people. A crowd of us always go for a meal afterwards, a curry, bit of a party if you like, and a sort of post-concert wind down. My cello was safe and comfy in its case lying down on the back seat of my car. It even had two seatbelts around it and the alarm was on.' He shook his head in disbelief as the next part of the story formed in his mind.

'When we came out, perhaps midnight or quarter past, I could hear a car alarm but never thought in this world it'd be mine.' Bannister visibly shuddered as the memory returned. 'It bloody well was! The alarm was blaring, headlights flashing, smashed side window, the whole caboodle. I ran the last twenty yards, and I never run. Anyway, the cello was still there but the case had been tampered with and the side pocket holding the bows was open. They were gone.'

'More than one bow then?' Stanier said.

'Oh yes, always take a spare, but it would stress me out to have to use it in concert. I paid a fortune to replace the bows with half-decent ones.'

'You reported it to the police?' Brenan asked.

'Straight away, and the police were there quickly considering it was what they'd probably just term minor theft. It was Saturday and I guess it was a busy time for them. The officer couldn't spend much time with me as something serious had happened nearby. He gave me a crime number and had to leave. It seemed up to me to try to tie up loose ends and so I asked the restaurant staff about any CCTV on the car park. They did have a system and let me view it. Just my luck though, as it didn't cover where my car was parked. It did capture a few cars entering and leaving and a few people wandering about. I left a voicemail for the constable dealing with it in case he needed to view it.'

'And they stole nothing else?'

'Never even opened the glove box.'

Stanier had been scribing away at a witness statement throughout the conversation. His ability to scavenge all the necessary detail and useful minutiae whilst also disregarding unwanted dross had been honed through countless major enquiries.

'Lovely place you've got here,' Brenan said admiringly, as Bannister signed the form.

'Thank you,' Bannister said. 'Yes, it's wonderful for my practice. No chance of disturbing the neighbours with walls this thick. That's always the problem with cello, those deep resonant notes travel like whale song.'

Forrest was nursing a pint of Falstaff and munching at a beef bap in the *Smithfield* when the pair met up with him. A major incident team would sometimes manage a pub carvery on Sundays, but not this Sunday.

'How are things going up at Park Hills?' Stanier asked.

'All but done now,' Forrest replied. 'Mortuary at eleven tomorrow morning for the skeletal analysis. We'll have a four o'clock finish today with it being Sunday and let's hope for a breakthrough tomorrow.'

Chapter 26

Day 15 Monday 29th April

THE MONDAY MORNING briefing began with a synopsis covering the most interesting events of the past two weeks. Forrest was hoping for more connections to the old triple murder case – anything that might give more leads to Kobe's identity.

His news of the connection to school cello burglary created furrowed brows. This was interesting.

He expanded on the information. 'It gives us a pretty strong link between murderer, abductor, rapist, baby abandoner, petty thief and now this school cello burglary.' He caught Brenan's eye. 'Eve, if you can update us on the additional cello bow business.'

Brenan explained the details of the wrongly stolen school violin bow and the tenuous connections to Mr Bannister's loss. 'As yet, we have nothing to firmly connect Bannister's theft. It happened forty-odd miles away in Birmingham city centre, but it certainly looks as though the thief was only looking to steal cello bows. Okay, so one was an extremely valuable one. Maybe that alone was the reason. It could be a totally unconnected separate issue. But couple that theft with the fact that it occurred three weeks after the cello was stolen from Birchfield High School, where the wrong bow was taken. Couple it again with the fact that Bannister, in point of fact, lives quite close – just ten or twelve miles away from the Birchfield estate – and it starts to get interesting. Add to it the fact that he had performed a cello display in Sherwood's music shop in Hanley and that adds even more. As I said, we don't need to get tunnel vision on anything, but an open mind on all the features is something we have to keep.'

Brenan's mobile pinged an incoming message as she finished off. She looked at the screen and then read aloud. 'Madeleine will be with us after lunch. She's been working on some ideas over the weekend and might have the beginnings of something interesting.'

Forrest brightened. 'Let's hope so, but we'd better get off to the mortuary.'

Brenan was having guilt pangs about not letting Scott in on the "ring" business. She deserved to know, but Forrest's orders had been firm.

Forrest did the driving for the three-mile journey to the Stoke Royal Hospital. The state-of-the-art "super mortuary" with all its high-tech facilities was now *the* place for most of Staffordshire's suspicious death examinations.

Forrest, Stanier and Brenan were regulars when it came to post mortems and knew to arrive early. They'd be meeting other members of the police team there and parking on the busy hospital site was always a nightmare. The DCI reversed into one of the few remaining spaces and joked on the resemblance of his black Skoda Superb estate to an undertaker's car. 'Could have parked this outside the door and not got a ticket.'

'Don't count on it, boss,' Stanier said from the rear seat. 'Even the Coroner had one a few months back. She was livid.'

They entered through the hospital's bustling main entrance and made their way along a fifty-yard corridor filled with a two-way moving pavement of humanity. Everyone was heads-up, eyes searching for signs. Wheelchairs and trolleys, paramedics and porters all seemed in a race to go one way or the other. The lift down from the ground floor delivered them instantly into a different world. Each wide, well-lit corridor became quieter and more deserted with every arrowed "MORTUARY" sign they passed.

The final door was grey-painted and heavy looking. Its sturdy digital lock was backed up by a wall mounted visitor's buzzer and intercom. Brenan applied a thumb to the button and a voice responded via the small speaker. The lady's tone was set at an optimum pitch for the most usual customers, bereaved and tearful relatives. The single word, 'Hello,' successfully conveyed both sympathy and concern.

'DS Brenan, DCI Forrest and DC Stanier, for the post mortem,' Brenan said, inwardly cursing herself for continually forgetting her new rank.

The intercom voice changed to a chirpy. 'Oh hi! Two ticks.' The door opened on Bridie McClelland, a smiling-faced and blue-uniformed Anatomical Pathology Technologist, or APT. 'Come on in. We've got the CSI team and the pathologist here already.'

The three followed Bridie through to the facility's break room, a long, narrow and windowless space. A sink, cupboards, and other kitchen effects stood at the far end. The diminishing low sound of a kettle suggested boiling point was close. CSI manager George Stodford looked up and signalled a greeting to the new arrivals. He was standing alongside fellow CSI Wendy Hulme and photographer Alex Jones, who was spooning coffee into waiting mugs.

A number of comfortable chairs and a couple of tables were arranged along one wall. Forensic pathologist Timothy French sat cross-legged at a table studying an inch-thick pile of notes and looking ten years less than his actual fifty-five. His slate grey pinstripe suit jacket hung over the chair back. The tail of a mauve silk tie had been tucked neatly in between the buttons of his snow-white shirt. He looked up from the paperwork and pushed his spectacles into place from the tip of his nose. His greeting was directed to Forrest. 'Morning, Dominic.' He eased up from his chair, right hand extended.

'Morning, Tim.' Forrest shook the hand and half-turned toward Brenan and Stanier. 'You've met DI Brenan and DC Stanier.'

'Ah, yes! Briefly up at Park Hills. It's Yvette, right? On the Glendenning case a couple of years back as well?'

'That's right, sir,' Brenan replied, mind now temporarily riveted onto a memory she someday hoped to forget – the horrific Glendenning child murder.

Stanier reached forward and joined in the handshaking. DCS Brown arrived in the room, car keys still in hand. He homed in on French who was still on his feet. 'We're a bit short on the bone count then, Tim?'

'A little, Geoff, but your team have done a bloody spectacular job in the circumstances and I'm confident there's been no post-death dismemberment. All down to animal scavenging. We've got most of the larger bones apart from the mandible, left ulna and right tibia. The majority of other missing bones are, as to be expected, small foot and hand bones, a couple of fingers, several teeth and some of the tiny ones from the ears.'

'Hmm,' Brown made a concerned face. 'So how's that leave us for a dental ID? It'll be some time before we get DNA through.'

'Not easy and certainly not today. It's not just the missing mandible; quite a few teeth have gone astray from upstairs and little or no sign of dental work.'

'Damn,' Brown cursed. 'I would've liked to have given some kind of positive closure to the parents today.'

With that, the door opened again and APT McClelland, now in a green apron over blue scrubs, politely ushered the lady beside her into the room.

City Coroner, Lucy Johnson, was a pert and slim fifty-six-year-old former barrister. Her auburn, recently coiffed, Princess Anne hair style suggested she'd not be going into the PM suite. Her smart grey pencil skirt was another indicator that she would not be getting changed and had opted for a seat in the viewing room. 'Morning, everyone,' she said, but then concentrated attention on DCS Brown and pathologist Tim French. 'Geoff, Tim; here we are again.'

'Yes indeed, ma'am, a tragic and intriguing case,' Brown said.

French responded similarly. 'Lucy, nice to see you again.'

McClelland looked around the room. 'We all here now?'

'Waiting on Debbie Gibson, the forensic anthropologist,' French said. 'She's juggled a few appointments to do this one and we definitely can't do it without her as we're talking just bones. She's texted me, running a tad late. Traffic.'

The APT nodded. 'Okay, I'll listen out for her.'

The DCI's decision to only have his main team players attend the PM brought the police numbers down to a manageable eight. DCs Jennifer Baines and Dennis Rawlins were now working as close liaison with the Hunt family and needed to be in the know. They would be doing some note taking, along with Ed Stanier, from the viewing room. Detective Chief Superintendent Brown's last-minute arrival increased police numbers up to nine, but he too had opted for the viewing room. The three Crime Scene Investigators would be heavily involved in the examination room itself, Alex Jones as photographer, whilst George Stodford and Wendy Hulme would be working as "dirty" and "clean" CSIs, specifically bagging, labelling and recording exhibited items.

Debbie Gibson walked briskly into the break room at ten minutes after eleven. The sense of high voltage which existed about her was intensified by her bright red hair and piercing blue eyes. A crack of static would not have been out of place with each eagerly shared handshake. She was a vital person, interested in everyone and everything. She offered her apologies by way of an observation. 'Bloody M6! Roadworks everywhere.' Gibson was accompanied by her secretary, Janet, a stern, round and grey-haired woman, who would be note taking.

Bridie McClelland now got things underway. 'Right, ladies and gents, we have a skeleton this morning and so this is a forensic skeletal analysis rather than a post-mortem.' She turned to Gibson and unfurled a hand in her direction. 'A welcome to forensic anthropologist Deborah Gibson. First time here at the Stoke Royal, but your reputation as the country's foremost in your field certainly precedes you.'

Gibson's simultaneous lift of the shoulders and lop-sided grin was a playful imitation of coy embarrassment.

DCI Forrest sat back in his chair to give a relaxed résumé of the background to the case. A few comments were thrown in by George Stodford and Mr French.

Gibson listened intently, eyes concentrating on the speaker of the moment but saying nothing.

As McClelland had pointed out, the examination was to be a skeletal analysis and, as such, Gibson was the accepted specialist. French was happy for her to take the lead and they would collaborate on the findings.

French turned to Gibson. 'As I said in my email, Debbie, there are a few interesting features about this. I've made my own mind up on them. So hopefully you'll concur.'

'No pressure then,' Gibson said, faking a grimace.

Bridie added the usual advice. 'Scrubs, aprons, and wellies are ready in the changing rooms. We won't be using visors today as this is a skeletal only job. Anyone observing from the viewing room, its first on the left.'

Chapter 27

THE POST MORTEM suite, currently empty of living souls, was a forty-five feet long cathedral of powerful overhead lighting, stainless steel surfaces, gleaming tiles and wall-to-wall cream painted body storage cabinet doors – two hundred and nine of them. Four heavily-engineered metal autopsy tables stood down the centre, each one occupying yards of working space and set upon its own tree-trunk-wide hydraulic steel lifting pedestal. One of these, the bariatric table for the examination of extra-large patients, was half as big again as the other three. A stainless-steel body tray, again the larger model, had been placed upon this platform and covered with a crisp white sheet.

The viewing room, a spacious seated area, looked into the suite via two huge, glazed windows. Above these, and abutting the ceiling, were two narrow but unglazed slots which allowed spectators to also hear what was taking place. The Coroner, the detective chief superintendent, DC Stanier and DCs Jenny Baines and Dennis Rawlins took their seats in the viewing room alongside two other mortuary staff. Their five-minute wait ended as, stage right, the changing room door leading into the post mortem suite opened.

McClelland led the group over to the bariatric table. Its larger size would allow the bones to be positioned into a slightly exploded and more accessible arrangement.

Gibson and her secretary, along with French and the CSIs were followed by Brenan and Forrest. All were dressed in blue hospital scrubs with a disposable neck-high and knee-length, green plastic apron. Mauve nitrile gloves and white wellington boots completed the ensemble.

Alongside the autopsy table stood a large, wheeled trolley which supported a black plastic body bag. Another, smaller trolley had been positioned parallel to this. Gibson made an eyes-wide head movement in Stodford's direction indicating she was starting, and used scissors to cut the body bag's plastic seal. CSI Alex Jones dutifully photographed each event whilst Wendy Hulme, as "clean" CSI, bagged, labelled and recorded each exhibit item.

The dull purring of the bag's heavy-duty zipper being drawn back along its full length preceded a captured glimpse inside. Differently sized transparent polythene evidence bags jutted unevenly, each one containing its cargo of associated and carefully recorded bones: left hand, right hand, right arm and so on. The soft rustle of plastic continued for some time as each bag was opened and its contents removed under the scrutiny of the note taker. French and Gibson collaborated to set the bones out in their appropriate places, conferring occasionally until accuracy was achieved.

The final "in-life" but slightly exploded position of the bones on the table presented a rudimentary, but also very graphic, illustration of the human being that once was. The laughing, the crying, the running and walking, the happy and sad times of this person were locked forever in what was left: biscuit coloured bones set against a stark white background. A small, lidded plastic evidence box formed part of the assemblage and was placed part way down the table. With its lid removed it seemed to contain several minute fragments of bone.

Even to the non-experts these human remains now on the table presented an unmistakably weathered, tan appearance – worlds apart from the archetypal notion of stark, bleached-white bones.

A few dried brown leaves and flecks of dark soil were dusted free into plastic receptacles on the third table. A couple of small snails had somehow survived the adventures of the past days and were also removed.

French took up a place close to the edge of the table alongside Gibson. Both experts had small lapel microphones clipped to the neck-hem of their scrubs tops. Dictaphones were already running in an inside pocket and note-takers readied their pens.

French cleared his throat for his usual preamble and then set his resonant voice into action, giving the time, date and place. He went on to read from McClelland's list of names present before briefly describing the bones and where they had been discovered. He then offered the stage up to Gibson. 'This is your show, Debbie, so over to you.'

The anthropologist continued to stare down at the disjointed jigsaw puzzle and, without looking up, leaned forward over the table and sniffed a few times. 'No smell whatsoever and no immediate signs of any remaining soft tissue. Mandible missing.' She picked up the skull and smoothed her gloved fingers across its forehead. 'Brow ridges on the skull are virtually non-existent and neck muscle attachment is much less pronounced than that of a male. Both features are indicative of this being a female.' She turned the skull and held it upside down in her left hand. 'Spheno-occipital not completely fused, so I'd estimate age at seventeen, eighteen… Nineteen tops.' She replaced the skull on the table. 'Of the two hundred and six bones normally to be found in an adult skeleton, we do seem to be short of a few. In light of the circumstances of animal scavenging this is to be expected. The CSI team has done well. As I say, the mandible, along with all of its teeth, is one of the missing items. Several teeth are also missing from the upper jaw. Due to the clean socket holes, I believe these to have fallen out post death. The lack of dentistry and missing parts make a dental identification demanding and certainly not possible today.' She turned to DCI Forrest. 'Do we have the dental chart for Poppy Hunt?'

Brenan had anticipated the request and stepped forward to hand over a plastic laminated copy of the document. With the skull now upside down and back on the sheet Gibson rotated the dental chart in her hands lining the diagram in sync. She made a few low-voiced "Hmms" before giving her opinion. 'This person was patently older when she died than the fourteen-year-old who went missing eleven years ago. Doesn't stop it being the same person, though. There is no dentistry to be seen on any of the few remaining teeth in this skull and Poppy's chart only shows one small filling to an upper right first bicuspid – a tooth which has disappeared from this upper jaw.' She turned the skull and showed the empty tooth socket to her audience.

'Now that proves nothing either way. We certainly can't prove identification from this. It will have to be down to the DNA. Looking at the quality of these bones we shouldn't have any problem at all there.'

French, keen to have some input but conscious of Gibson's greater expertise, pointed at the bones in the region of the neck area. A single tooth which had been discovered some distance away had been identified as being from the upper jaw. This had been placed on the cloth a few inches down from the skull. A few inches further down lay four tiny, separated segments of what, when held back in place, would form a small horseshoe-shaped bone. 'Hyoid bone looks interesting. What do you think?' he said, looking at Gibson.

'Yes.' Gibson gingerly shuffled the four pieces to a useful area of table and coaxed them into their in-life shape. 'The hyoid bone – or neck bone – is actually made from three separate pieces of bone which, over time, will fuse together to form the distinctive shape. The fact that its normal three pieces have fallen apart during decomposition is again indicative of a younger person, because it, too, had not yet fused. Also, the fact there are four pieces suggests a fracture to the hyoid. Indeed, I can see that the fourth section is a piece of one of the greater horns of the hyoid.'

French's face indicated his agreement. 'You're thinking possible strangulation. But it's only ever going to be a "possible", right?'

'Correct,' Gibson said. 'Without any tissue or other signs of injury, very difficult to prove. A fracture of the hyoid can often suggest strangulation. This one is, without doubt, fractured. As all the parts were found, it's unlikely to be the result of the animal scavenging. Again, microscopic analysis is the only way forward.'

'Completely agree with all of that,' French said. 'Not all strangulations lead to a fractured hyoid. As you say, it doesn't give us a definite.'

Gibson then picked up and closely examined the ends of each of the longer bones, the rib ends and some of the vertebrae. The three separate areas of the pelvis came under her scrutiny, as did a further look at the upper jaw for signs of wisdom teeth. 'Definitely female, aged seventeen to nineteen. Pretty serious weathering on the bones.' She looked up at George Stodford. 'So, no insect debris at the scene for the lab to help us to determine how long she's been there?'

'No, nothing,' Stodford replied. 'And, as we discussed earlier, no signs of burial, with the possible exception of the right hand, which might have been the work of animals. The body may well have been just pushed into the undergrowth. If so, I guess that might have accelerated decomposition and led to the animal scavenging.'

Gibson was non-committal other than a slight sideways tilt of the head. 'No clothing?'

'Nothing at all,' Stodford replied. 'All we found at the scene was the ring which was recovered from the right hand. That was removed by me at the scene. I have it here if you need it.'

'No, that's okay. I recall from the notes it was on the right hand small proximal phalange – little finger.'

Stodford explained more. 'Yes, the bones of the right hand were found ten metres from the centre of the locus. As I say, it was the only piece which appeared to have been buried. It was discovered an inch or so beneath the surface in a metal detector sweep. We may not have found it if not for the ring.'

'Yes, I've seen the *in situ* photos, and it certainly looks to be the work of a fox. You've been lucky to get it so intact. The animal must have cached it but never came back.' Gibson had seen this type of scenario many times.

The two experts moved a little further down the table. With both hands, Gibson again lifted one of the three sections of the pelvis and slowly rotated it, examining the contours, folds and crevices. 'Sciatic notch quite open, the pubic bone is rectangular. All supporting the likelihood that this is a female.'

She replaced the pelvis on the table and turned back to French. 'I went through the notes and photos you emailed me last night, Tim, and was interested by these.' She tapped a finger against the small plastic box. 'I concur with your thoughts one hundred percent. That is what they are.'

Brenan turned and shot a puzzled glance at Forrest. What did this mean?

French spotted the exchange, gave a small, embarrassed cough and explained. 'Sorry about this, Dominic, not something I've personally come across in the actual skeletal form very often, so I wanted Debbie to give her opinion before mentioning it.'

Gibson extracted one of the bones with a pair of plastic tweezers and held it up to examine it more closely, hand steady as a rock. 'So, you've got a jigsaw with extra pieces.'

The minute proportions, no more than three quarters of an inch in length and hardly an eighth of an inch across, created some squinted focus from the others.

It was clear that Gibson knew exactly what the item was and what it meant. 'Have you got callipers or a surgical micrometer? I need to accurately measure the length.'

Bridie turned to the instrument cabinet, found what was required and handed it over.

Gibson placed the bone on the edge of the table and carefully closed the measuring device against its ends. After recording the read-out, she again used the tweezers to hold the tiny object out with an extended arm for all to see.

'This is a completely intact bone. It measures nineteen point five millimetres. It's a clavicle; the first bone to fully ossify as bone in a fetus. Its length indicates a possible gestational period of around eighteen to twenty weeks. Once I have measured the other bones, we might get to a more accurate age for this baby. This young woman was pregnant when she died.'

Chapter 28

IT WAS QUARTER past two when Brenan, Forrest and Stanier emerged from the mortuary. They took a quiet late lunch in the hospital restaurant. The standard fish, chips and peas was good, but only eaten out of necessity. The cop's survival mentality had kicked in big style: *eat when you can, even though your last job made you feel like shit.* The latest sickening news of an unborn baby had somehow added an even deeper and more horrendous aspect to the case.

The three continued to sit at the table, their cleared plates long gone. Conversation was sparse. Brenan lifted her eyes and contemplated Forrest. She'd been wrong about him. There was no doubting that he was as obsessed as she was about finding out who Kobe was and, for that matter, finding Poppy – when there was still a chance she was alive. That was an ambition they could no longer achieve. Forrest looked tired. That dapper turnout wasn't quite there today and – now she thought about it – nor was it yesterday. The usually gelled, smart, dark hair was a tad untidy, the shirt collar less than well ironed.

Forrest looked up. 'So, we're inconclusive on a cause of death at the moment, but the bastard's strangled her. We've had an upbeat enthusiastic team up until now and, yes, they've all had their doubts since the skeleton was found. But now we've got this ring it's going to be a kick in guts for morale. So, we're still chasing the murderer, but the hope that Poppy would be rescued was always the core objective. That's what's kept everyone keen to get to work and do their bit. I'll have to let the rest of the team know about this pretty soon, but we can't risk the parents finding out through a leak. I'd really like DNA confirmation first.' There was an element of anguish in his voice.

Brenan was wearing her own gloomy face. The job of telling the Hunts would probably fall to her and Ed. She also felt guilty about not telling Madeleine about the ring. She'd be devastated and, even though she was not a police officer, she was accepted as one of the team's lead investigators.

Brenan gritted her teeth and decided to spit out another point that had been bugging her. 'Poppy's ring was initially described by the parents on the Misper form as being worn on the right hand, third finger.'

Forrest looked at her. 'Yes, I picked up on that too. It was actually on her right hand, little finger. So, was it a mistake by the parents originally, or had it become too small for the third finger? Pregnancy? Growing older? Putting on weight?'

'What about telling the team then?' Brenan said. 'And the parents. We did promise to keep them fully informed on everything, no matter what.'

Forrest positioned his elbows on the table and rested his chin on the backs of his hands. He blew out a long sigh. 'Okay, I'll tell the team tomorrow at the briefing. But don't breathe a word until then, not even to Mad. I think she'll be devastated. As for Mr and Mrs Hunt… I guess we'd better tell them tomorrow after the briefing. We must keep to our promises.' He got to his feet. 'Nasty job, Eve. Are you and Ed okay with it?'

The pair gave the standard show of fake indifference.

'I guess. After tomorrow's briefing then?'

They walked back to the car park.

It was half past four when they arrived at the MIR. Madeleine Scott was head down and rattling away at her laptop. 'How's it going, Mad?' Brenan said, pulling out a chair next to her and forcing a bright face. A rather non-committal, abridged summary of the skeletal analysis had already gone around the MIR. The team were not much the wiser following the "awaiting lab tests" précis.

'A hard slog and repetitious, but getting interesting,' Scott replied. She gave a smile of greeting to Forrest and then turned back to Brenan. 'The spit sample kits you sent off for me from Poppy's parents have really made a difference. They were fast-tracked through the genealogy site. It's cost a bit more but really speeded things up.' She spotted Forrest's grimace and wondered if he was still worrying about spiralling costs. She couldn't know that the man had other things on his mind. 'I'm officially managing both parents' genealogy accounts now as well as the one for Jason,' Scott said, as she manoeuvred her mouse and clicked up a different screen. 'I've shown you this before. It's Jason's DNA hits. Two hundred and thirty-seven people throughout the world who have sent in DNA samples and are proven to be related to him.'

The onlookers were familiar with the rows and rows of names. They also understood that buried somewhere in this multitude of innocent individuals was a tenuous ragged link through to the identity of the man they wanted.

'Now I have Poppy's parents on file, and all their own DNA hits, it's shortened my list considerably. I've been able to compare the three different sets: Jason's, David Hunt's and Laura Hunt's. I've been able to strike out those relatives David and Laura share with Jason, effectively removing the maternal side – that's Poppy's side – from Jason's DNA hits. It allows me to concentrate on the remaining ones. The father's.'

'So, how many are you left with?' Forrest asked.

'Seventy-two. There are a few more which I can't afford to ignore, and which may still hold the correct link, but they'll only have a small chance of involvement. Anything after a fourth cousin is still a bit hit and miss as to whether it comes down the maternal or paternal side. I can't rule anything out, but I can concentrate, for the time being, on the strongest paternal links.'

Scott clicked her mouse again and a grey screen appeared. Rows of the pink or blue squares were spread across the screen. All were linked by a network of lines. Names and dates were included in the squares. It was a family tree. She scrolled the entire screen view downwards with her mouse-wheel to reveal more of the squares, but with older dates showing. It was extensive and clearly there was more to see if Scott had chosen to go even further down. Instead, she pulled the view back to the most recent details and pointed at a particular blue male square which had a highlighted name. 'As an example,' she said, 'Ronald Dixon here is a relation on Jason's father's side. He shows as a 3rd to 4th cousin with a DNA share of 97 centimorgans to Jason. You'll remember that a centimorgan is the value used to calculate the share of DNA between people. We all have about 6,800 centimorgans so Dixon's share of 97 with Jason is very small, but it's still there. It appears that Mr Dixon started to investigate his ancestors about ten years ago and he's been building an online family tree since then. He's allowed it to be publicly viewable. Most genealogists do this, as that will often generate more leads. Evidently, he's used all the usual things researchers use: family history from surviving members, photograph albums, census records, births, deaths and marriage records. He's applied to registry offices and even purchased some copy records where he needed to. He's looked out church records and cemetery records, researched microfilm records of old newspapers for interesting tales about long forgotten family members.

'He's made a pretty extensive and comprehensive job of it all. The tree he's created so far details dozens of his ancestors and distant relatives both dead and living. Of course, there are branches he hasn't investigated. Maybe he ran out of the information to go further along that particular route but, even so, this sort of thing could lead us to Kobe. He could be dangling at the end of one of these branches.'

Brenan stared, fascinated at the screen. 'Are there many of the seventy-two who have started trees?'

'About three quarters are in some way connected to trees that either they, or someone else started. Some are extensive and others only contain a handful of names. None of the seventy-two can be ruled out. I've done quite a few checks on census records that I can access. Census records from 1841 to 1911 are available but under the one-hundred-year rule, we can't get at any after then – yet. The DNA hits I've had back only tell me that those people are living and blood-related to Jason. They don't tell me what part of the country they come from. Where I've got family trees attached to those people, I can look at their ancestors and search for them on the old census records. So, anything from 1911 or further back I can research and I've spotted something interesting. A large proportion of Kobe's ancestors originate from up north – Durham, Sunderland and around there. I've still got a lot to get through but, as yet, I've not found a single one with any Stoke-on-Trent roots.

Stanier joined them and stood silently, applying his detective's mind to this complex web, trying to make it fit with things he knew. He leant forward and uttered a single word. 'Miners.'

Stanier was well known for his economy and this singular utterance puzzled his colleagues.

'He comes from a mining family,' he explained. 'In the early sixties, hundreds of miners from up north were rehoused in North Staffordshire to work in the pits around here. The coal mines up there were in decline but ours were still thriving. Many mining families were installed in new houses on the Burrow Hill estate, right alongside the Birchfield, and lots on the Birchfield itself. The new estates up at Biddulph took big communities in. Coalvale, north of Birchfield, was another purpose-built estate mostly for miners. Literally, hundreds came from up north and were set on at all the local pits.' Stanier scratched his nose. 'Those pits are all closed now too, but a lot of the miners' descendants still live in the area.'

Scott set about polishing her glasses as she gave her opinion. 'That would fit, Ed, that would certainly fit. You see, going back to Ronald Dixon, I've already searched births, deaths and marriages and, from what I can figure out, he was born in Durham, got married there in 1973 and has kids living up there. So it seems that his side of the family never moved down here. Now that you've mentioned this mining connection, it makes sense of a lot of things. I've already checked the available census records against Mr Dixon's traceable ancestors. They all worked in the pits up there. It didn't strike me at the time as it was the main industry for that area, but now you've brought this up, well… it fits.

'Dixon's family was, in the main, a mining family. Sadly, his dad, also a miner, was killed in a pit accident in the late fifties. Maybe the subsequent Coal Board pension enabled his mum to keep the family up there rather than migrate to Stoke. He seems to have done okay for himself and became a chartered surveyor. We've got to remember that he's a very distant cousin of Kobe with perhaps a common ancestor of nothing more than a several times great grandparent. I picked on him as an example and it's doubtful someone like him would even know of the existence of the relative we've named Kobe, or even any of Kobe's close family. On the other hand, people like Dixon, blood relatives, may be able to suggest characters from the extended family who *did* move here. Those people could be much more closely related to Kobe.'

Brenan said: 'So, it'll be pretty certain that some of the Durham connected targets on your list will be descendants of mining families who moved here and are still here.'

'As in Kobe,' Stanier said.

Scott eased back into her chair, contemplating the remarks but still staring at the screen. 'If we could somehow narrow this group down to families who *did* move to Stoke-on-Trent with the mining migration in the early sixties, I could then concentrate on them.'

Forrest had been silently soaking up the information. 'We've already worked out some broad age parameters for Kobe.' He looked directly at Scott. 'We've agreed from the date of his first known attack on Sarah Powell back in 1999 and from the flimsy description she gave, coupled with other bits that he is now aged between thirty-eight and forty-five.'

'Even that is sketchy,' Brenan said, with more caution than usual.

'Agreed,' Forrest said. 'But we *can* allow ourselves a few gambles and if it goes pear-shaped we can still backtrack.' He set his stare on Scott. She was the expert. 'So, if Kobe *is* between thirty-eight and forty-five, what is most likely to be his relationship? That is to say, to the male family member, the head of the family, who upped sticks and moved to Stoke in the early sixties to work in one of our pits?'

Scott put a hand to her forehead as imagination joined forces with maths. 'As Eve says, "sketchy". He could have been a late or early arrival to the family. His father could have been as young as eighteen or much older. But if we are to use those possible ages then he was born between 1974 and 1981. So he could not have been born until *after* the mining communities settled here which Ed says was in the early sixties.' Scott moved her hand down to her chin and stared at the wall for more inspiration. 'It's more likely that the miner was Kobe's grandfather and that might make his *father* perhaps a teenager in the early sixties when the family arrived.'

Stanier threw in a suggestion. 'So, Kobe's father would have done some of his schooling here, and quite a bit of his growing up. He's gone on to produce a son – Kobe – and the odds are that the relationship which spawned that child was with a local, Stoke-on-Trent, girl. It could well be that some of Jason's DNA hits also link back to local people through Kobe's mother.' Stanier held Scott's gaze, unsure of his new found rationalisation of DNA links. 'How would that fit, Madeleine?'

'Perfectly, Ed, but she definitely hasn't sent a sample in. If she had done, as Jason's grandmother, that would have shown as a massive twenty-five percent DNA share. We've got nothing anywhere even close to such a big hit. She could well be lurking out there on the estate, though, waiting to be found.'

Frank Milton had listened in to the conversation. 'There might be some records still available through the Mineworkers' Pension Scheme or even old National Coal Board records. I had a lot to do with many of the retired miners and their families over the years when I was working on the estate. What Ed says is absolutely right. Certainly, most of the miners on the Burrow Hill estate were from Durham. There may even still be details of those incoming families going back into the sixties – names and maybe the original addresses.'

Forrest nodded at Milton's suggestions. 'And some of those names could even still fit with Jason's blood relatives – Kobe's relatives on Madeleine's working list.' The DCI narrowed his eyes as he decided to ask Milton a question. 'How do you feel about working alongside Madeleine on this angle, Frank?'

'No problem, boss. This has all been a bloody tonic for me.'

Chapter 29

Day 16 Tuesday 30th April

A WAVE OF despair passed around the next morning's briefing as Forrest explained Monday's mortuary findings. The fact the skeleton was that of pregnant young woman who had almost certainly been murdered, were horrific features in their own right. But the positive identification of Poppy's silver ring cast the darkest of shadows over the whole affair.

The discovery of the skeleton at the Sarah Powell rape scene had always fostered the possibility of the worst of outcomes. Without evidence to the contrary, the ongoing hope that Poppy was still alive kept the team buoyed. Forrest sensed the gloom now descending. He recognised how much this could affect the ongoing job – catching Kobe.

'The dental ID is looking impossible,' Forrest told them. 'So we have to wait until we've got DNA.' He took a stern look around the room. 'We promised the parents we'd keep them fully informed, so they'll be told about this today. Nevertheless none of this must get out to the press, not until we've got DNA.'

Madeleine Scott surreptitiously wiped a tear from the corner of her eye and tried to imitate the steely resolve which seemed to be the standard for the rest of the room. She'd yet to learn that the detectives' "act" was just that.

'As for the age of the skeleton at the time of death,' Forrest continued, 'the anthropologist is confident from how well-formed and fused certain bones are that the woman was between seventeen and nineteen. The younger of those ages would create an overlap between Poppy's pregnancy with Jason and this unborn child. So it's likely she was more towards the eighteen or nineteen side of things. It all seems to suggest that she died and has been there for, perhaps, six years.' Forrest reconsidered his words for a moment. He didn't want to give false hope that the skeleton wasn't Poppy. He wanted to be factual. He really needed that DNA.

'A lot of forensic tests will be carried out on the earth samples and the bones, but remember this body wasn't buried, just hidden in undergrowth. It's decomposed down to a skeleton quickly. That, coupled with the years it's been there, make it so much more difficult to confirm any of these dates forensically. The pathologist has also mentioned that it's entirely possible for a woman to conceive as early as three weeks after giving birth, especially if she's not breast feeding. We know Poppy wasn't breast feeding for more than a couple of days because Jason was found soon after his birth.'

Forrest gave his audience another grim stare. 'We can't avoid the possibility that there were other births or miscarriages in the two years between 2008 and 2010 when Poppy was taken and Jason conceived.' He then went on to give an outline of the genealogy and mining community aspects which had come to light. 'PC Milton is now working with Madeleine on thinning the list of Jason's DNA hits down.' He'd fixed his line of sight on Frank Milton in his back-row chair. 'They're hoping to achieve a workable number of the stronger links. That will be ones with Durham connections somewhere in their past. If, and when, that comes together, teams will be allocated target families for DNA swabs.'

Milton's closed-eyes acknowledgement of Forrest's words imparted his own despondency at the terrible news.

Charlie Sawyer's fidgeting indicated that he had a point to make.

'Yes, Charlie.'

'I've tried to keep up with this genealogy and DNA stuff as we've gone along and even had my own personal lecture from Madeleine…'

'*WAHAY!*' A spontaneous and raucous cheer went around the room cutting into Sawyer's comment. 'Watch him, Mad, he's a dark horse,' came another comment.

The charade of police black humour and indifference was kicking in to ease the team through this difficult time and get them back on track.

Madeleine Scott's neck and cheeks flickered with a chameleon-like crimson surge. Her closed-eyes shudder not only brought an outburst of laughter, but also eased her complexion back to normal. She was now an accepted member of the team and quickly learning how to deal with the particular blend of humour that went with it. She was also learning how this bunch dealt with emotions.

'As I was saying,' Sawyer said, head shaking with fake dismay, 'the DNA profiling method used by the police is different to the genealogy method on the public sites, as used by Madeleine. Our police one seems to be quick with a result, but not as far reaching. So, for our buccal swabs, where would they be analysed? By the NDNAD or the sites that you use for family tree work?'

Scott nodded as she answered. 'All of the work I have undertaken is through the publicly available genealogy sites. I'm doing that as an authorised manager of Jason's DNA and as a manager of Poppy's parents' files too. My official aims are to trace family trees. The fact that my actual aim is to find his father is effectively part and parcel of my family tree research. We already know that Kobe's DNA is not on the genealogy sites because it would have shown up when I first input Jason's DNA as fifty percent match. If we do reach the stage of sending detectives out to take buccal swabs from identified targets, then that would be the cross over to a criminal investigation. They would have to go to the police NDNAD. Hopefully, the lines of enquiry resulting in those targets would be so strong that we'd only be looking for Kobe himself or very, very close relatives.'

Forrest interjected. 'Yes, and so close that, even with the more limited scale of NDNAD familial testing, it would give a good clue to that person's relationship to Kobe.'

'And, from that, a firm pointer to Kobe himself,' Brenan remarked.

'Thanks for that,' Sawyer said. 'And the sooner we get to that stage the better.'

With the briefing over, Brenan and Stanier dawdled over a mug of tea before collecting their statement pads and deciding who was in the driving seat. Their heel-dragging was understandable. Neither was keen to tackle the first job of the day. If the press got hold of the "ring" story it would go viral and the link would soon be made with the eleven-year-old Poppy Hunt missing person case. Their pledge to the parents to keep them up to speed with all major breakthroughs was going to be honoured. It was one awful piece of news that they wished for many reasons they did not have to break.

Forrest's text pinged up on Brenan's phone as they exited the lift on the ground floor. It had the flavour of his usual directness about it: *Eve, my office now.*

Forrest's complexion had paled in the five minutes since Brenan last saw him. The three sides of A4 email printouts lying on his blotter bore the Forensic Science Laboratory logo. Even reading upside down this was obvious. Forrest planted a spidered hand down onto the paperwork, swivelled it and pushed it across to Brenan.

She dragged out a chair, smoothed a hand across the top page and started to read, but Forrest's voice summarised the entire scientific collaboration in three words: 'It's not her.'

Chapter 30

BRENAN STARED, UNBLINKING, at the tiny growth of poorly-shaven dark stubble on Forrest's top lip. It was a strange, fleeting distraction in a moment of monumental importance. It was Brenan's way of dealing with the confusion.

'It's not her,' Forrest repeated. 'It's not Poppy; it's another Misper.'

It was eleven-thirty before all the teams had been contacted, postponed their ongoing enquiries and made it back to the MIR. It was rare to call an *ad hoc* briefing in the middle of a working day, but this latest news was explosive. It was vital that everyone knew.

DCS Brown's twenty-mile dash from his Stafford office augmented the seriousness. He sat alongside DCI Forrest whilst Brenan, Stanier and Scott took up other spaces.

Forrest quietened the room with the customary tap of drinking glass against table top. The buzz of comments and dragging chairs died away. 'Right,' he began. 'You've no doubt already got the drift of this so, yes, the skeletal analysis was emailed to me this morning along with DNA results for the Park Hills scene. The victim is *not*, repeat *not*, Poppy Hunt. The DNA profile positively links the skeleton to a profile that's been on Missing Persons DNA Database since 2011.' He waved the paperwork with his left hand. 'Georgia Martina Esposito, seventeen years and three months old. She went missing from the West Mids police area in early 2011.'

Forrest folded back one of the pages to confirm the detail. 'The fetus bones have provided us with DNA which conclusively proves that Miss Esposito is the mother.' His pause lingered for seconds. 'Kobe *is* the father.' The room went silent. 'Officers from West Midlands are attempting to contact Georgia's parents as we speak, and two of their detectives will be here first thing tomorrow with full details. They'll be bringing photographs and CSI detail along with their HOLMES data to link the whole lot up and fill us in fully on the circumstances.'

Forrest then turned to Brenan. She'd been researching dates and it had been agreed that she would take it from here. She clasped her hands on the table top in front and began: 'Everything points to Miss Esposito being kidnapped, raped and held prisoner in the same way that we believe Poppy Hunt was. It's a certainty, although possibly not provable, that Miss Esposito was murdered… strangled.'

Charlie Sawyer was, as ever, on the ball with where this was leading. 'The bastard's killed this new girl. I don't think there's much doubting that. The question that now comes back into play is, has he yet killed Poppy? I can't see that there's anything to prove or disprove that.'

DCS Brown answered. 'You're right, Charlie, and until such time as we have evidence to the contrary, we must assume that Poppy is still alive. Our attempts to keep the press out of the loop on Poppy Hunt's involvement have been justified and may well have protected her. Kobe must now know that we've found Georgia's body, and must know that we will identify it as her. She is, as we all know, a Misper from Birmingham with no connections to Stoke-on-Trent. No signs of any clothing were found and, even after eight years, we would expect there to be something. He's stripped the body and hidden it well. My bet is that he thinks we haven't a chance of tracing it to him and even less of connecting it to Poppy or his other crimes.'

A voice chimed from the back of the room. 'What about Poppy's ring, though, sir? That does connect the two cases.'

'Absolutely it does,' Forrest agreed. 'So why was she wearing it? Has Kobe put it on her body hoping that, if we found it, we'd believe it to be Poppy? Maybe to stop us looking for her? I can't believe he's that stupid. We've been using DNA for identification since 1995. I think it's more likely that he hadn't even noticed it was there or didn't realise its significance. We can be pretty sure from what we do know about the time frames that Poppy and Georgia have been in captivity for quite a long overlapping period. Chances are that they've been together and possibly even been able to offer some solace to each other. Poppy may have given her the ring. Maybe there was even some plan hatching between the two of them for us to connect the two girls to the same kidnapper. Perhaps Poppy had something of Georgia's. I don't know, but it definitely connects the two cases. That hackneyed phrase you've used every day until the skeleton was thought to be Poppy just re-entered the vocabulary big time: if Poppy is still alive. And it just became a lot more significant. As we said from the outset, we need to identify Kobe and tail him. We need to get him to take us to her before he gets chance to kill her. Before he does a runner and leaves her to die. Before he gets locked up and goes "no comment".'

Brenan and Stanier still had a job to do at 27, Meerham Gardens. They'd be delivering better news than they were first intent on, but the additional dreadful circumstances would not be much comfort for the Hunts. The fact that someone else's child had died at the hands of the man who had kidnapped their own daughter would give a graphic illustration of his capabilities.

Forrest was sitting alongside Madeleine Scott when they arrived back at the MIR. It was seven o'clock and most of the team were still hard at it. Brenan and Stanier's dour expressions reflected the harrowing hour and a half they had spent with the Hunts.

Giant-sized flipchart pages were spread about on desks and even part of the floor. The workings of family trees and distant cousins were being fathomed by the DCI in an effort to lend some additional elbow grease and brain cells to Scott's intensive labours.

'You managed?' Forrest asked, looking up at Brenan.

'Hmm, just about,' Brenan said. 'Got the doctor in again for David. He's worse than Laura at the moment.' She gazed around at the paperwork. 'What's to do?'

Forrest smoothed a hand across one of the charts. 'Some of these family trees are huge, especially when you try to link them to other trees that might be connected. The computer programme is good, but the size of the screen restricts the overall picture of how it all works. Frank has been researching the mining families coming into the area and it's beginning to look promising.

Brenan found Milton where he'd temporarily set himself up for quiet research in a side office down the corridor. He had, from somewhere, acquired a second monitor which was running in tandem with his laptop. His hunched-over-the-desk stance fitted perfectly with what was undoubtedly intense concentration. His right hand busied a desk top mouse back and forth, shifting a single cursor between the two screens.

'How's it going, Frank?' Brenan intruded.

'Oh, sorry, boss,' Milton said with a start. 'Miles away then. Pretty good actually. As we discussed, I'm concentrating on Durham-based mining families who may have moved to Stoke-on-Trent.' He pushed his mouse aside and swivelled in his chair. 'There have been several migrations to Staffordshire pits over the years even going back into the fifties. A lot of Welsh miners came then and many of them went to pits in Cannock, but plenty also went to Hem Heath just up the road and were housed on the purpose-built Coalvale estate nearby.' The constable shook his head. 'God, I've worked around here all these years and never realised why it was called "Coalvale". Anyway,' he continued, 'there have been other influxes from up north over time: Cumbria, Tyne and Wear and Northumberland all provided experienced manpower. Lots of those miners were taken on at our nearby pits in Biddulph, Longton, Hanley and Hem Heath.' Turning back to his computer he pointed at the second screen. 'The main Durham arrivals though, came around 1964 and large numbers were housed in NCB homes on the Birchfield and the newly built Burrow Hill estate which adjoins the Birchfield.'

'Okay,' said Brenan. 'How are you getting names and addresses?'

Milton dipped his head towards the second screen. 'This is the website for the Durham County Record Office. Madeleine has geared me up on here and a lot of it is freely available to genealogists for research. The site also holds what remains of the old NCB colliery records for all of the Durham pits, and a wealth of information on the miners who worked at them. Now, some of that information is data protected as it contains exactly what we're after – names and addresses of possibly still living people. As we're police officers investigating serious crime, the new Data Protection Act allows us access. Their data controller has effectively plugged me in. These are the lists of miners formerly employed at certain County Durham pits who migrated to North Staffordshire, there are literally hundreds. As I say, the main migration from Durham came en masse in 1964.'

Brenan listened, impressed as Milton gave more. 'Now, on the other screen you'll see that I've got a selected list taken from Jason's DNA hits. These are all the ones Madeleine has so far identified as being on his father's side – so, Kobe's ancestors. She's narrowing it down even more by only selecting the ones with connections back to Durham.'

'So you're hoping to find people on one screen with a surname common to people on the other screen?'

'In a nutshell, boss, yes. And if it were that easy it would be great but, as Madeleine has explained, the names could have changed on either side of the fence due to marriage so, if we get nowhere, we may have to dig deeper into family trees.'

Brenan gave Milton a concerned stare; she knew he'd got health problems. 'You alright with this, Frank?'

'Lovin' it, boss. Feel like a proper copper again.' He swivelled back to his desk.

Chapter 31

Day 17 Wednesday 1st May

FORREST HADN'T EXPECTED a full welcoming party on the police station steps the next morning. The welter of camera flashes joined forces with several thrust-forward microphones and panning TV news cameras. A barrage of shouted questions drove home the fact that Georgia Esposito's death was now common knowledge.

He made it through the security door and upstairs, head down and hands thrust in pockets, with nothing more than a promise to the reporters of an eleven o'clock update.

'How the hell have they got wind of Georgia's death already?' he said, as he entered the MIR and tossed his coat over a chair back.

'Who knows?' Brenan replied. 'We're now involved with another force and more relatives. Nothing's really been lost, boss. You were going to have to tell them today anyway.'

Two detectives from West Midlands Police had arrived early to make a start inputting their information with the HOLMES computer team. The briefing was never going to make its usual eight o'clock as it was important to load the new data. All facets of the multiple cases needed to be compared electronically. They also needed to set up the overhead projector and screen to better explain the case to their Staffordshire colleagues.

One of the terminal operators gestured to Forrest as soon as the data was fed into HOLMES. 'Sir,' she said, 'we've got a date collision flashing up.'

Forrest was at her side and staring at the monitor within seconds. He was unsure what she meant but the urgency in her eyes showed that this was important. 'Explain.'

'The date of the theft of Mr Bannister's cello bow coincides with the date now input for Miss Esposito's disappearance.' She jiggled her mouse back and forth. 'And,' she added, 'it looks as though she was last seen within one hundred metres of where the theft took place in the Broad Street area of Birmingham.'

This bombshell automatically stalled the briefing even further. All the potential speakers needed to be *au fait* with this latest twist and how it might affect what they had to say.

The West Midlands Detective Sergeant eventually got into his tale at ten o'clock. He explained that he had known nothing of the Esposito case until two years previously. Georgia went missing a full nine years ago, when he was still a probationary uniformed constable. His initial contact with what was now a cold case was one of the first jobs he was given as a newly appointed detective sergeant. The review he carried out took a full four months but, despite his painstaking work, gathered no new leads.

DS Daniel Delaney's voice held a slight twang of Black Country accent. 'The Esposito Misper case was treated as a major enquiry from the word go,' he said. 'Georgia worked as a waitress at the Italian Restaurant, *Pasta Roma*, in Edwards Wharf off Broad Street in the Ladywood area of Birmingham.' He pointed the remote control at the overhead projector and a four feet high, head and shoulders colour image of the missing girl showed up in pale contrast on the screen at the end of the room.

The intended straight-face expression required for what had originally been a passport photograph had not been completely successful and a certain Mona Lisa grin lurked within the cheeks. The youthful dark-haired, dark-eyed beauty of the girl created many an anguished glance.

'Georgia was British born, but has an Italian father,' Delaney continued. 'Date of birth 15th October 1993. She finished her shift at half past eleven on the evening of Saturday the 15th of January 2011. It's a busy part of the city.'

Delaney continued with his commentary, clicking through several different camera views of the area as he did so. 'Lots of businesses, restaurants, pubs and entertainment centres. There's plenty of parking, both on-street metered, and public car parks. She left as usual by the restaurant's kitchen rear door and would have then found herself in a small service road at the back.'

More images came on-screen. 'Normally, she would have turned right and right again bringing her onto Edwards Wharf and to the front door of *Pasta Roma* from where she would have been able to get a bus home. Edwards Wharf was a well-lit road with plenty of privately operated CCTV even back then. No CCTV picked her up, so it seems likely she was abducted somewhere near the rear of the restaurant.' Delaney went through a series of different pictures of the back, front and sides of the immediate area. 'The alleyways and small service roads adjoining the back of the property all give access through to different premises and to main streets and car parks. It's an interconnecting maze, but a fairly short walk would take you to the private car park of the *Taste of India* on Broad Street. This is where Mr Bannister's car was parked. On foot, this would take less than two minutes, but the thing is you can't drive between the two places.'

'So Kobe has parked close to the rear of *Pasta Roma*?' said one of the team. 'Walked to Bannister's car at the Indian restaurant, stolen the bows and then walked back to his vehicle?'

'That seems like the logical explanation, and then possibly come across Georgia by chance and abducted her,' said Delaney.

'And no CCTV at the rear?' another voice asked.

'Nothing. So Kobe, as you call him, has been lucky in that respect, but CCTV and ANPR at other locations did both collect information that was looked at by the original enquiry and retained. Some of it was interesting at the time and remains so. But now we've got this clear connection through DNA to your case *and* the stolen cello bows I think all the footage should be viewed again.'

Delaney reset the projector image and the screen displayed a black and white video sequence of a strip of pavement, a road and the pavement opposite. It was grainy and poorly lit. The setting showed no traffic or pedestrians but a twinkle of lights from cars on the main road and the occasional January snow flake proved its captured reality. A time/date banner flowed along the bottom of the image indicating that the selected part was recorded on 15th January 2011 at

23:53hrs and with seconds clicking ever onward.

'Now this is CCTV from a bathroom store on Lock Street, which runs off Edwards Wharf. The time was found to be out by eleven minutes. It was fast, so the real time was 23:42. Georgia is believed to have left three or four minutes later than her half eleven finish and so this van –' he froze the picture as the headlights of a vehicle started to brighten the screen on the right – 'was pretty well in the right time frame.' He then alternately pressed the *Start* and *Pause* buttons on his laptop, jogging the images forward until a small van filled the screen sideways on.

Delaney turned to the audience 'Also, take into account that Lock Street is little used of an evening other than for parking. The vehicle has been identified as a Mk 6 Ford Escort van. The model was manufactured between 1992 and 2002 and went virtually unchanged externally throughout that entire period. Even if it was one of the last to be built, it was already at least nine years old. You can see the "55" badge on the front wing. That concerns the payload. Ford did a 55 and a 75. This one, the 55, is capable of carrying five hundred and fifty kilos. His speed as he passes the shop has been calculated at thirty-two miles per hour. It's a short street so he's accelerated hard. You can see that his heavy use of the right foot has kicked out a lot of exhaust smoke. This suggests a worn engine and experts also added that it was more likely the diesel engine model.' Delaney jogged the image further until the van had gone from the screen. 'The glare from brake lights as he disappears from view shows that heavy braking was needed at the junction with Broad Street, where he was headed. It's a dual carriageway so he *had* to turn left, but obviously we can't see that. You'll notice that any sighting of a number plate is impossible and all we can say is, "driver only" – absolutely no visible features other than a dark indication of a profile. Baseball cap by the look of it, and that fits with one of your sightings, but not much help. There were other vehicles on different CCTV systems which were all looked at, but this one remained key throughout.'

Delaney switched the screen to yet another image. 'I mentioned

ANPR and, back then, there was only one such automatic number plate recognition camera anywhere nearby that picked anything suspicious up that we failed to get to the bottom of. All the experts have pored over this and are as convinced as they can be that this is the same van you've just seen in Lock Street.'

The screen was now filled with a reasonable quality night-time video. It showed a colour picture of the seven broad, undivided lanes of Birmingham's Aston Expressway. A multitude of red tail lights and blinking amber indicators streamed away from the camera against a reflected sheen of wet road surface. The oncoming glare of headlights in the opposing lanes were indistinct – this camera's work concentrated on the city's outbound motors. As the vehicles sped into the distance, a small rectangular white box holding the registration number ghosted itself alongside each one. A few were defeated by the conditions, but most appeared to have been successfully collected.

We remain convinced,' Delaney said pausing the image, 'that this is the same van heading out from Birmingham on the A38(M) towards Spaghetti Junction.' The detective sergeant successfully created an on on-screen shaky white arrow pointing at a white van in lane two. Beside the targeted van hovered a white box complete with a registration number. 'Again the experts are convinced that it's the same and the timing fits perfectly – two point three miles covered and five minutes twenty seconds elapsed.'

'So, give us the bad news on the reg number then,' a voice enquired from somewhere.

'Exactly,' Delaney said, knowing full well he was in a room of like-minded cynical detectives. 'All the more reason to suspect that this *was* the vehicle we were after. It was a ringer.' He accepted that the van could have been just a piece of unconnected minor crime which had been wrong place, wrong time but knew this was unlikely and so did everyone one else there.

'Some thought had gone into ringing this van. The number on it was not any old number. It was the correct number for an identical Ford Escort van – a 55, diesel, white, 2002 model which was still taxed, MOT'd and on the road making regular journeys up and down the M6 between Manchester and Birmingham.'

'So he's clocked it somewhere on his travels and got some plates made up,' Brenan said.

'Yep, looks that way,' Delaney replied. 'It is possible that, in his efforts to be so precise with model, year and type, that his own van was really a 2002, diesel 55 and it's certainly white.'

'Probably well and truly scrapped by now, though,' chimed Charlie Sawyer.

'Yes, it'd be a minimum of seventeen years old if it still existed.'

'We've got five sightings of a van on the *Sandstone* enquiry,' one of the HOLMES operators said. 'It's variously described, but the possibility that it's white and a Ford Escort does crop up. The last sighting of Jennifer McQueen, the first victim, puts her getting into such a van.' He looked down at his notes. 'It was June 2005, and there was no ANPR anywhere nearby back then.'

Forrest took over as Delaney wound up his input. 'For sure, all this new info will generate a lot more actions. We're expecting another four DCs from West Mids to help us out and there's likely to be some shuffling of the type of actions and areas of the enquiry you'll be dealing with.'

Brenan smoothed the top page of her notepad before beginning her own update. 'The skeletal analysis cannot definitively prove Georgia's age when she died. It can only estimate it to be between seventeen and nineteen. Now, at present we know that she was officially reported missing on Sunday January 16th 2011, when she was seventeen years and three months old. We know that she actually went missing just before midnight on the Saturday, so that's the 15th. We also know that she died eighteen to twenty weeks into her pregnancy.' Brenan consulted her notes. 'That would place her earliest dates of death between roughly Saturday 21st May and Saturday the 4th of June 2011, aged around seventeen years and eight months old. Technically her latest date of death would have to be her nineteenth birthday, so October 15th 2012.'

Brenan let everyone digest the theory before continuing. 'We've proved that the father is Kobe, and any suggestion that he could have met her before the night of 15th January 2011 and fathered the child she was bearing is absurd.' Brenan gave a tilt of the head and added. 'But, okay, it has to be considered. Nevertheless, we will not be calculating our dates on that possibility.

'So, she was kidnapped twenty-four days before Poppy gave birth to Jason. Because of this, it also seems likely that, unless the two girls were kept separately, they actually *met* each other. Georgia could well have helped with the birth. We now know that Georgia was wearing Poppy's ring and we have to consider how she came by it. Did Poppy give it to her? Or was it given by Kobe?

'We've got several new lines of enquiry but every time we get a fresh lead it carries with it a host of additional questions.' She rested her elbows on the table. 'Has Kobe really gone all the way out to Birmingham to steal the cello bows? Was Georgia really an opportunist abduction? My own gut feeling is "yes" to both questions. But how has he come to know about Mr Bannister, his cello bow, the concert, the curry afterwards and his car?

'Before we jump to any conclusions, we can't be sure of the date of Georgia's death. The dates I've given are a starting point. The actual cut-off date is governed by the anthropologist's opinion of her age at time of death – a maximum of nineteen. As I've already said, that would take her to 15th October 2012.' Brenan looked up from her notes. 'She's been there between seven and eight years.'

Chapter 32

IT WAS MIDDAY when Stanier and Brenan arrived back at Brian Bannister's home in the village of Oulford. The resonant strains of the musician's cello were unmistakable and sailed high above the underfoot crunch of gravel as the pair headed for the front door. They stood for a while taking in Bannister's skilful creations. Even with the thickness of the solid stone walls and heavy oak door, they easily picked out some unknown-to-them classical piece. The rich lower notes of his instrument burrowed through to the outside world with ease. There was a sudden halt to the sound as Brenan interrupted with a rap of the brass door knocker.

Shirt sleeves rolled, glasses on forehead and tie-less, Bannister opened up. An earlier phone call had warned him of another visit, but it seemed he'd become lost in his music. 'Come on in,' he said, cello bow still clutched in right hand.

The necessity of a DNA buccal cheek swab was the first job to get out of the way before the three sat down on tall stools either side of the high work top of a kitchen island. With another mug of Bannister's Nespresso coffee apiece, they got down to business. The musician had not been fazed by the DNA request. 'Fully understand,' he'd said after a partial update on the story from Brenan. 'I've certainly got nothing to hide and I'm happy to help out any way I can.'

Bannister's face registered disbelief as Brenan gave him more disturbing details.

'It seems that the offender is inclined to steal virtually anything rather than go through channels which may lead a route back to him. Buying, scrounging or borrowing have never been given a second thought. He'd rather travel all the way to Birmingham and back if it gives him the opportunity to steal a bow from you without anyone seeing his face.'

Bannister shuffled forward on the stool, head still rhythmically displaying his concerned confusion. 'How could he know? If, as you suggest, he's from somewhere around Stoke-on-Trent, how could he possibly know I was going to be in concert that night in Birmingham, and then in the restaurant afterwards?' Additional head shakes followed. 'And my car… How would he know my car?'

After a few more thoughtful moments he was on his feet and rooting through a kitchen drawer. 'Keep my old diaries in here.' He returned to the work top within moments and placed two small hardback *Forward Planner* diaries down. The years he had selected were 2010 and 2011.

'I don't keep a daily diary as such,' he said. 'Just these planners for forthcoming appointments, gigs and whatnot; perhaps the occasional mention of something important – like my stolen bow.' He snorted. 'Helps me out with my tax form as well.'

He leafed through the later diary until he came to the relevant entry made out in his own neat fountain-penned blue ink script for the 15th January 2011: *6 pm. Brum concert.*

'Well, there's my entry for the concert that night. We were due to start at seven o'clock and I like to get there an hour before. The M6 can be a nightmare at that time, so I'd be on my way by half four.'

There was more writing beneath the concert reminder: *Car broken into – bows stolen West Midlands Police Crime ref 964/ 16.01.11.*

'Hmm,' Bannister grimaced. 'Don't really need any reminders for that, but the terrible story you've related puts my little annoyance into perspective.' He flicked the pages backwards. 'I got these out for a reason. I'm beginning to feel that I might be able to make a suggestion – only a suggestion, mind – on how he's come to know so much.'

The two detectives were now upright on their stools, hands flat on worktop and eager to hear the theory.

The musician muttered to himself as he flicked back through the 2011 diary. 'No… Must have been just before Christmas.' He took the 2010 diary and thumbed it open at December. He turned a page or two before he landed on Saturday the 18th.

'There,' he said, tapping against an entry. 'This could be the answer.'

Brenan leaned over to read a couple more lines of Bannister's tidy handwriting.

Sherwood's, Hanley 11a.m. Cello Demo and talk: £536 raised – Help for Heroes.

'Yes. Interesting thing, though,' Bannister explained, 'is that I rarely do this sort of thing, but I'd been raising money for the *Help for Heroes* charity off and on. I called into Sherwood's one morning for some music. I've known the owner for years and he suggested the demo idea along with a raffle and a bit of an auction for the charity. I said I'd get a couple of tickets for one of the big Birmingham concerts as a prize. It was an opportunity to nurture a bit of musical interest in the locals as well. It snowballed from there and a few other businesses put in prizes and auction lots. Old Sherwood stumped up fifty quid to go with the tickets for a restaurant meal after the concert. As I said before, some of the orchestra wander over to the *Taste of India* after a big concert, so the idea was that the lucky couple would sit with me and the conductor. It was advertised in the Sentinel and on Radio Stoke and turned into a really successful event.'

Brenan took on a serious expression. 'So who won the tickets?'

'Oh, no worries there,' Bannister said. 'Delightful couple from Newcastle. They're now converted classical music buffs. Often see them at concerts. I should be able to find their details from somewhere, but what I was thinking was that the full details were given both on the tickets and in the Sentinel. In fact, the Sentinel did an article after the event and published a photo of me with them at the shop.'

The two detectives looked at each other. 'So,' Stanier said, 'if our man had been keeping an eye open for cellists – as you do! –' he smirked at his humorous aside – 'then the Sentinel newspaper, and maybe even a visit to Sherwood's music shop for the demonstration, would have supplied him with the time, date and place of both concert and curry house.'

Brenan nodded agreement with Stanier's theory. 'No doubt a half hour spent in the car park near Sherwood's after the demo would have been enough for Kobe to clock you loading up your cello into the back of your Mercedes. He'd have number plate, colour, model and all he needed.'

Bannister looked surprised at how quickly the detectives had reached a possible conclusion from his input. 'That would fit, that would certainly fit,' he said. 'But who is Kobe?'

Brenan blushed. 'Forget I said that.'

Chapter 33

ROOM 410 HAD evolved steadily throughout the two weeks since Brenan and Stanier first moved in. Even though still in need of redecoration, it now sat seriously well with its title: "Major Incident Room". The numbers of investigators and support staff had swollen in keeping with the rising body count and serious offences tally.

The ten feet long whiteboard Brenan had organised as one of her first jobs seemed ridiculously oversized back then. Fixed centrally to a wall, it was now anything but the blank canvas it had started out as. A plethora of victims' photographs and names formed a central line. Suspect vehicles, theft and burglary offence details were dotted about. Some were circled and others emphasised with exclamation marks. Boldly applied and variously coloured marker-pen arrows snaked around the board to join each of the diverse facets. One centrally drawn large square hung suspended by a spider's web of these pointers. The single word etched into the box in red capital letters sat where a photograph would be if one were available: "KOBE".

Different desks, spaces and tables now filled the extensive floor area providing a day to day workplace for some of the specialist personnel who were essential to an MIR: Exhibits Officer, Inside Sergeant, Outside Sergeant, CCTV/Video Investigator, Actions Officer and HOLMES operators – all had staked claims. Genealogist Madeleine Scott and PC Frank Milton both merited in-house spots. Brenan and Stanier as a key investigating team were more out of the office than in, and frequently found themselves evicting squatters from their own original pole positions. The now twenty-two strong team of outside detectives would more usually make use of the six smaller semi-derelict offices on the same floor when paperwork and phone enquiries called. The seemingly inexhaustible supply of red stacking chairs had been spread out variously across the top floor.

Morning briefings were seriously first-come, first-served when legs needed the weight taking off them. Desk-ends and window ledges made for a second-best option.

Another new expert had briefly joined the team. Facially, forensic psychologist Graeme Andrews looked both young enough and green enough to be a brand-new police probationer. The similarities ended there. The professor's youthful features belied not only his actual thirty-seven years but also his subtle grasp of the workings of the most evil and violent of criminal minds. He had studied the case during his train journey down from Edinburgh the day before. Such abstract ideas would not have been contemplated by cops of a decade or so earlier. But now it had become accepted practice, especially in drawn-out cases, serial killings or events where other lives might still be in jeopardy. This affair seemed to fall into the category: *all of the above.*

Andrews' flying visit whilst en route to a London conference had been time enough for him to present his profile verbally to Forrest, along with a promise of a follow-up written report and updates along with any new information. 'No father figure in the family,' he summarised. 'An alcoholic mother is a possibility, finding it hard to make ends meet – prostitution as a last resort maybe. It could explain the prostitute murders. There certainly seems to be a bond between him – Kobe, as you call him – and Poppy. Hopefully there still is and hopefully she's still alive. I'm not so sure that the relationship fits with Stockholm syndrome. The fact that Poppy has, over several years, manipulated the situation so successfully that he's running errands for her, and taking big risks into the bargain, seems to give *her* some control over *him.*'

The psychologist hoisted the belt of his thirty-inch waist skinny jeans. 'But she's got to be careful. Every day is a knife edge. We know what a monster he is. It seems he's taken Georgia Esposito as a second sex slave. There could be others.' Andrews made a *'who knows?'* face. 'But something went wrong. She – Georgia – stepped out of line, and he's killed her. It doesn't matter how strong the bond may seem to be with Poppy, he could snap at a second's notice and kill her –' Andrews clicked his fingers – 'just like that. We have to be careful. He must be agitated already. He knows we've found Georgia's body and, from what you say, a few things have been going on throughout the estate. Okay, the general public haven't got enough info to put two and two together, but your offender has every reason to be suspicious about every little bit of police activity.'

Andrews picked up his briefcase, intent on heading for the lift. He had a train to catch and his transport to the station was waiting.

'Others?' Forrest said. 'You said there could be others.'

'He'll still be using prostitutes. Sex rules his life. It's a strong possibility that there have been others – maybe still are. Must go! I'll be in touch and I'll email a report.'

The young man turned and made for the stairwell, briefcase in one hand and the other raised shoulder high in a parting gesture. Forrest shook his head at all that nervous energy and wandered through to the MIR.

He was still there and going through more family tree work with Madeleine Scott at four o'clock, when Brenan and Stanier arrived back. Their visit to Brian Bannister had turned into another comprehensive witness statement with all the new information and leads.

Forrest swivelled in his computer chair, but his finger remained glued to a large chart of paper spread across Scott's desk. 'How've you gone on with Bannister?'

'Good. In fact, *very* good.' Brenan explained how they had worked out Kobe's complex unearthing of the details allowing him to steal the cello bows. 'Clearly,' she added, 'Georgia Esposito *was* an opportunist abduction. He must have come across her as he was going back to his van.'

Forrest turned back to the desk and homed in on where the tip of his still-glued finger rested against the surname "Carr". 'Madeleine and Frank have started to find some hope of leads back to families in the area connected to Kobe as blood relations. This family is one of three at the moment. That's two households on the Burrow Hill estate and one on Birchfield itself.'

Scott was keen to impart what had been discovered. 'We've got to these addresses through Frank's work on the old National Coal Board – NCB – records. These would have been the homes of Durham miners who moved over here way back in 1964. They were all NCB houses then. The problem is that Frank has already checked the electoral register and found that the names no longer match. The houses were sold off by the NCB and are now all owned by people with entirely different names.'

Milton entered the office part way through Scott's explanation. His facial expression imparted the word, "Whoa!" and immediately broadcast that he'd turned something up.

'What is it, Frank?' Forrest asked.

'Well, sir, I've been waiting for access to some of the more recent crime files. You remember asking me to take a look at any possibilities that Kobe was still up to his petty thieving?'

'Yes, go on,' Forrest said, stimulated by Milton's enthusiasm.

'Well, I was about to start on the electoral register when I saw that I'd now got access to the latest crime files, so I had a quick shufti. Searching the system was a piece of cake and I was able to quickly dig out any classification of crime I wanted. There's some stuff you've got to see.'

Forrest, Brenan, Stanier and Scott trailed behind Milton and followed him into the side room he'd been using. A laptop and second monitor were still lit up on the desk.

'Look at *this*.' He settled into his chair as the four took up arms-folded positions to watch over his shoulder. 'I input the postcodes covering the Birchfield and Burrow Hill housing estates.' He spoke as he moved the cursor back and forth across the screen and clicked at different boxes. 'I searched on all burglaries except house burglary. I included theft and stealing pedal cycles and that way should have been covering all Kobe's previous MO. So, gardens, sheds, garages, nicking bikes. I hadn't thought about it but doing it that way it's also included shops and businesses – which I wasn't really interested in.'

Milton's cursor hovered over a particular high-lighted crime reference. He clicked and the screen changed to show the details.

'Here we are. A shop called *Book Worm.* It deals in second hand books. It's on David Road and has only been in business for about twelve months. It was broken into about four weeks ago.' He flitted the cursor about to highlight additional detail. 'It was a weekend burglary. The shop was closed on the Sunday so, between six o'clock Saturday 6th April and the morning of Monday the 8th April, when the break-in was discovered, the offender smashed a rear window and climbed in. Didn't make much mess and just stole certain books, but also had a look in the till and drawers, probably after petty cash. There were a few reasonably valuable books on the shelves but nothing life-changing, and the burglar didn't bother with those anyway. It was as though he knew what he was after and where it was.'

'So,' Brenan said, 'sounds as though the thief has been in the shop posing as a customer during normal hours, browsing to check out what he wanted and getting to know where it all was. Setting himself up to steal what he needed.'

'Yep, that would fit,' the old PC said. 'There are literally thousands of books in stock and yet he's taken just a handful.'

Stanier asked the question that was on everyone's mind. 'Arnold Bennett?'

'Mostly Charles Dickens, and because of that I almost discounted the possibility of a connection. I did look more closely, though, and discovered that one book *was* an Arnold Bennett. It was actually described as a "play" but had been produced as a hardback book titled *What the Public Wants.*

'Can't say I've ever heard of it before now,' Brenan said.

'No, me neither, and that's the reason why I jumped the gun on this one and phoned the shop owner. I had to give him a bit of a tall story that I was looking into his burglary rather than give away the fact that it might be connected to other things. He tells me he'd had it on display in the window advertised as *"A Rare Arnold Bennett"* but admits that was a bit of a sales ploy as it's not really worth much, just scarce.'

'So the chances are that Kobe spotted it in the window,' Brenan suggested.

'That was my thought.'

Forrest looked unsure. He didn't want to get too excited about the theft of a handful of old books just because one happened to be an Arnold Bennett. 'Hmm. Completely different MO, though, Frank,' he said. 'You do realise that, if this really is Kobe, it means Poppy *is* still alive and that would be pretty bloody amazing news. But it's not a lot to go on.'

'There's more, sir,' Milton said, cycling his mouse wheel and taking the cursor down amongst the list of stolen property. 'The Dickens books themselves could be seen to be similar in taste to Bennett's and, with a bit of imagination, that could add weight to the theory. But take a look at these two. They're very different.' Milton clicked to increase the font size of the last two stolen books on the list.

Successful Self-Dentistry.

Cure Tooth Decay.

The ten second silence which followed allowed some thinking time as the group tuned into Milton's idea. Brenan was first to latch on. 'She's had no dental care in eleven years. The poor sod's got bad teeth.' Brenan cut her own sentence short and found herself staring down at the floor, and then: 'I think she really is still alive.'

Chapter 34

Day 18 Thursday 2nd May

THE ATMOSPHERE AT next morning's briefing was a peculiar mix of optimistic elation and cynical doubt. Everyone wanted Poppy to still be alive but, to some, the evidence was thin. It seemed more a case of: *We can't prove she's dead, but we can't prove she's still alive.*

'Yes, I know it's not concrete,' Forrest said, feeling the uncertainty. 'But we've got to have faith. We're putting out some new actions for enquiries into the book shop burglary. There was no burglar alarm and no CCTV fitted at the place. It was originally viewed as a fairly inconsequential break-in and not much of an investigation was done on it. We're only three weeks behind on this one and there could be something that's been overlooked. We're back to square one in some ways because, once again, there's a chance Poppy is still alive. The difference is that we're closing in on him now.'

Forrest got to his feet. He stared around the room, grim-faced and tired, but determined. 'I'll put my neck on the line with this. I think Poppy *is* still alive.' He folded his arms, pressed his lips hard together and gave several emphasised nods. It was a display of gritty, strong-minded resolve. 'When we identify him – and we will – it will be a full-on twenty-four hours a day surveillance until we know where Poppy is being held. I'm *not* giving him chance to go "no comment" and leave her to die, and I don't want him getting spooked into killing her to dispose of the evidence. Kobe is turning out to be a bizarre creature. He keeps showing signs of actually caring for Poppy, but we also know what a mad bastard he is.'

Brenan's eyes stayed to the front throughout Forrest's words, but she grabbed a surreptitious, corner-of-the-eye glance before he finished up. 'Let's nail him! Bring me some good news!'

The rumble of chairs and immediate chatter began before Forrest got to his feet. Approving looks passed between the different teams at Forrest's clear-minded determination.

Frank Milton arrived alongside Scott's desk not long after the briefing finished. The wad of printouts in his hand were the product of several hours of overtime the night before and an off-the-wall idea from Scott. She'd suggested that if, somehow, they could pinpoint each household on the two estates where the family name was also a family name common to Durham it could to some degree by-pass the problem of changed addresses. It was never going to be a sure-fire pointer to Kobe's front door but might provide a few short cuts.

Using digital copies of the relevant pages of the electoral register, Milton had converted the information into a computer-searchable document. The resulting list of residents – eligible voters aged eighteen and over – had topped thirteen thousand by the time Milton added his final keystroke. He was pleased the computer had been able to do all the hard work, as a manual attempt at the task would have taken him into retirement.

A simple Google search had given Milton a list of surnames particularly common to Durham. The annoying frequency of Smith, Brown and Jones caused those three names to be temporarily "put on the back burner", to use the constable's expression. A few other nationally common surnames were also put on hold for another day. It left Milton with a total of twenty-eight, good, old-fashioned, dyed-in-the-wool Durham names. The constable's second task of using the "Find" facility on his keyboard to seek out families bearing any of these names from the Birchfield and Burrow Hill estates gave him a total of two hundred and five addresses. With the sum total of family homes on the two estates standing at almost six thousand, it certainly cut down the numbers.

'There you are,' he said, handing over. 'I've put it on a memory stick as well. I've been doing my best to keep up with this, but I'm not sure how this idea is really going to help.'

'It might not, Frank,' Scott said, swivelling in her chair. 'But I'm coming up with several of Jason's paternal-side DNA hits – Kobe's relatives connected to family trees with links to Durham families. Many of these show from early census records as mining families from the year dot. One or two are now showing up through your NCB records as having migrated to Stoke-on-Trent for work. It's over fifty years since those original people came here. There's no coal mining as such around these parts any more. All the living relatives of these people have turned their hand to other things now. Most, if not all, have moved from those original houses, but you know from your local knowledge that many still live in the area.'

Milton was keen to agree. 'Yes, and I guess Kobe's a prime example of that.'

'If I start getting a few surnames with the possibility of stronger DNA links to Kobe and can connect them to those mining families who migrated from Durham… These families, these addresses –' she waved the paperwork Milton had handed her – 'it might provide a quicker route through to Kobe's front door.'

Scott knew the word "might" figured strongly in her theory, and that the ultimate signpost to the right man lay with a DNA hit directly on Kobe or via a familial search through the police system on a very close family member.

As the teams got on with their own enquiries, Scott persistently burrowed her way through several different family trees at the same time.

Working on her own separate copy/pasted versions of these private family trees, she was able to add new ancestors and relatives. Consequently, none of her work would interfere with the online genealogy work of the individuals whose background she was looking into.

Come late afternoon, the team assigned to re-investigate the book shop burglary had discovered that a private CCTV system at a nearby house did indeed have something of value.

Forrest, Brenan and Stanier stood clustered around a 48-inch TV screen which had now been installed in the MIR for specific CCTV and video investigations. It was better quality than the projection system and allowed the operator to pinpoint finer detail. Its installation had been another surprise to Brenan on Forrest's changing mind-set on financial budgets.

DC Tom Finlay, sitting at a desk to one side of the screen, explained as he went through the sequence. 'We've been lucky to get this. It's come from a house about seventy yards along David Road from the book shop.' Finlay clicked his mouse button to start the sequence. 'As you know, David Road is a fairly busy thoroughfare during daytime. This clip is timed at 2:57 a.m. on Monday 8th April – so, just over three weeks ago. If the man you'll see in a moment is the burglar – and there's really no doubt on that – then the break-in was the Sunday night/Monday morning. You'll see that it's quiet, no traffic. It's dark, and the only artificial lighting comes from a street lamp out of view of the camera. This is a colour camera but shows as black and white in this poor lighting.'

The TV showed a small front garden area which had been converted to a space for the two cars parked there. Two wheelie bins stood inside the brick pillars of a gateless opening. The pavement, the road itself and, further on still, the opposite pavement, could be picked out. Beyond this, an increasingly darkened and lacking-in-detail view disclosed the sketchy features of a steep grass incline up to the service road of the houses opposite. Parked cars and a solitary bedroom light were barely visible. Movement to the left and high up on the screen drew the eyes of the watchers as a small light-coloured van with only sidelights on progressed slowly forward along the service road from the left. It stopped, lights now off, between two other cars. Several minutes passed before the van's interior light flickered in the distant gloom indicating that a door had been opened and closed.

The indistinct, grainy figure emerging from the driver's door gave away nothing until the man – for it soon became apparent that it was a man – took several stealthy but loping steps closer to the still distant camera. Six feet two inches was the agreed estimate of the rucksack-carrying and baseball cap-wearing outline as he took the shorter route down the turf incline. With head furtively swivelling left and right, he gave a nervous tug at the peak of his cap, stepped onto the pavement and started across the road. His agonisingly closer-and-closer-to-the-camera stealthy steps were encouraged onward by the below-the-breath comments of the watchers. 'Keep fucking coming, Kobe. Just a bit closer.'

The man's sudden diagonal route across the road would presumably set him on course for the alleyway leading to the back of the bookshop. It also took him out of shot before any details of clothing or facial features were given even half a chance. 'Damn!' Brenan's frustration was matched with more expletives from her colleagues. 'See him pull at his cap. He's CCTV conscious, that's for sure.'

'Twenty-three minutes before he gets back,' said Finlay.

'Right,' Forrest said as the video continued to play, 'Eve, get some house-to-house arranged. Pay particular attention to that house with the bedroom light on – always a chance someone might have taken a look through the window. Make sure we've not missed any more CCTV from other nearby houses too.'

Finlay fast forwarded the sequence, commentating as he did. 'Only sixteen vehicles, all cars, pass along the road while Kobe's away and it's plain to see that he's picked a quiet time to cross both ways. I'll get this enhanced, but I think we'll all agree it's unlikely to show any useful detail. As for the other passing vehicles, we're sideways on and consequently not a chance of number plates, although two do have taxi door-stickers which we should be able to read.'

Finlay pressed the play button and seconds later the same figure appeared from the left trotting diagonally across the road and up the grass verge – a solitary, smudged black outline. The vaguely bulging profile of the rucksack was the only change perceived by the concentrating, squinted eyes of those watching. A single brief flicker of yellow light signalled the opening and closing of the van door. The slow and careful lights-off journey as the vehicle exited screen right along the service road was watched without comment.

'So what have we got on the van?' Brenan finally said.

'I've done some research already. It's a Ford Transit Connect,' Finlay explained. 'Lot of people get thrown by the word Transit and think it's a big van but, no, it's not that much bigger than Kobe's old Escort van – so he likes his Fords. The Connect came out in 2002 and is still in production today, although my expert tells me this is a first-generation model which went through fairly unaltered until 2013. Difficult to track it down any further just yet. The model did undergo a facelift in 2009 but the changes were pretty minor and, from this distance, we can't see anything other than it's light-coloured and probably white. It could be as old as 2002 or even up to 2013.'

'So this doesn't seem to have taken us any further,' Forrest said.

Brenan folded her arms and continued to watch the still-running film. 'Have you watched this right through?'

'Fast forwarded it yes and slowed it when anything interesting popped up,' said Finlay.

'Strange that we've got him coming in from the left and disappearing to the right,' Brenan said. 'He's had to go to his right when he's driven off because that service road is tight and impossible to turn around in, and that would attract attention. He'd have to join the main road – David Road – further on up the service road. Now, dependant on which end of the estate he lives, you'd have expected to see the van being driven along David Road either shortly before he arrives or shortly after.'

Finlay sat back in his chair and sighed. 'See what you mean. I've certainly watched right through for half an hour after and there was no sign of a van coming back along David Road. I'll take a closer look before and after.'

Back in the MIR, Madeleine Scott was nudging her computer cursor across three good-sized monitors. Forrest had authorised the additional expense without a second thought. Indeed, after working alongside her for a while on the complexities of family trees and seeing the potential value, it was his idea. He now rarely went to his own office, preferring to keep fully in touch with all developments.

Brenan had been surprised more than once with the change in the previously budget-obsessed DCI during the eighteen days since the enquiry had first started. She also noticed that stress was taking its toll, as it was with everyone. Forrest still looked presentable at the morning briefings, but Brenan's eye for detail picked up on the non-too particular morning shave and the always clean, but occasionally not well ironed shirt. She knew his circumstances and a couple of times recently she'd wondered how he was coping in his solitary private life.

'You okay, boss?' she said, after another snatched lunch break.

Forrest was standing against the bank of windows staring out at nothing in particular, left hand pressed against his lips.

'What…? Miles away then. Yes, okay. I was thinking we've got so many leads, but nothing seems to go anywhere.'

'Look, boss, me and Mad are out for a meal tonight and maybe a bevvy or two. It's "Pie Night" at the *Sythe*, and John Eardley has said he'll find us a table whatever time we make it. Why not join us? We're getting a taxi.'

Chapter 35

IT WAS CLOSE to half past eight when Brenan and Scott made it to the lounge of the *Southwood.* Brenan waved at John Eardley behind the bar. The big man was his usual florid-faced and bare-armed self. Those all-important jerky final pulls of the beer pump were vital to create the perfect pint and not a moment for interruptions. His raised eyebrows joined with a smiled response and a nod in the direction of the one remaining empty table.

'I tried to get him to come along, Mad,' Brenan said as she pulled out a chair. 'He's making himself ill. He looked really rough the other day. Apparently, he was still going through stuff at midnight.'

Scott said nothing. She was feeling the strain herself and noticed in Brenan's eyes that Forrest did not have the monopoly on fatigue.

Eardley appeared beside the table. 'Mad, Eve... Should be busy tonight but I'll catch up with you later. Steak and ale pies are already sold out, but the steak and blue cheese are extra delicious – or take a look at the specials board.' A grin spread across Eardley's naturally mischievous face. 'I've got Deuchars IPA on draught at the moment, if you fancy a beer, and it's good. Any detective worth his – or *her* – salt will know that Deuchars IPA is Detective Inspector Rebus's beer, unless I've got my Ian Rankin completely wrong.' The mischievous face had now split into a grin. 'Just thinking, Cadet Brenan, whatever this big case is, you might solve it more quickly with a page or two from Rebus's book.'

Eardley's humour lifted spirits within moments and the two women were grinning again for the first time in a few days. The agreement that passed between them quickly saw the delivery to the table of two pints of cream-headed, crystal clear amber Deuchars IPA.

'Pints, ladies?' The voice from behind was steeped in mock surprise.

Brenan turned to see Forrest, showered, shaved and now in jeans and sweat shirt. 'Boss?' She couldn't quite believe her eyes.

'Popped home and got myself sorted,' he explained. 'Got a taxi. All work and no play… Not going to get nicknamed Jack. And we're off duty, so it's Dom.'

Prompted by Eardley's earlier Rebus joke, a pint of Deuchars swiftly arrived for Forrest too. 'Might just work,' he said, as his first taste took the liquid level down by an inch and left him with a moustache of white foam. 'Gorgeous. I needed that.' He wiped a hand over his lips.

The home-made steak and blue cheese pies all around matched Eardley's description. The *Sythe*'s speciality, peppered chips and garden peas, made it clear why the pub was so popular.

The mood was lifted, the stress relieved and some of the worries temporarily pushed to one side. It was inevitable, though, that conversation still wended its way back to work.

'I've got six particular family trees I'm working on now which are looking promising,' Scott said, as the second round of Deuchars arrived.

Forrest nodded his interest as Scott went into detail.

'Along with all the DNA hits I've had back from Jason's profile, there are these six people that I'm concentrating on. Each one shows as a fairly distant cousin to him and of course they are all from Jason's paternal side, so a slightly closer relative of Kobe.'

She looked from Forrest to Brenan and back. 'Another attraction for spending time on these six is that they've all done quite a lot of family tree work and made those trees publicly available. Looking at the trees I can see numerous male ancestors who show up on old census lists as being miners in and around Durham years ago. They were all from dyed-in-the-wool mining families and so all connected through the bloodline in some way or other to Kobe. Each one of these "census- traced men" –' she made finger quotes as she spoke the phrase – 'passed away years ago, but their genes have continued through their offspring. Hence the eventual arrival of Kobe and then Jason. Taking these six target family trees a bit further has increased the numbers of Durham-based male blood relatives of Kobe, but they're just names, so no DNA.'

Scott paused and sat back in her chair. 'What is interesting, she continued, 'is that, from these six different trees, I have now discovered fifteen men cropping up on Frank Milton's lists of miners. Back in 1964, all these men were Durham-based miners who moved to Stoke-on-Trent to work in the pits here.' Prefacing her next point with a huge '*and*', Scott continued, 'all fifteen were installed in NCB houses either on the Birchfield or Burrow Hill estates. Again, these details come from Frank's Durham NCB archive research. I even have the addresses they moved to, but all of those houses were sold off by the NCB into private ownership years ago. The names currently listed on the electoral register show that completely unrelated people now live in each one. The council tax department and property registers both confirm there are no connections between the current occupants and my fifteen family tree miners.' She made an emphasised downturned mouth before adding: 'After all, it was fifty-five years ago when they moved in.'

A full twenty seconds of silence followed as Forrest assimilated this information. Brenan had already heard a summary of Scott's news during the car journey. She carefully studied the DCI's expression for any sign of elation or even puzzlement, but the poker face stayed intact. 'So,' he finally said, 'these fifteen men could all be related in some way or other to Kobe?'

'Absolutely, unless there's been a little hanky-panky going on somewhere in the distant past.' Scott's eyes widened behind her specs as she made the comment. 'They should all have had some sort of a DNA share with Kobe.' She shrugged before adding more. 'I say "had" because that fifty-five-year gap now makes them all very old. Some, if not all, of them could be dead.'

'You can find that out, though?' Forrest said.

'If they've already died, you mean? Yes, I've got their dates of birth and I'll find more out tomorrow. I'll also be attempting to find what addresses the families have moved on to. Each one of these men may share only a handful of centimorgans with Kobe.' She lifted her pint mug and took a sip. 'So, either a distant relative, or as much as a full twenty-five percent – as in Kobe's grandad! We'll only ever prove that bit if the person is still alive and we can get a DNA sample, though.'

Forrest stroked his chin as he thought things through. 'I've said it before, if we do identify Kobe, our biggest worry is spooking him before we've located Poppy. We need to find where the descendants of these men are now living and then, somehow, get DNA samples to see which family, if any, is the closest to him.'

'You said it,' Scott reiterated, 'which family, if any. Until we get some good DNA pointers, we're never going to be sure that we're even on the right track. I could be completely out with this. But I don't think I am.'

Brenan sat back in her chair and gazed at the ceiling. 'It might even mean a covert attempt to get DNA from completely innocent people – without their knowledge.' She was aware of the legal implications and the criticism such action could bring.

'Hmm, not easy,' Forrest said. 'But I'm happy to cross that bridge when we come to it, and do whatever is necessary.' He looked up from his beer at Scott. 'You've already explained that we can't use the genealogy firms where we are directly investigating crime. So, any covertly obtained DNA can only ever be sent to the police NDNAD. Okay, so we'll be a bit limited on what we learn if it's a very distant blood relation. But, if we've got our man – as in, Kobe or a really close relation to him – the NDNAD will be able to tell us and then we're in business.'

Brenan sneaked a crafty sideways look at Forrest. He was surprising her as each day went by. She could not fault his determination to put Kobe behind bars. His belief that Poppy was still alive and could be rescued had become unswerving over the last few days.

Scott's eyes were also fixed on Forrest. 'I've put all my money on the Durham mining families who moved to the Birchfield and Burrow Hill estates in the 1964 migration, ones who match Frank's list. Tomorrow, I can start work on trying to match any of these fifteen surnames to that list of two hundred and odd Durham-surnamed families. It's hit and miss, I know, but it could save us time if we strike lucky. I'll be working up other family trees at the same time.'

Ironically it was Scott who eventually dragged the conversation away from work with her praise for the quality of the *Sythe*'s food and drink. 'Best pie ever,' she said, pushing her cleared plate to one side and savouring the last few dregs from her current pint glass. The food and the beer suited them all. So did the chat about music and sport, as a relaxed and friendly evening wore on.

The girl who had served them returned a few more times to replace emptied glasses with full ones before a school-bell type clanging from behind the bar signalled last orders. Brenan performed the honours by introducing Forrest to John Eardley as the pub landlord sidled over and settled into a seat at the table.

'Heard a lot about you, Mr Forrest,' Eardley said, giving Brenan a sly wink (he could be well behaved at times). Brenan returned the sly wink but added a surreptitious frown. Forrest had risen in her estimation during the last couple of weeks and she'd rather Eardley forgot about any whinging she might have done about him in the past.

Forrest gave the standard reply: 'All good I hope.' Then added: 'I remember you, John, when you were a DS. I was a uniformed PC, a probationer. I'd arrested a couple of Scousers on the town for a bit of serious shoplifting. They decided not to play ball. They'd got the better of me and I was heading for a serious pasting. You appeared from nowhere. You were out shopping with your wife! They suddenly wished they'd never even heard of Stoke-on-Trent.'

Eardley gave his head a scratch. The action matched his furrowed forehead. 'Bloody hell!' he said, cheeks creasing into a wide grin. 'Was that you? That's got to be thirteen or fourteen years ago. Just before I retired.' Eardley thought for a moment. 'And a couple of days later I found a bottle of Scotch in my office drawer. There was no need for that, lad.'

Brenan and Scott caught each other's eye and smirked. "Mr

Forrest" had quickly become "Lad". Knowing Eardley, if Brenan was doomed to always be known as "Cadet", it seemed likely that DCI Forrest was stuck with "Lad".

'You've no evidence,' Forrest remarked on the whisky accusation, as he tried and failed to keep a straight face.

'We didn't need evidence back then, lad!' Eardley's response generated a bout of impulsive hilarity which set the standard for the next hour or so.

It was half past one when a taxi arrived in the car park and the sniggering threesome stepped outside. 'Keep it down – the neighbours'll have the police on me,' Eardley slurred from the doorway. His added hiccup caused an extra round of stifled laughter.

Forrest's purposeful attempt at bagging the front passenger seat was thwarted by Scott. She stepped in front of him, made a grab for the handle and was seated and clipping on her seatbelt all in one movement. He could do nothing other than push the door closed and watch as she turned and grinned at him through the glass. She then screwed her face into an emphasised and conspiratorial wink.

The DCI climbed into the back seat alongside Brenan, their hands touching momentarily as each fastened seatbelts. They turned to each other in the gloom. Brenan clenched her jaw trying hard to keep a grin in check. Forrest's own face took on a comical expression of concern, all teeth and high eyebrows, as Scott furthered her mischief by ordering the driver to drop her at the Premier Inn first.

'Mad paid for our taxi out, so I'll get this half,' Brenan said delving into her handbag as the taxi stopped at her own apartment.

'Not a chance,' Forrest said.

'I'll give you a tenner. It soon mounts up this time of night.'

'No, Eve, my treat. It's been cracking tonight. I really needed it. Mad is a nutter and John Eardley is... Well, a right hero.'

The couple turned to each other. Forrest considered a friendly peck on the cheek – just a *good night and thanks* sort of thing, but Brenan had pulled the door catch and was out of reach before his mind could catch up. 'Night, boss. See you in the morning,' she said and pushed the door closed.

Chapter 36

Day 19 Friday 3rd May

BY FIVE MINUTES to eight the next morning, the teams were sitting, standing or with backsides perched on desk ends ready for the briefing. The chatter, the ringing telephones, the clatter of teacups and the buzz of printers provided what had now become the everyday background racket. Charlie Sawyer's latest joke drew a guffaw of laughter from one group of detectives. It also prompted a loud 'tut' from DC Vicky Potts who had overheard.

Brenan breezed in, a Tesco bag on one arm. 'Tea kitty's low,' she said above the din as she piled a box of teabags, jar of coffee, milk and sugar on a small table alongside the kettle. 'I'm delegating. Charlie, you're in charge of the kitty and shopping from now on.'

'Oh, boss! Why me?'

'Number one, you drink more tea than anyone else; and, number two, I caught wind of your punchline. Very sexist.' She sniffed the air. 'God! I've just caught wind of something else. You lot are disgusting! Someone open those windows!'

Madeleine Scott was at her desk, monitors filled with data and hand covering nose in an attempt to filter the air. Forrest entered, pale face, bloodshot eyes and forced smile.

'Morning, Mad,' he managed. 'You're early.'

'Not really.' She looked up at the wall clock. 'I wanted to get stuck in. Some of this is really showing promise now.'

'Right, settle down,' Forrest said, before giving the okay to DC Tom Finlay who had now found himself with the title of *CCTV/Video Coordinator.*

'Going back to the bookshop break-in,' Finlay began. A trawl through more of the footage from the same camera has revealed a sighting of what could be the same van thirty-three minutes earlier.

We have it timed at 2.24 a.m. driving right to left down David Road. If this is Kobe, then it's a further example of how cagey he is. He must park up some distance away before driving back to the service road and leaving the van to commit the burglary. There were a few cars about then, so he was maybe waiting for a quiet spell. After he's broken into the shop, he returns to the van and drives away to the right. The service road exits onto David Road out of camera shot but the van does not appear again. This suggests he has driven away to the right and headed towards the southern side of the estate. The fact that the van has originally come from the right, again points to this.'

Forrest interjected. 'We can't be one hundred percent sure that it is one and the same van, but common sense suggests it is, and on this latest sighting we have a much better view. Tom?'

'Yes,' Finlay said. 'As it drives right to left along David Road, it comes as close to the camera as it could do. We can now tell for certain it's white. We can also tell from the rear light cluster that it's the earlier model from before the 2009 facelift. This conclusively puts it as being registered between 2002 and 2009. We're working on the issue with PNC to see if we can obtain registered keepers and addresses of all such vehicles. But the only way that might help us would be if it's actually registered to him under its real number, and that's doubtful. It's a good bet that it's on false plates, whatever its history is. You all know the form. It could be knocked off and on ringer plates. It could have been officially scrapped. Many possibilities.'

Forrest rested an arm across the desk and leaned forward. 'Having seen how cunning Kobe's been so far and his elaborate ringing the changes with the last van, it's likely that this one is another ringer and not even registered to him. How about ANPR Tom?'

'No luck on the night that he's done this job. Problem is, there are no ANPR cameras on the estate. The closest one is nearly a mile away on the main Leek Road. I've drawn a blank on sightings of what might be the van on the night, but I'm not giving up on that angle.'

The briefing was stalled at this point when the door half-opened and Crime Scene Manager George Stodford peered in from the corridor. The expression he shot at Forrest and Brenan indicated he needed a word.

They put things on hold and joined him.

'You requested tests on all the condoms recovered at Park Hills, Eve,' he started.

Brenan nodded.

'We found thirty-seven in total, some going back years. Almost all had been knotted and flung into the undergrowth at the edges of the different pull-ins along the pathway.'

'So indicating they'd been chucked from parked cars after sex,' Brenan suggested.

'Exactly that. The semen contents from most of them were degraded through time and weather conditions. Several, which look to have been dumped recently, have also suffered from the effects of the spermicide within the condom – it degrades the DNA. But,' Stodford went on, 'the lab was able to get profiles from eight. Tests suggest that ten to twenty-one days is the average time limit for any usable DNA to survive. So that would be ten to twenty-one days before we arrived at the crime scene on Thursday 25th April. We have four condoms of semen giving four different full DNA profiles, none of which figure on the NDNAD either as a crime scene stain or as the profile of a known individual. Two others provided partial profiles and, again, a manual check of the markers on these suggests no connection to our case. And then there are these other two.' Stodford was looking down at his paperwork. 'One contains semen which is a partial match to Kobe. It's slightly degraded, but it's him alright. The last one contains a full match to Kobe and must have been deposited recently, probably a few days before we arrived at the scene.'

Stodford looked up from his paperwork momentarily. Forrest and Brenan had both become fixed in "pause" mode, paralysed from the toes up, as though a button had been pushed. 'But that's not all,' he added. 'This last one is so recent that good quality vaginal cells were also recovered from its exterior – a full DNA profile of the woman.'

Brenan jolted out of pause mode, leaned her head in a little closer and mouthed a single word: 'And?'

The significance of the findings crinkled Stodford's eyes down into a squint as he started his sentence. 'The woman *is* on the NDNAD. Anna Maria Elena Albescu, a Romanian immigrant. She came here in 2010. She's now thirty-three. Convictions for GBH and several other assaults, shoplifting, possession of Class A and soliciting for prostitution. She's appeared in court in Manchester, Nottingham and Stoke-on-Trent.'

'Right,' Forrest said, now out of pause mode himself and almost on fast-forward. 'You say that the condom was deposited recently. Can the lab give us a definite date?'

Stodford turned the corners of his mouth down. 'No, they can't. Park Hills became a crime scene on 25th April, so it was before that. The vaginal cells would be susceptible to the weather and so their shelf-life would be a few days at most. The condom had been knotted; its contents were in perfect condition. The lab's guess is no earlier than the 19th April.'

Forrest turned back to Brenan. 'So, if he hasn't killed this woman too, then we might have a witness with a good description. Maybe even a name, an address perhaps, more vehicle details. Eve, put the bones of this together and get a team dedicated to tracing this woman pronto.'

'I'm on it,' Brenan said, but her look of astonishment was beginning to fade as her mind took in *all* the implications. 'So he's shagging prostitutes again, like he was fourteen years ago – and murdering some of them back then.' She looked at Forrest but said nothing more.

'I know what you're thinking, Eve. Why is he going with prostitutes when he's got his very own sex slave incarcerated somewhere nearby? And, is it another pointer that she is now dead after all?' The DCI puffed out his cheeks and blew out hard as if to no longer even consider such an idea. 'No, I'm not even going down that road any more. The book shop burglary was April 8th and he was still pinching for her then. Yes, he's been with this prostitute after that date, but I don't think this animal ever stopped using prostitutes. And, thinking about it, that's exactly what the psychological profiler suggested.'

Forrest's stoic attitude, right or wrong, lifted Brenan from the darker thoughts that the ultimate goal might be lost.

'We need some serious obs fixing on our red-light areas,' Forrest said, as the pair stepped back into the MIR. He explained Stodford's new information to the team. 'All we've got at the moment is the van, a sketchy description of Kobe and the file on this Albescu girl. Time for ROCU to make amends for Perky's cock-up.' He spotted DC Finlay. 'Tom, I'm going straight over to HQ to see the DCS and get some heavy string-pulling done. Get everything on the van and the bits of description we have on Kobe. Run me off a copy of Albescu's CRO file, along with her mugshot. Email it all to DCS Brown's secretary and get her to print it off ready for my arrival. This could be the breakthrough we've been hoping for.'

Chapter 37

IT WAS HALF past eleven when Scott waved Brenan and Stanier over to her desk. The pair dragged out a chair either side and settled in to hear her latest. Of the three monitors on her desk, the centre one showed the full names of the fifteen former Durham miners she was concentrating on. The men's dates of birth were listed along with their old Durham addresses. The new Birchfield and Burrow Hill addresses they moved to in 1964 were typed in another column. The additional letters "NCB" showed that each house had originally been owned by the National Coal Board. More detail scavenged by Scott proved that all fifteen men had gone to work at the large Hem Heath pit four miles south of the city centre.

'I've got more work to do on each one of these men, more family tree research to establish marriages, children and grandchildren. All of the fifteen houses were sold into private ownership. The NCB firstly sold them to the council and then in the eighties the sitting tenants were allowed to purchase under Maggie Thatcher's Right to Buy Scheme. One way or another all fifteen properties were in private hands by the late eighties. The initial buyers were those sitting tenants, but not necessarily the original mining fifteen. Over twenty years had passed since they'd moved in, remember.'

'So now you're trying to establish where the original men, their families and eventual offspring went?' Stanier said.

'Exactly that,' she said.

'Can't you get anything through the old rating records?' Brenan said. 'A sort of paper trail from one house to another?'

'These houses were sold back in the eighties, thirty years ago. Many of them went into the hands of private landlords in no time. The deeds and Land Registry records are little help with tracing previous tenants and no help at all in tracing where they went to. What we do have, though, is full names, dates of birth, marriage records, children's names – genealogy stuff recovered from family trees connected to those fifteen first families.' A smile stretched her lips mischievously – this was her territory. 'Many of the family surnames are common-to-Durham names, so a lot fit with the list Frank has put together.'

She was holding two pieces of A4 copy paper. 'I know this is hit and miss but it could be a short cut. Take a look.'

Frank Milton heard mention of his name and was now standing, hand on the back of Brenan's chair, head craning for a look at the details printed on the pages.

'These are the fifteen men I've been looking at.' She laid one of the sheets flat down on her desk top. The names were printed in a bold large font. Most of the surnames seemed fairly common names which would not usually have given rise to any particular interest. Scott was quick to point this out. She was also quick to make a comparison. 'You see here in Stoke-on-Trent you're used to your Johnsons, Williams, Hughes, your Coopers and your Taylors and plenty more common-to-Stoke names. These are names that have been plentiful going back years in these parts. You probably wouldn't think it unusual if you came across someone with the surname of Armstrong, Nicholson or Richardson. I doubt if any of the other names on Frank's list of Durham names would come over as earth shattering: Walker, Pilkington, Miller, Carr, Robson, Bell and Walton aren't that peculiar…' She left a pause. 'But those names are *not* really old Stoke-on-Trent surnames. On the other hand, they and the others on Frank's list do crop up frequently in and around Durham. Many of my fifteen bear these, and other, common-to-Durham surnames which appear on Frank's list. Of the two hundred and five addresses he's earmarked on the two estates, these fifteen surnames all appear several times.'

Brenan pursed her lips as she concentrated on Scott's ideas. 'But surely the chances of tracing the right families from such a list are pretty bloody small. I mean, you've only got surnames. Admittedly, the same surnames as some of the fifteen, but to narrow it down through DNA checks is… well… a mammoth job.'

Scott shook her head. 'No we're not just looking for surnames. I'm still working the family trees remember. I'm digging out full names and dates of birth of the fifteen's children and grandchildren. That is beginning to turn up individuals aged eighteen or over living at the two hundred and five addresses with a matching forename and surname.'

'How many so far?' Stanier asked.

'I've only worked one tree through to the present day so far and it's produced sixteen children and grandchildren in total. Two of the males bear the right forename and, of course, surname as two of *those* descendants of the fifteen men, so the idea works. Both houses are at the southern end of the Birchfield estate.' Scott placed another of the sheets of paper down onto the desk. 'But this next one I'm going to show you is interesting. He comes from the second family tree that I've started to build from the fifteen.' Scott manoeuvred the page into the centre of the desk. It had one name printed onto it along with a date of birth and address:

Arthur Ernest Pilkington DoB:17th June 1924, Birchfield Lodge, Pringle Crescent, Birchfield, Stoke-on-Trent.

'This chap does figure on Frank's list, although his home is not actually a house. What has made him easier to find is that he's actually one of the fifteen. He's an original from my list. He's a Durham miner who came to Stoke-on-Trent back in 1964. Still alive and kicking at the ripe old age of ninety-four.'

'Wow,' Brenan said. 'And Birchfield Lodge?'

Frank Milton threw in his local knowledge: 'The care home back of the *Bottom Knocker*. My grandma lives there.'

Brenan had already started making arrangements by the time Forrest arrived back from HQ. The group were clustered around Scott's desk and it was four o'clock before Forrest was fully up to speed with the developments.

'So,' he said, 'you're saying that Mr Pilkington is almost certainly a blood relation of Kobe, but not necessarily a close one.'

'That's right,' Scott said. 'From the age of the old chap, the best we could hope for would be that he's Kobe's grandfather. He is almost certainly related, but the worst-case scenario would be that he is nothing more than a distant cousin with no contact or knowledge of Kobe's side of the family at all.'

'He's our best shot yet, though,' Forrest said. 'We need his DNA, but we know we can't bowl up and ask for it. Everything has to be done covertly.' He turned to Brenan. 'What background have you got on Mr Pilkington so far, Eve?'

'Well, first things first,' she began. 'I'm guessing that DCI Perkins' familial search would have got a hit on him if he'd already been on record and was closely related. Nevertheless I ran his details through the system and he's as clean as a whistle. No convictions, not even a motoring fine. So, no DNA profile to look at. But Mad's worked her wizardry.' She turned and nodded for Scott to explain.

Within a few mouse clicks, Scott's monitor brought up the detail and she began to read: 'Arthur Ernest Pilkington, born on Tuesday 17th June 1924 at Easington, Durham. He's obviously from a mining family as he's one of my fifteen. His father and grandfather before him all worked down the pits in and around Durham. He was one of seven kids: three lads, four girls. All three lads became miners, but both of Arthur's brothers moved to work in a pit at Whitehaven. They died in a terrible disaster there in 1947 along with another one hundred and two souls.' Scott had everyone's attention as she gave them the stark facts.

'Arthur Pilkington,' Scott continued, 'stayed at Easington Pit until 1964 when he upped sticks and moved to Stoke-on-Trent and into one of the NCB houses on the Burrow Hill estate. That original house was sold off into private ownership and, as to an actual address he went to, I'm struggling at the moment but, clearly, he stays local. I should be able to trace any children's names and ages and maybe the same for grandchildren if there are any. The electoral registers don't give dates of birth but his is an unusual combination of names. Couple that with the fact that he's in a care home, indicating advanced age, and it's him alright.'

Forrest pulled up a chair. 'Bloody difficult. We're going to need someone on the inside before we can work out how we're going to go about this.' He looked around at the gaggle of detectives. 'Ideas?'

Frank Milton was first to speak. He reiterated the fact that his grandmother was a resident at Birchfield Lodge. 'I get to visit her most weeks. I know most of the staff on a friendly sort of basis.'

'What about Mr Pilkington? Any clues?' Brenan asked.

'Hmm,' Milton went into thought mode. 'The home is on three floors: ground, first and second. The ground floor is the kitchens, laundry and admin, so no residents' rooms. It was built about fifteen years ago – I remember them doing it. There was always petty theft going on – wood, tools and whatnot. My grandma has a room on the first floor. I know most of the current residents on her floor by sight and one or two by first names.' Milton thought for a second. 'You know, each resident has their name and photograph on their own door. It's most likely that Mr Pilkington is up on floor two. I've probably seen most of the residents from up there at some time or another and I'll possibly recognise him when I do see him.' Milton pulled a "*why not?*" face. 'It certainly wouldn't be considered odd for visitors to wander about on different floors or corridors with relatives. A lot of people do exactly that for a bit of exercise. I could pop up after Gran's had her evening meal to visit her and have a mooch around.'

Chapter 38

FORREST GAVE THE green light to Milton's plan and it was seven o'clock when Brenan and Stanier waved *au revoir* to Madeleine Scott. She was still bent forward in her computer chair, engrossed in her work and unaware of their departure. The pressure was on everyone and building.

Brenan and Stanier headed out to the *Bottom Knocker* pub, where they had arranged to meet Frank Milton after his undercover assignment at the care home. The chance for a surprise visit to the landlord, Nicholas Mazewski, was never to be sneered at, if only to keep him on his toes.

The pub's deserted, uninspiring main room was called "The Fettler's Lounge". It was another tongue-in-cheek reference to a particular occupation in the old pottery industry. Mazewski stood, arms-folded and brain-dead, back resting against the doorway through to the bar. The lack of any noteworthy televised sport and the absence of other human beings offered no respite from the mind-numbing flicker of the pub's nine differently tuned 50-inch TV screens. The usual out-of-context music blared from another source.

'Sergeant Brenan,' Mazewski acknowledged as he came out of his coma. His peculiar high-pitched voice was somehow able to penetrate the din. He was unaware of Brenan's temporary higher rank.

'Prick!' Brenan responded, making full eye contact and using a false *good to see you* face. She knew Mazewski was too thick to be an accomplished lip reader and her bright-eyed grin was enough to convince the steroid-pumped gorilla that she had called him by his first name.

Stanier successfully turned his shoulder-jogging snigger into a sneeze and polished the performance with handkerchief to nose.

'Turn this bloody row down!' Brenan instructed.

Mazewski obeyed. 'What's to do, Eve?'

The detectives had discussed tactics during the drive down. They would certainly not be taking this licensee into their confidence but may be able to surreptitiously wheedle information from him on side issues.

'Thanks for giving us the nod on Devonish Crescent last week,' Brenan softened up. 'You'll have heard that it turned into a bit of a fiasco. That's the trouble when other departments come poking their noses in.' She was confident the main issues behind the operation had been kept from the public.

Mazewski smiled, pleased at the praise and now eager to grass-up even close relatives for a chance of similar "matey" tributes from Brenan.

The conversation swung between football, pub business and what the local toe-rags were up to. Mazewski's insistence on an update on paranormal activities in the pub would provide Brenan with plenty of over-a-beer laughs next time she saw John Eardley. Stanier successfully turned the tête-à-tête momentarily to the subject of the care home which backed onto the pub's rear car park.

'Birchfield Lodge, you mean?' Mazewski responded, eager to help.

Stanier's charade of researching care homes for his grandfather covered the brief discussion. 'Yes that's it.' He said. 'Any good? I mean is it a nice place?'

'One of the best around apparently. Expensive, though, from what people say. Often get staff, relatives and some residents in for lunch – do 'em a special rate.'

Frank Milton caught up with them twenty minutes later. They'd found refuge from the TV glare in the only out-of-the-way corner of the place. Mazewski was back behind the bar as a trickle of customers started to make an appearance. At least he'd kept the music down.

'How've you gone on, Frank?' Brenan asked, as the constable pulled up a chair alongside.

Milton made a grateful thumbs up at Stanier for the pint of bitter now sitting in front of him. 'Well, I've found Mr Pilkington. He *is* on floor two, as I suspected – so that's Room 28.' He dug into his jacket pocket for his phone, pressed at the screen and then turned it towards them.

The image showed the head and shoulders of a round faced and smiling elderly gent. The name "Arthur Pilkington" was printed in bold red letters along the bottom. The alignment was slightly out of kilter. A large number "28" was also visible along with an unintended narrow framing of light grey painted woodwork – Milton had snapped the photo from the ID picture on the gentleman's bedroom door.

'Nice work, Frank,' Brenan said. 'Anything more?'

'Maybe a bit more than we could have hoped for.' Milton pulled a small white envelope from his inside pocket. The flap had not been sealed and its slightly deformed shape indicated that its contents were something other than a standard letter.

The two detectives eased forward for a better view as Milton delicately slipped a folded white tissue from the envelope. 'I took my gran to the upstairs lounge for half an hour as a cover for my mission.' He looked upwards, mimicking a plea for forgiveness, as he delivered the sentence. He was not comfortable with his actions, but the gravity of the situation mitigated his feelings of guilt – a little.

He carefully unfolded the tissue explaining what had taken place. 'This wasn't intentional, but it was too good a chance to miss. As soon as I saw the chap's photo on the door, I knew I'd met him before, actually chatted a couple of times. Nice bloke.' Milton grimaced. 'All the more reason to feel a bit guilty,' he said, adding a head shake. 'He's definitely a Durham man; still got a broad accent. I'd told him I used to be the local copper on the estate, and we'd shared a few humorous moments talking about the different local idiots who were always causing trouble. So, you see, it didn't seem that out of place to knock on his door and see how he was doing.

'In point of fact, I thought he'd left or died as I'd not seen him in a while, but he'd moved upstairs to a different room. Anyway I knocked and there he was watching TV. He was pleased to see me, remembered me. No dementia there, but he has got health problems as well as his age. You see, he's diabetic. He has to have a couple of insulin injections and regular blood tests each day. It's just a prick of the finger.' The constable set his stare on the now unfolded tissue. A fingernail sized red spot of what was evidently dried blood was clear to see soaked into the tissue. 'So when I saw this in his bin and got the chance to pocket it, I thought, "Why not?". It's a finger dab from his evening's blood test, and if it helps us lock this bastard up and maybe even find Poppy…'

Brenan looked at Stanier. She was having difficulty hiding her astonishment. 'No need for any guilty feelings, Frank. You might have saved us a massive load of work.'

'The DCI has told me to take the weekend off,' Milton explained, as they got out into the car park. 'Wife's birthday party tomorrow, so got to make that one. Don't mind turning out if there's anything I can help with, though.' Milton headed towards his car and home.

Brenan and Stanier were back at the MIR by half eight. Two of the HOLMES operators were still rattling away at keyboards, the crime scene manager was doing similar, and Scott was busy working out an extended family tree with two flipchart sheets Sellotaped end to end.

Forrest entered, bleary eyed and biro behind ear; he'd overheard Brenan's voice. He gave his eyes a rub. 'How's Frank gone on?' The story sharpened him up. 'Superb work. It's Saturday tomorrow, so it would be Monday morning before we could get the sample down to the lab.' He broke off for a second. 'But maybe that's not such a bad thing. I'm researching something at the moment and, if it comes off, it could make our DNA test requests a hell of a lot easier.' Brenan made an inquisitive face, but it was clear he was keeping this secret to himself until he was sure of his ground.

Forrest looked at Scott. 'So, we'll be hoping to learn what family relationship, if any, exists between Kobe and Mr Pilkington. Is that going to be possible, Mad?'

'Depends. It will be a simple comparison between Pilkington's DNA from the tissue and Kobe's crime scene stain from one of the murders. I can't see it being classed as a familial search – it's nothing more than a straight comparison of the two. It would be easily possible using the algorithms available on genealogy sites, which would give you a pretty definite idea as to their relationship, if there is one. We are stuck with using the NDNAD for any searches like this and so, yes, they'll be able to tell you if they are *very* close relatives – sibling, child or grandchild – but anything much less than that will get sketchy and require masses of detective work. They'll still be able to say they're probably related, but putting a label on that relationship will be guesswork unless, as I say, they're very close.'

Forrest nodded. 'Still sounds like a starter for ten to me.'

Brenan held the door ajar. 'I've got all the details, boss. It'll take us half an hour to get the paperwork if we do it between us, and then it's over the road for a pint.' She looked back into the room, taking stock of the stressed-out faces. Who's coming?'

Chapter 39

BY QUARTER PAST nine, the standing room only, rammed lounge of the nearby *Smithfield* pub had been swollen a little more by eight of the MIR staff. It was Friday Karaoke night and Madeleine Scott was belting out Meat Loaf's *Paradise by the Dashboard Light.* Brenan and Forrest winced at the din as they squeezed through to join the team. Scott graciously accepted the crowd's huge cheer as she finished the eight-and-a-half-minute rendition by way of an arms-outstretched, exaggerated curtsy, drawing even louder cheers.

Forrest and Brenan were both clutching glasses by the time the *Smithfield*'s latest star squeezed back through the crowd to join them. Her ear to ear grin was enough to bring the rest of the group to additional fits of laughter.

'She's nuts!' Brenan yelled above the racket into Forrest's ear.

With a mouthful of lager on board and lips tightly sealed, it was all Forrest could do to keep his laughter in check but, without doubt, he agreed.

Ed Stanier needed no coaxing to take the microphone for his half-good attempt at local boy Robbie Williams' *Angels.* Brenan was dared by Scott (a foolish move) to perform and stunned the crowd with a raunchy foot tapping version of *Valerie.* The shouted-above-the-noise debate which followed was centred on whether Amy Winehouse or The Zutons first recorded the song. Forrest was never going to be goaded into singing *My Way* at any price.

It was ten past twelve when the team called it a night, made it through the door, and wandered back towards the police station car park. Scott shouted, 'see you in the morning,' and headed off for the short walk to her Premier Inn. Everyone had, for a change, been careful with the drink. This was not just for the sake of the serious consequences of a breathalyser, but also because the stakes on the investigation were upping each day. The stress was increasing. They needed to let their hair down occasionally but also had to be ready to give their best at a moment's notice. Forrest, though, wasn't sure of Brenan's actual alcohol quota. 'Need a lift, Eve?' he said, pulling out his keys.

Brenan was already fumbling in her bag, but was slow to explain that she'd only been on shandy and was okay to drive. In fact, she never got chance to start the sentence. The sight of a helmetless uniformed constable jogging over to them looked likely to put going home on the back burner.

'What is it, Peter?' the DCI asked apprehensively, as the gangling young man came to an uncoordinated halt in front of him.

'Spotted you from the window, sir. We've been trying you and Inspector Brenan on your mobiles for a while now. A DS from the Regional Organised Crime Unit is after you. They've brought a woman in you've been after. Alberto or something.'

Forrest looked around at Brenan. 'Albescu. The prostitute.'

It was a few minutes after one o'clock when Brenan got her first sighting of Anna Maria Elena Albescu. The glimpse through the spyhole into Interview Room 3 showed the thirty-three-year-old Romanian prostitute seated, arms folded, staring at the door. She pushed out her tongue and raised a single finger in the air as she perceived the flicker of movement. The ROCU team had done well to find her so quickly. She'd been picked up early in her working evening, before she'd pulled a punter.

'Nice,' Brenan said, looking around at Forrest and then pressing on the door, clipboard pinned beneath her right arm.

Forrest followed her in and the pair noisily dragged out chairs and sat, Brenan opposite and Forrest at the table's end.

Pinch-faced, haggard and corpse-like, the woman looked old enough to be her own mother. A series of self-inflicted tattooed foreign words littered the backs of her hands. Her forearms, from the rolled-back sleeves of her moth-eaten red cardigan downwards, showed manic badly drawn pictograms mixed between red and scabbed over injection track marks. Ragged canines flashed between black gaps as she spoke her first harshly accented words.

'Vot the fuck!'

The three words were enough for the detectives to get the drift that the woman was not pleased about her detention.

With introductions out of the way Brenan added the legal requirements. 'You're not under arrest and you're free to leave at any time.'

The woman made a display of slowly getting to her feet and edging out from behind the table.

'But we'd like you to stay and talk to us.' Brenan moved her eyes from Albescu and landed them on the chair, as if willing the woman to sit by some super-power. 'I think maybe you can help us and, in return, maybe we can help you.'

Albescu sat. 'Iz zis being recorded?'

'No.'

The next hour was a difficult one – a mix of trying to explain the urgency and importance of the situation without giving the game away. Albescu was a serious drug addict, so the two police officers knew from experience that she could not to be trusted with secrets.

Pizza, Pepsi and a pile of chocolate helped fend off the woman's approaching drug cravings.

Although she looked totally out of it for most of the time, Albescu was surprisingly astute and alert. As the chat wore on, a small element of trust and understanding started to grow between the three of them. It was as though she accepted that this was something pretty out of the ordinary, something maybe ground-breaking enough for her to actually want to help the police – and maybe get some benefit from it herself.

Their questions concentrated on one particular punter she'd been with at least once. The fact that they seemed to know about his white van and the place where they'd had sex increasingly puzzled Albescu. When they actually took her there on a virtual trip via Google Earth and pinpointed the spot precisely on Brenan's laptop, Albescu's curiosity got the better of her. 'How do you know zeese things unless either me or he told you?'

They were stumped for a reply which would not give away any clues about DNA. Brenan's irritated sigh was followed by her short and spontaneous statement. 'A young woman's life may depend on you telling us what you can about this man.'

It was more than she wanted to give away, but Albescu immediately sat back into her chair and began to nibble at non-existent fingernails. Forrest's eye contact with Brenan went unseen by Albescu. It looked like she was going to talk.

'So, no prosecution?' Albescu said, sitting forward again, stare fixed on Forrest. Even though Brenan had done most of the talking, she'd remembered his senior rank from the introduction.

'No,' Forrest said, 'we're not interested in soliciting, so no prosecution.'

'And help? How you help me? I need doctor. I need money, clothes food, place to stay.'

A tear swelled in the corner of a sunken eye socket and hung there until a single blink released it to meander down a pallid cheek and drop onto the table.

'We'll help you as much as we can. A doctor yes, and Social Services to sort you some regular benefit. They should be able to get somewhere for you to stay.'

'There's been so many, but, yes, I remember him.' She pointed at the laptop screen with its frozen Google Earth picture of Park Hills. 'When he started driving all the way out there, I knew it was a bad move. It was supposed to be a fifteen-minute blow job. That was what he said anyway. Turned into a nightmare. He tried to kill me.'

Chapter 40

Day 20 Saturday 4th May

BRENAN STEPPED INSIDE the MIR the next morning, yawned, dumped her handbag on the desk and draped her jacket over a chair back. Scott was already seated, laptop switched on. She looked up at the wall clock as Brenan stifled another yawn. It was five minutes before eight. The lack of sleep etched into Brenan's face bore similarities to the weary glance Scott had received from Forrest as she'd passed his open office door ten minutes earlier. She put a finger to her lips and considered the situation for a moment. Last night wasn't a particularly late or hard-drinking one, at least not for her. Puzzlement creased her forehead as the last sighting of Brenan and Forrest came back. They were heading across the car park together just after midnight and deep in conversation. The puzzlement morphed into suspicion.

'You look tired, Eve,' she said, vision remaining fixed on computer screen. 'Have a late one?' Her pupils crept to the right corners of her eyes.

Brenan's own tired eyes instantly narrowed down into a discerning stare which she aimed at the back of Scott's head. 'You could say that.' She moved behind Scott's chair and closed her mouth up against the genealogist's ear. 'Spent the night –' her voice was secretive, hushed – 'most of the night anyway – with the boss. Or should I say "Dom"?'

Scott swivelled before the sentence was finished, eyes now saucers. 'Noooo,' she whispered back, extending the single word to a ridiculous length and not really managing a whisper at all.

Charlie Sawyer's announcement, 'Teas's up,' prevented any further discussion as two dozen individuals clamoured to get mugs before the morning briefing began.

Forrest, looking worn out, entered a couple of minutes after the dot of eight and patted an extended hand downwards into the air for everyone to take a seat. 'Interesting development last night,' he started.

Scott caught Brenan's eye for a conspiratorial wink at Forrest's choice of words. Brenan merely wrinkled her nose by way of reply.

'Yes,' Forrest continued, 'DI Brenan and I drew the short straw as we were about to both head for home. The Romanian girl, Anna Albescu, was pulled in by ROCU late on and we ended up interviewing her. By the time we'd finished and got Social Services out to try to get her poor, miserable life back on track it was gone half four.' Forrest added a rider to his statement: 'So don't let me hear anyone else saying they're tired – not today anyway!'

Brenan slowly turned, looked across at Scott and mimicked her friend's wink of a few seconds before. She also managed a tired but very definite serves-you-right grin.

Forrest, unaware of the episode, began a summary of Albescu's interview. 'She's been back and forth between here, Birmingham, Nottingham and Manchester over the past couple of years and picked up a few convictions along the way: soliciting, drugs and assaults.' He shook his head. 'Unfortunately, that's not all she picked up, according to the doctor – something else that doesn't bode well for Poppy's health.'

Brenan busied herself with fixing the most recent photograph of Albescu onto the whiteboard as Forrest ploughed on. 'The woman is so ravaged by years of drug and alcohol abuse, it's a wonder she can remember anything, but she certainly does. She's only been with Kobe once, and once was enough. The condom proving her sexual connection with him, as you already know, was found at the exact spot identified by Sarah Powell as her twenty years old rape scene. It is also where we found Georgia Esposito's skeleton. Dozens of other condoms were found and at least one other also contains Kobe's semen. Albescu is adamant that she's only been with Kobe the once, and I believe her. Who the other woman is – was – we may never know. She could even be another murder victim.

'We know from forensics that Albescu's vaginal cells could not survive more than a few days on the condom out in the open. She remembers that Kobe picked her up on a Sunday night. We effectively closed Park Hills down when it became a crime scene on the morning of Thursday 25th April. Her session with Kobe was therefore almost certainly the evening of Sunday 21st April. Forrest took a look around the room. 'Any questions or points so far?'

The silence allowed Forrest a quick sip at his tea before he was back into the tale. 'Anna initially complained to Kobe about him wasting her earning time by driving out there. She was used to going somewhere near her patch, but Park Hills was nearly a fifteen-minute drive and she was not happy. The deal she'd struck with him was for oral sex – "a fifteen-minute blow job", as she described it. He got nasty and threatened her. He put her through a variety of full sex acts and made a pretty serious attempt at strangling her. She says she felt as though she was fighting for her life and then another car pulled in nearby and he calmed down. He actually paid her more than the going rate and dropped her back at her pitch about an hour later. Just before midnight.'

Forrest picked up his notepad and flicked pages back and forth. 'Now, getting to the van,' he continued. 'Anna remembers little, other than that it was a small white van. Scruffy, smelly and with a mattress in the back where they had sex. She remembers rope, tools and vehicle number plates, several of them wedged between the mattress and the van's sides.'

'So he's been changing plates regularly then,' a voice suggested.

'That looks a certainty,' Forrest said. 'Anna has been doing what she does for several years now.' Forrest's eyes drifted over and landed on the photograph that Brenan had fixed to the whiteboard. 'And, whilst she's certainly not come out unscathed, she *is* still alive. Her lifestyle has definitely taken its toll, but she's got a pretty good idea of how to look after herself. She's explained that one thing she would always do when she got into a vehicle was to have a crafty look around for anything she could use as a weapon, if needed. Tools, wheel brace, jack, anything she could clump the fella one with if things turned nasty. A car number plate edge-on between the teeth would "come keen" as she put it, hence her good recall of those.'

Forrest made a despondent face as he looked around the room. 'Now to the all-important part – Anna's description of Kobe. Not a lot of use. Height-wise, she reckons he was maybe a tad over six feet, perhaps six-two, but bear in mind she never really saw him standing. He's either been in the driving seat or lying in the back of the van. It's always been dark and the only times he did stand up were when he stepped from the driver's door, in the dark to pull the seat forward and climb into the back. Facially she can't tell us much apart from what she called bad skin, an awful complexion. But that also means she's sure he had no facial hair. He was wearing a baseball cap all the time, even while he was on the job. She can't be sure on the hair colour but edges towards dark. He smokes and reeks of fags.'

'Anything more on the baseball cap? Colour, motif?' the question was thrown in by one of the female detectives.

'No ideas on any motif, but she's sure it was dark in colour – black or dark blue.'

'What about the sex acts? Anything peculiar we should know?' The question came from DC Vicky Potts who had been working as dedicated liaison with rape victim Sarah Powell and had taken her detailed witness statement. 'I'm particularly interested,' Potts continued, 'due to the violence used on Sarah. Yes, I know the circumstances were different and Anna, to begin with, was a willing partner, but the violence used on Sarah with the ramifications of attempted murder may be part and parcel of the buzz he gets from what he does.'

'Good points, Vicky,' Forrest responded. 'We're still working with Anna on this and, at the moment, all her explanations are by way of note taking, so no witness statement as yet. She's not keen on the idea of a formal statement, but we do need one. I was thinking you might be the best person to have a word with her on this.' Forrest's face held a hopeful expression. He knew Potts was necessarily spending a lot of time with Sarah Powell and didn't want to interfere with that relationship.

'Speak to you after, boss, but Sarah's doing fine now and I'm sure it won't cause difficulties.'

'Okay,' Forrest said, and turned to look at Brenan. 'Now, for the answer on what we've got from Anna so far on Kobe's sexual predilections, I'll hand over to you, Eve.'

Brenan's shrug and comment, 'Thanks a lot, boss,' brought a ripple of laughter from the team. She perched herself on the edge of the table in front of the whiteboard, casually folded her arms and began to speak. There was no blush of embarrassment, just a calm and professional explanation – a mixture of fact and measured opinion. 'Whilst Anna's memory on some things is poor, any situations that touched upon her own safety seem to have stayed with her vividly. We know that Kobe's been offending for years. It's more than likely there are additional victims, women like Sarah Powell who survived but didn't report the matter to the police. There could even be more murder victims, and that's something suggested by our psychological profiler, Mr Andrews. His latest report fits the emerging patterns. He draws attention to the usual themes for sex offenders where the violence increases with each offence committed. If we take Sarah Powell as being one of Kobe's earlier victims, we can see how he's then progressed through the three *Operation Sandstone* killings. Clearly his use of violence becomes more extreme. His attempt to murder Sarah by strangulation seems to have been lacking in determination, thank God. With the three *Sandstone* girls, the violence and determination are now there and actually increasing in intensity. The first girl, Jennifer McQueen, was manually strangled, thumbs pressing so hard into the throat they actually penetrated the flesh and crushed the hyoid bone. The next two, as you know, show more premeditation and more determination – a ligature tightened from the side with some kind of twisting implement. In both cases, it squeezed the neck so tightly as to crush the bones and cartilage in the neck down to a diameter of barely three inches.'

The audience, mostly hard-nosed detectives, sat grim-faced, taking in Brenan's reminders of what they already knew about these earlier cases, but also accepting the theory of increasing violence. Anna's story was beginning to reveal as fact some of the conjecture often put forward by the experts. Brenan explained more detail of the actual sex acts carried out on Anna, correlating them with the known sexual violations against the other victims. 'Oral, vaginal and anal sex. Factors which correspond in full with the attack on Sarah Powell. Sarah was anally raped after the vaginal rape which resulted in her pregnancy. All three of the *Sandstone* murder victims suffered exactly the same kinds of defilement but in what order those sex acts took place, we do not know.'

In some of the more recent briefings Madeleine Scott had confidently held her own when she'd had a speaking part. She knew how to strike a good balance of humour and professionalism. Her outline on the in-depth work that led to Mr Pilkington's genealogical connections received interested nods. She left it to Brenan to mention that a possible DNA sample had been obtained from the care home and would be analysed.

When the briefing was finished Scott called Brenan over to her desk eager to update her on the latest interesting features she had uncovered. 'I'm working my way through another family tree from one of the fifteen ancestors of Jason's father.'

'Right,' Brenan said, 'so once again you're thinking this is a relative of Kobe who moved to one of the estates from Durham around 1964?'

'That's right. This family connection first shows itself with the input of a DNA sample to one of the publicly available genealogy sites two years ago by a lady from Hartlepool named Lesley Martin. Her maiden name is Carr, a popular Durham surname and one which has cropped up before. Sure enough, her family does originate from Durham and her own extensive work on a family tree shows this. Both of her parents, Joan and Stuart Carr, are still living and now in their early seventies. They are inhabitants of the village of Plawsworth, just outside Durham. Lesley Martin's grandparents on her dad's side, also named Carr, are both now deceased. That grandad was not a miner, he was a teacher. He didn't move down here and so *he* is unlikely to be the connection. He did though, have two elder brothers, Percy Carr, a miner, born in 1927 and James Carr, also a miner, born in 1930. Percy was badly injured in a mining accident in 1953 and couldn't work in the pits again. These three brothers would all be great uncles or, as some people would say, grand uncles to Lesley.'

Scott halted and looked around at Brenan with that "are you still with me?" face that she'd taken to using during complex explanations. Brenan's irritated blink urged her to continue 'Now, James, the youngest of the three brothers, worked at Shotton Colliery, close to Durham. Records show he married Christine Elizabeth Richardson at St Nicholas's Church, Durham, in 1954. They had three children, John, born in 1955, Sarah in 1957 and Henry in 1959. The family upped sticks and moved to Stoke-on-Trent in 1964 when James was offered a job at Hem Heath colliery. I can trace this branch of the Carr family to living at an NCB house on the Burrow Hill estate between 1964 and 1976. I believe that James Carr *is* therefore our likely Durham mining connection with a DNA link through to Jason. James Carr would have been eighty-nine if he'd still been with us, but he's not; he died eight years ago. Of his children, both John and Sarah are still alive, but disappeared from local records by 1979. Sarah married and emigrated to New Zealand whilst John is a graphic designer working in London. Henry, on the other hand, stayed in Stoke-on-Trent. His birth records show his full name as Henry Peter Carr, born on 17th April 1959. He was four when he arrived in Stoke and so he schooled, grew up and lived locally. He married and set up home with his new wife on the Birchfield estate at –' Scott checked her screen again – '17 Cavalry Place. At least I'm pretty damn sure he did.'

'Okay,' said Brenan, ever the cynical detective and wanting proof. 'So how can you be sure it's the same Henry Carr that you think you're tracking down to that address?'

Scott had anticipated Brenan's question. She'd got to know her well now and knew no criticism was intended, nor any attempt to put obstacles in the way. Brenan needed to be sure. She wasn't going to fall into the same kind of trap Perkins had done. The genealogist confidently explained: 'There are a handful of families living on the Birchfield and the Burrow Hill estates named Carr. There's only that one address where there is a Henry Peter Carr. Ed has carried out a DVLA check which reveals he has a driving licence. The birthdate registered to him is the 17th April 1959, so the same date. It's got to be the right Henry Carr. He is effectively Lesley Martin's first cousin once removed.'

Brenan blinked again as she assimilated the term and how it could connect Henry Peter Carr with Jason and, effectively, Kobe. 'Okay, but everything you've said so far is conjecture. The only two people whose DNA is available for you to compare are Lesley Martin's and Jason's. That's the DNA connection you've used from Jason's sample and that's what you've used to dig into Lesley Martin's family tree.'

Scott went to answer, but Brenan held up her hand to stop her as she pressed on with her thoughts. 'You mentioned before about DNA shares… the percentage that people share with relatives and how that can be used to work out their *possible* relationship to each other. So, if Henry Carr had a son, he would be what relation to Lesley?'

Scott didn't even need thinking time. 'Second cousin.'

'So.' Brenan prefaced her next question, 'taking the conjecture further, if that son does exist and *is* actually Kobe, and he had a son himself – as in Jason – what would be Jason's official relationship to Lesley Martin?'

'Second cousin once removed.'

Brenan's continuous slow nods could have given any self-respecting car rear-window bulldog toy a run for its money. But the jigsaw was piecing together in her mind. 'Okay, you mentioned before that the DNA share shown on the genealogy site can give an estimate of the actual relationship between the two people. What, then does it suggest is the relationship between Lesley Martin and Jason Fitzgerald?'

A huge grin appeared on Scott's face at how Brenan's grey matter had put it all together. She started to explain. 'The association between Lesley and Jason shows on *Geneaus DNA* as being a possible third to fourth cousin. Now as I explained before, at that stage the term third to fourth cousin is a generalised term used to cover a lot of possibilities. It's a rounded-up piece of terminology which fits with the DNA share that exists between them.' She turned briefly to look at her screen. 'They share 135 centimorgans across eight segments and technically that could cover a couple of dozen possible relationships. But, the computer can go into it in more detail by using the hundreds of surveys carried out in other similar DNA shares. It can actually make a prediction using that centimorgan share as to the most likely relationship. That prediction does in fact come out as a second cousin once removed.'

'So,' Brenan said. 'Now we need Henry Carr's DNA profile too.'

'Yes. I've still got work to do on establishing what children Henry Carr has produced, but I'm minded to leave that until we maybe get that DNA sample. We've already got Arthur Pilkington's, so that should be looked at by the lab first.'

Brenan stared down at her desk and remained silent for several seconds. 'I guess that makes sense. We could get excited about any one of the fifteen and waste time if they turn out to be not closely connected.' She turned to look at Stanier. 'So we need to put priority on getting these DNA samples as these names come into the frame. Did we get Henry Carr's driving licence photo along with his DVLA check?'

Stanier slid the enlarged photocopy of Carr's driving licence picture across the desk. It was a nine year old, lacking-in-detail, photo-booth shot. Whether or not it would be good enough to confirm the man's identity – if they got to see him in the flesh – was another unknown.

Brenan looked at the face. 'We need to get Henry Carr's DNA if we're to rule this connection in or out. We need it fast and, until we know who's to be trusted, we need to do it covertly. We've still got to work this on the basis that Poppy is alive and in danger.'

Chapter 41

AD HOC SURVEILLANCE had always been part and parcel of a detective's routine. Lurking in the shadows in a parked car or watching a target from a derelict building often disturbed set plans and social lives.

Brenan pulled her Ford Fiesta into the residential cul-de-sac that was Cavalry Place at half past three. With Stanier in the passenger seat, she drove slowly enough to take a good look, but not so slowly as to appear suspicious. The local knowledge between Stanier and herself had been enough to create a mind's eye picture of what to expect and it was as near as damn it to being accurate.

The thirty-six semis were separated by a narrow curving sweep of asphalt. The uneven flagstone pavements and turf verges were dotted with concrete lampposts. A turning circle at the far end might have been useful but for parked vehicles. A squadron of satellite dishes high up on many of the left-hand properties attempted to drain the southern sky of its deluge of TV drivel. There was the usual Birchfield mismatch of privet hedge and panel fencing boundaries. Pavement-parked cars and vans did nothing for the ambience. There were plenty of streets on the estate which were decent enough places to live. There were also many which had dropped off the other end of the scale. Cavalry Place was a few rungs down the ladder but not that bad.

Number seventeen, Henry Carr's three-bedroomed abode, was on the left-hand side before the turning circle. Tidier than most, with neat garden and trimmed hedge, the place showed signs of regular maintenance and care.

The registration numbers of the grey SEAT Ibiza on the drive and the Fiat 500 on the road outside were surreptitiously jotted by Stanier. His covert furtiveness continued with a crafty wink at the lady who was busily posting Aldi flyers through letter boxes. The ruse had worked well during Scott's last piece of surveillance so they were trying it again. Brenan and Stanier needed a quick overall recce of the place themselves. Scott's closer "nosy" might just hand them some unexpected nugget. Perhaps even a fleeting glimpse of Henry Carr himself.

The threesome met back up as agreed outside the shops, and Scott hopped into the back. 'Okay?' Brenan asked without turning.

'Yes, not as heart-stopping as the last episode. You clocked the numbers okay?' Police jargon was now becoming second nature to Scott.

'Yes,' Brenan confirmed. 'PNC comes back in Henry's name for the SEAT and Marie Taylor for the Fiat.' She looked up at the mirror, directing her comment at Scott. 'Perhaps she's a visitor but worth a thought for your research, Mad.'

'Okay. The current electoral register only shows Henry and his wife as the resident adults so, as you say, perhaps a visitor.'

Brenan's eyes were still on Scott. 'Anything then? Any gems of information to report?'

'Nothing really. I tried for a crafty peek through the bay window as I was posting. Saw someone's feet. The telly was on – snooker.' Scott grinned as she started her next sentence. 'Mr Carr can't be that bad a chap, though. He's a Liverpool supporter. He's got the Supporter's Club mini bear on the dash of his car.'

Stanier gave a slow nod. 'Yes, I spotted a Liverpool mini strip in the back window too.'

Brenan was puzzled. 'Bit odd him being a Liverpool supporter and living on the Birchfield. Stoke City or Port Vale maybe, but Liverpool?' She turned completely in her seat and looked at Scott through the head rest. 'Hope we've got the right Henry Carr. We don't want to waste any more time.'

'It's the right man,' Scott said. 'Lots of people support teams from other areas nowadays. I'm a Liverpool nut myself and I live in Milton Keynes! That's why I noticed his mini bear.'

Brenan looked surprised. 'Hmm, you learn something every day. Still, whatever Henry's sporting choices are, we've got to stay focused on our objectives for him. We're looking to find a way to surreptitiously get hold of his DNA. Not an easy task even if we knew a bit about him. Any kind of source for that DNA sample would be worth a try: a fag end, a glass he's used, clothing, gloves, a hat, a hairbrush – anything personal. Our own efforts today haven't taken us very far forward with ideas. We still know pretty much nothing about him. Breaking into his house and pinching all the bloody toothbrushes is about all I can come up with.' She narrowed her eyes as she held Stanier's gaze on her last comment. 'Only joking, Ed. But, unless we get lucky we're going to have to get proper surveillance in place. That will involve the ROCU team and that'll take up more time.'

Stanier looked nonplussed, implying only partial agreement with Brenan's ideas. 'We could at least do with a look at Henry Carr in the flesh and get a bit more background before we hand over to ROCU. From what I could see of Cavalry Place, it's a bloody awkward place for obs, even by the experts. Parking's a nightmare with that narrow road, and any stranger cars are going attract attention. I didn't spot any empty for-sale or to-let houses. ROCU obs might take ages to set up. Even then we might not get a result.' He turned to Brenan. 'As for your toothbrush... *joke*, well, let's not forget I know you!'

The journey back to the MIR was a quiet one and, as they pulled into the car park, Scott's out of context comment did not seem to warrant a reply: 'Liverpool are playing Newcastle United tonight.'

Scott repeated the remark as Brenan unclipped her seatbelt and switched off the engine. She then leaned forward between the two headrests to add some more. 'They're playing Newcastle away. Sky Sports match. It could be a real nail biter. Liverpool are looking good for the Premiership title and need to win this one.'

Brenan caught Stanier's eye, bemused by Scott's seemingly off-the-wall comments. She wasn't much of a soccer fan and expected a similarly puzzled look from her colleague.

Stanier's enlightened expression signalled that he had tuned in to Scott's thinking. After all he *was* a football fan. 'You're thinking Henry will be watching the match,' he said, turning in his seat.

'If he's anything like a Liverpool fan, he wouldn't miss it for the world. I was hoping to settle in with a pint in some pub and watch it myself.'

Brenan was now in on the idea but was still sceptical. 'If he's watching it from home, it's a non-starter, though.'

Scott gave a sceptical look. 'He'd got no Sky dish, so probably not. Anyway, it's no fun without some atmosphere – and a pint! He'll be going to the pub and that's a definite!'

The three were out of the car now and making their way across to the police station. 'What time's the match?' Brenan was looking at Scott.

'Quarter to eight.'

'If you're right on this, the chances are he'll be watching it from the *Bottom Knocker*. We'll need to tail him from home to be sure, *and* we've still to get a look at him yet. That driving licence photo is crap.'

'Can't see him going anywhere else,' Stanier said. 'The *Bottom Knocker* is a ten-minute walk for him. He won't even need to drive.'

It was five o'clock when Brenan got back. Forrest listened to the full update. Some planning and additional input from Stanier and Scott took the time through to six. Forrest understood as well as anyone that the Henry Carr connection could be a huge red herring. Nevertheless it was interesting, and a lead that had to be treated seriously. Time was, as ever, of the essence, and this new facet had to be bottomed quickly. They needed to get hold of the man's DNA without him knowing. Time to hatch a cunning plan.

Chapter 42

AT HALF PAST six, Brenan and Stanier settled into a spot of in-car observations. Brenan flicked down her sun visor and shuffled a little lower in the driver's seat to get the right angle of vision up Cavalry Place towards the Carr household. Stanier, sitting beside her, did likewise and unclipped his seatbelt.

Their earlier shufti had given them the lie of the land and so, even from this fifty-yard viewpoint, they could see the roof of Henry's vehicle and the garden gate. Confident of spotting a person or vehicle emerging from the driveway, they waited. If Henry Carr did go out, he would have to walk or drive right past them. It was a feature they hoped to deal with "if and when".

It did seem likely that Henry Carr was a completely innocent man, and the intention of acquiring his DNA without consent had entered the minds of all involved. The possibility that this might be the only way to save Poppy's life, if she really was still alive, balanced the scales of morality.

In the Fettler's Lounge of the *Bottom Knocker* pub, Forrest and Scott settled into comfortable seats. The poster outside advertised only one event: *Newcastle V Liverpool 7.45.*

Mazewski was going to be busy tonight. The Premiership title could rest with this game. Liverpool needed to win if they were to stay in with a chance. Birchfield estate football fans of all persuasions were steadily filling the huge room. Mazewski, along with tonight's five bar staff were already feeling the pressure as pint after pint was pushed across the woodwork. More and more customers filed in, ordered drinks and took up favoured TV viewing spots.

Forrest waited until the back of the Mohican-haired landlord showed he was busy at the furthermost till before squeezing through the sea of bodies to catch the eye of one of the bar-staff. Mazewski did not know the DCI from Adam but, after Scott's recent visit with Brenan, she could possibly be recognised. The fewer people who knew the Old Bill were in, the better.

Forrest was soon back alongside Scott, clutching two foam-topped pints. If the pub *was* to be Henry Carr's chosen venue for a night out, it had the potential to be a long one and they'd be sipping this pint slowly. On the other hand, if Henry was *not* the football fan they had him down for, or if he decided to go elsewhere, the whole ideal could fall flat.

It was seven fifteen when Forrest's mobile vibrated in his inside pocket. He poked a finger into his left ear to drown out the noise as he answered Brenan's call.

'He's out. He's on foot. It's definitely him from the driving licence photo – looks a good bit older though. He's a big guy, six-one, six-two, overweight, dark hair, greying, 'tash, long sideburns, blue jeans, red T-shirt, pale green zip-up bomber… And get this: he's smoking. Got to go.'

Brenan closed the call. Forrest knew from experience that she was doing whatever was needed to avoid suspicion. He nonchalantly leaned over and spoke into Scott's ear, giving her an update whilst pointing at nothing in particular on the nearest TV screen. The acted, stifled laugh he gave added authenticity to the charade. Scott played ball with her own fake laughter.

Seven minutes passed before Forrest's phone lit up again. He pressed it tightly to his ear to overcome the din around him. The rounded tones of Brenan's "in-car" voice from her last call had now been substituted for a slightly higher and breathy pitch. Car engines and road noise formed a background muted roar – she was in the car park. 'We're in business! He'll be coming in in five, four, three, two, one...'

Forrest caught Scott's eye. His directional dip of the head to the entrance door coincided perfectly with Henry Carr's steps over the threshold. His upright posture and 180-degree scan of the Fettler's Lounge as he made for the bar, were robotically comparable with most arrivals. He was looking for his drinking partners. Brenan's description quickly assured the two "watchers" they now had the eyeball on Henry Peter Carr. The term "eyeball" was a piece of police jargon Scott would undoubtedly have used, given the opportunity. "Knobhead" was another overused term in police circles, and Scott may well have chosen it as an identifying feature for Carr. His boastful, swaggering gait, jutting chin and puffed-up chest tagged him unreservedly with this title.

Had Scott also been in the position to give an opinion on the likelihood of this man being closely related to young Jason Fitzgerald, she would have selected her words carefully. It was nothing more than a brief squint across a crowded pub, nothing more than the opinion of a self-employed genealogist, a self-taught DNA detective. But the build, the colouring and the mannerisms did not rule Henry Carr out.

There was little likelihood of anyone noticing the interest the two strangers were taking in a pub regular. Tonight was set to be mega-busy and "standing room only" had already been achieved.

Carr quickly joined forces with a bunch of friends at their usual end-of-the-bar spot. Mazewski turned the sound up to "match-level" as kick-off approached and a necessary shouting match for drinks orders ensued. Forrest's mobile vibrated with a text message from Brenan:

He ditched his fag before he came in. Flicked it over someone's hedge so I doubt if we can get that one. Chances are, he'll be out at half time for another – that will do but, as discussed, we'd be better with at least two sources.

She and Stanier were now in the Fettler's Lounge and eyeballing Carr from a different angle.

The background chatter quietened as the kick-off whistle shrilled. "Oohs" and "aahs" from the room then started up in sync with the live crowd noise from the sound system. Occasional swearing followed footballing misdemeanours or missed chances as play started to warm up.

Scott and Forrest gave up their seats to move in closer to Carr, as Brenan and Stanier craned heads for fleeting glimpses across the crowded room, hoping for inspiration as to how they could manipulate the situation to their advantage.

Spotting that Carr was tilting the last few dregs of his first pint into his mouth, Scott wriggled her way through to the bar, squeezing in between him and another punter. She held her own emptied glass forward, faking an attempt at catching the eye of the girl behind the bar. The tension in the room suddenly increased and a roar began to build. All eyes were TV-glued as the ball and a number of red-shirted Liverpool players closed in on the Newcastle line. A chance at goal was now a certainty as a Newcastle defender lost his footing. Scott, the only person not riveted to the match found her eyes being dragged by magnetic force to the screen as she fought with her Liverpool-supporting mind-set. Here was the best possible distraction being handed on a plate. Henry Carr and all those around him stiffened into an upright posture, heads up, chins forward, bracing themselves as the still-building roar increased. Liverpool's van Dijk rose up, seemingly in slow motion, before powerfully connecting a header from just six yards out. Henry Carr automatically swung his right arm back behind him to carelessly plonk his emptied pint glass onto the bar top as the ball flashed past Newcastle's keeper, Martin Dúbravka. The pub went wild, and only fifteen minutes had passed.

Scott pushed her way back through to Forrest. He'd struggled to see exactly what had taken place and now felt a tinge of guilt that his own eyes had visited the screen as the goal was scored. Scott's wide-eyed smirk seemed to indicate good news. 'Couldn't get a drink!' she shouted above the din. 'It's bloody crazy up there! I was lucky not to be trampled!' She was holding a still-empty pint pot in her right hand. Oddly, in view of the manic back-slapping and celebrating which still gripped the entire pub Scott held the glass with awkward delicacy – by its base rather than its top rim. She flaunted one of her cheeky winks at him.

It was an easier job than expected for Scott to sneak the pint mug outside. The car park and even the fag-end littered smoker's corner were completely deserted. It was as though the entire population of the Birchfield were inside the pub. Brenan followed her down the steps and pointed the remote key over at the car.

With the glass hurriedly bagged and stored out of view in the rear footwell, the pair were quickly back inside. The thunderous cheer they'd heard indicated that they'd missed out on some more action and Scott needed an update. Stanier gave the news that Newcastle had equalised.

Plenty more football drama followed, but half time brought with it Stanier and Brenan's attempt at snaffling a backup DNA source from Carr. As expected, their target trooped outside for a fag, along with about fifteen other people. The only way Stanier could get close enough was by smoking himself. Being a former smoker, this was a habit he now abhorred with a vengeance. It was, though, a case of needs must, as he'd lost the heads-or-tails decision with Brenan. He lit up a previously cadged-in-readiness cigarette and sidled over.

Henry Carr, in an eager attempt to ruin his own health, quickly smoked himself through a full two half time cigarettes. A check of his wristwatch as the fifteen-minute period drew to a close coincided with the pumping-up of the pub's sound system. The change from commentary box chat and adverts back to crowd noise signalled the imminent second half. Carr stubbed out the remnant of his second ciggy and along with the other smokers, about-turned and headed back up the steps. Two solitary figures stayed outside.

Back inside the Fettler's Lounge, and now a full ten minutes into the second half, Forrest and Scott craned necks to capture a distant thumbs-up from Brenan as she and Stanier re-entered.

The foursome saw the match through until its exciting finish with Liverpool winning three goals to two. Scott was ecstatic. They then all beat a hasty retreat to *The Southwood Inn.* John Eardley's beer was much better than the *Bottom Knocker*, and the surroundings more suited to a debrief.

On the face of it, the three possible samples they had procured – one beer glass and two cigarette stubs – were nothing more than that: possibles. The hope that at least one might give Henry Carr's full DNA profile was now in the lap of the Gods – and the skill of the forensic scientists.

Forrest's main reason for choosing this quieter and more secure spot to mix business with pleasure was that he had some news which, hopefully, would impact the evening's work. He explained that his afternoon had been spent on a number of phone calls and something he'd been researching. A text message he'd received part way through the Newcastle-Liverpool match was the result of those calls. The Chief Super had given up with his attempts to ring Forrest direct and had finally resorted to SMS. The technology Forrest had been researching was still in its infancy and wasn't yet common knowledge in the UK. The green light Forrest had been given had finally come from Forensics Services and the NDNAD FINDS Strategy Board. It was something which looked likely to speed up the results of any urgent DNA tests the team might be submitting to the lab from now on.

Forrest furthered his initial explanation. 'So, the machine is currently under evaluation by the NDNAD. There are only two fully working models in the country just now and we've acquired full and immediate use of one, along with the undivided attention of a scientist who works for Thermo Fisher, the American firm that invented it.'

Brenan, Scott and Stanier listened as Forrest explained more. 'It's called RapidHIT ID, and it does exactly what it says on the tin. It's a totally automated technique linked directly to the NDNAD and requires nothing more than the input of the actual sample believed to contain DNA. It self-processes the sample and extracts the DNA, compares it with the database and can churn out any match within ninety minutes.'

Forrest looked around at his three-person audience. It would have been a tough call to decide who looked the most astonished. Scott was first to speak. 'Wow! But what about familial tests?'

'Good point. In keeping with the same capabilities of the usual physical tests done through the lab, it can produce familial tests. However anything smaller than a twenty-five percent DNA share would create challenging problems. Loads and loads of possibles, exactly the same as a standard familial test done on the UK police system.'

Brenan looked between Scott and Forrest. She was now more sure-footed with her understanding, but was still looking for a sign of agreement as she offered her own hypothesis. 'So a fifty percent match has to be the father of Kobe. That's what we're after – the father. *And* we're not comparing against the entire database? We're merely comparing one sample against another?'

Scott shuffled forward in her seat. 'If we got back a fifty percent match of Arthur Pilkington or Henry Carr, or any of the others we might test against Kobe, yes, it means that person is Kobe's father. A brother or sister would also have a fifty percent share, but some simple tests would show them as siblings fairly quickly. The age difference would make a sibling relationship unlikely. I would imagine the Thermo Fisher scientist will carry out this test as a matter of course.'

Forrest said: 'This means that we should be able to get Arthur Pilkington's sample and then Henry Carr's done pretty well on a same day process. The one issue is that any covertly obtained samples won't be coming from easily tested spit or buccal swabs. The scientist will have to treat the items to enable the machine to extract the DNA first.'

'So when?' asked Brenan.

'The scientist is travelling up with a couple of technical engineers from London with all the kit tomorrow. I'm hoping we'll be ready to go by Monday morning.'

Chapter 43

Day 21 Sunday 5th May

THE FOLLOWING DAY, Sunday, brought with it the traditional MIR treats of a one hour lie-in and the possibility of a pub carvery lunch – enquiries permitting.

Madeleine Scott enlightened the briefing with her progress on the genealogy connections to Henry Carr, but left it to Brenan to discuss the clandestine operation which had hopefully collected his DNA.

Forrest's news on the revolutionary RapidHit DNA device caused a stir and a few "what next?" comments. The Thermo Fisher scientist and her team were expected to arrive with their gear by car after lunchtime. Rooms had been arranged at a decent hotel close to the Staffordshire University forensic facility where they'd be based. Staff at the university would be ready to receive them in spite of this being their usual weekend off.

The more relaxed nature of the Sunday briefing developed into something of an open debate on what was actually known about the device. Conjecture and hunches could have gone on all morning, but Forrest closed the briefing after half an hour. Several teams had appointments arranged with people they'd not been able to pin down on weekdays and others were working on paperwork and Internet research. Scott's three screens were soon churning through endless lists of names and historical documents. Everyone had plenty of paperwork to plough through.

The carvery lunch at a large chain establishment nearby was a little rushed but, for a change it did actually happen. It got most of the team together for almost an hour of cheap and cheerful food and chat. Fact was, after nearly two weeks without a day off, all the team were also hoping for a rare "on-time" finish at the end of the day.

Forrest's mobile pinged up a text message as he was finishing off his dessert. The RapidHit team had arrived.

It was two o'clock when Forrest and Brenan arrived at the locked front entrance to the forensic training facility on College Road. The building served as one of the county's foremost teaching establishments in that field. All the latest hi-tech equipment could be found there, along with some of the country's brightest brains in these disciplines.

Despite the seemingly deserted, closed-down Sunday afternoon campus, the doors were eagerly unlocked and opened up from the inside by forensic scientist Dr Simon Duncan. He'd been looking forward to their arrival.

As the forensic science course leader, Duncan, a thirty-seven-year-old with a PhD in chemistry behind him, had only recently become aware of the ground-breaking capabilities of the Thermo Fisher RapidHit machine. He was understandably keen to get such an early chance to work with the device in its evaluation stages *and* on a real live case.

Dr Duncan was accompanied by a face familiar to the police officers. Philip Lowe had retired from Staffordshire Police as Detective Chief Inspector some five years before and was now a senior lecturer at the facility.

A round of introductions followed before the lift took them to the third floor of the modern and airy building. Bright afternoon sunshine flooded into the wide corridors from multi-windowed lecture rooms as the group made their way. Empty seats and desks faced wall-sized whiteboards. A plethora of scientific and electronic gadgetry, along with all manner of chemical paraphernalia, stood awaiting student return tomorrow.

Security had already been made clear by Forrest. It was important to get the whole set-up installed and operational before the deluge of students, with their inquisitive sharp minds and prying eyes, could spot something out of the ordinary.

The group arrived in the good-sized three room lab suite which had been set aside exclusively for their work. They were met by Thermo Fisher scientist, Dr Mary Blackstone and technician Michael

Carver. These two were part of a seven-strong team from the Massachusetts based firm who, until yesterday, had been working from New Scotland Yard. They were understandably keen to show off their "pride and joy", especially on a real criminal case of such importance.

Scotland Yard Detective Inspector Arjun Patel, a National DNA Database liaison officer, had driven up with them to oversee the security of the connection with NDNAD and the correct use of its files. The overriding stipulation had been made that none of the information or intelligence obtained through the use of the device could be presented as evidence in any court case. It would all eventually be duplicated via conventional methods using accepted experts at Home Office accredited laboratories. Nevertheless, every single action would be disclosed fully and comprehensively to CPS for any subsequent court hearing. As SIO, Forrest was aware of the number of high-profile cases which had been lost simply by failing to divulge even the most inconsequential detail.

A deep clean of the suite had already taken place and, even though results would never be used in court, the avoidance of cross-contamination was a high priority. Protocols had been rigidly installed by DI Patel. CSI-style suits, hoods and face masks would be the order of the day in the middle "Observation" room of the suite. Admittance to the third "clean" room which housed the RapidHit machine, was strictly out of bounds to all but Dr Blackstone.

The police team were surprised that the actual commissioning of the device was already complete. It now stood alone in the clean room, working its way through an automatic test routine to establish its accuracy and the reliability of the connection to the NDNAD. The data it was producing appeared as a steadily rolling page after page string of characters on the monitor alongside technician Carver, who occasionally glanced at the screen.

The group chatted amiably over coffee in the entrance room, the strong American accents of the two Thermo Fisher boffins adding extra flavour to the discussion. All the details on the case, along with mobile numbers and other contacts, were exchanged. Blackstone showed interest in the unusual work of Madeleine Scott and hoped to meet her to expand on some similar work that had borne fruit in the USA only a few months before. Brenan handed over the sealed samples from Pilkington and Carr.

With the RapidHit test run successfully complete, Blackstone explained that Mr Pilkington's blood-stained tissue would be the first sample to be tested. 'The machine takes an average of ninety minutes to obtain the DNA profile and compare it against NDNAD records. As you're only requesting a comparison against Kobe's crime scene stain, it'll take a little less, but I will then be having a long hard look at the resulting matching chromosome pairs – if there are any. Hopefully I'll be calling you later on.'

The four were back at the MIR by half past three and lethargically making an effort to get on with their own research projects. Forrest disappeared into his office to take on some paperwork and Scott tried hard to tune her tired eyes and mind into a new family tree. The HOLMES operators unenthusiastically clicked away at keyboards updating the system from new witness statements and action form results. The rarity of the big pub lunch and a stress-free hour now combined with the near-silent telephones and a lack of "across the floor" chatter to fashion drowsy faces all round.

Forrest re-entered the MIR rubbing his tired eyes and looking for all the world as though he may have unintentionally grabbed forty winks. 'Anyone for a brew?' he said, heading for the kettle. There was mumbled agreement all round but his mobile halted the idea. The screen lit up to display Dr Blackstone's name as he pulled it from his pocket. 'Yes, Mary,' he responded, pressing a finger against the phone's loudspeaker icon.

'Got you a result on Mr Pilkington, Dominic,' Blackstone announced, although her strong American drawl gave them: "reesult" and "Domnic". 'Not as good as we'd hoped, but nevertheless a result. Arthur Ernest Pilkinton is, without doubt, related to the crime scene stains from the offender you call Kobe – but don't hold your breath. There are some matching chromosome pairs. Sadly, we don't have access to the algorithms that the genealogy sites use, so we can't make an accurate estimation of the relationship. I can tell you that it's a pretty small DNA share. It could be as small as only two or three percent, so you may be looking at nothing more than a three- or four-times great grandparent, going back centuries even.'

Forrest looked nonplussed by the news. 'Okay, Mary, nothing lost, but it does show us the idea works.' He made a thankful bow of the head at Scott as he spoke. 'So we can cross Pilkington off. Any ideas when you'll have a result on Henry Carr?'

'We have to do some more self-tests yet,' Blackstone replied. 'We'll be back in action first thing tomorrow.'

Chapter 44

Day 22 Monday 6th May

THE NEXT MORNING, Brenan settled into her chair in front of a packed MIR. She hoisted her black and grey pinstriped slacks an inch with a spontaneous tug above the knees and made herself comfortable. Her jokey public sacking of Charlie Sawyer from tea duties received a unanimous cheer from the room. It had been more because of his failure to keep stocks well supplied than as praise for his recent interesting results on the history of the Birchfield site. His response – hurt face and outstretched upward palms – also got a laugh.

Madeleine Scott didn't join in with the merriment. She was under pressure to keep up with the massive workload she'd set herself and seemed unusually stressed. Her silent flitting of computer cursor across three screens as various updates were given went unnoticed by most people.

Forrest gave the results of the Pilkington sample. 'We're getting close now and, even though this particular event doesn't take us forward a great deal, what it does do is prove that Madeleine's work does exactly that – it works.'

Scott called Forrest over to her desk when the last points had been discussed. The DCI watched and listened as she took him through the latest string of names and details she had built from another Durham miner. A living relative had again been traced to a nearby Stoke-on-Trent address through the distant bloodline connections to young Jason Fitzgerald.

'This is another name that's come from one of my fifteen most interesting players on family trees,' Scott said. 'I'll keep on going through these and coming up with names. I'm trying to take the Henry Carr tree a bit further, but one thing has me puzzled…'

Forrest's mobile interrupted the conversation: Mary Blackstone.

'Mary,' he said and again put the phone on speaker.

Blackstone's thickly accented drawl came over more loud than clear, but the message was patently obvious. 'You got yourself a fifty percent match with Henry Carr, Dominic. This guy is Kobe's daddy for sure.' Blackstone was unaware of the manic response her words had created in the MIR, but the magnitude of the news she was delivering made her raise her voice. 'Now, we didn't need to test any further, but we did. Young Jason's DNA was compared as a crime scene stain alongside Henry Carr's and, sure enough, he shows up with a full twenty-five percent match. Henry's the boy's grand-daddy, make no mistake.'

Forrest thanked Blackstone, closed down the call and turned to Scott. His grin was visibly eating into the stress and fatigue that had started to show on his face over the last few days. 'So, Mad, are you going to give me Kobe's name?'

Scott's eyes had been locked on Forrest throughout the short telephone conversation. The elation on everyone's face did not seem to quite harmonise with her own look. She'd paled a little in colour and her shoulders had slumped. She was almost single-handedly responsible for getting them this far and yet there was apparently some doubt nagging away inside that razor-sharp mind.

Brenan was puzzled. 'What is it, Mad? There's a problem?'

'I wasn't expecting a result like this so quickly. I thought I'd be having to trawl through numerous other possibilities. I was about to tell you that I've only just got round to taking a cursory look for any children Henry Carr may have.' Her expression seemed to be showing defeatism – a first for Scott. 'There is no son registered to the marriage of Henry Carr and his wife, only a daughter.'

The room went silent. 'Henry has only ever been in the one marriage,' Scott falteringly added. 'There is no son registered to him as father.'

A pin could easily have been heard dropping to the floor of the MIR if someone had wished to test the phrase.

Brenan rose from her chair and placed a comforting hand on

Scott's shoulder as she calmly broke the silence. 'Don't beat yourself up on that score, Mad. We'd never have got this far but for you. It's a setback, yes, but we know for certain that Henry *did* have a son and that son *is* Kobe. It seems that the old sod did a bit of wild oats sowing when he was younger. We mustn't lose sight of the fact that we've got a psychological profiler telling us all about Kobe having no father figure in his life. It looks like that bit was right.' She turned to Forrest. 'Strategy meeting boss?'

Forrest, Brenan, Stanier, Scott and one of the detective sergeants convened to Forrest's side office. Sufficient chairs were squeezed in. 'Okay,' Forrest said. 'Suggestions?'

'Ask Henry Carr outright,' the detective sergeant proposed.

'It may come to that,' Forrest said, 'but not until we look into the situation. A lot could be lost if he's in contact with this son and wants to protect him' He turned to Scott. 'Madeleine?'

'I've come across several situations where the father did not even know about a child. It's usually been where the child was the product of a casual relationship and the mother was either unsure who the father was or wanted no more to do with him. Henry Carr may not even know about Kobe. And, by the way, Henry's daughter was christened Marie. She's now married and named Taylor. So that's the Fiat that was parked outside.'

Brenan leaned in towards the desk. 'We need obs on Henry, a full ROCU job. I appreciate Mad's thoughts, but we need to know if he is aware that he has a son and, if so, whether he has any contact. We must begin serious enquiries into him. We're out on a limb. We're still in the dark really. We may *have* to get him in and confront him. There seems to be no help likely to come from the NDNAD as Kobe's mother hasn't shown up through the familial tests.'

'That's right,' Scott said, 'but I will look more closely again at Jason's genealogy DNA results. If you remember, by removing all the blood relatives on Poppy's side, we narrowed down the field to Kobe's side, but that would still include both Kobe's mother as well as his father.'

Forrest got to his feet, indicating the meeting was over. 'Great,

Madeleine. If you can look at that, I'll get ROCU to arrange obs. Eve, you and Ed start digging deep into Henry Carr.'

Brenan and Stanier made the *Southwood* pub their first port of call. They had been keeping the main features of the case from the public and, even now, were still inclined to only let the most trusted of outsiders in on the full facts.

Landlord John Eardley, as an ex-colleague and friend, had some inkling of what was going on. His wide-eyed silence as the meat of story was laid bare was eventually broken by a short sentence which accurately revealed the level of his shock: 'Fuck me!'

'We'll pass on that one, John, if you don't mind,' Stanier said. 'But now you can see what we're up against and why we've been so cloak and dagger.'

Eardley led the pair over to a quiet table. Lunchtime meals were finished, and he was happy to leave his two staff to earn their pay. Brenan slid the driving licence photo of Henry Carr across the table.

'I know him,' Eardley said without blinking. 'Big Liverpool fan. He's one of Nick's clientele, but just for football matches. Whenever he wants decent grub and ale, he comes in here – most Fridays and Saturdays, him and his missus. He's a bit of a bighead, not really my cup of tea, but he's a pretty good customer, so you make allowances.'

The details Eardley was able to relate about Henry Carr since he'd been coming into the pub were numerous. Whether or not any would be helpful in tracking down the illegitimate son remained to be seen. The landlord spent a full three quarters of an hour, chin supported by right hand, teasing trivia from his memory banks. On the face of it, the casual conversations he'd had with Carr, going back perhaps five or six years, were nothing more than friendly chit-chat. But it was now up to Brenan and Stanier to disseminate, to sift and filter, to put the details under the microscope and see if the identity of Kobe's mother was there right under their noses. And with it maybe even Kobe's name, date of birth and address.

Chapter 45

BACK AT THE MIR, Stanier read from the jotted notes he'd made during the meeting with Eardley. 'Right,' he began, 'Carr used to work as a self-employed painter and decorator. Had his own firm. He retired a few years back but still does a few foreigners… just cash in hand and no taxman. Before that, in his younger days, he worked at a potbank.' Stanier turned a page. 'Falcon Pottery in Hanley. It's long since closed.' Stanier looked up from his notes. 'We know from Mad's investigations that he was born 17th April, 1959 in Peterlee, County Durham. He's always supported Liverpool rather than Stoke-on-Trent teams. From what John Eardley thinks, it's something he latched onto as a young lad. He's only ever spoken about having a daughter – Marie – and, again, that fits with the Fiat parked outside on Saturday. John's pretty sure him and his wife have always lived at the Cavalry Place address and he's only ever been married the once. He goes out for a pint two or three nights a week; uses the *Bottom Knocker* on football nights but gets in the *Sythe* most other times. In his younger days he played guitar in a local group called the Falcones – no doubt from his time at Falcon Pottery. He played centre-half for Eastvale FC in his early twenties for a couple of years. He did his cartilage in and that stopped that. He seems to have been a bit of a lady's man in his younger days.'

Forrest sat back in the chair he'd commandeered. 'That bit fits.'

'He had bypass surgery a while back and manages to get a couple of holidays abroad in each year. Not long changed his car to the SEAT Ibiza he's got now. He plays a good hand of crib and darts and could have made the *Sythe's* pub teams in both but didn't want to get into the wife's bad books.'

Forrest was impressed at Eardley's detail. *Typical old cop,* he thought. *Could do with him coming out of retirement.* He set his gaze on Brenan. 'Okay, Eve, work all of this any way you like. On the face of it, it all seems to be dross, but you know as well as I do that there might be something hidden away in there that could get us home and dry. Use anyone you like from the team to help out if you need to – apart from Charlie. He's coming up with some good stuff. ROCU are sussing Henry Carr's place out now and hope to be set up within a couple of hours – full twenty-four-hour surveillance.'

Not for the first time, the thought crossed Brenan's mind that Forrest was doing an all-round good job. His determination to crack this case and find Poppy – if she was alive – was matchless.

She sauntered over to Scott's desk as Stanier got stuck into a spreadsheet based on Henry Carr's known life. 'How goes it Mad?'

Scott turned in her swivel chair. 'Not good, Eve.' She looked glum. 'I've put all my eggs in one basket now to try and track down Kobe's mum, but there's very little, if anything. I've had to look outside the Durham miner's fifteen. I'm concentrating on people local to Stoke-on-Trent, but there's been nothing really. It's as though hardly any Stokies have sent in DNA samples for family tree research.'

Brenan smiled at Scott's spontaneous use of the word "Stokies". She was becoming fluent in the local dialect as well as police jargon, but looked like she needed cheering up. 'I think you've done your bit, Mad, so don't fret. If she's not in there and there are no connections to her, then you can do no more. Look, it's curry night at the *Sythe* tonight. I'll treat you.'

Scott turned back to her screen with nothing more than a half smile and a downhearted, 'We'll see.' She had, though, been listening carefully to Stanier's update on Henry Carr's background.

The office clock was showing ten past four as Scott signalled with her eyes at Brenan. The detective inspector was barefoot; she'd kicked off her shoes for comfort. She pressed her toes down onto the cool vinyl floor tiles and coasted her computer chair the few yards over to Scott. 'What you got?'

'Took it on myself to dig into The Falcones, Scott said. 'That's the group Henry Carr played guitar for. The local newspaper do a supplement every month on interesting articles and things from the past. They call it *The Way We Were*.'

Brenan blinked. She knew this and often purchased the publication herself. Her own picture had once appeared a few years ago. It showed her as a seventeen-year-old in her cadet uniform. John Eardley had jokingly threatened to post it on the *Sythe*'s notice board. 'Go on, Mad,' she encouraged, now keen to hear more.

'Well they brought out a *Way We Were* back in 2015 featuring local nightclubs, entrepreneurs, musicians and groups back through the years. The Falcones, back in their day –' she glanced at her screen for reference – 'which was from 1978 to late 1981, were doing okay-ish, they described themselves as "Mod Revival" and locally had quite a following. They even cut a record, *Little Dreamer*. It got to 145 in the UK charts.' Scott pulled one of those faces that she was so good at: a square mouth, a show of teeth and wide eyes. It was a Wallace and Gromit-style shock horror expression. 'So, no more tries at that but, as I say, locally they seem to have done okay.' She moved the cursor over to her central monitor and opened up the forty-four-page online publication of *The Way We Were* from 2015. A front-page title gave a clue to the overall theme: *Potteries Club Land – "The Place" To Be.*

The choice of words was a witticism on the name of a long since demolished Hanley nightclub. *The Place* had been one of the city's most successful entertainment venues from the sixties through to the nineties. Scott clicked some more to reveal double-page spreads filled with black and white photographs, together with anecdotes and memories about local nightclubs, entertainers, groups and promoters. She stopped as pages 14 and 15 opened up with the dedication: *The Falcones – The Group That Nearly Made It.*

The seven photographs accompanying columns of text catalogued the progress of the group and loosely explained how they suddenly ceased to be. Details of successful venues and recollections of devotees from the band's era made for a nostalgic trip back in time.

Scott touched a finger against one of the photos. 'There's our man.'

Having seen Henry Carr in the flesh there was no doubting it was him, regardless of the passing of several decades since the photograph was taken. His sharp hairstyle, jutting chin and arrogant body language spelled out the words "gigolo" and "boaster".

Carr had been captured standing in the centre of a group of teenage girls, arms draped around the shoulders of the two nearest. His guitar was pinned between his knees. Doe-eyed, fawning expressions seemed obligatory for all of the girls. A line of text described the scene: *Falcones lead guitarist Henry "Bumper" Carr with fans after a gig at the Crazy Cat Nantwich in 1979.*

Brenan had now gone into gritted teeth mode. 'Looks like a right bastard.' She spat the words.

Stanier joined them. 'Agreed.'

The other photos showed the group on stage. The text put names to the faces of other group members and the different venues as well as giving recollections of performances and songs. One photo taken on stage from behind the group looked out onto a shoulder-to-shoulder standing audience of mostly screaming girls. The text beneath read: *The Falcones, Stoke Town Hall July 1980.*

Brenan's finger made a beeline for a petite, dark haired girl squeezed up against the stage. The picture had caught her mid-scream, arms outstretched and eyes riveted into an idolising upward stare. The youngster and the other jam-packed fans had unwittingly created the archetypal pop group photo.

'Same girl,' Brenan hissed. 'Same bloody girl as in the other photo.

'Only looks about fifteen,' Stanier added. 'Sixteen tops.'

Scott processed the remarks. 'Hell of a long shot, but Nantwich in one picture, Stoke in another. She's certainly a fan.'

'A young groupie more like, following him round,' Stanier suggested. He stepped back over to his own laptop. 'But not such a long shot, methinks.' He pulled in his chair against the desk and clicked his mouse, lighting up the screen. 'I've downloaded these photos from the same newspaper source. Eastvale FC, Carr's football team. They were in the Staffs County Senior League; still going now. They've produced quite a few pro players over the years. I've been looking for any photos from around the time we think Henry Carr was playing for them. It looks as though Henry's fleeting musical career came along around the same time as his fleeting football one. Eastvale hit the local newspaper back in 1981 when Henry was playing, and they actually won the Staffordshire Senior Cup. I'm pretty sure I've got the same girl on a club photo.' With that, he clicked his mouse to bring up lines of thumbnail .jpg images. After an adjustment of his spectacles he selected and enlarged one picture full screen. 'This is the one.'

The good quality colour photo showed a party in full swing: a packed room, grinning young men in suits, a large double-handled metal trophy aloft against a background of held-high sloshing beer mugs. The Eastvale club banner could be seen draped along the back of a bar. A tall figure in a slick grey suit caught the eye standing right of camera. The hair now styled into an Elvis quiff, with three-inch sideburns, looked freshly combed. Jacket sleeves were hitched to the elbow, narrow tie tucked between shirt buttons: Henry Carr, "Bumper" to his mates.

The jutting jaw and swagger were there again. The hairstyle had changed but Carr looked a similar age to his pop group pictures. The girl on his left was unquestionably the same girl but the similarities to the other picture stopped there. Notwithstanding her closeness, in this picture there was no draped arm around *her* shoulders. Another young lady stood on Carr's right: older, perhaps even a similar age to Carr himself. Her confident grin had been frozen for all time in blatant and suggestive eye contact with "Bumper". The younger girl's attempted smile-for-the-camera had been thwarted by a preoccupied vacant stare. The words "worry" and "anxiety" might as well have been etched in biro across her crinkling forehead. To the casual observer or everyday newspaper reader, there wasn't anything particularly noticeable about her. The eyes of the cynical investigators, though, immediately probed the detail on offer and homed in on the ever so slight tummy bump.

'She's bloody pregnant,' Brenan said, moving down to the line of text beneath – *Stock photo: Eastvale FC Clubhouse – Victory celebrations. April, 1981.*

'Okay,' Brenan began. 'No tunnel vision. It might not be Henry

Carr's baby and, for that matter, she might not even be pregnant, but the few photos we've looked at picture Carr with that same young girl on three separate occasions. Twice in the Stoke-on-Trent area and once way out at Nantwich. That's what? Twenty miles away? The football party was several months after the pop group photos. But, if he was the Jack the Lad he seems to have been, some of the other faces may give us more background. If this hunch is wrong and we can't covertly find Kobe's mother, then maybe we'll pay him a home visit after all.' Brenan almost snarled. 'I'm developing quite a dislike for Henry bloody Bumper Carr.'

Brenan was on her feet now, hands behind back and pacing. Anyone who knew her also knew these were not moments for interruptions. She'd reached the end of the room and turned before she spoke again. 'If he's turned down a place in the *Sythe*'s pub darts team for fear of losing credit points with his missus, he's a bigger spineless bastard than he looks. He deffo won't want his wife knowing about the skeletons he's piled up in his cupboard. The bastard will have to play ball.'

Brenan came to a halt alongside Scott's desk. Her screen still showed the Falcones article. Up to this point she had only scanned the parts that jumped off the page. She now took a closer look prompted by a hazy memory from a small photograph heading a short column to the right of the page: *YourMemories.*

The picture showed a respectable looking gent. It was this face which now caused Brenan's forehead to wrinkle with puzzlement yet again. The text immediately confirmed her recall:

Hanley music shop owner, Roy Sherwood, managed the Falcones during their short career. "I was looking after several local bands at the time," the 67-year-old recalled. "The Falcones could really have made the big time but, as happens with so many groups, there was an acrimonious split and they all went their separate ways."

Brenan looked at her watch: five minutes before six. She turned to Stanier. 'Get your jacket, Ed.' She looked back at Scott as they hurried for the door. 'Send those photos to my phone, Mad... Please!'

Chapter 46

ROY SHERWOOD HAD locked the store's entrance door to cash up. The window shutters had already been lowered. With keys in hand and jacket over arm he was about to set the burglar alarm and leave for home.

Brenan's knuckled rap startled him. His suspicious frown washed into a sigh of relief as the two warrant cards were pressed against the glass. It only took a second to recall the name. 'Inspector Brenan,' he said, as his fumbling fingers unlocked and opened up. 'Lucky to catch me.'

After introducing Stanier, Brenan lost no time in outlining what they needed to know. She still remained economical with the facts.

'That article for *The Way We Were*? Yes, that's five or more years ago. The Falcones were top drawer back in the day. Like the article said, they nearly made it and could have done if they'd stuck together.' Sherwood clamped his lips in a show of dismay. 'All Bumper's fault. Good lead guitar but a right nasty piece of work.'

'How so?' Stanier said.

'The Falcones were pottery workers from the big Weatherby's factory just up the road. The building *had* been Falcon Pottery. It's been closed years now.' Sherwood studied the ceiling for a moment as he grasped old memories. 'Lozzer Lucas on drums, Grib – that's Alan Gribble – on bass guitar, Bumper Carr as lead guitar and Bernie Quinn on guitar and keyboards.' He became momentarily apprehensive and then started again. 'I said nothing more than "acrimonious split" for that newspaper article. But there was a lot of bad feeling at the time and I guess even now some people wouldn't want the truth digging up.'

The three were by this time seated on stools around a large drum kit display. 'You see,' Sherwood explained, 'Bumper Carr was a nightmare to keep in check. A loud-mouthed, brash bighead – and he couldn't keep his dick in his trousers.'

Brenan's cheekbones tightened as she held a grin in check at the shopkeeper's colourful description. It seemed a little out of character for him. But, then again, she reconsidered, Sherwood *had* been a pop group manager back in the era of sex, drugs, and rock 'n' roll.

'Excuse my French,' Sherwood added, reddening slightly. 'But I'm sure you've heard worse, and it's the truth. It was down to his behaviour that the group split up.'

'So I'm gathering there was a particular incident?' Brenan asked as her phone chimed with an incoming WhatsApp message.

'More than one. Several very young lasses were besotted with him. I wanted shut of him before he dragged the group down and then it came to a head with Maisie.'

Brenan and Stanier waited. It was clear that Sherwood was about to tell them what he knew.

'Maisie Quinn was guitarist Bernie Quinn's little sister. She came to most of the gigs and sometimes used to travel in the van with the group. Anyway Bumper was giving her a seeing to and there's no doubt it started before she was sixteen. There were a couple of nasty fights between Bumper and Bernie over it. Carr was seeing other young girls as well.'

Brenan held her hand up. 'Hang on, Mr Sherwood,' she dipped into her pocket for her mobile and then worked the screen to bring up the photos Scott had sent. Picking the one showing Carr surrounded by fans, she pinched the screen outwards to enlarge the girl whose face appeared in the other pictures too.

Sherwood's nod confirmed it. 'Yep, that's Maisie. I remember that picture.'

Brenan next selected the backstage photo and enlarged the same girl's image.

'Yep, her again! Crazy Cat, Nantwich.'

Brenan repeated the process with the football club party.

Sherwood shook his head. 'No, not seen that one before, but that's Maisie for sure, and looking mighty glum.'

'I think she'd got reason,' Brenan said. 'I think she was pregnant.'

'That doesn't surprise me, but it is news to me. I'm guessing the group had pretty well split by then, and I heard no more from them apart from Lozzer, the drummer. He went on to play with some good bands. This would be when Bumper was playing football for Eastvale. I gather that you know who the other woman in the photo is?'

Brenan shook her head.

'That's Rose,' Sherwood said. 'I'd heard tell he'd got her pregnant too, but word was he actually married her.'

Forrest listened intently to the full update as soon as they got back to the MIR. 'I'm hanging my hopes on Maisie Quinn being Kobe's mum,' Brenan said. 'I know that, with a character like Henry Carr, it's always going to be yet another gamble, but it does fit with what we now know. Certainly, Madeleine has already confirmed that Carr's wife is named Rose. She's also discovered that they were married at Hanley Registry Office on 20th March 1982, and that their only child, Marie, was born on 22nd April 1982. So, a bit of a shotgun wedding. Mad is now pulling the stops out on the name Maisie Quinn.'

Forrest swivelled in his chair to look at Scott as her printer churned out a single A4 sheet. She lifted it from the tray and held it, arm outstretched, to Forrest. 'There we go, boss.' She turned back to her own screen and read out the details. 'Maisie Janet Quinn born 11th February 1965 to Margaret Doris Quinn – maiden name Tagg – and Robert Ernest Quinn.'

An email pinged on Scott's laptop as she continued to explain. 'Maisie registered the birth of her own child, a boy, with Hanley Registry Office as being born on 19th September 1981 at the City General Maternity Hospital.' She calculated on her fingers. 'Making her sixteen years and about seven months old when she gave birth. The name and occupation of the father have been left blank.'

Brenan's teeth were gritted with anger again. 'So, she's kept her secret to herself, hence the reason why it appears that Henry didn't get done for having sex with an under-age girl.'

Scott was still scrolling through her screen details. 'Doesn't look as though Maisie ever got married from what I can see.'

Forrest found himself having to ask: 'And the boy's name?'

'Well, plainly he's kept his mother's surname,' Scott answered. 'So Quinn, Jeremy Henry Quinn.'

'God help us. She's even used Carr's first name as a middle name.' Forrest turned to Brenan and Stanier. They knew what was next, but he was going to say it anyway 'We've got a full name and date of birth now. I want every kind of check we can think of: Criminal Records Office, DVLA, Intelligence Officer, credit rating, Social Security, Housing Department, income tax, the bloody works – and more. I want an address within ten minutes. Two free pints for the first one to get it.'

The entire room turned back to computer screens or grabbed telephones.

Brenan thought she'd won the bet when she swivelled in her chair on the count of three minutes and forty seconds. 'Got him! CRO check. He's only got a bloody criminal record, hasn't he?!'

Forrest paled as though a plug had been pulled from his jugular vein. 'What? How the hell?'

'Don't worry boss, it was yonks ago when he was a teenager, and before compulsory DNA had got off the ground for juveniles. His prints, mugshot and everything have been on file but not his DNA. Kobe never left any prints behind.'

Brenan added a few more keystrokes and quickly accessed the file. With two more clicks the front facing and side profile colour mugshot picture of Jeremy Henry Quinn filled the screen. A Criminal Record Office number was strung along the bottom edge.

A staring-eyed, hollow faced youth glared back at the camera. The ravages of a serious acne war looked to be at its peak. Skin had been replaced by a veneer of raspberry yoghurt which without doubt would have left his cheeks and forehead gouged and cratered for all time.

'This guy is fitting the bill more and more. Remember Anna Albescu's account – the bad skin?' There was a hint of controlled excitement in Forrest's voice. 'So, how long ago was this picture taken, and what were his convictions for?'

Brenan moved the screen half a page down into the text fields. 'That picture was taken in October 1995. He was up at Fenton Juvenile Court. Assault and three counts of theft. He'd be fourteen then. He'd had several youth cautions before that. It looks like he slipped through the DNA net, which didn't start including juveniles until 1996.'

'So, the address?' Forrest questioned, stepping behind Brenan's chair.

She read the details. '16, Magdalen Close, Birchfield at the time. Magdalen Close is right over on the north side of the estate, so that bit doesn't fit with the ideas we dug up from the bookshop video.'

'Point taken, Eve, but that was only ever conjecture.'

'No, boss, I think it was right.'

The voice came from behind the group and belonged to Frank Milton.

Chapter 47

'QUINN DEFINITELY MOVED from Magdalen Close,' Frank Milton said, as he set a gritty stare onto the mugshot. 'I remember that little turd well.' He bowed his head towards the screen. 'I actually locked him up for that last conviction – the assault. He was a dangerous bastard even as a youngster. He carried out a nasty attack on a young lad, an eleven-year-old. The deeper I dug into the case the more concerned I got about Quinn. You see, it turned out that he'd developed a very unhealthy interest in the boy's thirteen year old sister and, on the way back from school one day, Quinn grabbed the girl and tried to drag her off. Her younger brother was a brave little bugger and he managed to pull a few lumps of hair out of Quinn's head. Quinn beat the lad senseless. The business over Quinn's initial attack on the girl all took a back seat and was put down to horseplay but I was never convinced on that score. A couple of weeks later the family's two pet rabbits were beheaded and that, I'm certain, was down to Quinn, but couldn't prove it. I had him in for it, but he'd learned the stock phrase "no comment" pretty well, even at fourteen.'

'What about the thefts?' Forrest asked.

Brenan checked her screen for detail. 'Shoplifting. Odd, though to take a juvenile to court for that. He must have got through a few cautions before that step.' She scrolled further for more detail. 'Yes, not your usual bag of sweets from the local tuck shop. On his last one, when he was thirteen, he nicked a large camping knife and some rope from the outdoor pursuits shop in the town centre.'

Forrest turned back to Milton. 'This guy's got an interesting background. You were going to make a point about the address, Frank?'

'Yes, boss, he's not there now. I'm pretty sure Quinn lived with his mother at that address. She got a new bloke in her life and the three of them moved over to the south of the estate. It was somewhere close to the *Bottom Knocker*.' Milton suddenly became silent, as though his power switch had been flicked off. 'Bloody hell!' he started again. 'Evesham Gardens. It was a detached bungalow at the end of Evesham Gardens, a little cul-de-sac. It's at the side of the *Bottom Knocker* and backs onto Birchfield Care Home. I'll bet it was him who was pinching all the building materials when they were putting the care home up.'

Forrest was amazed that Milton's incredible local knowledge continued to give even after all the years that had passed. 'More than likely, Frank,' he said with a chuckle. 'But we'd better try and prove that he's our man before that.' The comment generated a ripple of laughter from the room. Forrest turned back to Brenan. 'Eve, get teams concentrating on pinning down the actual address and the occupants. Our first objective will be getting the eyeball on Jeremy Quinn and covertly obtaining a DNA sample. We're going to need proper obs on the place.' Forrest lifted his head to pick out DC Sawyer. 'Charlie, close liaison on this. Your new-found expertise and contacts with the Planning Department might help us with details of the building.' Sawyer returned an enthusiastic thumbs-up.

Madeleine Scott had continued to rattle her computer keys as she'd listened to the interesting points that were being made. She swivelled her chair and interrupted Forrest before he could start his next point. 'Got it! Electoral register. 10, Evesham Gardens.' She ripped the page from her printer before it had completed and read the detail. 'Three eligible voters residing there: Milner, Desmond Terence; Quinn, Maisie Janet; and Quinn, Jeremy Henry.'

'Great work, Mad,' Forrest said. He turned to Stanier, 'Ed, run a DVLA and CRO check on the name Milner.'

Stanier was inputting the details before Forrest turned back to the room, still talking. 'Remember, we have to be sure Quinn is our man, and we need to try and establish where – or, indeed, *if* Poppy – is being held. If she really is still alive, she might not even be at this latest address, so here's where the obs will come in.' He turned back to Brenan. 'Eve, trace the energy suppliers for that address and get them to do some sort of evaluation on the usage.' He paused to compile a better explanation. 'They're so bloody good at calculating how much energy we all use. See if they can come up with an idea of how many people might be there from the amount going on the bills.'

Brenan was eagerly on top of the novel idea. It was certainly worth a try.

Forrest swivelled back to PC Milton. 'Get stuck into Jeremy Quinn, Frank. See what you can find out. I'm thinking education, occupation, acquaintances.'

'I know for sure that he went to Birchfield High,' Milton advised. 'He was there when I dealt with him. Not sure if the school will still have records, and I can't recall coming across him again after that, but I'll start there.'

Stanier had one of his results back within two minutes. 'Boss, DVLA check on Desmond Terence Milner comes up to that address with a driving licence which gives a date of birth working out as August 2nd, 1952, making him fourteen years older than Maisie. It's also given me the green light for a full PNC Criminal Records Office check which comes back negative. He's got a clean sheet. No previous.'

Forrest looked up at the wall clock: almost half past seven. 'Okay, great work. Frustrating as it is, most of the enquiries and organisation we need to do won't be possible until tomorrow. I'm standing ROCU down from the obs on Henry Carr's pad and getting a representative in for tomorrow's briefing. I'm going to have to swap them to this new address.' He turned to the office manager. 'So, full eight o'clock briefing tomorrow.' Swivelling back, he fixed another stare on Frank Milton. 'Gold star for you again, Frank, and I think the two pints prize goes between you and Madeleine.'

'Cheers, boss,' Milton said coyly. 'Pencil me in for another night, though, if that's okay. I need my beauty sleep.'

'Don't we all!' Forrest rubbed a palm down a stubbly cheek. He turned to Brenan. 'My stomach thinks my throat's been cut and you'll still get the consolation prize of a least one pint.'

'Fair do's, boss. I was telling Mad it's curry night at the *Sythe*, and John says he'll hold us a table.'

Scott had been rejuvenated by the latest progress and seemed back to her usual enthusiastic self. Even Ed Stanier decided to grace them with his company for this outing. His lunchtime peanut butter sandwiches had gone uneaten again and he needed something more substantial. His pledge to be making an early run for home, though, put him in the driving seat. There was no firm intention to have several pints, but it was agreed that things could turn out that way. It would likely be a taxi back for the other three.

The intensity of the case was building by the hour but, until the next morning, most enquiries would get no further than an unanswered telephone, a locked office or an unmanned email account. Frustrating as it was, Father Time had a way of making people take a break. As the journey to the pub got underway there was no surprise or objection when Forrest suggested a "quick shufti" at the new target address. Indeed, Brenan had the idea in mind herself.

Dusk and half past eight approached as Stanier pulled his car, sidelights on, into the curving sweep of Evesham Gardens. This was one of the estate's more upmarket spots. Ten homes populated the wider-than-average cul-de-sac: two sets of semi-detached either side, and two detached bungalows at the end of a turning circle. They quickly worked out that one of these bungalows was number ten. The foursome would not be hanging about and hoped the recce would go completely unnoticed by the locals or put down to a driver taking a wrong turn, in the worst case scenario.

The tight turning circle and parked vehicles forced Stanier into a casual three-point turn at the end. His slow and intentionally indecisive exit from the street was an act he'd played out many times. It was a ruse used when a potential joint needed casing for a later search warrant. The charade faithfully produced the look of a lost and bemused driver.

Stanier pulled up in the car park of the *Southwood* ten minutes later and the four took a moment deliberating over what they had each been able to glean.

'Fairly tidy looking street, apart from the target home,' Brenan said.

The three other voices chimed accord with this. 'Yes,' Forrest added. 'Stands out like a sore thumb. I'll bet the neighbours love them.' Forrest had now turned in his front passenger seat to Brenan and Scott. 'Big van on the drive. I got part of the reg.'

'Got it,' Brenan said, patting the note pad on her lap. 'As you said, big van – a Peugeot, I think, so not the little Ford Connect we were hoping for. I'll PNC it tomorrow.'

'Double garage, though, so there could be something in there,' Scott added. 'Quite a sizeable place, three- or four-bedroomed, by the look of it.'

'No lights on that I could see,' Forrest added. 'And it certainly looks pretty bloody dingy and uncared for. Weeds growing through the tarmac, some of the guttering hanging off, and was that a settee in the garden?'

Within five minutes the four were settled around a table in the *Southwood*'s lounge and getting personal service from the landlord himself. The place was its usual busy-busy with every other space taken up by early-doors hungry punters. John Eardley took the orders and promised to join them as soon as things quietened. The Deuchars IPA had been such a popular tipple that Eardley had ordered more in. "Curry night" meant what it said and, as long as everyone liked chicken rogan josh, they would all be happy. They did and they were.

A few surreptitious scans of the other clientele were taken between poppadoms and main course in case Henry Carr was in, but he was not. There was an eagerness to talk of nothing but the case. They all had ideas and hunches, but this was not the place, not just now at any rate. By default, the conversation turned to the more pleasant aspects of life. As usual, humorous stories about the job and the characters found their way between holidays, sport and music.

Ed Stanier paid up his portion of the bill and beat a hasty retreat by quarter past ten.

John Eardley, a perspiring red bulk of unhealthiness, took over Stanier's vacant chair. He mopped his sweating brow with a handkerchief and blew out a long sigh as he took the weight off his feet.

It was twenty past eleven and last orders had been and gone along with the other customers. The few remaining staff wouldn't be far behind them.

'Any more for any more?' Eardley asked, placing his own Deuchars down onto a beer mat.

The offer was appreciated but they'd all still got pretty full glasses and a hangover was not something anyone wanted at this stage of the game.

Forrest had discussed John Eardley's situation with Brenan earlier, even though he'd already made his mind up that the man was completely trustworthy. They'd both agreed he should be privy to all the additional detail. His local knowledge and sharp observations had already paid dividends.

'So, you've only got this at the moment?' Eardley said. He was holding Quinn's photograph towards the light for a better look.

'Yes,' Brenan said. 'Taken back in 1995. He was fourteen.'

'Very difficult to match that Neanderthal to how he must be now, but I'm betting with acne like that he's been left in a bit of mess.'

Forrest made a small unnoticed shake of the head in wonder at Eardley's perception.

The big man tapped down onto the photograph. 'This scrote is now, what? Forty? '

The three nodded in unison.

'And you say he's a gangling tall fellow? Baseball cap, yes?'

More nods.

'Bloody difficult when I've got to try and add twenty-six years onto him. From what you've said, Nick Mazewski would be your best bet. The *Bottom Knocker* is right alongside Evesham Gardens, but I can understand the reluctance to take him into your confidence. He's a loose cannon at the best of times.'

The conversation moved about during the half hour it took to finish up drinks. Police characters from years gone by to local crooks and misfits busied the dialogue into a comedy act by landlord Eardley. The resulting outbursts of belly laughter temporarily sidelined the stresses of the case, until tomorrow. The flicker of car park lights gave notice that their carriage had arrived.

Eardley waved the three off from the doorway and the pub's lounge lights were out before they piled into the taxi. Scott once again accomplished stage one of her matchmaking endeavours by ducking past Forrest and hopping into the front passenger seat.

Forrest smirked but was content to slip into the back seat alongside Brenan. They buckled up as Scott accomplished stage two: instructing the driver to drop her off first. The DCI's second bout of eye-rolling was met by Brenan's perfectly matched look as they turned to each other.

Scott made a mischievous grin at the back seat couple as the car pulled up outside the Premier Inn. 'See y'all t'morrer – as they say rind 'ere.'

'Mad,' Forrest shook his head as the door was closed.

'Yes… mad Mad,' Brenan concurred.

Chapter 48

Day 23 Tuesday 7th May

THE NEXT MORNING'S briefing necessarily lingered until nine o'clock. Yesterday's developments had brought about some changes. Many of the mostly two-person teams were given different priorities and some of their other, more mundane, actions would be temporarily shelved. The ROCU Detective Sergeant busied himself with some serious note-taking and posed questions to help him set up full observations on the new address.

The tone and decisive quality of Forrest's closing words got everybody sitting up and taking notice. 'So,' he said, 'we've now traced three people to this bungalow.' He gritted his teeth. 'And I want to know the full ins and outs of Meg's arse on every bloody one of them by lunchtime, so let's get to it.'

'YES BOSS!' the two words were delivered in complete unison and full voice against a background of rumbling chairs as the team got to their feet.

Brenan watched Forrest shuffle his papers together. A hint of a smile curled her mouth upward at the edges as he left the room. The almost imperceptible nod of her head continued as the door closed behind him. 'Shaping up nicely, boss,' she said to herself.

By nine-fifteen, all the outside investigating detectives were either out on enquiries or engrossed with telephone or computer research in other rooms.

Scott had been the only one to show a degree of uncertainty. Her expression seemed torn between grin and puzzlement. She beckoned Brenan over for a word. 'Meg's arse? Who's Meg, and what's her arse got to do with anything?'

The two hands which Brenan clasped to her face could not stifle her laughter sufficiently and an outbreak of infectious sniggers took over those still in the room. 'Meg's arse,' she finally managed to get the words out. 'It's an old Stokie saying. It means he wants to know everything about everything.'

It took a few minutes for the mirth to die down and another half hour before Brenan's own snippet of "everything about everything" was the first new information on 10 Evesham Gardens and its occupants.

Forrest peered around the door and quietly perched himself on a desk edge as Brenan scrawled details onto the whiteboard in green marker and explained her findings to the remaining group. 'The van on the drive,' she said. 'Is registered to the man himself: Jeremy Henry Quinn. PNC tells me that it's a Peugeot Boxer, long-wheelbase, high top, diesel. Quinn's particular model comes in a fetching shade of vomit, which is apparently called, "Horizon Yellow". It was first registered in 2008. He's been the owner since August 2013. It's taxed, MOT'd and fully insured through AXA. Only him on the policy, and a full sixty percent no claims bonus. A surprisingly careful driver.'

The kettle was boiling for a mid-morning brew by the time Ed Stanier had more to give. He was standing, paperwork in hand. 'Right, Desmond Terence Milner, date of birth August 2nd, 1952, so that makes him sixty-six – sixty-seven in August. I can't find a vehicle registered to him, although he's still got a valid licence and will have until he's seventy, when he'll have to reapply.' Stanier loved his detail, but sometimes went over the top. He continued. 'I've got his National Insurance number now and the Department for Work and Pensions have confirmed that he's been in receipt of a state pension since his sixty-fifth birthday.' Stanier checked his notes. 'He receives almost six-hundred quid a month for that. Now, HM Revenue and Customs have kindly been able to open their books in view of the serious nature of the investigation. They tell me that he is also in receipt of a sizeable occupational pension through his former employers. That's British Rail. I've done some work on this aspect and discovered this is all paid into a joint account he holds with Maisie at the Nat West in Hanley.'

Stanier signalled a "thank-you" to the HOLMES operator dishing out the tea as he finished off. 'I've got the same checks going through on Maisie Quinn.'

Scott had swivelled in her chair to take on board Stanier's detail. She adjusted her specs to read out her own latest. 'Okay, a bit more on Desmond. Not local to Stoke – actually born in Cannock. I can't get into any recent census records, so not much luck on previous addresses yet. He has been married, but his wife, Lynette, appears on a death certificate back in 2002 – cancer. He doesn't show up living at the old Magdalen Close address at all. He is, nevertheless, at 10, Evesham Gardens with both Maisie and Jeremy on the 2007 electoral register. It seems that all three set up in the new home together. So, if he's retired at fifty-five, then he's set up home with Maisie quite soon after his retirement.'

Forrest had remained on the desk edge throughout the updates. 'Hmm,' he commented when Scott finished. 'Making some sense there. He's probably used his pension commutation to buy the bungalow. Perhaps he's the cash cow.' He flipped over a page of the reporter's wire-bound notepad on his knee and started with his own news. 'ROCU have already carried out an obs survey on Evesham Gardens and, as we concluded ourselves yesterday, it's a difficult one. There are no available properties in the street and any "stranger" vehicles will stand out like a sore thumb. They're applying for the NCA's director General to authorise intrusive surveillance, so we can hope for phone taps, Internet monitoring and vehicle tracker. In the meantime, they're setting up a "Joey" maintenance gang around a British Telecom street cabinet which is on the pavement inside the turning circle.'

Scott pushed her mouse to one side. This was interesting stuff, the like of which was rarely shared with the public. She'd also now acquired another piece of police jargon for her ever-increasing vocabulary – "Joey" – although this time the meaning was pretty obvious. Forrest ploughed on. 'They'll have a van with the right logo, the right overalls, the cabinet keys and a few tools. Just as long as they don't start fiddling with the wiring and cut anyone off, it should be okay until something better can be fixed. Apparently, Quinn's van is parked on the drive almost completely shielding the garage door and obscuring any decent view of the bungalow's front door. The garage door appears to be a full double-sized roller shutter type and ROCU say that the chances are that it is electrically operated. Now that will be from a battery-operated remote fob. Like a car key. They have an electronic code grabber and are confident that they're close enough to grab the code both for the garage door and for the van. Obviously, someone from the bungalow has got to operate the remotes so that the grabber can lock onto the signal. If it works, we'll then have easy access to both the garage and the van if and when we need it.'

'Any movement yet, boss?' Stanier asked. 'And what about "follows"? Are they set up?'

Scott's eyes darted from Stanier and back to Forrest as she fought to keep up. *"Follows"?*

'They're still setting up, but the van's not moved yet,' Forrest explained. 'As for the follows, yes they've got a decent team with three cars and two motorbikes nearby. They're short on female walkers, though.'

Brenan raised a finger and both eyebrows. 'I've done the course, boss, only last year.'

Forrest supressed a grin. He was expecting this. 'Yes, Eve, I know, and if ROCU has to go on foot they may need you. The one thing they hadn't catered for was the covert obtaining of Quinn's DNA. If he does go on foot, then that's the likely best chance we'll get – a discarded fag-end, a glass in the pub or whatnot. It would be a lot less dodgy than getting in the van or bungalow unseen. They've left me a couple of radio and earpiece kits and I've had CSI put together a few forensic bags and swab containers, but they'll need your handle, Eve.'

Scott had done well so far. She'd worked out "Follows", but was now stalled for a moment by "Handle." A wave of recognition released the tight lines of her furrowed brow as she concluded that this would be Brenan's dedicated surveillance radio nickname.

Brenan reddened, wasted a few seconds by clearing her throat and then meekly offered, 'Pickles, Angelica Pickles.'

The room erupted. 'From the *Rugrats*? The kids cartoon TV show?' one of the older DCs laughingly questioned.

Brenan slumped back into her chair and puffed out a lengthy sigh as she accepted it was best taken on the chin. 'The very same. Someone suggested I looked a bit like her, so I was stuck with it.'

'Okay, thanks for that, Eve. I'll pass it on.' Forrest was doing well to keep his grin in check, but it was pretty clear he'd already known Brenan's handle before he mentioned the subject. He got back into his update. 'The front curtains look to be permanently closed. The ROCU DS has suggested that there are two viable properties nearby giving line of sight. One is the Birchfield Lodge care home, which abuts the back gardens of numbers 9 and 10 Evesham Gardens. The other is the side car park of the *Bottom Knocker* pub.' Forrest set his eyes on DC Sawyer. 'Get back down to the Planning Department, Charlie. We're going to need blueprints of the bungalow when kicking-the-door-in time comes around. Take a crafty look at the care home and the *Bottom Knocker* or anywhere else that might be a better OP.'

Frank Milton held up his usual hesitant finger and caught Forrest's eye. 'Bit of an update on Jeremy Quinn, sir,' he began. He flattened out the relevant page of his notepad. 'Quinn was removed from Birchfield High after his assault offence. He went into a children's home in Newcastle until he was sixteen and finished off his schooling at the Thomas Fisher school in Newcastle. He moved back in with his mother then and started at Stoke Technical College. He completed several building courses,' Milton turned a page. 'He's done City and Guilds in bricklaying and structural engineering and an NVQ level 3 electricians' course.' Milton looked up at Forrest. 'He was described as an odd young man but nevertheless a good student. I can't actually find any details of him working in the building trade. For that matter, I can't find details of him working anywhere unless he's been doing foreigners. He's been on the dole for years.'

Forrest let out a long low whistle. 'This guy is beginning to look so bloody interesting. Eve, have we checked HQ Firearms Department to see if Quinn legally owns anything?'

'Done it. boss,' Brenan said. 'No shotgun or firearms certificate. No record of him ever applying.'

Stanier shuffled the paperwork he'd got together and began. 'Desmond Milner is listed as "Injured Party" in a burglary at his previous home in Cannock.' He traded a glance with Scott. 'So I've got that Cannock address for you now, Mad.' He turned back to Forrest. 'My main point, though, is that *he* did used to legally own a shotgun. All the records are still held with our firearms department at HQ. It seems that his shotgun was stolen during that burglary and the theory was that the shotgun was the sole reason for the break-in. It happened back in 2007, in the same week Milner was due to move to Evesham Gardens. He'd actually applied to transfer the weapon to that new address.'

All eyes were on Stanier; this was a worrying twist.

Stanier continued. 'It's likely that Quinn was involved with the house move and, if so, would have known about Milner's shotgun and cabinet. Now I'm not trying to put two and two together and make five, but we also know that Kobe has got plenty of access to power tools. Apparently, an angle grinder was used to steal the weapon from its gun cabinet.'

Forrest stared at the floor for a couple of seconds as he digested the worrying possibilities. He thanked everyone for their input, turned and disappeared back to his office.

It was not long before he was back, mobile-in-hand and determined expression. 'The van's on the move. ROCU have a three car and a motorcycle follow going on.'

Chapter 49

BRENAN AND STANIER were out on the police station's forecourt and dashing for Stanier's Audi within one minute. Brenan ignored the car's seat belt warning chime, fixing the Bluetooth Jabra earpiece/mic into place, and switching on the ROCU surveillance radio. A flurry of action and urgent voices blurted out as she flicked over to loudspeaker. The overheard commentary told them that the ROCU team were getting a full and professional follow underway.

The fact that the Audi's rear passenger door also banged shut as Stanier lifted the clutch and spun wheels was no great surprise. Scott was not going to miss this.

'You'll get us shot,' Stanier said, eyes on his rear view mirror as the genealogist fumbled with her seat belt.'

Brenan turned and spoke through the headrest. 'No Aldi flyers today, Mad. This is serious. You must stay in the car with Ed.'

The surveillance radio chatter eased down for a couple of minutes as bums were shuffled for comfort, seat belts and mirrors adjusted, sat-navs engaged and maps spread on knees. The controlled commentary which followed came from several different voices. It painted a picture in Stanier's mind of where the follow was happening and the general direction it was headed. It was his job to stay out of the action and unseen but close enough to drop Brenan if she was needed.

'Mongoose to the team,' the radio chimed. 'I have the eyeball, and he's taken a right, right, right onto Leek Road… Two vehicles separating us. Traffic is heavy, speed is twenty.'

Brenan picked her chance to transmit. 'Pickles to the team. I am mobile and available for walkies.'

A different voice responded. 'Pedlar to Pickles. Thank you, Pickles. Not too close please. Watch this space.'

'Mongoose to the team. He's left-hand lane now and indicating left.' There was a pause, then more commentary: 'Slowing… Red traffic light ahead. Be prepared for a possible stop in traffic. Yes, it's a stop, stop, stop and, unless he changes plan, he'll be turning left up….' Another voice was helping out with road names in the background and then. 'Yes, Mongoose back. Lights are green, he's taken a left, left, left, heading up Kilnbank Road towards Hanley centre.'

Unhurried, Stanier used a series of backstreets to close in.

Scott, in the back seat, was bolt upright, wide-eyed and listening as the different radio handles – Mongoose, Growler, Pedlar and Wings – professionally played out their parts. The lead "eyeball" vehicle was occasionally swapped so as not to allow Quinn to be suspicious of a tail in his rear-view mirror.

The journey took the clandestine caravan of police followers on a four-mile trek across the city before Wings, the motorcyclist with the current eyeball, radioed in. 'Leek New Road heading out of town, indicating left.' The measured gear changes and motorcycle's engine noise were clear behind the voice. 'And it's a left, left, left onto Norton Retail Park. It's going to be McDonald's, Aldi or the pub.' A short delay followed before the commentary cut in again. 'It's a left, left, left into McDonald's. I'm taking a right into Aldi – don't want to get blown. And Target is stop, stop, stop in McDonald's car park. I've got him located. Leave me with the eyeball. He's distant but can't go anywhere. Suggest a walker.'

'Pedlar to Pickles. You local enough to take this?'

Brenan responded as she clambered from the passenger seat, flicked her radio pack onto earpiece and stuffed it into her handbag. 'Pickles back. Yep, out on foot now, on the main road right on top of the footpath through to the entrance. If he's going for a Big Mac, I can be inside within a minute.'

'Wings to Pickles, I still have the eyeball. He's out, out, out from the van and walking across the car park heading for McDonald's entrance. Red T-shirt, camouflage combat trousers, dark coloured baseball cap. He's gone inside. Eyeball lost.'

'Pedlar to Pickles. Go for it.'

Brenan pushed the forensic evidence bags into a pocket and peered through the glass entrance door. She picked out *Red T-shirt, Baseball Cap and Combats* immediately – it had to be the man from the van, it had to be Quinn. He was standing, arms folded, and leaning against the wall near to the counter, apparently waiting on his order. Another customer paraded back and forth from entrance to counter, engrossed in mobile phone chat and no doubt also waiting for his order. Brenan scanned some more before going inside. The only other customers were a group of four animated schoolgirls in the seating area – all mobiles in hands and coffee cups on table.

'Pickles to the team. I have the eyeball. I'm going in.'

'Pedlar back. Okay, Pickles. Good transmission. We're listening, we're nearby. Best of luck.'

Brenan had thought through her next moves in the precious minute between knowing where Quinn had gone and actually seeing him herself. Now she was going to squeeze as much detail as she could from the situation and maybe even grab an opportunity to secretly get his DNA. She could only hope it could all be done without raising a hair of suspicion beneath that grubby baseball cap. She pushed the door open with her left hand whilst her right hand barefacedly held out her Samsung J10 at arms-length. The phone's forward-facing camera was running on *video record* and pointing directly at the slouching, sullen-looking and gum-chewing Quinn.

Brenan uttered a loud girly giggle as the door closed behind her (not something she was known for). Her free left hand casually smoothed hair from forehead to nape of neck. 'Getting it cut on Thursday, Mel darling,' she spoke the words loudly, brashly, like the type of person Brenan herself would often describe as "needing a slap". 'I'll maybe go redhead,' she continued. 'What do you think?' She touched her fingers against the Jabra earpiece and gushed some well-acted laughter at the conjured response from her non-existent friend. 'Yours looks nice like that – it really suits you,' she added, eyes still on screen. 'Look, I'll ring you later and we're out Friday okay? Just in McDonald's now – coffee fix and snack. Byeee.'

Quinn's two dark eyes lifted their gaze from the tiled floor at the sound of Brenan's voice and locked onto her with the power of an electromagnet. No shrinking violet herself and extremely worldly-wise, Brenan had been the subject of similar stares more times than enough. Plain fact was, though, that none of those other gawpers, oglers or lechers came even close to this intense and venomous X-ray. With her eyes fixed on the phone screen and its moving captured images of Quinn, Brenan found herself battling both a leaping heart rate and blossoming flush of crimson which wanted to climb from shoulders to cheeks.

A finger against the phone's "camera" icon stopped the recording and served as an end to the fake video call. She slipped the phone into her shoulder bag and approached the counter. She was a yard away from Quinn now and could feel the intensity of his predatory stare increasing. The voice of her old surveillance instructor was shouting inside her head: "No eye contact!" It was a difficult directive to stick to at the best of times, but now Brenan felt Quinn's stare burning even deeper. She fought against a shudder somehow sensing his illusory defilement of her actually taking place.

Riveting her eyes up onto the automated order screen, she battled against even the slightest squint towards him. One outstanding number showed on the board: *152*. The words *Being Prepared* sat alongside. The other customer had left, so 152 had to be Quinn's. Brenan's stare stayed glued until the information suddenly changed: *152 Please Collect*. Quinn's feral 20/20 vision detected the update regardless of his baseball cap's long peak. The X-ray petered out as he turned and stepped over to the counter. Brenan stifled her staccato breaths, moved in behind him and carefully regained her composure. She had to stay in control – had to reinforce her innocent customer charade and get more detail.

Her senses drank in all that was on offer about Jeremy Henry Quinn as he lifted his tray and turned. He was an arm's-length away from her.

Everything about Quinn looked bad to Brenan. Her involuntary blink and shudder might as well have been accompanied by that digital camera shutter noise of a mobile phone as she took in every facet close-up and personal.

A second wave of panic strove to turn her legs to jelly as she herself became the starer. Quinn's seamed and cratered, apple-crumble skin was stretched across a jumble of ever-masticating sharply edged facial bones. He existed as a slowly-rotting hybrid reptile whose DNA profile she no longer needed in order to satisfy herself that this was indeed the man they were looking for. This *was* Kobe. Her raised hackles and creeping flesh, though, would never be enough to satisfy a court.

A robot inside Brenan's head somehow manipulated her voice box as the lady with the "Dianne" nametag and McDonald's grey uniform beamed a smile from the kitchen-side of the counter. 'Bacon and Cheese Flatbread and a regular coffee please, duck.' Brenan's verbal delivery appeared authentic and nerve-free right down to the "duck" Stoke-on-Trent vernacular. 'Run it through twice please, duck,' she added. 'Like my cheese well melted.'

'Eating in or out?' Dianne asked.

'In please, and table service thanks,' Brenan's routine response came from years of enforced detective's "eat-when-you-can" lifestyle. It had granted her total familiarity with the systems of McDonald's, KFC, Burger King and other fast food outlets.

Quinn, tray held out in front, had retreated to the eating area. From behind the counter, Dianne's eyes followed him. She traded a look of disgust with Brenan and made a point of waving a flattened hand in front of her face. Brenan responded in kind. She'd smelled Quinn too.

Brenan paid for her order and found herself in another exchange with Dianne. 'God, he stinks,' the woman said. 'Strange man. He comes in most days. Wish he'd go elsewhere.' She pushed a plastic order number across the counter. 'Two minutes max, my dear,' she said, and disappeared into the kitchen.

Brenan walked into the eating area and chose a table near the window. She was three down and on the opposite side from Quinn's chosen table. He was facing away from her, his red T-shirt showing a curving line of knotted vertebrae and the rhythmically stirring jagged shoulder blades beneath. A savagely pockmarked neck with coarse, unbarbered dark hair sat below the black baseball cap.

It didn't take Brenan long to comprehend the motive behind Quinn's chosen spot. He was right opposite the schoolgirls and enjoying an unbroken line of sight beneath the table where young smooth white legs and ankle socks fidgeted, tapped and shuffled.

She fixed a laser stare on the back of Quinn's head as he methodically tore open one of his two large McDonald's brown paper bags. The chomping jawbones stopped as food was pulled from the bag. The vile fingers went up to the mouth and Brenan, unsighted, could only presume that it was chewing gum which Quinn now thumbed into place beneath the table top. Her still bounding heart missed a beat. DNA-wise this was promising, but something else as well would be even better. Her involuntary 'great' was said in the lowest of voices but was picked up by the rest of the surveillance team and a voice came through in her earpiece. 'Pedlar to Pickles. Appreciate your situation but update if poss.'

Brenan held her now switched off mobile to her ear as a cover for her mouth movements during a low-voiced update via the Jabra ear/mic. The lump of chewing gum looked like a potential winner but, if she was to get more, she may need help. Her murmured update and idea for a distraction were conveyed via the hi-tech equipment without the slightest suspicion. She finally looked down at her slender, packeted flatbread and still-lidded plastic coffee cup which had arrived, and forced herself to tuck in.

The schoolgirls didn't hang about for long. It was pretty clear from their sudden silence and worried, exchanged glances that Quinn's unwanted attentions had frightened them off. Brenan stared down into her half-empty, now cold coffee as she assembled more and more data on the monster that was Jeremy Quinn. Those girls looked to be the exact same age as Poppy when she was taken. She looked back up, taken off guard by Quinn's sudden activity. He was piling his rubbish onto his tray and preparing to squeeze out from behind the table. McDonald's assistant Dianne was hovering in the background waiting to grab anything he didn't clear away himself and wipe the table.

Brenan's secretive radio command held some urgency. 'Pickles to the team. Come in ASAP – as in, now!'

'Pedlar back. Understood. Five seconds.' The door opened and an anorak-wearing bearded scruff ambled up to the counter, immediately forestalling Dianne's plan and diverting her to serving duties.

Brenan was up, tray of rubbish held out in front and planning to beat Quinn to the disposal slots should he actually have enough social conscience to clear his own table. Predictably, he did not. He left his tray of garbage on the table and was quickly out in the car park and heading for the van.

'Pickles to the team. He's out, out, out, and heading for the van. He's got his second MacDonald's bag with him. Eyeball lost.'

A burst of radio chatter filled Brenan's left ear as she swept Quinn's entire table leavings into the evidence bag. A shoulder check satisfied her that Dianne was still busy with the bearded scruff. Chewing gum next, with all the potential DNA richness Quinn's saliva and cheek skin cells might bring with it. An apprehensive, corner of the eye, shufti took in the outline of new customers at the entrance. She kneeled to peer beneath the table, mind now made up to disregard any puzzled or disgusted looks that might come. She was going to get that dollop of sticky grey mush whatever happened. Her use of the buccal swab and its snap lid plastic container for storage would have delighted any forensic scientist and she managed it without witnesses.

The scruff entered the eating area, tray held out in front. He hadn't opted for table service. He gestured a massively over the top wink at Brenan as he took a seat and she headed for the door. She returned the wink, unable to suppress an ear-to-ear grin at her success. She'd pulled it off and her heart was thudding with the thought of the breakthrough this might bring.

Chapter 50

BRENAN'S MOBILE CALL prompted Stanier and Scott's return to the drop off spot. She jumped into the passenger seat. 'Right,' she said holding up her booty: plastic buccal swab tub and transparent evidence bag. 'Let's go see our DNA lady.'

They listened to the continuing ROCU surveillance commentary as Stanier got the fifteen-minute journey underway – Quinn seemed to be heading back home. Brenan switched off as they drove into the Staffordshire University car park and then hurried across to the entrance. She Whatsapped her McDonald's video through to the MIR as they took the lift to the third floor.

Mary Blackstone, technician Carver and DI Patel were waiting in the entrance room to the forensic suite.

'Okay,' Blackstone said, as Brenan completed the tale, 'I'll run tests on all the items eventually, but initially I'm concentrating on the chewing gum.' She narrowed her eyes with mock-suspicion. 'Now, you're certain it's his?'

'Absolutely,' Brenan said. 'It was right where I saw his hand go, and the only other pieces were rock hard and in a different spot – been there ages.'

'That's good then, Eve. Chewing gum is one of the best sources for DNA we could wish for. I will have to carry out some forensic procedures to extract it, though, so it's going to take a bit longer than the ninety-minute machine test.'

They left the forensic team to their work and made it back to the MIR for half three. Forrest was standing, arms folded, trying and failing to play down the enthusiasm he could feel building. 'Sounds promising,' he understated. 'Well done. Quinn went straight back to Evesham Gardens and it's all quiet there again. ROCU will update us if anything happens.' He held crossed fingers aloft. 'So we're waiting on a result back from RapidHit, but it looks like you've already made up your mind.' He looked over at the whiteboard as he spoke. A full-face, high quality picture of Quinn had been lifted from Brenan's Whatsapped video. It now took pride of place in the centre of the board alongside the *Kobe* nickname. A large red question mark was also in place.

'Too damn right,' Brenan said with a slow shake of the head. 'I've come across some bloody evil people during my time as a cop, but that one…' She gave a low whistle as her eyes landed on Quinn's photo. 'That one takes the biscuit.' She slumped into her chair and smiled her thanks as a coffee appeared on her mouse mat. Her eyes were then drawn to a new office addition. An A4 poster had been blue-tacked to the grubby plasterwork alongside her desk. Rugrats star, Angelica Pickles – blonde-haired, wide-mouthed and thin-legged in all of her cartoon glory – leered out from above the printed title: *Det Insp A. Pickles.* Brenan threw up her arms in surrender as sniggers turned to laughter. 'Okay, you got me. I thought it wouldn't be long.'

The healthy banter was a welcome relief, but didn't last long enough. Brenan clicked her emails up onscreen and sat reading for a few moments. One message got her attention 'This is weird,' she said. 'I've had a reply back from EON, the energy suppliers for 10, Evesham Gardens. They've been puzzled by the low usage at the property for years. In both gas and electric, the overall annual totals have never come near to the predicted usage for a property of that size even for one person. For the three legitimate residents that we believe are living there, they say it's way, way off beam.' Brenan thought for a second. 'He certainly smells as though he never has a shower, but what about his mother and her partner?'

Forrest was now alongside. 'So what's he doing? Bypassing the meter?'

Brenan was still reading the detailed report. 'Apparently not. EON has changed the meters three times over the years and checked everything thoroughly. They can find no faults or interference.'

Forrest was frustrated. 'Something's not right. Get a team onto the actual power distribution service supplying the area. See what they think. This doesn't fit very nicely with our hope that Poppy's still alive. She'd make the numbers in that place up to four.' He disappeared into the corridor and back to his office.

Brenan made a note of her latest job and watched the door close behind Forrest as the rest of the team returned to their desks and got back to work. She took a step back from the whiteboard and stood, arms folded, pondering the changes that had taken place over the twenty-odd days since the case began. Back then, just two small, lonely photographs occupied the centre of the vast white empty space – Poppy and Jason. Now a crazy collage of different faces, snapshots, names and details filled almost every inch. The labyrinth of coloured lines and arrows connecting one feature to another resembled a zany version of the London underground map. One common denominator, though, was that these lines all now funnelled downwards, dragged as though by gravity into a central deep drain – one photograph. The large question mark alongside Quinn's staring face served as a poignant reminder that the evidence was not yet there.

It was quarter past four when Forrest swept the door open, mobile phone held aloft as though it was Exhibit A. His grin would have put any Cheshire Cat on the back row. He directed his voice at the device 'Okay, Mary, for the benefit of about fifteen tired people, tell me again what you just told me.'

Blackstone's American accent came through on loudspeaker. 'You've got him, Dominic. I've only done the chewing gum yet, but it's a one hundred per-cent match with every goddamn crime scene stain attributed to the guy you call Kobe. Jeremy Henry Quinn's your man, as sure as eggs is eggs.'

Brenan stepped over to the whiteboard, licked her finger-end and rubbed the question mark alongside Quinn's photo out of existence.

The cheer rattled the windows of the MIR and caused a few uplifted heads on the floor below.

It was a fact that Brenan had already convinced herself Quinn was Kobe, but she was nonetheless elated that the science was now proving it. She turned to share the moment with Scott. If anyone deserved praise for getting them this far, it was her.

The genealogist's back was all that was on offer: black blouse, blue jeans and the trade mark red high heels. Her forehead rested in her right palm, auburn locks pushed backwards by fingers, bony elbow point on desk. The oversized glasses lay discarded across her keyboard. Brenan hesitated with her congratulations. She quietly pulled her chair in alongside as she spied a tear creeping out from beneath Scott's hand.

'Hey now,' Brenan said softly, arm now around shoulder. 'What's this about?'

'I never thought we'd get this far,' Scott sniffed. 'There was so much against us. Now we've done it, but we might still be too late if this electricity thing is right.'

The clunk of glass bottle on woodwork startled her. She blinked through teary eyes to focus on Forrest now kneeling at the side of her desk, chin resting on folded arms and peering around the side of the litre bottle of Shackleton malt whisky. He'd heard her reply to Brenan; he'd spotted the mascara smudges. 'It was you that got us this far, Mad. More's the bloody pity you were cheated out of being a cop because of some crazy eyesight regulations. You're welcome as a detective on my team any day of the week. If Poppy's there we'll get her back.'

The bottle managed a dram apiece with a little over for late comers.

'ROCU phoned me,' Forrest said, after the glasses had been cleared. 'The static obs team watched his return home, but they're frustrated with their OP. Quinn's parked in pretty well exactly the same spot on the drive and they can see nothing. They can't even be sure if he went in through the front or side door along by the garage. He'd got the other McDonald's bag with him; they could see that much. So is that food for someone else? Poppy, maybe?'

'Still no sightings of the other occupants then?' Stanier asked.

'No, nothing at all. They'll have to pack in the fake BT maintenance gang before the day's out and, unless we can help out with a decent OP, it'll be down to parked cars – not good.'

Charlie Sawyer pushed the office door wide and stepped inside.

He had a wallpaper-sized roll of documents under his arm. 'As requested, boss, the original plans for the bungalow.' He unfurled the blueprints on a table top as he spoke.

'The two bungalows, nine and ten, were built in 1981 by a different contractor than the earlier parts of the estate. These were freehold properties and pretty upmarket compared to the council houses. Number ten was built as a three-bedroomed. It's got a lounge and two of the bedrooms on the front along with the porch and front door.' He pointed at the plan as he spoke. 'The third bedroom is on the back right-hand corner. The dining room looks out onto the back garden and the kitchen is on the back left-hand corner. Now, what we'd call the back door comes directly from the kitchen and is more of a side door which opens onto the pathway between the house and the garage.'

Sawyer now made a smug face. It quickly cracked into a grin as he spoke his next sentence. 'Due to the topography of that particular spot…' He was expecting the long mocking, 'Whoooo!' which came at the use of his new-found planning word. He waited for the teasing to die down before continuing. 'Yes, due to the… geography, the entire back is overlooked by the Birchfield Lodge care home which actually stands two metres higher than the bungalow. There could be several rooms in the care home which would be ideal for an OP.'

Sawyer shifted his attention to the large square on the plans marked as *Garage*. 'Now, the garage is a double and is detached, so a totally separate building. The vehicle entrance door is a full-sized double and ROCU have already worked out that it's electric. There's a four foot wide path running between the bungalow and the garage and the plans also show another conventional, inward-opening side door to the garage. The building line of the garage is stepped back from the building line of the bungalow by six feet. If you wanted a decent line of sight towards the property's front door and the front of the garage, then you'd get it from the car park of the *Bottom Knocker*.'

Forrest stared at the plans as he absorbed Sawyer's ideas. 'We could do with eyes all over this place.' He said. 'ROCU need a decent view back and front. The locals, and maybe even Quinn himself, will start getting interested in that BT maintenance gang putting in so many hours pretty soon. The only other option they've got is a blacked-out van on the *Bottom Knocker*'s car park. That won't last more than twenty-four hours before someone starts taking a closer look. Forrest turned and gave PC Milton the heads up. 'You okay to work through a bit, Frank? I could do with you taking a closer look at the care home. With your granny being there, I'm guessing you know the manager. I was wondering if we could get somewhere indoors, or even in the grounds, as an OP for the ROCU team. We'd have to be sure we could trust the staff and that the surveillance team couldn't be seen by Quinn or anyone else for that matter. Difficult, but vital.'

Milton's enthusiasm had increased by the day. 'I'm game to give it a whirl, boss.' He grabbed his jacket.

Forrest singled out Stanier. 'Ed, can you go with Frank on this.'

Forrest now turned back to Brenan. 'We need to test the water with Mazewski. I know you're not happy about him, but maybe if he gets an inkling of the seriousness of this – perhaps the chance to think he's played a part in saving someone's life…?'

'Desperate situations require desperate measures, so let's give it a try.' She pursed her lips. 'Maybe an approach from the *big boss* could get him to play ball long enough for us to get the job done.' She added a single raised eyebrow to her "Big Boss" metaphor.

Madeleine Scott turned through one hundred and eighty degrees in her computer chair and set her eyes on Forrest. 'Not wanting to speak out of turn, boss, but I'm guessing you were hoping to get these new observations points sorted for tonight?'

Forrest suppressed a grin. That was Scott's first reference to him as "boss". She was definitely part of the team now. He'd got to know her pretty well and it was clear that she'd got a relevant point to make or had picked up something he'd missed. 'Okay, Mad, spell it out.'

'Liverpool are playing Barcelona tonight – UEFA Champions League semi-final. Starts at eight. *Bottom Knocker*'s going to be manic and I'm guessing it'll be rammed full come kick-off. If you want to get him to play ball today, you'd better get a move on.'

Chapter 51

IT WAS HALF past six when Forrest pulled his Skoda into a parking slot outside the *Bottom Knocker*. He looked around at Brenan next to him and Scott in the back. 'We'll play this by ear. I've not met this chump before, but at this moment in time we need him.'

The low number of cars in the car park suggested that most of the football fans would not be turning up until closer to kick-off time. It was a good thing; they needed a quiet chat.

Mazewski was down in the cellar changing barrels when they arrived inside. They took up a free table away from the TV sets and waited with a shandy apiece.

'Eve?' Mazewski said, wiping his hands on a bar towel as he eventually strolled over to stand alongside them. 'What's to do?'

Forrest was introduced and the obligatory handshake ensued. 'Hmm, the big boss, eh? Nice to meet you.' Mazewski's high pitched voice foiled any chance of deciphering between honesty and deceit.

Mazewski's "big boss" comment threatened to bring on a grin and forced Forrest to avoid eye contact with Brenan. He'd decided to play hardball on the issue and needed to keep his authority intact. 'That's right. The big boss.' He successfully kept his charade of stern and uncompromising complete. 'Sit down,' he instructed.

Mazewski obeyed, already feeling the underdog. 'You'll have suspected by now that we're looking into something very serious,' Forrest explained. 'I believe that you can help us with our enquiries.'

'Always willing to help the police,' Mazewski lied, but nevertheless was beginning to feel that he may have to do exactly that.

Forrest was light on the detail but heavy on emotion. 'Do you know what a police officer's prime duty is, Mr Mazewski?'

'Nicking crooks at a guess,' came the octave-too-high answer.

'No, that's well down the list. It's the protection of life.' Forrest shuffled his chair in closer and gave Mazewski an unblinking stare.

'We have a life to save and you could help us, but it will require your unrelenting confidentiality.'

Mazewski had become wide-eyed. 'So, how's this going to involve me?'

Hook, line and sinker was a phrase which went through Forrest's mind as he leaned in even closer and added more cloak and dagger. 'We need to keep a twenty-four hours a day watch in your car park. I can't tell you any more but we're looking to place a couple of undercover observations vehicles there.'

Mazewski joined in with the furtive leaning-in-across-the-table. 'Right,' he said, now feeling part of the team. His surreptitious left and right glance around the table preceded a question. 'When's it all going down?' There was almost a hint of an American accent as he settled properly into character.

'Not sure yet, Nick,' Forrest said, feeling the time had come to dispense with the hardball routine. 'Secrecy is vital on this. One word in the wrong place could scotch the entire operation and someone could die.' Inside his head, Forrest winced at the fact that there was a lot of truth in what he was saying.

On the "worried-face" scale, Mazewski was scoring a full ten.

Forrest relaxed back into his chair, now in total command. If he could have managed a surreptitious wink at Brenan and Scott, he would have done. 'So, perhaps a tradesman style van – blacked out windows – couple of cops hiding inside, for starters. What do you think?'

Mazewski's usual silly smirk looked to have been permanently removed. 'I have a better idea. You could use my beer cellar. It's got windows at the ground level of the car park. We've got plenty of time before the match. Come on, I'll show you.'

The three followed, as Mazewski led them behind the bar and through a central door into a small room. The light from the cellar beneath shone up through the still-open trapdoor. A wooden staircase took them down below. The expansive space was low-ceilinged and split into two large areas. A chill coolness mingled with the malty smell of beer. A stillage along a whitewashed brick wall supported a regimented line of metal beer kegs. Variously coloured plastic pipes curled their way upwards to the ceiling and then onwards to beer pumps above. The occasional flexing and twitching of the piping corresponded with clicks and whirring as bar staff up above pulled pints for the increasing number of customers coming in. The adjoining area was a wines and spirits store.

'Over here,' the landlord encouraged, stepping towards a ten-foot length of eighteen-inch-high hopper windows. These were at comfortable eye-level and looked directly out onto the tarmac surface of the car park. A series of metal security bars failed to spoil the view.

'Ideal,' Brenan said, gazing unobstructed at Quinn's front porch and garage door, whilst pretending to show interest in the full expanse of car park also on view.

'As long as you keep the lights off and stay back from the windows, no one outside will see you, day or night.' Mazewski said. 'But then I'm guessing it'll be a daytime job.'

Forrest gave a shrug. His serious face reinforced his authority. 'In an ideal world we'd need it twenty-four/seven – and from now.'

Mazewski gave his own shrug. 'Okay, not a problem.' He delved into his pocket and pulled out a huge bunch of keys. He singled out and unclipped a particular chrome mortice lock key and led the way around into the storage area.

A sloping wooden beer keg chute led up from the concrete floor and terminated in a square wall hatch which presumably was at ground level with the outside car park. Alongside the wall hatch was a sturdy-looking wooden door also giving access to the car park. A set of stone steps led up from the cellar floor to this door.

'Only gets used for deliveries,' Mazewski said as he handed over the key to Forrest. 'That door goes straight out onto the car park and as long as I leave the alarm off down here you can come and go as you like – straight in or out any time.' He cocked an ear toward the open cellar trap door leading up to the bar. The sound of customers' voices and the general bustle from above indicated a big increase in numbers. 'In fact,' Mazewski added, 'you'll be best leaving that way. The pub's filling up now and you don't want to attract attention. I'll do all the barrel changes myself, so no other staff will see you.'

Forrest gave Brenan a satisfied look. This had worked out better than expected.

Mazewski's face tightened into a graver expression as he organised his next few awkward words. 'One thing you should know,' he said. 'This place is haunted.'

Brenan and Scott struggled to keep grins in check. They knew of Mazewski's obsession, but Forrest was not in on the secret. His narrowing eyes met with Brenan's along with a *what-the-hell?* stare. Brenan's stiffened cheeks implied that she'd fill him in later.

Mazewski left them to it, climbed the stairs back up to the bar and closed the trap door.

A telephone call to the ROCU team initiated a swift change in plan. They upped sticks from the BT maintenance sham and, courtesy of their very own entrance door down into the beer cellar, three of them installed themselves. With tall stools set back from the windows and an array of video and sound recording kit the officers gave an approving nod. 'Bloody brilliant.'

Stanier and Milton also came up with the goods. Milton had known the care home manager since his gran first moved in as a resident. He was happy to stake his reputation on her trustworthiness. It made Stanier's decision to let her in on the full secret a lot easier and this clinched the deal. She was horrified, but also grasped the importance of keeping the circumstances close to her chest.

A first-floor unused resident's room was commandeered. The remotely controlled video camera installed there gave perfect line of sight onto the back of Quinn's bungalow and included the pathway between it and the back of the garage. Plugged into a mains socket and with state-of-the-art HD capability, the unit could transmit twenty-four/seven across the forty yards of gardens and car park to Mazewski's beer cellar. None of the other overworked staff members at the home had any inkling about the clandestine set-up. Things were looking up. It was now a watching and waiting game.

Chapter 52

AS THE BIG match's half time whistle blew, and with Liverpool leading one-nil, the background noise in the *Bottom Knocker*'s beer cellar dumbed down to an acceptable level. It was replaced by the muted voices of broadcasters and football pundits nit-picking the game so far.

The surveillance team were satisfied with the set-up and continued to tweak swiftly towards "running like clockwork". Two TV monitors showed the views from both the care home bedroom and the beer cellar window. Two radio transceivers stood on a makeshift beer-keg and wooden-planking table alongside the monitors and other pieces of electronic gadgetry. The three ROCU team members now manning this hastily cobbled-together base wore Jabra radio earpieces to help with the silent running of the operation. The car and motorcycle follow team members were discreetly standing-by in covert radio contact at various spots around the estate.

Frank Milton booked off duty directly from the care home. Scott and Stanier opted to stay on at the *Bottom Knocker*. Neither could think of a good enough argument to suggest this was vital to the operation, so readily admitted that, in reality, they wanted to watch the football.

There wasn't much Forrest, Brenan, Stanier or Scott could do tonight unless something happened at the bungalow. Spotting that was down to ROCU.

'So what's this ghost business?' Forrest said to Brenan as he cranked the Skoda's steering wheel hard right and drove out of the *Bottom Knocker*'s car park.

Brenan shuffled for comfort in the front passenger seat as she began. 'Nick has had a bit of a thing about this since he first took the pub over. He even had a vicar in once to do an exorcism. For all his hard man front, he's a right big girl's blouse.'

Neither of them was that interested in football. A decent pint at the *Southwood* and a bite to eat sounded like a better idea. Mobile phones would put them in touch if anything cracked off at the bungalow. As an afterthought, though, Forrest and Brenan had both pocketed a ROCU surveillance pack and squeezed a Jabra earpiece in place – switched off, but there just in case.

It was approaching ten o'clock when Forrest's mobile phone vibrated. John Eardley had already delivered the news that Liverpool had pulled off an amazing four-nil victory, and Forrest was sure the call would be Ed Stanier. 'No doubt they'll be after meeting up for some decent beer,' he said, as he flipped open his phone.

He was surprised to read the caller's ID: *DS Hawkins ROCU.* 'Yep?' he said grin dissipating.

'He's on the move, boss. We saw him come from the back door almost an hour ago and go into the garage by the side door. There are no windows, so no chance of a peek inside. We were getting pretty concerned about what he might be doing in there and I was about to update you when he came out of the side door. He put some rubbish in the bin and then walked to the front and shifted the van away from the garage. He's then used a remote to raise the main garage door, so we've managed to grab the transmitter code. He's back inside the garage now and I'm guessing he's got another motor in there.'

'Well done,' Forrest said, pressing against his left ear to click on his Jabra. Brenan read the situation and did likewise.

Hawkins continued to explain as the rumble of music from the *Bottom Knocker*'s lounge above him formed a backdrop to the excited urgency in his voice. 'These electrically-operated doors usually automatically turn on a light, but it's all still dark. I'm guessing he's disconnected the bulb. We can't see in as we're sideways on… Oh, wait… Exhaust smoke. He's started up another vehicle.'

Muted, indistinct conversation between the two other beer cellar team members suggested hushed radio commands were also being given to the follow team. This chatter now started to come through in Forrest's earpiece as his Jabra connected. He squinted hard to concentrate on the sergeant's words rather than the follow commentary.

'Yep, eyes on the vehicle now,' Hawkins informed. 'Reversing out – small white van and the number is… Fuck! Can't see… Can you read that, Jed?' Another voice, unclear, but reading out a registration number, then Hawkins again: 'Yep, got it now, it's NM07TLG. Pretty sure it's a Ford Connect. Garage doors are closing. He's out onto the road.'

Forrest and Brenan were on their feet and heading for the exit as the flurry of radio babble from their Jabras got full attention.

'Control to Pedlar. You on top of this?'

'Pedlar back. Yes, yes, yes, ready for the pick up as he turns out of Evesham. Confirm vehicle description and registration plate.'

Forrest and Brenan were now sprinting for the Skoda as the follow team's stream of radio messages flooded into their respective left ears. The DCI's hand-out-in-front frantic press of his car remote key initiated a flicker of the vehicle's amber indicator lights and they jumped in. Forrest chucked his still-connected mobile into Brenan's lap and spun the wheels as they left the car park, seatbelt-less for the first two hundred yards.

Hawkins' voice came through Forrest's mobile, now on loudspeaker. 'You still with me, boss?'

'Yep!' Forrest yelled as he calculated a route avoiding contact with the follow. 'We're listening to the surveillance commentary and we're heading back to the *Bottom Knocker* ASAP in case there's a chance of a shufti while he's out.'

'Okay, boss, but cool it before you get close. Don't want to alert the natives.'

Forrest made a slightly irritated face at the phone. He'd already killed the speed but accepted the comment was well meant.

The surveillance commentary started to flow more smoothly as the team got their act together. The intermediate remarks hinted at difficulties, though. There was little traffic about; it was now well after ten o'clock and dark. These were problems which could make a vehicle follow difficult, especially if the target driver was surveillance conscious. Unless Quinn had been lucky over the years, the chances were that he was one of the slipperiest of customers to ever draw breath. There was little doubt that his eyes would be more interested in what was going on behind than even the road ahead.

It meant that constant "eyeball" changes needed to be made. Any following traffic had to present as nothing more than a casual everyday interchange of different shapes and lights. Quinn's rear-view mirror needed to show him nothing more peculiar than a handful of disinterested individuals doing their everyday thing. Other gimmicks included swapping from sidelights to headlights and even occasional main beam when a car switch was initiated. The commentary painted a picture of a non-stop stream of ingenious trickery and gave confidence that Quinn had not got a clue he was being tailed.

Forrest pulled into the *Bottom Knocker*'s car park and steered the car to an unlit area at the far end. He switched off the motor, sat back into his seat and turned to Brenan's greyed-out shadow.

'She's in the bloody garage,' Brenan muttered. '*That's* where he's keeping her or that's the access to it.'

Forrest's silhouette seemed to contain only half-hearted agreement with the theory. He grabbed his still lit-up phone to continue the conversation with Hawkins. 'Right…' He stretched the word out to add thinking time. 'We need to look in there while he's away. You've got the code, so you can open and close the door?'

'Yes,' Hawkins said. 'All we've got to do is point and press. It'll work easy from here.' Hawkins' intake of breath and corresponding sigh were both easily picked up by Forrest's phone. It was clear the sergeant had something serious to add. 'The follow's going well,' he started. 'But, by my reckoning, he could well be heading for the red-light area.'

'Shit!' was Forrest's single word. This was the last thing they needed.

'Exactly,' Hawkins said. 'We absolutely cannot take the risk of allowing him to pick up a prostitute. If he does, and she gets killed, it will literally be *shit*-street and the sack for everybody.'

Forrest's long exasperated sigh into the mobile gave notice to Hawkins of his increasing frustration.

'If it comes to that,' Hawkins went on, 'we'll *have* to nick him and that'll mean blowing the whole job.'

Forrest caught Brenan's outline easing forward. There was a *clunk* as her seatbelt unfastened. 'What're you doing?' he said, as the next *clunk* came from her opening passenger door. He'd worked out what she was up to. He grabbed her right arm and pulled her back. 'I said, what the fuck are you doing?' Forrest's still-illuminated mobile tumbled down onto the floor mat.

'You're hurting me,' Brenan hissed, trying to pull her arm free. 'I'm going in. I'm going into that frigging garage. If she's there, it doesn't matter if we have to blow the job. We can nick him anyway.'

Hawkins' voice, still on loudspeaker, yelled from the mobile: 'Hello! Hello, boss! You still there?'

'And what if she's not in the garage?' Forrest was yelling himself now. 'What if she's somewhere else? Somewhere we don't know about. Just wait! Give me a second; let me think. There may be something we can do.'

Brenan's taut muscles slackened. She relaxed back into her seat and tugged the door back into place. Forrest released his grip and bent forward to pick up his phone. His cheek brushed hers as he did so. 'Sorry,' he apologised, eyes not daring to meet hers as she slowly rubbed the affected limb.

Hawkins' voice came on Forrest's mobile again. 'You still there, boss?'

'Yes, still here,' Forrest said, struggling to find his usual calm tone. 'Here's what I want you to do. Keep the follow going. Tell the team not to let the bastard out of their sight for one second. Get on to the nick. Phone them. Tell them to do whatever it takes to get a couple of uniform cars down into the red-light area – Trafalgar Road, Decade Avenue. The controller will know all the working girl's hangouts. See if he can detail a couple of PCSOs or a real beat bobby into the area. You'll have to give them the vehicle details, but ensure no one approaches it or lets the driver know they're interested in him. We need to make it look as though we're blitzing the area with patrols for the prostitution problem like we sometimes do when we get a lot of complaints. We want to make life so difficult for him that he goes back home thankful he's not been clocked. Make sure the surveillance team are *au fait* with the idea and keep the commentary running. We could save the operation yet.' Forrest left a five second pause. 'If a girl gets in with him, we'll have to pull the plug – we'll have to nick him. Ring me back as soon as you have an update.'

Forrest turned back to Brenan. She was still rubbing her right forearm. He gently placed his hand on the spot. 'Sorry, but you're so bloody impetuous. I'm as keen to get Poppy back as you are.'

Brenan shook her head. Despair, tension, hype, stress, fear and emotion were all swirling inside her mind, and she knew for sure that Forrest was going through the same thing. 'It's okay,' she said. 'Didn't really hurt anyway.'

Forrest gave a short but exasperated sigh at Brenan's remark. They could both hear the ROCU surveillance commentary constantly updating through their earpieces. It was clear from the familiar road names that Quinn really was homing in on the red-light area.

Forrest closed his eyes, making the darkness darker. 'Look, we're still unsure about the other two people at the bungalow. We've not seen hide nor hair of them. We can't even be sure if they're in there or not. I agree that this is our best chance for a sneaky look in the garage but I'm coming too.'

'No, Dom… Sorry… boss. You're needed out here on top of the situation and, apart from that, I'm betting that, if she is in there, the last thing that's going calm her nerves is some big, hulking strange man appearing from the shadows. I've got my surveillance radio. I can update you. I can call for help if needed. She's either in there or she's not. It's dark. No security lights. Door up, in, door down. Two minutes and out.'

Forrest stroked his stubbly chin and looked over to where the lights from the pub showed the last of the football fans heading for home. 'Hmm, big, hulking strange man, eh? Okay, Eve, go for it. I'll update Hawkins.'

Chapter 53

IT WAS QUARTER to eleven by the time Brenan completed the four-minute walk from the pub car park and down Evesham Gardens to the front of number ten. The street itself was quiet at the best of times. It was not that late, but she was confident she had not alerted any nosy neighbours. She even managed a small, but tension-relieving snigger at Forrest's "strange hulking man" response.

'Yes, got her on camera now,' Hawkins' voice informed from Forrest's mobile. The DS had sounded a bit worried about the idea, tetchy even. The suggestion of Brenan going in at all, never mind on her own, sounded dodgy. Hawkins' tetchiness came even with Forrest's much senior rank. The surveillance part of this operation was, after all, ROCU's province. Hawkins nevertheless went on to agree that it might be a chance not to be missed. Quinn was still two miles away and being watched closely. The other two supposed occupants had not even been seen yet.

Forrest closed the call down and sat back to listen in to the surveillance commentary on his Jabra. Hawkins had arranged two separate channels. One covered the vehicle surveillance and the other would be for Brenan's *ad hoc* garage recce. It was a simple matter for anyone to switch channels should they need to.

'Pickles to Base on channel seven, signing in.' Brenan's voice came through in Forrest's ear. He'd opted to pay close attention to Brenan's channel for the moment.

'Okay, Base back,' Hawkins responded. 'Let me know when you want the door up. I can stop it as soon as you've got enough clearance to duck inside, and put it back down until you're ready to come out. Remember, no big light. It could show between door and concrete. So torch only and, again, not until the door is right down.'

'Pickles back. Understood. There are no lights on in the bungalow. I'm going to take a quick shufti in the bin first and see what he's dumped in there. Pickles over.'

Hawkins tutted at Brenan's update. She'd only been switched on ten seconds and was going off-piste already. He watched on the monitor screen as she disappeared down the path between bungalow and garage. Her black outline then materialised on the other monitor from the care home.

Brenan's careful and silent tip-toe steps took her past the kitchen door on her right and then past the garage side door on her left. The wheelie bin stood against the corner of the bungalow. She silently tugged the handle, satisfying herself that there was hardly any weight to its contents. Ever cautious that a sudden light could alert someone she decided to make do with second best. With her phone's camera set to "flash" she opened the bin's lid enough to slip her hand inside and snapped off several random photos. The semi-shut lid kept all but a glimmer of the photo flashes successfully hidden.

She was back at the front of the bungalow within a minute and hidden between the corner of the big van and the edge of the garage, contemplating the situation. Quinn had left sufficient space to raise the garage door with his remote fob as he came down the street. It would allow him to drive the smaller van straight back in and close the door behind himself.

Back in the beer cellar, Hawkins monitored both radio channels whilst the other two operatives kept eyes glued on the video monitors. Makeshift screen hoods had been created from old pub promotional posters to shield the glow from anyone in the car park.

The surveillance commentary was beginning to sound worrying.

'Growler… Still with the eyeball and not happy. He's kerb-crawling. Paying a lot of attention to single females. Still on Trafalgar Road. He's slowing… stopping… No, he's on the move again! He's taken a left, left, left into Duckham Road. Need to swap eyeball. I'm going straight on.

'Yep, Mongoose taking the eyeball, and left, left, left into Duckham Road. Only one hundred yards separation and no covering vehicles between. Very dodgy – don't like it. Could get blown. Where the fuck are the cop cars?'

Brenan, unaware of the action, decided it was time. She took a deep breath. 'Pickles to Base. Door up.'

A muffled rumble began within a second of Brenan's command. The big door shuddered as its black, plastic-coated aluminium slats began wrapping around the top tube to haul its weight upward. The additional muted creaking was only heard by Brenan.

'Base to Pickles, okay?'

'Pickles back. Yes, good. Just a bit more. Okay, door stop.'

Three feet had been enough for Brenan to duck into the unknown. It gave less chance for a nosy neighbour to spot anything. It was a good thing Quinn had disconnected the automatic light.

'Pickles back. Door down.'

Hawkins obeyed and Brenan stood watching as the gap between floor and door slowly diminished. The blackness of the windowless space became total as the last few inches of the world outside disappeared. A repetitive ticking from the motor's relay pulsed on for another fifteen seconds. Brenan stood unmoving, eyes useless, heartbeat thudding in her temples.

'Hello. Anybody here?' she finally managed, voice hardly more than a whisper, but loud enough to be heard. 'Poppy, I'm a police officer. I'm here to help.' Silence, just the sound of Brenan's flat shoes against the gritty hard floor as she shifted her weight from one foot to the other.

She fumbled her mobile from a pocket, cursing herself for not getting the torch app ready beforehand. Her index-finger homed in on the icon. Despite its brilliant white glare the single LED bulb's effectiveness was only half good. The perfect circle of light changed the blackness to a shadowy gloom, animating all manner of peculiar shapes and outlines as she shone around.

The immediate disappointment at not picking out any evidence to suggest Poppy was, or ever had been in there brought a long sigh from Brenan. She shuffled forward, taking in what detail was on offer. Oil patches stained the floor. Wooden planks were piled against a wall, along with builder's scaffolding poles and clamps. A battered electric concrete mixer took up a corner. A heavy industrial

Kango jack hammer and transformer lay beneath a maze of cabling. *All nicked*, was the thought that came to mind.

A sudden thump from a corner jolted Brenan like a coiled spring into a one-footed, phone-held-out-in-front swivel. It was as though the phone were a gun and in that second she'd wished it had been. The glare lit up a waist high, six feet long rusting monolith of a chest freezer. The thump had been followed by the subdued metallic jangling of the machine's compressor.

'God above,' Brenan sighed to herself, chest pounding.

'Base to Pickles. You okay? Did you say something?'

'Pickles back. No, all okay, but not looking good in here. No secrets so far. No hidden doorways. No steps going down, just a load of knocked-off gear. I'm going to have a good look through.'

'Base to Pickles. Okay, and I don't need to mention the importance of not disturbing anything. I've got more commentary coming through in my other ear. I'll get back to you.'

In the beer cellar, Hawkins seated at the broken pub table he'd commandeered as a desk, took in the latest ROCU commentary.

'Pedlar with the eyeball. Not good. He's stop, stop, stop and window-down. Chatting with three working girls. Uh-oh. One of them is going around to the passenger side. It's looking like end of… No! Hang on! Here comes the cavalry – a cop car. It's worked. It's spooked him, *And* it's an off, off, off, heading down Duckham Road. Wings can you take the eyeball.'

In Quinn's garage, Brenan felt a little more at ease now. She was confident she'd get a good early warning if Quinn did start back. Her brainwave to video the inside of the garage with her phone was something she could have kicked herself for not thinking of before. She enabled the torch app to stay illuminated during the video and started to pan around.

Second hand power tools stood stacked on a bench, mostly dust covered. A couple of old model mountain bikes looked to have been untouched for years. There didn't seem to be much which had been stored recently. A cardboard box of books had been pushed under the bench. Brenan pointed the phone. Arnold Bennett's *Riceyman*

Steps lay on the top. 'Oh my God! Where are you Poppy?' Brenan barely breathed the words but, in the beer cellar, Hawkins picked it up – and so did Forrest in the gloom of his car.

'Okay, Pickles?' Hawkins voice came through on Brenan's Jabra.

'Yes, I'm okay.'

Hawkins gave the latest Quinn update. 'They're still following him, but there are quite a few uniforms about now and it's looking like he's been frightened off.'

'Pickles back. Thanks. Let me know if he starts heading for home. I'm not going to be much longer, over.'

Brenan continued to carefully work her way around the garage, pointing her phone at every corner and every patch of floor. Each wall, the ceiling and all the boxes and tools were videoed. She took particular attention with her shots of a two feet high plywood-sided reel of blue nylon rope.

She was finally confident that she had done what she could and was about to radio Hawkins to raise the door when the freezer's thermostat clicked its compressor off. The machine's slight clunk of power-unit against internal framework turned her attention back towards it. *Why had Quinn got such a large freezer?* He seemed more of a takeaway man, and certainly wasn't the type for entertaining or cooking. The low, low electricity bills didn't tally with this constantly-on, old, inefficient unit, either.

She wandered over, hand held out, video still running, light still shining, and took a closer look. Something wasn't right. The hairs on her neck started to prickle into life as she pointed the phone at the rust-pitted chrome handle jutting from the front of the lid. She gripped it with her free hand and gave an upward tug. It didn't want to open, but there was no lock mechanism. The resistance it offered was unyielding; the rubber seals had long since perished and iced it shut. Her racing thoughts flashed back to how her first freezer used to do this in the days when you had to defrost them every few months. This was different, though. This lid hadn't been lifted in years. It was frozen solid.

'Base to Pickles. Looks like target's on his way back. You'd better be getting out of there.'

Hawkins' voice was clear enough on Brenan's Jabra, but somehow the words didn't register in her mind. Her eyes and every shred of her consciousness were now fixed on that freezer handle.

'Base to Pickles. Respond please.'

Forrest was now out of his car and standing alone in the shadows, one hand pressing hard against his earpiece as he agonised over Brenan's failure to answer.

In the garage, Brenan placed her mobile down onto the concrete, its light shining upwards, its video churning ever onwards and amassing wasted memory megabytes of garage ceiling. Her two hands were now able to take a firm, ten-fingered grip on the freezer handle and pull. It took three tries before the ice gave way with crusty, scrunching *snap*.

The phone captured Brenan's ashen look and outstretching hand as she bent to recover it from the floor. A crystal-clear image of the freezer with its lid gaping by three inches started to embed itself on the phone's memory card as Brenan moved up closer.

'Base to Pickles. Respond immediately or we'll raise the door and come to get you. He's heading back and you're running out of time.'

'Fucking wait, will you?' Brenan's voice stammered back, all concepts of radio etiquette consigned to the bin.

'One minute, Pickles, and that door goes up.' Hawkins voice was severe.

The image on Brenan's phone jogged in and out of focus as it recorded her right hand pushing the lid completely backwards. The picture then hovered, noticeably trembling, as it pointed down into the freezer and captured a nightmare.

Chapter 54

BRENAN'S MASSIVE INTAKE of breath created a hollow, uncontrolled moan from the back of her throat. The small, stifled sound broadcast such terror across the airwaves that the eyes of the two men who heard it widened like saucers.

Forrest was already running.

Hawkins was on his feet, nose pressed against window, mind battling to comprehend a scenario capable of prompting such horror.

Brenan staggered back a pace as vomit churned in her stomach and threatened to claw its way upward. The corpse's solid permafrost face looked to have been chiselled from a block of Carrara marble. A clutching frozen hand had morphed over time with the shoulder it rested against. No visible lines of separation remained but an opaque glimmer of red nail polish was somewhere beneath the sparkling surface.

'Door up! Door up! Door up!' Brenan's pitiful plea was already being answered. Hawkins had pressed the button and the outside world was beginning to appear.

Hawkins' voice came back in Brenan's ear. He didn't need any more clues to know that something awful had happened, but had to make sure Brenan stayed in professional mode. They couldn't afford to lose everything through a small mistake. 'Okay, Pickles! We know something bad has happened, but make sure you're leaving it as you found it. You've got about two minutes max.'

Brenan gulped down a mouthful of sick and forced herself into robot mode. She took on another huge breath, stepped over and slammed the freezer lid back shut. She snatched one last look back inside, thankful she'd managed to hold onto her stomach contents, switched off her phone video, ducked under the door and stepped back into the real world.

'Door down, door down, door *bloody* down!'

Forrest met Brenan at the end of Evesham Gardens. He'd slowed to a walk when he spotted her distant figure. She was head down, hands deep in jacket pockets and shivering as though she was cold. He put his arm around her shoulder and held her in tight as they made their way back to the car. Her breaths were short, disjointed, staccato, as though she'd lost control of her diaphragm – more like sobs, but without tears.

Quinn's van passed them as they stepped into the shadows of the pub car park. Forrest's earpiece gave notice that the surveillance was finished and the target "housed". The distant gear changes of an unseen vehicle heading away was more than likely the last "eyeball" of the day heading for his or her guest house or Premier Inn.

Stanier and Scott were parked up alongside Forrest's Skoda and had already received something of an update from Hawkins. Scott jumped out and rushed over to Brenan to put another consoling arm around her shoulder. She added a few quiet words of comfort, but Brenan managed nothing more than constant head shakes in reply.

Forrest knew only too well that a full debrief of Brenan was vital. He and the rest of the team needed to know exactly what she'd stumbled across in the garage. He could also see that she was teetering on the edge of a nervous breakdown. He'd seen it before in cops; been close to it himself even, especially when work had shattered his marriage. He'd always thought Brenan was impervious to stress and mental torture. She was a real hard nut, an unreadable one. He stood and watched from the other side of his car as Scott did a good job – sensible, compassionate, but not over the top. Brenan's shoulders were relaxed now and she'd lifted her head, but still not said a word since that "Door Down" radio shout. He looked at his watch: 11:45 p.m. He opted for the most usual and effective CID therapy. 'Pint?'

John Eardley didn't even flinch at Forrest's telephone appeal. 'Course you can, no problem. I've just seen the last of the staff out and shut up shop anyway. I'm all on my lonesome. Come to the side door.'

Forrest had invited DS Barry Hawkins along too. As the

surveillance team boss, he needed to know as much as possible. The ROCU team had all done a great job, but it was better for Brenan that the gathering should be confined to a small group.

Eardley had sussed out that there was a problem from the urgency in Forrest's voice. He led the way through to the minimally-lit empty pub lounge and quickly picked up on Brenan's agonised look. She barely managed eye contact, never mind her usual grin.

Forrest was happy to have Eardley in on the latest facts – the retired detective's knowledge and experience might even help. Evidently, it was going to be some time before the conversation got down to the nitty-gritty, though. Brenan plonked herself down into a chair and sat, elbows on table, head buried in hands. Eardley slid a tumbler of Johnnie Walker Black Label over to her; everyone else was on pints. Brenan sighed and dipped her head in thanks at Eardley. She reached down for her handbag and delved in one-handed for her phone. After a few finger-presses, she started the garage video rolling. It was the first the others even knew about its existence. She handed it to Forrest, stood up with her glass and wandered through into the equally empty and even darker bar room.

The others positioned chairs around Forrest and watched in silence. The mounting tension when the freezer loomed from the shadows upped heart rates. It also hinted that things were about to get much worse. A gasp went around the table as the woman's frozen features filled the screen. It came in sync with the recording of Brenan's gulp of terror, her own silent scream.

Scott's ashen pallor took on a luminescent glow in the dimly-lit room. This was all new to her. She'd never seen a dead body before this case and now images were cropping up every day. Forrest realised she was struggling. 'Go see how Eve's doing, Mad.'

Scott went through and found Brenan sitting on a red leather bench seat and staring up at the ceiling. 'You okay?' Scott asked, as she shuffled in next to her.'

Brenan nodded twice. 'Will be, yes.' She looked down at her glass. 'Could manage another.'

Scott picked up the glass and stood. Brenan took hold of her wrist. 'Is it her? Do you think it's Poppy?'

'It might be, Eve. John suggests putting it up on his big TV for more detail. I don't think I can watch it again.'

Brenan got to her feet. 'You need to – and so do I.'

The others looked up, surprised to see the pair back so quickly. Brenan took her phone back from Forrest, touching at the screen to turn on *wireless projection* whilst Eardley used his TV remote to turn the on the wall-mounted set and enable *screen mirroring*. In no time, Brenan's video was coming through in fifty-inch HD as the group sat staring, arms folded. Scott took a couple of deep breaths and prepared herself.

Forrest snatched a quick look at Brenan as the film approached its horrifying closing stages. Her gritted teeth and unblinking stare showed the mettle of the woman. She'd been to hell and now she was clawing her way back.

The most horrifying frames of the recording arrived with the trembling representation on screen of the woman's crystalline sparkling face.

'Just a minute,' John Eardley said, hands gripping at seat armrests and easing forward. 'Go back! Go back a few seconds and then pause.'

Brenan handed her phone to Forrest. 'You do it, boss. My fingers won't do as I tell them.'

Forrest dragged the video progress bar back a tad and pressed *Play*. The TV screen mirrored the phone's output. 'Stop!' Eardley said as the marbled features took over almost half of the large screen.

Eardley was on his feet now, touching the television. 'See! Another face – a man! There's a bloke in there with her.'

A gasp went around the room as the outline of a second frozen head was made out in the depths beneath the woman's body.

Several seconds elapsed before the phrase "Oh my God!" was uttered as one by the entire group.

Forrest looked around at Brenan. 'Eve, that's not Poppy. I think that's Quinn's mother and her boyfriend. That's why we've not seen them. Looks like they've been in there years.'

Chapter 55

Day 24 Wednesday 8th May

THE ENTIRE TEAM piled into the MIR for next morning's briefing. The ROCU sergeant, Barry Hawkins, had come along too and squeezed in alongside Ed Stanier. Brenan's garage film took priority. It would be scrutinised later in detail by experts but this interim showing was the best way of getting the full message home. The shockwave it created was palpable – two more bodies and such horrendous circumstances. These were all experienced detectives but this enquiry had entered a league of its own. Several corner-of-the-eye glances at Brenan were stolen and much private self-analysis got people wondering how they would have coped.

The facial features of the "Ice Maiden", as she'd already been nicknamed, were receiving frame by frame attention. It was impossible to make any considered opinion but there was now no doubting that the female was a person much older than the twenty-five years that Poppy would be. It had also become apparent in a couple of frames, that a blurred inch or so of something blue could be made out in the region of the neck. This particular shade seemed to match that of the nylon rope which had made so many appearances throughout the case. Whether or not the body was Quinn's mother could never be proven until a forensic examination took place.

The features of the male occupant of the freezer were more difficult to gauge and too distorted even for the driving licence photo of Desmond Milner to be of any help. Teams had been working flat out on the background and whereabouts of Maisie Quinn and Desmond Milner since their names first cropped up. What had been discovered added more certainty that it was indeed them.

The bespectacled, praying mantis figure of the ROCU finance

investigator, Detective Sergeant Ron Bickton, got to his feet to say his piece. 'Jeremy Quinn,' he started. 'Receives £74.35 per week Job Seeker's Allowance which goes into a bank account in his name. That is with Barclays in town. He has a debit card on that account and uses it a few times each week.'

Bickton pressed a finger against his tongue to assist with page turning and continued. 'His mother, Maisie, receives £110.55 per week in respect of Employment and Support Allowance, and her money goes into a joint account which she holds with her partner, Desmond Milner. That account is with the NatWest, also in town. Maisie receives some additional benefits which I've yet to calculate and these all go into that joint account.'

Another page was turned, allowing Bickton to give more. 'Milner is in receipt of a state pension of around six hundred quid a month and a private pension from his former job of around eighteen hundred a month. Again these go into his joint account with Maisie. Both Milner and Maisie have debit cards on that joint account. Maisie's card has not been used for over ten years. It's been reissued a few times but has never been used. Milner's card is used regularly, though. But, and it's a big but, I do not think Milner is alive. When Quinn paid for his McDonald's yesterday, the bank has been able to tell me that he did so using Milner's card. It seems likely that all the other use of Milner's card was actually by Quinn.'

An exhalation of breath went around the room as it was accepted that Maisie Quinn and Desmond Milner were both dead.

Bickton continued. 'The few direct debits that are running are all on Desmond and Maisie's joint account. That's energy bills, water bill and council tax. Vehicle road tax and insurance on the big van also come from that account. There's a phone line with Vodafone but it never makes or receives any calls at all. It's used solely for very limited Internet use.'

'Can we tell what that use is?' a voice asked.

'Sadly, no. I'm afraid in the real world, and unlike the TV programmes suggest, we can't. All I can say is that it is limited, so much so that it is possible that the user has had their wings considerably clipped. I can't confirm this, but it's possible that something called "whitelisting" may have been used. It would restrict access to anything other than a handful of sites. It could be a way of stopping the user from making contact with the outside world.'

Brenan felt her stomach churn as more details of Kobe's vice-like grip on Poppy emerged.

'Now,' Bickton continued. 'We've only been investigating Jeremy Quinn for a short while and from that know not much more than that he's a sex fiend and eats McDonald's.'

'Probably fit in here,' a voice muttered.

Bickton allowed himself a shake of the head at the remark and continued. 'Having scrutinised the accounts historically, I can add that he makes regular cash withdrawals on his own account from ATMs. The Milner/Quinn account has similar ATM withdrawals and no doubt these are down to Jeremy Quinn too. He averages two hundred and fifty to three hundred pounds per week which is usually withdrawn on a Friday morning. He's not using that all on prostitutes and the general consensus is that it's for his weekly shop – all paid in cash with no trace back to him, and no clues as to what he's buying!'

Forrest gave a thumbs-up to the detective for his information. 'Thanks, Ron, and heaven forbid this all continues until Friday to check that out.' He homed in on another face. 'Our resident CCTV/Video and vehicles expert, DC Tom Finlay, has some update for us on the van Quinn was using last night. This is the smaller white van.'

Finlay gave a sardonic smile as he willingly accepted that he was now also "a vehicles expert" and began to read from his notes. 'The vehicle was filmed by ROCU during the surveillance and is identified as a white Ford Transit Connect van. I'm confident from the various different angles and shots we have that it's a first-generation model and, from the rear light cluster, a model issued before the 2009 facelift. There's a small dent noticeable on the nearside top corner and after another look at the bookshop burglary video, which is pretty poor quality, that does seem to correspond. It's almost certainly the same vehicle. Last night it was bearing the registration plate NM07TLG. It is, of course, a ringer, but a carefully prepared one. The real NM07TLG fits to perfection everything about Quinn's van, right down to colour and possible year of production. That real one is also taxed, MOT'd and insured and lives with its legitimate owner in Shrewsbury.'

Finlay now brought up Brenan's McDonald's video. It gave the team a good opportunity to see exactly what and who they were dealing with. He had another point to make. 'We've been looking closely at this. It captures some excellent footage of Quinn… Kobe.'

Finlay froze a particular frame of the video. It showed a full-length frontal image of the man. 'You'll see that he's wearing multi-pocketed combat style trousers. Take a look at the right-hand hip pocket. There's definitely something in there – more than a handkerchief.' Finlay jogged a couple of frames further and the audience watched as Quinn's stance twitched robot-style into a slightly different pose. 'See now,' Finlay's pointing stick was touching the screen alongside the pocket. 'Just a flicker of blue. Exactly the blue for the same rope again. It's too indistinct in this picture to be sure, but I'd have a fiver on it.'

The silence in the room demonstrated that Finlay's lecture was being treated with huge importance. But the detective was not finished. He had another even more cautionary note to add. 'Let's move on to a slightly better angle.' He skipped through a few seconds of the film to where Brenan's phone had caught Quinn lifting his head and setting Brenan with his x-ray stare. In doing so, he slightly shifted weight from one foot to another. Finlay paused the shot and touched his pointer, this time at Quinn's right leg. 'Now, if you look lower down you can see there's a flap-topped shin pocket. It's probably got a Velcro fastener by the look of it. The stitching outline shows it's a deep pocket and from the way it's hanging there's something heavy in there.' He deftly skipped the film a frame at a time and then back and forth. The liquid motion of the material flowed over the object allowing the imagination to suggest possibilities. 'Certainly something narrow and heavy and perhaps as much as ten inches.'

Finlay's narrative caused no surprise and it took less than a second before several voices harmonised one word: 'Knife.'

Forrest had already discussed the issues with Finlay and made an appreciative nod for the way he'd got the important messages over. 'We can see how careful Quinn has been over the years,' he added. 'Any PNC checks done on his van would, on the face of it, return a perfectly legit vehicle. We also know from prostitute Anna Albescu that he has other number plates in the van. No doubt these are swapped occasionally and probably also fit the vehicle's exact description. DC Stanier's enquiries into Desmond Milner have given us some serious food for thought. Did Quinn steal his shotgun? Was the shotgun ever really stolen? Or is it another red herring? So, be aware that there could well be a shotgun somewhere *and* it looks very much as though Quinn carries a knife.'

DS Hawkins mentioned that the night shift observer had been relieved by the day crew at nine o'clock. He'd confirmed there had been no movement overnight. His tale of a peculiar midnight occurrence, though, had been compared with the landlord's "haunted pub" stories. The story created some laughter and there was little doubt the ROCU detective in question would be wishing he'd never mentioned it.

Forrest grinned at the story, pleased it had lifted spirits slightly if only for a minute. He got back to the job in hand. 'Okay, Charlie,' he said to DC Sawyer. 'I believe you've come up with a few bits of interest in the line of your own new found expertise – basements, cellars and underground workings.'

'Hmm, well boss,' Charlie began, 'I am starting to discover some interesting puzzles about the site that the Birchfield is built on. I can't really call these "facts" as there's so little hard evidence. I am, after all, going back seventy years and more. I've previously discussed the existing underground structures that we know about. They're all in buildings erected when the estate was constructed in the fifties or later. These are all documented at the Planning Office and have *all* been physically checked out by me. The old Stoke-on-Trent planning archives still hold full architectural blueprints in the form of "hard drawings" for the original creation of the Birchfield and later Burrow Hill estates. It seems that the reason for lacking evidence of building work or earlier structures is down to the Germans. On 16th January 1941 a German bombing raid hit Stoke-on-Trent, demolishing a row of cottages at Etruria and several buildings in Hanley town centre. Many of the public records had been removed for safety to a building within Hanley Park. Bad move! This building was destroyed along with all the records. Nothing exists in relation to any historic buildings or developments for most of the Stoke-on-Trent area from before 1942.'

Sawyer relaxed back into his chair as he started to explain what he had managed to discover. 'Very certainly, back through the ages, much of the ground where the Birchfield Estate now sits would have been farming pasture. In the absence of any surviving records I've made a few discreet enquiries with some of the locals…'

'*In* some of the loçals,' a voice from the back suggested, bringing with it some laughter.

Sawyer gave the comedian a disdainful look. 'And, as I suspected,' he continued, 'there were several farm buildings in the area all from well before the Birchfield development in the fifties. In view of the lack of public records I've probed a bit more and spent a couple of days on Wikipedia research, along with an afternoon's library swotting. I came up with a couple of interesting historical articles. It transpires that, prior to and during the two wars, the land had been earmarked for a number of Government-backed projects. These included an aircraft parts factory. This was proposed in 1937 to work in tandem with a sister factory which did see completion alongside the then Meir Aerodrome three miles away. A local historian confirmed this, along with a story which existed – more as a myth than reality – that the Government also proposed a military use for the land when the Cold War was hotting up. They were looking at it to build a nuclear bunker as a regional seat of Government. Apparently, the building on that site never got past planning and surveying stages and was eventually built at an existing military site at Hack Green near Nantwich – the Secret Bunker, as it's now known, a tourist site.'

Forrest gave Sawyer a wide-eyed look as if encouraging him to embellish upon what he'd discovered. The fact was that the interesting summary had still not established the presence of any unrecorded below-ground structures.

Sawyer lifted his shoulders. 'I can't make stuff up, boss,' Sawyer responded to Forrest's expression. 'But I have tracked down one of the few remaining builders who worked on the construction of the estate in the early fifties. He's eighty-three now and I'm seeing him this morning.'

'Okay, Charlie, good work. Let me know as soon as you get anything more.'

Chapter 56

A HUDDLE DEVELOPED around Brenan's desk as the last of the outside teams left. The wheelie bin photos had now been transferred from her phone and printed off.

Forrest called DS Hawkins over. 'This could be interesting to the surveillance team.'

The three A4-sized pictures all showed the bin's grey plastic inner sides brightly lit by the camera's flash. Almost three quarters full, the topmost rubbish consisted of McDonald's cartons, paper cups, lids, brown paper bags and food remnants. The most recent was likely from Quinn's outing the day before.

'DNA?' Brenan said, and gave Forrest a stare. 'Wish I'd grabbed some of this yesterday. We really do need to get the contents of that bin.'

'Agreed,' Forrest turned back to Hawkins. 'If his extra McDonald's purchases were for someone else –as in Poppy – then there's got to be a chance of DNA on that rubbish. A test could hit the jackpot and prove conclusively that she's still alive and actually there somewhere.'

Hawkins agreed. 'We're going to have to pick the best time, though. We can never be sure we're safe while he's in, even at night.'

'It's bloody odd how he came from the garage,' Brenan said. 'The video was a distant shot of him lifting the bin lid, but if we can get Poppy's DNA off anything in that bin…' She turned to Stanier. 'Ed, get on to the council and find out when the bins get emptied for Evesham Gardens.'

The task took Stanier two minutes. He turned back, phone still in hand, 'Bins get emptied tomorrow, any time from half seven onwards.'

'Well, that gives us a bit of breathing space,' Forrest said. 'I'm going to have to give Mary Blackstone a call. She's been asking if they can get back to London now they've identified Kobe's DNA. We could do with her hanging fire for another day at least.'

Brenan agreed. 'What's really bugging me, though, is what was he doing in the garage for nearly an hour before he went out trying to get himself a prostitute? I've been in that garage. In the dark, yes, but I did video it and I've been through the film more times than enough now. There's no sign of other rooms or even access and certainly no signs of habitation.'

'Our vehicle man suggests the possibility that he was changing the number plates over.' Forrest said. 'We know how careful he is about that sort of thing.'

'Surely,' Brenan said, 'that's a fifteen-minute job, tops.'

'Agreed,' Forrest said. 'It's weird.'

It was Hawkins' own idea to collect a quantity of McDonald's rubbish to substitute in place of what they might remove from Quinn's bin. 'Just in case he happens to chuck something else away and gets suspicious. Best safe than sorry.' He said his goodbyes and set off back to the *Bottom Knocker*'s beer cellar with the promise of an early update if anything was happening.

Forrest didn't have to wait long. It was shortly after eleven when Hawkins made the call. 'Target's on the move, boss. He's in the big yellow van and we've got a follow going on. Could be McDonald's again.'

'Okay, Barry. We'll leave him in your capable hands, but shout up if you do need anything. What do you think about the wheelie bin? Is it a good time now, while he's out? I'm gathering he's not pushed it out to the pavement for tomorrow's collection yet.'

'It was on my mind too, boss. It's still in place right out of sight down by the back door. If he puts it out for tonight's collection, it'll be right out on the pavement, so now might be a better option. I was thinking of sending one of the lads in BT overalls down the path and quickly grab some of the bits and pieces more likely to have DNA on them. I've managed to snaffle a good bag of similar crap from the McDonald's on Victoria Road. Got a few funny looks, but hey ho!'

'Thanks, Barry, and, yes, go for it. Let me know.'

It was twenty-five minutes before midday when Charlie Sawyer bowled into the MIR, hot meat and potato pie in brown paper bag ready for an early lunch as soon as the moment presented itself. Forrest spotted him pass his office doorway and followed him in. Charlie set about putting the office kettle on for a brew as he started with his update.

'Interesting chat with my latest gem of a witness, sir,' Charlie began.

'The builder?' Forrest said, as he pulled out a chair and settled to listen.

'Yes. As I said, he's eighty-three – eighty-four next month – but sharp as a knife. He did well out of the building trade and went on to own his own large building firm. He lives with his son's family in a big place just up the road at Endon.'

Brenan and Stanier repositioned their seats to hear Charlie's tale, whilst Scott gathered some cups together.

'His name is Cyril Clewlow. He was sixteen when he started as an apprentice bricklayer. Now, that was with a local firm who had one of the contracts for the Birchfield estate. His first seven years from 1952 were spent working on that project. He learned his new trade as he went along and saw first-hand what problems were involved and how they were dealt with. He recalls that there were quite a few old farm buildings that had to be demolished. The remains of some ancient pottery works were also discovered. The whole area was littered with stuff like that and his bosses turned a blind eye to it as much as possible. They didn't want the archaeologists putting a stop to progress. What is interesting is that they encountered several more recently constructed foundations. A number of huge concrete platforms, metres down, held work up for weeks. These were too massive to break up or remove, so architects had to revise some of their plans. A few entire streets had to be relocated or shortened. Some of his older colleagues had actually worked on these structures before the Second World War. It was part of the shelved aircraft factory I spoke about. No planning documents recording any of this had survived the wartime bomb destruction. Cyril believes that the actual completion of this second factory failed because of the uncertainty surrounding the Meir Aerodrome and because of the looming war. Meir Aerodrome closed in 1952 – around the time they started on the Birchfield.'

'So what's your theory, Charlie?' Brenan asked.

'Well, from what Cyril has told me, there certainly were basements or underground areas incorporated with the foundations for the factory. He's actually been inside one that they discovered where it was possible to excavate down a side. He said it was massive… big enough for three or four cars and dry as a bone. His boss told the team to keep their mouths shut and fill it back in. The costs would have gone through the roof and the firm he was with were likely to lose out.'

PC Milton had listened to Sawyer's information. He got up from his chair and wandered over. 'Interesting, Charlie. I've mentioned before that I was still working the estate at the time the Birchfield Lodge care home was built. Absolutely loads of building materials were stolen from the site right from when they first started on it. I seemed to be visiting every week over the thefts. It meant I got to chat with the foreman quite often. I can certainly confirm some of your story in more ways than one. The plans for the care home had to be altered too. They discovered a metres-thick, unlisted brick foundation. It was going to skyrocket the total spend to break it up. It was easier and cheaper to move the whole plan back three metres.'

Forrest sat in the nearest chair. 'Thanks, Frank, that's good.' He looked over at Sawyer. 'Work with Frank on this, Charlie. See if there's any way, any way at all, to discover the footprint of this building.'

It was ten minutes past one when Forrest's mobile started to ring. The caller ID showed *DS Hawkins*. He snatched the device from his desk and answered. 'Yes, Barry.'

'Target's back home. Went in through the front door. He paid a visit to Aldi for a few groceries – cash in there – and then on to McDonald's. Same as before, he's eaten in himself and then taken another bag of food back home. Couldn't clock his order but a pretty bulging bag and he paid on a card like before.'

'What about the wheelie bin?'

'Yep, all sorted. Worked like a dream. Jed was able to offload quite an assortment of DNA possibles. He's got McDonald's paper cups, paper food wrappers, bags, some food remnants – looks like bits of bap, burger, flat bread. Some's pretty fresh, some's a few days old. He's topped it back up with similar garbage just in case the target pulls the lid up. It's all here waiting for you.'

'We're on our way,' Forrest said picking up his car keys and making for the door. Brenan wasn't waiting for an invitation, she was right behind him.

Brenan's phone pinged an email as the journey got underway 'From Western Power,' she said reading through. 'They supply all the electricity to the Stoke on Trent area. They've done a computer analysis in conjunction with EON, the power providers for 10 Evesham Gardens. They now confirm that there's an unaccounted-for drain on the power supply to the care home. He's somehow tapped into their wiring and with them being a substantial user it's gone unnoticed. He's probably been thieving the electricity since the place was built.'

'No surprise there then Forrest said as they arrived in the *Bottom Knocker*'s car park. A text to Hawkins allowed them unnoticed entry into the beer cellar by the delivery door.

Hawkins and two other ROCU detectives were there. 'Our ever-helpful landlord has even supplied us with a kettle and some brew making kit,' Hawkins explained. 'He's been great, actually, not half as bad as we'd been led to believe.'

'Hmm,' Brenan was not too sure. 'You managed the wheelie bin okay then?'

'Yep,' DC Jed Marshall said. He was pouring the tea and still decked out in a pair of BT overalls. 'It's all there.' He pointed to a black bin liner. 'No problems at all.'

'Good work,' Forrest said. 'We'll get this straight down to the university and see if our scientist can find anything.'

'Are you working late again tonight, boss? Chances are that the target will be out on his travels again, and if he does have another place maybe he'll be going there.'

'Yes, Barry, I'm not thinking of going home anytime soon.' He held up the bin liner. 'The results on this could well intensify things one way or the other.'

Hawkins struggled to hold a grin in check. 'I've got the *Ghostbuster*, DC Mark Singer, doing a twelve-hour night shift for us again tonight.' Hawkins grinned. 'I reckon he wishes he'd never mentioned that now. The team have had a laugh at his expense. They reckon the only spirits down here are in Nick Mazewski's bottles.'

Forrest and Stanier delivered the wheelie bin contents to Dr Blackstone at three o'clock and made it back to the MIR for half past.

Forrest took Brenan to one side to discuss their next moves. The surveillance and follows so far had done nothing to support the idea that Quinn was keeping Poppy anywhere other than at Evesham Gardens. They needed to decide how long they were going to let the observations run in this current limbo state. It was agreed that if and when a decision was made to arrest Quinn, it would be during a follow whilst he was away from the bungalow. It all added to the frustration and increasingly made Forrest feel as though he was treading water.

He'd been back in his office for some time when Hawkins telephoned with more updates on Quinn's peculiar visits to the garage. 'Thanks, Barry,' he said, as the call concluded and he gently replaced the receiver. In point of fact, he would have felt so much better if he could have smashed the phone with a lump hammer.

Forrest decided to wander back into the MIR rather than damage police property. He set his mind on running through the garage video yet again to see if they'd overlooked anything. Mary Blackstone's mobile call put the idea on hold. She wanted to discuss her latest findings face to face.

Forrest tipped Brenan the wink that some ground-breaking news must be afoot and quickly grabbed his car keys. It was only fair that Stanier and Scott should not miss out on this and the four piled in together.

It was quarter past five when they arrived. Blackstone stood looking from a window, mesmerised by road chaos down below. She turned, smiled a greeting and peeled off her gloves. Her attempt at a straight face soon cracked into a grin. She mouthed the word, "Wow!" before she even said anything.

She plonked herself down in front of a twenty-six-inch monitor. 'I've recovered full DNA profiles of four individuals from the items you delivered today.' She deftly fingered the keyboard as she spoke. 'That was no real surprise to me. Several people at McDonald's and possibly police surveillance agents could be expected to leave traces. It's this profile which I recovered from the lip of a paper drinking cup and again from a piece of cheese burger which is the one you're going to be interested in.'

The group leaned forward in unison as a string of characters appeared on Blackstone's screen. 'As I say, this profile was collected from a paper cup and also from a remnant of food. Now you'll see that the profile is made up of these sixteen pairs of numbers. They all correspond to the sixteen analysed areas of the donor and this makes up the searchable profile.' She looked back. 'You all with me?

'Preceding the pairs of numbers,' she continued, 'we have an XX sex chromosome…'

Scott couldn't help herself. 'A female.'

''S'right,' Blackstone agreed, and clicked her cursor to bring up another line of characters to sit parallel with the first one

The eyes of the detectives homed in on this new addition. 'This lower string of characters,' she said, 'you will see matches the top one exactly. It is identical.' Her pause was huge. 'It is taken from the MPDD. It *is* Poppy's.'

Brenan's legs had gone weak. She stumbled against Forrest for a second. 'Sorry! Sorry, boss.'

Forrest seemed lost for words for a few seconds – and then: 'You were right. You never lost faith – all of you. She *is* alive and now we've got to get her back!'

Chapter 57

'FOCUS, EVERYONE!' THEY were back in Forrest's car out in the car park of the University forensic facility. It was Forrest's voice which had broken the still-stunned silence. 'Focus!' he repeated. 'So, Poppy's alive and that's the best news we could wish for. Quinn's not visiting anywhere else. He's taken that food in there; he's put that rubbish in the bin. She simply has to be there somewhere. It may even mean locking him up on his next outing and going in half-cocked, hoping for the best.'

'Hoping for the best?' Brenan's question had some sarcasm attached to it. Her own rash thoughts about going in half-cocked the night before were in her mind, his calling her impetuous and grabbing her arm.

Forrest tried hard to keep his slightly hurt expression in check. 'Yes, maybe even hoping for the best.'

'Sorry,' Brenan murmured, hating herself for a moment.

In the rear seat, Stanier and Scott exchanged a sideways glance.

Forrest's mobile interrupted any more thoughts. It was Hawkins at the pub OP. 'You able to come over to us?' There was some urgency in his voice.

They pulled into the *Bottom Knocker*'s car park and covertly made it down into the cellar within fifteen minutes. Forrest kept the DNA results to himself, at least until Hawkins had explained whatever was important enough for this visit.

Hawkins introduced the group to the man standing next to him. 'This is DC Singer. He's our night duty observer, but he's come in early. Something's been bugging him.'

The detective started into his tale. He looked tired from his morning's failed attempt at a couple of hours' sleep. The penny had already dropped that this was the now infamous cop who claimed an encounter with Nick Mazewski's pub ghost.

‘Ah, DC Singer,’ Forrest said out of good manners, but with the thought in his mind that this was likely to be a waste of time. ‘Heard a lot about you.’ There was an element of derision in the remark.

Singer was used to police mickey-taking. It was part of the job and anyone could be a target. This time it had been him. ‘Yes, boss, I could have kept quiet about that, but it was particularly weird. So much so that you’d best know what happened.’

Forrest was puzzled. He looked at Brenan and her expression suggested she was none the wiser.

‘Well, boss,’ the man began, ‘I’m not one for the supernatural. Interesting, I’ll give you that, but I’ve always found there’s usually a reason, an explanation. So, anyway, I’m sitting here in the dark last night watching the screens and feeling pretty bored. I’d not long settled in. I could hear the landlord upstairs – the customers had gone and I guess he was clearing up. It’d be around midnight.’

Singer played along with the cynical response he was getting with a half-good try at a terrified face: wide eyes and a show of teeth ‘The witching hour had arrived!’ he said, before his expression slid back to “severe”. ‘I started hearing a sort of distant wailing sound. I couldn’t quite tune my ears into it as it was so faint. Obviously, I’ve heard about the landlord’s stories, but I knew I wasn’t imagining it. It set me up nicely for several hours down here on my own, I can tell you!’

Forrest held up his hand. He was getting annoyed. ‘I haven’t got time for this.’

Hawkins stepped forward, ‘Boss, I think you should hear this.’

Forrest gave a reluctant blink and Singer continued. ‘Now we all know what a bunch of piss-takers coppers are. If I’d mentioned ghostly noises and things going bump in the night without proof, I’d never have heard the last of it.’

The comment generated a little scornful laughter.

‘So,’ Singer continued. ‘I got to thinking about how to prove I wasn’t going crackers. I decided to try and record it.’ He pointed over at the silver flight case of ROCU hi-tech equipment. ‘The sound was so distant and intermittent that I struggled to position the microphone to pick it up. I felt my way around in the dark to establish where the noise was loudest. I'd only got the two TV monitors on low light, so it was pretty gloomy. I banged my shin on a beer keg but eventually decided on this...'

Singer stepped over and patted a hand down onto where a six inch, heavily painted, cast iron sewerage pipe fed down from the pub above and disappeared into the concrete floor. 'I wasn't too successful with recording at the start but, when I pressed the mic hard up against the pipe, I could see the waveform on the recorder's screen. It was clearly picking something up much better than my ears could ever do. I left it running until about three o'clock when it seemed to stop altogether. I burnt the recording to a disc and took it back to my hotel. I was knackered and didn't get chance to listen until after I'd tried for some sleep.'

Singer switched on. 'Listen to this.'

A hiss of white noise started to flow from the machine's speaker, a few clunks were picked up and the sound of a chair being dragged to one side. It was clear that this had been the start of the detective's search in the dark for the best spot. A dull thump came as another detectable sound, along with Singer's exasperated voice: "Bastard".

'That's when I banged my shin,' he explained. This brought some humour to what was, so far, a puzzling episode.

'Right, this is where I hold the mic right against the pipe,'

The background sounds faded out as faint nuances and indistinct resonances softly filtered through from some far-away place. The mocking humour was gone in an instant. Now each head assumed a cocked-to-one-side attitude, testing hearing to its limits. The frequency and pitch of the sound swayed back and forth before a more rapid staccato version gave the human ear a definite grip – something to guarantee that this was not imagination. A single, deep, reverberating echo, much louder and bolder than before started to penetrate through.

'It's music,' Scott suddenly said. 'It's an instrument.'

Hawkins nodded. 'Our thoughts too.'

Forrest's left hand momentarily touched Brenan's forearm. He was staring blankly at the wall. 'A cello?'

Chapter 58

FORREST IGNORED THE speed limits in their dash back to the MIR. Different tasks were still being debated as the four hurried up the police station's steps.

Stanier was straight into his job with a phone call to Poppy Hunt's old music teacher, the flamboyant and extrovert Miss Phoebe Halton.

Brenan only racked her brains for a few minutes before she arrived at a solution to her problem: where to get her hands on a couple of stethoscopes. Her prayers were answered by a call to the duty police surgeon, and the equipment arrived at the public enquiry desk downstairs within an hour and a half.

Phoebe Halton presented herself at the same desk – not far behind the stethoscopes – at eight fifteen, wearing jeans, white pumps, yellow T-shirt and with her brow knitted into a frown of extreme puzzlement. The full and no-punches-pulled update Stanier gave her quickly converted her frown into a bout of head shaking. 'My God, what a terrible story! Yes, I'll help in any way I can.'

It was now half past eight and Forrest was almost finished with an update to DCS Brown when his mobile came to life with a call from ROCU. 'Could be on the move soon, boss,' DS Hawkins said. 'Same as before, he's shifted the big van backwards and raised the garage door.'

Forrest switched on the surveillance radio pack and fumbled in a pocket for his earpiece. The surveillance radios had a limited range but he needed to listen to the follow if there was going to be one.

Hawkins gave more. 'Yes, the white Connect van is now out. Garage door's going down and it's an off, off, off.' His surveillance speak was coming through loud and clear on Forrest's mobile and in broken fashion on his earpiece.

'Base to the team. Important update. Same vehicle, different plates.' Hawkins then spelled out an entirely different registration number which was now showing on the van, before dedicating his voice to Forrest's mobile. 'You get that boss? He's switched plates again. I'm just getting PNC done.'

'Yes, I'm with it, Barry, and I'm listening in. We need another look inside the garage. Ed Stanier and Eve Brenan are on their way up to you. They'll be bringing Madeleine and another member of the public. She's fully briefed and may be able to help us. Unorthodox, I know, but needs must. Play it by ear and see if you can get Eve and Ed inside the garage while Quinn's on his rounds.'

Stanier pulled into the *Bottom Knocker*'s car park and within one minute he, Brenan, Scott and Halton were descending the beer cellar's steps. Hawkins couldn't help his customary circumspect police mind-set as yet another outsider joined the team. It was rare for members of the public to have such close access to intrusive police surveillance activities. This operation seemed to be doing exactly that on a very grand scale.

Scott took Halton over to where the sewerage pipe fed down the wall to the floor. They were both fully up to speed with DC Singer's peculiar story and knew what was required of them.

The pinnacle of strangeness arrived for DS Hawkins as the two women made themselves comfortable with beer kegs to sit on, before each fitted stethoscopes into their ears and hunched close to the pipe.

Hawkins looked bemused but got back to the job in hand. He quickly went through a plan with Stanier and Brenan on how to get them back into the garage unseen during Kobe's absence. 'You'll both need a Jabra, but one radio pack will suffice. If it looks like Kobe's on his way back, I'll give you an estimate on how long you've got. Inspector Brenan had a close call last time and we don't want that again.' He arched an eyebrow at Brenan. Her traumatic visit to the garage was still firmly on his mind. 'Are you okay with this, Inspector?'

Brenan returned a resolute nod.

It was approaching nine o'clock and, despite the lengthening days, the sun had set some time ago. The "No Lights" order for the cellar was imperative. Even the slightest breach could attract attention.

Miss Halton's profile somehow gave away her bewilderment. One moment she'd been at home sipping a gin and tonic and settling down for an evening's TV. Now she found herself at the heart of the most appalling set of circumstances in a pub cellar surrounded by police officers. It was, though, quite exciting.

A startling departure from the events came as the ceiling cellar flap opened and landlord Nick Mazewski appeared in all of his unsettling glory. 'Bloody hell!' his completely at odds voice shrilled. 'There's more down here than there are upstairs. Is it party time?'

Halton fixed Scott with an alarmed stare as Mazewski necessarily switched on a low wattage bulb. She now managed a more detailed look around at her new-found friends and surroundings. Mazewski got about his beer keg change-over, traded pleasantries, switched the light off and disappeared back upstairs.

'Well,' Halton said, as the cellar flap closed and returned the group to the gloom. 'There's plenty of booze down here. We could get pissed if things don't turn out well.'

Hawkins issued an elongated *shush* to quell the stifled laughter at Halton's joke. The noise needed to be kept right down. He tuned his hearing back into the vehicle follow and worked out that the team were again tailing Kobe in the red-light area. It was a possibility that had been foreseen and catered for. Two uniform patrols with a *heads-up* directive that their presence may be needed were already in the area. More diversionary tactics could soon be playing a part. The operation's cards-close-to-chest strategy, though, was no longer a priority. Poppy's life had always been their prime objective, and now the pressure was increasing.

Hawkins gave Brenan and Stanier the green light by way of a double thumbs-up. He'd calculated from the radio chatter that Kobe had been worried away from the red-light area by a police Incident Response Vehicle. He was heading further out of town, possibly to other hunting grounds and apparently unaware he was being tailed. 'Okay,' Hawkins reaffirmed, as the two detectives made their way up the steps. 'Channel seven and off you go. Let me know when you want the door up. Good luck.'

It was less than five minutes before Brenan's voice came through.

'Pickles to base. Door up.'

Hawkins did the necessary and the big roller shutter started to rumble upwards.

After a few seconds: 'Door stop.'

And then: 'Okay that'll do; we're inside. Door down.'

They had decent torches this time and a good quality camera. A meticulous video scan of the inside of the garage began, along with precise and easy measurements taken with a builder's laser tape.

Brenan threw her head back in a little show of resignation when Stanier gestured to the freezer. It had to come, but fortunately they both now knew what to expect. Brenan's upwards pull at the lid effortlessly did the trick. It would take months to freeze it so solidly again.

Stanier carefully filmed the gruesome contents taking particular care to zoom in on the two solid ice faces as Brenan shone the torch and quietly wished away those particular seconds of her life.

'I think we're all done now,' Stanier said, and switched off the camera.

Brenan grimaced as she pulled down the freezer's lid. She'd be glad to be out of here – again!

Something startled her, stopped her in her tracks. She swivelled back to Stanier. 'Shh!' Her eyeballs had lodged in their extreme left corners as her hearing sought to identify the nature and source of the noise picked up by her free ear.

Stanier was already motionless. He'd heard it too. It was only the total silence of that particular moment that had allowed such a vague and remote sound to be perceived. A sudden ROCU transmission on their Jabras and thump of the freezer's compressor coming to life killed any chance of hearing more. Brenan frantically ripped out her earpiece and stuffed it in a pocket. Stanier did likewise and then flashed his torch around the back of the freezer to find the mains switch. He needed to briefly silence the machine. His eyes landed on a wall mounted double power point inches away, but oddly both sockets were empty. His puzzlement grew as he took hold of the freezer's grubby cable which looped from the back panel. He ran it through his fingers down to where it snaked into a two-inch black hole in the concrete floor.

'Well that confirms the power supplier's email,' he said 'It's not plugged in here; it's drawing electricity from somewhere else beneath us.'

'Yes, all wired up the care home no doubt,' Brenan said as her torchlight hovered over the freezer's temperature control on the bottom edge of the unit.

There was no off switch, just a thermostat dial. Stanier knelt, took a good look at the setting and then turned the dial until the humming compressor clunked off leaving them back in total silence.

They both stood in the gloom arms by sides, torch beams lighting their shoes and listened wide-eyed.

'There!' Brenan said. 'Can you hear it?'

Not wanting to lose his fix on the oh-so-distant hint of sound or even have his hushed voice mask it, he merely gave three assertive and slow nods.

In the beer cellar, Phoebe Halton's trained musical ear had also picked up the same tenuous strains. Scott had set herself the job of putting some coffee together but quickly side-lined the idea when she realised Halton was on to something.

The music teacher's hitherto animated outline had taken on the stillness of a Greek statue. It was as though a wand had been waved. The subtle power of the stethoscope she held so tightly against the pipe permitted her to climb down into a well of resonances, hums and emotional echoes which, by some fluke, were being transmitted from another place.

The statue came slowly to life as Halton's silhouetted hand gently drifted in keeping with the haunting beauty of what she was hearing. Had there been even an extra glimmer of light, it may well have picked up the tears which trickled down her cheeks with the melancholy beauty of those distant far away tones.

She looked at Scott and directed her softly spoken voice. 'She's there! Poppy's there! It's so long since I heard her and so faint. She's come a long way…' Halton's voice tailed off as she comprehended the irony of her own sentence. 'She's playing something called Elegy. So haunting, so apt, so damned beautiful.'

In Kobe's garage, Brenan and Stanier battled to soak up more of the sound. Their circumstances denied them even the slightest of any audible definition, but they knew it was music, knew it was a cello. Stanier got down on all fours and pressed an ear close up to where the cable fed down through the hole. 'Seems a tad louder here,' he said, face illuminated by Brenan's torch.

Brenan suddenly left him to his own devices and began a frantic search through pockets for her earpiece. 'We've been out of touch for a while,' she hissed.

Hawkins' voice came through mid-sentence as soon as she pushed the Jabra back into place: "… Pickles, don't do this to me again… Don't know if you two are receiving or what, but that door is going up now."

"Pickles, back. Sorry, we got diverted. Is there a problem?"

The door had already started to rise.

"Problem, yes. Out now!"

Stanier was back on his feet. They both stared down at the growing gap. Stanier turned back into the garage. 'What is it?' Brenan said.

He darted back over to the freezer. 'I haven't reset the bloody stat.' He quickly swivelled the dial around to roughly the right setting and they dodged out into the fresh night air. Brenan's urgent radio transmission prompted the door into its rumbling downward journey before they'd left the driveway.

Chapter 59

'THE HEAT'S OFF.' Hawkins' voice came through as Brenan and Stanier neared the end of Evesham Gardens. 'He's been acting erratically. The boys in blue frightened him off from pick-ups a couple of times and it was looking like he was heading home, hence the panic, but he's set off elsewhere now.'

'You don't think he's sussed out that he's being tailed?' Brenan asked, when they arrived back in the cellar.

'Can't be sure. He carried out a classic "twice around the roundabout" manoeuvre. It's a trick used by top crooks to blow out a surveillance team. We always stick to the book – plenty of separation and at least one innocent punter between, so it didn't work but it was odd.'

'Where is he now?'

'In town. James Street multi-storey.'

'Difficult,' Brenan sympathised. She knew from experience of the complications a multi-storey could bring to a mobile surveillance. The eyeball was almost always temporarily lost with so many possible lefts or rights, multiple exits, different floors and the chance to slip away on foot. Attempts to tailgate and keep the eyeball would raise suspicion levels in the mind of a paranoid wrongdoer.

Brenan squinted over at Halton and Scott. Their two crouched outlines showed that they were now both plugged into the musical interlude and unaware of the unfolding drama. The occasional hushed comment between the two suggested an exchange of ideas.

Brenan switched her radio pack over to the surveillance channel, enabling her and Stanier an insight into both sides of the commentary.

A glimmer of headlamps on the car park, probably a pub customer, crept in through the slot of ceiling-high, barred windows. It flickered intermittently across Hawkins' face, revealing the worry etched into his forehead. Brenan listened with growing horror to the surveillance commentary.

'Growler to the team, still no eyeball. I'm on level one. Don't know if he went up or down. Get the exits covered and get a walker inside double quick. It's pretty empty in here. I'm parked and switched off, listening.'

'Wings to the team, got James Street exit covered.'

'Mongoose to the team, Bignall Street exit covered

'Pedlar to the team, on foot and inside now. No engine sounds to be heard. How about you, Growler?'

'Growler back. Nothing; no engine sounds. He must have parked. I'll drive to the top level. Pedlar, you do the lower ones.'

Hawkins was sitting, hands on knees and staring into the shadows as Brenan settled in alongside. He turned to her. 'Not good. Not good at all.'

'No tracker?' Brenan said.

'No. We got one on the big van last night. But this one's always been locked in the garage and, with him in the bungalow, it's been too risky to try opening the door.'

'Growler to thc team. No sign on upper levels.'

'Pedlar back. Likewise downstairs. Looks like he's driven straight through. We've bloody lost him.'

Brenan was already on her mobile to Forrest. 'Put out general obs for the van,' he snapped back. 'If he's picked a girl up, we're done for. I'm on my way to you.'

More commentary was coming through on the earpieces but a sudden sharp metallic *clunk* made Brenan and Hawkins swivel in their seats. Phoebe Halton was the culprit. She was holding a hammer she'd pillaged from Mazewski's tool box. She'd struck the cast iron pipe a hell of a whack for some reason and was now right-arm-back behind shoulder readying for another.

'What the hell?!' Brenan said, getting to her feet, voice louder than advisable. Hawkins' torch clicked on to illuminate the scene just as Halton crashed the hammer onto the pipe again. Halton punched out a flattened palm towards Brenan and ordered a loud 'Shhh!' She swivelled back to Scott. 'Well? Any good?'

'Yeah,' Scott nodded, stethoscope tubes waggling. Her left hand still held the device's diaphragm hard against the pipe. 'She's stopped mid-flow.'

Halton looked back at Brenan. 'We've sent her a message and she's heard it, but she'll not know for sure if it was really a message for her.'

Brenan instantly got the drift but wasn't too sure that the timing was right. 'Okay, but hold up on that for now. Things are happening.'

Hawkins was back on the radio. An update was coming in.

'Pedlar to base. We've got two working girls in an alley off Bignall Street. Apparently, this has been their pitch for a while now. It's cost us a few quid to get them to talk. They're saying that another girl, Sadie McVey, got into a white van that came out from the multi-storey ten minutes ago. The deal was a blow job and back on her pitch within a quarter of an hour.'

Hawkins faced back to Brenan. 'If he's picked up a girl and gone off for a casual blow job, then he doesn't know he was being tailed. He'd be panicking if he knew.'

Brenan agreed as she dashed for the stairs. 'Come on, Ed.'

With their Jabras still relaying the now frantic surveillance commentary they jogged across to Stanier's Audi A6 and were quickly off from the pub's car park.

The sharp flicker of blue lights and the distant blare of police two-tones grew brighter and louder as Stanier pressed the car up the steep incline of Kilnbank Road towards the town. Brenan grabbed Stanier's police radio from the floor-well and switched on. The chatter of several different units in a desperate search for Kobe's white van instantly spelled out to her that it was a futile quest. 'They've swamped the area already, Ed. He's gone. He was probably out of town before they'd even realised he'd left the car park.'

'Yes,' Stanier said. 'I'm betting he was using the multi-storey as a cut through. He knew exactly where he was going and where the prozzies would be.'

Brenan sat back in her seat. 'Pull over, Ed.'

Stanier did as he was told.

Brenan made a thoughtful face at him. 'A fifteen-minute blow job, eh?'

Stanier gave an exaggerated shake of the head. 'Sorry, boss, didn't know you cared.'

She ignored his joke and sat forward in her seat, eyes wide, as a piece of memory was recalled. 'That's what he said to Anna Albescu when he picked her up before he half murdered her. "A fifteen-minute blow job".'

Stanier was partially illuminated with the orange glow of a street lamp. 'It's not the smoothest of chat lines I'll give you that, but what's your point?'

'Park Hills, Ed.' Brenan was scrabbling one-handed in the car's glove box for Stanier's magnetic blue roof light as she spoke. 'Drive like your life depended on it.' She crooked an arm from the window and solidly fixed the already flashing unit in position as Stanier got stuck into a wheel-spinning three-point turn.

He drove as ordered, jumping two sets of red lights and a speed camera in a 60-mph dash east of the city. The surveillance radio equipment had a limited range and they weren't long into the manic journey before the commentary started to break up. Moments later, their Jabras fell silent. It did not take many minutes before Stanier was turning left from the main road and entering the semi-countryside region where lanes and tracks led off into the remote wooded area of Park Hills. Brenan hauled the roof beacon back inside and switched it off. 'Cool it now, Ed. Don't want to give the game away if the bastard is here.' There then began a slow cruise in the manner of a courting couple looking for a private spot.

Forrest was livid Quinn had been lost and was aware of the possible consequences. He hot-footed it from the MIR over to the *Bottom Knocker*, arriving in the beer cellar OP at the stroke of ten. The bungalow was the only location he could be sure of that Quinn would end up at. 'We need some better lighting down here now. Our secrecy campaign just took a back seat. Can't see us losing anything if we cover those windows as long as the camera can see out.'

Hawkins got to work on the windows with some of Mazewski's bar towels and, within a few minutes, one of the cellar's strip lights produced a better working environment. The ROCU's frantic surveillance commentary had now reduced to a few despondent messages. The last hopes of getting back on Quinn's tail would lie with a sighting of the van by the uniform branch.

As soon as he was up to date with the last sighting of Quinn, Forrest made a beeline for Halton and Scott. He'd been updated on his mobile about the possible hammer contact.

Halton explained what had happened.

'Yes,' Forrest said. 'It seems that the sounds have been heard by the pub landlord for quite a while now. But, without any kind of listening equipment, it was never even considered to be an instrument, let alone music. So you're absolutely sure?'

'Very. It's definitely live cello and, even taking into account the audible difficulties, I was able to pick up some nuances and style touches that were beginning to become part of Poppy's playing technique all those years ago. She was concentrating on a couple of different pieces, popular and classical.'

'So you're confident the banging on the pipe was heard?' Forrest asked.

Scott answered. 'No doubt at all, boss. She was playing that theme from the *Schindler's List* film.'

'I'd decided to try to make contact but it was played with such emotion...' Halton said, leaving a long pause. 'Such empathy. I could hardly bring myself to interrupt. I struck the pipe hard and she stopped immediately but after a few seconds started again, so I struck the pipe once more.'

'And?

'She stopped again. She hasn't started again since.'

At Park Hills, Brenan and Stanier completed one circuit of the more usual courting couple spots. 'Do you really think he'd be nutty enough to head out here?' Stanier said.

'Well, it's a big area and there are loads of secluded pull-ins and lanes. The main crime scene locus was all cut back by CSI, but they finished with it over a week ago. Quinn's certainly got a macabre affinity for it. Let's check out the exact spot – the crime scene locus. We'd better phone in as soon as we get chance. We've lost the surveillance commentary. For all we know they might have spotted him.'

After ten minutes of slowly driven narrow twisting track, the Audi's headlights picked out familiar large trees and swathes of recently scoured, strimmed earth. This was the place where, two weeks before, dense thickets of dog-rose and bramble had kept Georgia Esposito's bones hidden for so many years. Where Sarah Powell had been raped, where Anna Albescu had been half-murdered, and where who knows what else had happened.

The time was nearing half past ten. There seemed little doubt that the lack of any parked-up courting couple's cars in the area was down to the notoriety achieved with the discovery of Georgia's body.

Stanier's first-gear trundle gave him chance to delve into a door pocket for his telescopic baton. A Taser would have been handier but they were short on options. He slid the weapon into his inside pocket and brought the car to a stop right alongside the former crime scene. He switched out the lights and killed the motor. They didn't need a conference on their next move. They were both out, doors closed, standing, listening. There was no moon to help, and only the meekest of starlight reflected from the roof of the Audi which stood between them. Their outlines diminished even further as the car's interior light automatically faded out.

'Phones on silent, Ed.'

Chapter 60

AT THE BOTTOM KNOCKER, Nick Mazewski made an unannounced arrival down the steps from the bar's cellar flap. The now dimly-lit room allowed him to see all. He was stunned by the sea of different faces, the equipment and general activity. The presence of a lady doctor wearing a stethoscope puzzled him as much as anything. Forrest decided it was time the landlord was let into more of the real secret as the chances were looking likely that things would get even busier before the night was over.

Forrest's update left Mazewski holding a hand to his mouth in shock. 'Shall I put some chips on?' was his way of dealing with the matters. A rounded answer of, 'Yes, please,' saw Mazewski disappear back up the steps with a firm promise to clear the pub of stragglers and keep schtum on the issue.

Forrest turned back to Hawkins. 'What's happened to DI Brenan and DC Stanier, Barry? When did we last hear from them?'

Brenan and Stanier lingered, unmoving in the darkness, listening hard, eyes straining. Concentration peaked as their senses laboured to separate and discard nature's standard night time echoes, rustles and movements. After a couple of minutes Stanier's low voice came across car's roof. 'Shall we take another drive around? It's a big area.'

'No,' Brenan returned. 'The bastard's here somewhere.' She flinched as she finished the sentence. Stanier could only make out her outline. He couldn't see his partner's shoulder-high hand – that fingers-apart gesture, meaning: *wait, listen.* He didn't need to, though; he'd heard the sound too – distant and indistinct, but with a certain quality that made the hairs on the back of the neck start to prickle.

It came again and this time with enough inflection to separate imagination from reality, enough resonance to distinguish its human qualities, and enough emotion to scream the terror its choked echo wanted to scream.

A silhouetted copse ninety or more yards distant and near the top of a steadily rising incline was the spot that their senses pinpointed as the source of the sound. There was no definition, no detail, just black outlines of trees and bushes. Brenan dug into a pocket as they started jogging, hand fumbling for her phone.

They slowed to walking pace, hoping for another audible clue as Brenan's phone torch app abruptly bathed the immediate area in its piercing white LED light. Stanier pointed down at fresh tyre marks. Spinning wheels had recently cut through the surface turf. 'Gotta be this way!' He broke into a run.

The tiniest flicker of red gave the game away. Perhaps half an inch of vehicle rear reflector in the midst of bushes captured the torchlight and threw it back from over sixty yards. Another scream now: more resonance, more volume, more terror. The square outline of the van took on form and character. The white paintwork, both rear lights, the glaring yellow number plate all started to morph from a blur to becoming more defined with each step forward.

The van's two rear doors burst open and Quinn, alerted by the light, was out: trousers at knees, baseball-capped, startled, vicious face, wide-eyed – and holding a double-barrelled sawn-off shotgun.

'Police officers!' Brenan screamed, as they stumbled to a panting stop forty yards short, and wishing it was further. 'Put the gun down and walk slowly towards us!' She tried to keep her voice on an even keel. She needed to control the situation. She'd been in some tight corners before and this one was up there with the worst of them. Should she mention that they knew who he was? Maybe even that they knew about Poppy? Would it give them the upper hand or make this madman madder? She decided to test the water. 'Put the gun down on the ground and walk towards us,' she repeated. 'Don't make things worse. We need to attend to the girl in your van.'

'You fuckers are dead!' The shotgun's deafening roar came a nanosecond behind the orange football of flame which ballooned from one of its two muzzles. It lit Quinn's face long enough to illuminate the pockmarked snarl. The two seconds that followed were punctuated only by the blast's echo reverberating from an unseen black landscape.

Brenan was on the ground, right cheek pressed into the damp turf and trying to comprehend how her instinct had flung her away from danger before the trigger was pulled. Now her thoughts were on her partner. She whispered to her left: 'You okay, Ed?' Her eyes squinted through the gloom for Stanier, but he, too, must have dived for cover. She swivelled back and peered up the bank to keep a fix on Quinn's shadowy movements. His indistinct outline showed him one-handedly hoisting his trousers while sweeping the gun barrel left to right. There had been no attempt to replace the spent cartridge. He'd still got one shot left, though, and that could easily kill.

A few seconds went by as Brenan's mind raced through the possibilities, the probabilities and the options. Her phone had disappeared into the scrub somewhere. She couldn't see its light but, then again, neither could Quinn. It meant he couldn't be sure where they were. If he shot off his remaining round, he'd have to take the chance on reloading before they got to him. Brenan turned to her left again, puzzled at Stanier's failure to answer. 'Ed! ED!' she raised her voice as much as she dared. She was worried.

'Ed,' she called again. 'You okay?'

Stanier's voice was weak, barely audible. 'No, Eve… I'm hit. I'm bleeding pretty bad.'

A mere thirty seconds had passed since the gun's blast, but Brenan's body clock registered a full thirty minutes. She didn't know the extent of Stanier's injury, but he needed hospital and quick. The mental overload drilled even deeper with the thought that the prostitute in the back of Quinn's van was either dead or soon would be if she couldn't get to her.

Quinn's voice carried through the stillness with the rasp of a mechanic's bastard file. 'I know I got one of you.'

Brenan decided negotiations were at an end. Her temper overcame her fear. 'Drop dead, you piece of shit!' She kept down low and scrambled across to find Stanier. The detective had propped himself against a tree, legs splayed out in front and gripping his left thigh with both hands. 'It's bad, Eve… Femoral artery, I think… That's the trouble with being a cop… You see too much… get to know about things that are best not known about.'

Brenan leaned in close and unthreaded his tie knot. Stanier rambled some more but she spoke gently over his words. 'Keep the pressure on. Good job you're an old school cop, Ed.' She pulled the tie out. 'These new buggers don't even wear ties on promotion boards nowadays.' She pressed a little kiss against his cheek.

'The missus got me that one for Christmas… Other stuff, too… some books and nice single malt… Feel tired, Eve, so tired.'

'No nodding off on the job, Denry.' She squeezed a hand beneath the injured leg and threaded the tie through with it. She felt the sticky smear of blood, the tattered shreds of trouser. 'This'll hurt a bit, but it might wake you up.' She pulled hard on the two ends using all her strength and dexterity to blindly create a double knot. Stanier's stifled groan of pain turned into a closed-mouth whimper. Brenan had put a tourniquet on a man's leg once before and once on a woman's arm for that matter. The man was a road accident, the woman, ironically, a shotgun wound. The man died through massive blood loss. The gaping wound on Stanier's inner thigh seemed reminiscent of that injury and was still pumping even with his attempts at pressure. Her mind raced as her own blood supply was transformed into pure adrenaline.

The distant *click* of metal on metal signified Quinn's shotgun barrel snapping back shut. He'd replaced the spent cartridge.

The kidnapper's abrasive voice cut through the silence again. 'Two cartridges back in the tubes, lady copper. Bit of good fortune that you've survived – so far. I'd rather fuck you alive than dead, but we'll see which comes first.' He gave a laugh and started to casually saunter down the slope, shotgun dangling one handed at waist level.

Brenan wasn't going to give her location away with a reply this time and, anyway, she was busy. She gave Stanier's telescopic baton one last tightening quarter turn inside the knotted tie. 'Little trick I learned from Kobe,' she muttered, satisfied her creative surgical performance had finally staunched the blood. The words went unheard; Stanier was out of it.

Eyes now fully accustomed, she peeked through the trees to check on Quinn's progress. His slowly loping and cautious gait had brought him to within thirty yards. But that body language suggested uncertainty. He wasn't sure where they were. It wouldn't take him long to find them, though. Brenan thought long and hard – all of two seconds. She had to draw Quinn away from Stanier. She took in one huge and determined breath and then bolted out into open ground and sprinted towards the blackest bolt hole on offer. Sheer terror hurtled her forwards and threw her into a densely overgrown thicket which might as well have been the dark side of the moon.

Quinn's hatred pierced the night. 'Get you, you fucker!' He swung the gun upward at Brenan's darting outline and tugged at one of the triggers. The blast flickered a bonfire-orange pulse through the trees as it exploded upwards, shredding leaves and startling roosting crows into a crazy flapping retreat. It also recharged Brenan with even more adrenaline, impelling her forward like some deranged Olympic athlete. The solidly packed saplings and bushes she found herself crashing through had not seen the attentions of the CSI investigators or any other human interference for decades. Brambles ripped at her clothing and lashed her face and hands. Tree roots marshalled forces to rip every stumbling, panicking footstep out from beneath her. She tumbled out onto the lane, her arm almost pulled from its socket by a length of thorny dog rose snarled into a sleeve, and ran – but she was still thinking.

Brenan's suicidal ploy had worked and diverted Quinn away from where Stanier was lying. She needed backup right now and more than at any other time in her service. Her Jabra was out of range and her phone was lost in the undergrowth. She could only hope her partner's continued silence suggested to Quinn that he was dead. She also hoped that was not now a fact.

The madman's anger slid into the middle distance as his diminishing string of expletives proved that he'd not tried to follow through the thicket. Brenan's ribbon-cut face and hands, aching shoulder and bruised shins suggested he now had a physical advantage even greater than his male frame would usually allow. He also had a gun. She gulped in air and made the decision to take another pathway to her left and try to backtrack on Quinn. If her frantic notion was right, it could bring her out on the other side of the van. She knew Stanier's car was no use to her; the keys were in his pocket, along with his mobile. How she now wished she'd grabbed it.

Keeping to the grassy sides of the track she forced her exhausted limbs to jog quietly in what she hoped was the right direction. Quinn had gone silent, either that or he was too distant to hear – worrying unknowns. Minutes had gone by since she'd left Stanier and she was mindful that every single second counted. She furtively rounded a bend in the track, peering into the dense overgrowth on her left until eventually she captured a glimpse of white. It was Quinn's van.

She started to push her way through the bushes. What was Quinn's plan? Was he on his way back to the van? Had he abandoned it? Was he already there? Was the girl dead? Could she get back to Stanier and maybe even steal the van? A lot of questions, but she wasn't going to leave Ed, whatever happened.

With chest heaving and hands and face sticky with blood from a myriad of cuts, she crunched her way through, making more noise than she would have liked. Stopping for a second, she looked back down the slope, eyes searching for detail in the gloom. Huge oaks and birch trees shadowed the CSI's cut-back area, darkening the thick ground cover beyond into a crow-black featureless solid. She was unsure of Stanier's exact location but knew he was somewhere in the woods on the right. There seemed no sign of Quinn but, then again, he wouldn't advertise his return. A low wattage interior light, a necessary tool in Quinn's regime of perversion, was apparent as she approached the back doors and peered inside. Naked flesh: alabaster white legs and buttocks lay upon a filthy mattress. Tied wrists, blue nylon rope, dyed blonde hair, red shotgun cartridges, more of the blue rope but this length twisted and knotted around the neck. These things all blended to create a collage of heart-stopping horror. A twelve-inch hammer shaft lay by the woman's head, but had not been forced in between neck and rope; they had interrupted him. The legs moved and a muffled moan gurgled from the tightly gagged mouth. She was alive.

'I'm a police officer, I'm here to help. I'm taking the gag out, but you've got to keep quiet… It's me and you. He might come back.' She put one knee up into the van and reached forward, hooking her thumb into the gag and pulling. The girl coughed. 'I'm choking…. Chok…'

Brenan climbed inside on both knees, quickly breaking what was left of her fingernails, but managing to loosen the neck rope. The girl gasped as Brenan got on with her wrist ties. 'Thank you… Thank you. He was going to kill me.'

'I know, but we're not finished yet. It's Sadie, yes? He could be back. I've got no backup. It's just you and me…'

'No, lady copper,' Quinn's voice came from behind. 'There's three of us, and I do like a good threesome. No backup, eh…?'

Chapter 61

BRENAN TWISTED AND faced the two wide barrels of Quinn's shotgun. She was unsure if he'd reloaded the spent cartridge again or if he was still down to one, but it didn't seem to make much difference. She'd never been one for giving people thinking time. Tackling things head on and striking while the iron was hot were adages she'd been brought up with police-wise since her first arrest.

The two-footed back kick she produced carried every ounce of the power and aggression she could package, along with her very real will to live. Her hope to get the sole of at least one shoe under the shortened barrels of the shotgun and force it upward out of harm's way paid off, although a little more height would have been good. As well as achieving this all-important feat, the kick delivered an intestine tearing ramrod into Quinn's lower gut. Whether the pull on the trigger by Quinn was intentional or caused by the sudden vicious action would never be known. But the subsequent blast was so violent and in such close quarters that it threw the unprepared psychopath backwards into a stumbling failed attempt to regain his footing. The recoil wrenched the weapon from his grip and saw it tumble to the turf at the back of the van.

The twelve bore 00 buckshot rounds Quinn was using were deadly. Each cartridge, with its nine quarter-inch lead balls, could kill a deer and very definitely a human. The discharge missed Brenan's head by inches as it went on to explode through the van's roof.

It was an event the callous, murdering sex fiend was not expecting. No woman had ever dared or even got the chance to turn his aggression back onto him before.

Quinn was on his backside, legs straight and propping himself up on locked-out arms. Even in the poor light the astonishment on his pockmarked face showed clearly. But Brenan wasn't finished with him. She knew she had to completely immobilise him. She was also frighteningly aware that her adrenaline reserves were now at an all-time low. Her heaving chest and pounding heart rate were the consequences of the last ten crazy minutes and she was all but spent. In one movement she swivelled, slotted her toes down onto the edge of the tailgate and leapt like an Olympic butterfly swimmer off the starting blocks. Quinn wasn't quick enough to dodge to one side, Brenan's additional blood-curdling full-flight scream trapped him like a rabbit in headlights. He took the full force of her head-butt with all of its nose-breaking and teeth-snapping consequences. The searing pain was worsened for Quinn by two more similarly vicious head butts. Brenan was completely whacked now, though, and the flurry of clenched-fist punches she continued to deliver had no force in them.

Injured and bloodied as he was, Quinn grabbed Brenan's head with both hands and turned her onto her back. Her resistance came from burning muscles, from arms and legs which had turned to jelly. He sat on top of her and spat a mouthful of blood and broken teeth fragments into her gasping face. 'You're going to pay for this, copper!' His right hand grabbed fully down onto her left breast – nails penetrating through material. He bounced his buttocks hard down onto her stomach forcing a breath-expelling grunt from her mouth. His left hand reached round and slammed between her legs, forcing probing, scrabbling fingers into the crotch of her trousers. Her side-of-the-fist thumps at his chest were increasingly ineffective.

With a casual lifting of his right buttock Quinn delved into his hip pocket. The McDonald's video was running in Brenan's mind before Quinn's hand even got there. Her eyes took on the proportions of a *Star Trek* alien as she forced solid lead arms into more pitiful slaps. She knew what was in that pocket!

Quinn's blood-smeared features didn't mask his manic grin as he extracted the three foot length of blue nylon rope. Brenan's derisory volley petered out pathetically as the madman flexed the rope between his two hands just above her nose. He looped it over the top of her head and then pulled down sharply, bringing it behind her neck. Her ever-weakening struggles were casually ignored as he pushed one end into the knotted loop at the other end. 'One I made earlier,' he chuckled, and started to slowly pull on the rope.

'We know who you are, Jeremy.' Brenan choked the words out through her narrowing airway.

It gave her a second's respite as Quinn's muscles relaxed. He looked down at her, completely confounded. 'What?!'

'We know who you are, and we know where Poppy is. There are more fucking coppers in Evesham Gardens than Scotland bloody Yard right now!'

Quinn's jaw dropped sufficiently wide for Brenan to get an idea of the damage her head-butt had caused – not enough. She looked up at him, trying to draw on any reserves she had left to escape. He'd become motionless, staring out into nowhere. The pause lasted three, maybe four seconds. He had always looked like a madman, but now he was a broken madman. He snapped hard with both hands at the rope, flexed his shoulder muscles, felt the surge of blood as his own sinews stressed into quivering tension and started to haul the life out of her. Her back arched up from the turf, taking Quinn's weight upwards in one last reflex action before slowly sinking back as the darkness closed in around her vision and thoughts.

The two barrels of Quinn's shotgun pressed hard and cold into his right temple. He momentarily eased the tension on Brenan's neck, eyes moving in sockets to their extreme right corners. A sickly grin crept through the moustache of congealing blood which had formed on his crooked lips. 'Go on, pull the trigger. Let's see if you've got the guts.'

'You won't be seeing anything if I do, cuz you'll have no fuckin' head.'

Prostitute Sadie McVey rammed the gun hard into the bone of Quinn's temple to show she meant business. Her own dangling blue noose hung loosely from her neck. She was still naked and more of the rope hung from one of her wrists. 'Now leave her, you mad *bastard*!'

Quinn casually turned back to his work. 'This is how you kill someone. You can watch if you like.' He slowly started to pull the ligature.

Sadie's eyelids flickered as she prepared herself for the explosion and the recoil. She tightened her finger on the trigger. And pulled.

Her successive pulls on both triggers entered into the world of the frenzied, the hysterical even, as she continued to frantically repeat the process with an ever-increasing feeling of dread. Helplessness saw her shoulders slump as the weapon fell from her hands.

Quinn looked around. 'Helps if it's loade…' His sentence came to a premature stop as his wild eyes swept over and stared down the slope towards the track. Flashing blue lights peppered the black landscape, voices yelled instructions. Half-seen moving shadows between trees preceded a distant loud hailer voice: 'Armed police! Jeremy Quinn, put your gun down! Raise your hands above your head, and walk slowly out into the open.'

With the end of Brenan's ligature still around his palm Quinn sprang back to his feet. The action pulled Brenan's head upward in a sickening jolt and then saw it thump lifelessly back to the turf as he shook his hand free. The shotgun lay empty at the girl's feet. Quinn made a hesitant grab for it, but changed direction mid-stream. He'd never have time to grab cartridges and reload. He dashed the four yards for the van yanking the driver's door open. Another mid-stream change stopped him as his wide eyes were caught in a powerful searchlight beam. Three combat-clad Firearms Unit officers with night vision headgear scurried inside the tree line, assault rifles held ready as they made ground and hoped for an early view of Quinn. With seventy yards still to cover, they needed to establish the threat level. A couple of eager sounding barks from a police dog joined the mounting clamour.

Quinn's right hand made a scrabble for the flap of his trouser shin pocket. A tearing Velcro-rip preceded the sparkle of steel as a ten-inch hunting knife was drawn. He snatched the dyed-blonde locks of the prostitute and yanked her into a faltering, squealing backwards stumble. 'You're my ticket out of here. Now get in the fucking van.' The knife's point pressed hard into her neck, instantly drawing blood. An FU officer steadied his aim from fifty yards and calculated the risks between hitting a legitimate target or an innocent victim.

Brenan's left hand snatched out and grabbed Quinn's ankle. The panicking madman was taken completely off guard. The squealing woman turned herself from his grip leaving Quinn to violently kick away Brenan's grip. His desperate lunge for the open driver's door was spurred on by the intensifying shouts and dog barks. It also took him out of the FU's vision.

The van's engine roared into life under Quinn's panicking right foot and slewed around, rear doors flapping, in wheel-spinning, turf-churning lunacy. The quick-thinking Sadie grabbed Brenan's feet and swung her rag-doll outline in a sweeping semi-circle. Quinn's blurring tyres carved deep gouges where she had lain.

Quinn pointed the van down the slope, slammed his foot to the boards and started into a faster and faster gear-crashing one-way ticket to hell. Several figures dived for their lives as the wheels parted company with the uneven ground. The flickering speedo hit a full fifty miles per hour before the vehicle was stopped dead in its tracks by a parked and empty police firearms car. Quinn's ample-sized human frame, unrestrained by a seatbelt was seized by the forces of momentum and catapulted through the windscreen. He took half of the steering wheel with him but left most of his right leg behind. The airbag made a brave attempt at saving the murderer's life but managed to hold on to nothing more than his genitals. The remaining mangled remnants of Jeremy Henry Quinn were found in a sturdy English Oak some forty feet further into the wood. The tree was unharmed.

Brenan struggled to sit upright as a breathless Forrest and Scott ran up the slope towards her. 'Ed… Ed's been shot,' she said desperately.

'It's okay,' Forrest said as he helped her to her feet. She was shaking, unsteady, needing support. He put his arms around her and held her in close. She was doing her normal *Eve Brenan*: battling to keep her emotions under cover – trying to anyway. Forrest could feel those small spasms as she attempted to control the sobs. His voice was more of a whisper in her ear as he tried to comfort her 'We tracked you from your mobile phone signals and we managed to ring

Ed. That's how we got here so quick. They're with him now and paramedics are on their way.' More blue lights had joined the swarm down below.

Scott quickly handed over her knee-length Helly Hansen to the still naked and shock-shivering Sadie and helped her struggle into it.

'Is Ed really okay?' Brenan was glad of Forrest's arm around her shoulder as they slowly started back down towards the cluster of pulsating lights and flickering torches. Her question came with that usual scepticism – that *never-believe-anyone-until-it's-proven* philosophy – another Brenan trade mark.

'He's conscious,' Forrest said. He emphasised his reassurance with the slightest tightening of his arm, pulling her in a little closer. 'Reckon your Kobe-style tourniquet saved him.'

Scott and Sadie watched the two outlines for a moment as Sadie collected her thoughts. 'She saved my life,' the woman said.

'Looks like you returned the favour,' Scott replied.

Sadie dipped her head towards the diminishing outlines of Forrest and Brenan. 'They an item?'

Scott managed a little chuckle at the sudden out of context question. 'That would be good, that would be so good.'

Chapter 62

Day 25 Thursday 9th May

IT WAS HALF past two in the morning when Brenan, Forrest and Scott arrived back at the *Bottom Knocker*. Brenan had been cleaned up and bandaged at the hospital's Accident and Emergency unit. The phrase *dragged through a hedge backwards* was close to reality and it certainly fitted how she looked and felt. If it had been down to the doctor, she would still have been there – if only for observation on her neck injuries. The purple weals which stretched from throat to nape had been enough to bring some gushing TLC from Phoebe Halton. 'My God, you poor dear. Excuse my French, but thank God the bastard is dead!' It was a sentiment agreed by all. Nevertheless Forrest, Brenan and all the other investigators had suspicions that Quinn would be taking other terrible secrets to his grave.

Brenan's face and hands had suffered badly from scores of brushwood, thorn and bramble cuts, along with several to her legs where the material had been penetrated. Nothing required stitching and, as she was up to date with tetanus from her last roughhouse, she waved the doctor's concerns away with: 'Worse things happen at sea. I've got to get back.' She kept the pulled shoulder muscle a secret somehow but it was sore as hell.

Ed Stanier was in ICU. He'd lost a lot of blood and suffered some muscle damage to his leg. Brenan wasn't going to leave until his wife, Val, had arrived and they'd both been able to speak to him. Once she'd achieved that and convinced herself the medical experts genuinely believed he would make a good recovery, she happily switched her hospital gown for some decent clothing. Madeleine Scott's one o'clock dash to Brenan's apartment had provided jeans, trainers and all the other necessary.

A completely stunned Nicholas Mazewski was now doing his best to help out with snacks and coffee. His concern for Brenan, when he saw her, was confirmed by the large Scotch he supplied. She gratefully accepted.

Sadie McVey had been kitted out with some temporary clothing by one of the detectives and, despite the hour, was at the Sexual Advice Referral Centre for statements and forensics. Even though Quinn was dead, the entire usual procedure would still take its course. Brenan's phone call from hospital ensured that the girl would be treated well and helped. She promised to catch up with her as soon as she could.

The overall title, *Operation Denote*, had not been used much since it had been thought up. It was simply a file name. Its overriding objective had always been to find Poppy Hunt and free her from her eleven-year incarceration – *if she was still alive.* That unknown component, which was so often added to many a sentence, had fluctuated on a daily, if not hourly, basis. In doing so, it hauled the hearts and minds of the Major Incident Room team along with it in a roller-coaster of emotions. It had now become a rescue mission but still not one that could be bull-dozed headlong into. The circumstances suggested that Poppy was not in immediate danger, but the psychological effects on her were at the forefront of Brenan's mind. She'd been vocal with Forrest on that point, but he'd agreed with her from the off. In an ideal situation, he would let her know she was about to be rescued and that the world she had known for the past eleven years was about to be turned upside down – for the better. Whether or not a few hammer bashes at the sewerage pipe could achieve that, was something yet to be learned.

The team needed a temporary base. There were still a number of possible scenarios which could develop. The beer cellar had worked well so far but had its limitations. Nick Mazewski agreed to put the pub at their disposal. He was confident he could square things with the brewery come nine o'clock. It would stay closed to the public during the police operation. The Fettler's Lounge would be used as a briefing room and the large car park was also theirs.

There were a lot of dog-tired faces about, but sleep wasn't an option just yet. Several important team members, not involved in last night's action, were recalled to duty early. Charlie Sawyer arranged his blueprints and planning documents along one section of tables in the Fettler's Lounge before the five o'clock dawn chorus started. He'd assured Forrest of the arrival of a building inspector, a structural engineer and the Planning Enforcement Officer if needed by nine o'clock. A JCB was ready and waiting on a trailer at the council yard and its driver on standby.

Scott had stayed with Phoebe Halton as a second pair of ears at the sewage pipe listening post since the last time the cello had been heard. Her own passion for piano delighted Halton and created some eager conversation.

It was agreed that the search for clues on how to pinpoint Poppy's actual location and safely get her back would begin with a search of the bungalow and then the garage at eight o'clock. The last overheard spell of cello music strongly suggested that Poppy was not in immediate danger.

The timing would not only provide daylight to work in, but also allow for the quick response of any of the expert and technical help which might be needed. A temporary pathway had been cut through directly from the pub car park into the garden of the bungalow. It shortened the journey from several minutes to thirty seconds. CSI and forensics had already made an outside assessment.

The main team leaders all tried for a couple of hours' sleep on various bench seats in the Fettler's Lounge. DC Vicky Potts, though, commenced her in-car vigil outside 27, Meerham Gardens at 5 a.m. She'd be waiting on news from Forrest, but had been assigned the task of informing the Hunts whatever the outcome and as soon as news was available. Fluttering strands of blue and white police tape and a couple of arms-folded uniform constables now guarded the entrance to Evesham Gardens. The first reporter showed up at half past five after a phone call by a puzzled resident. He was quickly frustrated by shaking heads and total silence.

The arrival of eight o'clock on what was a bright May morning was broadcast to the Birchfield estate by the bell of St Stephen's church. Before the chimes had finished, CSI manager George Stodford held up the bunch of variously sized keys recovered from Quinn's van. The Yale latch key he chose was the one he was willing to bet a tenner on to open the bungalow's front door. As the sound of the bell's eighth chime died away, a certain irony went completely unnoticed. Twenty years earlier, that same bell had joyously pealed in celebration for the wedding of Kevin Powell's parents.

Stodford was right first time. The bungalow's door swung inwards. The sunlight, though, struggled to manage two yards into the pitch-black hallway. The CSI manager, in full forensic suit and face mask, pushed a little further and warily led his cameraman into the darkened passage under the beam of a powerful lamp. This would be a cursory assessment and an initial video sweep. They would be treating the scene with the same meticulous, evidence-gathering finesse as if Quinn were still available to be charged and taken to court. The priority now, though, was Poppy and how to get to her. Seeking clues to other, as yet unconnected, offences would be secondary. Only these two CSI would enter at this stage.

A police-only audience settled down into the comfortable chairs in the Fettler's Lounge as DC Tom Finlay selected the correct input on one of Mazewski's fifty-inch HD screens. Within seconds, Stodford's CSI video was streaming direct from the forty yards distant bungalow. Despite this not being an "in-the-flesh" viewing, it still somehow managed to present a spine-chilling and unnerving spectacle.

Finlay adjusted the TV's volume as Stodford's voice started to give commentary. His description enlarged upon the strangeness of the household and he started forward. A nitrile-gloved hand and white forensic jumpsuit sleeve made an occasional appearance on the screen as he pointed out targets for the cameraman.

Heavy, threadbare, dirt-caked curtains strained at their hangings in each room to completely block any hint of the outside world. Bare wires hung from ceilings and wall fittings. Not one single light bulb existed anywhere throughout the entire structure. The examination was only possible by virtue of the high-intensity lamp Stodford held. Strips of wallpaper had separated from plaster in varying degrees to hang part way down the walls in curled cylinders. Black mould concealed any idea of colour or pattern. Stodford's narrative mentioned, '…a strong musty smell,' giving rise to a theory that dampness and a lack of heating were the cause. Filth and decay pervaded every inch.

The building inspector was not privy to the film, but his theory that any route to an underground facility would have to be accessed through a floor hatch was common sense. His additional caveat that such a route to the underworld could be hidden by furniture, fittings or even a false wall added other considerations. Forrest had briefed Stodford on everything. Consequently, a good deal of the performance was taken up with floor space and possible access points.

It was as the viewfinder framed a bedroom door and slowly moved inside that the audience's hushed comments were silenced. A slow pan around the room brought wardrobes, drawers and cupboards into focus from a filthy black background. Piles of strewn and rotting clothing lay on the floor, together with old newspapers. Stodford's voice gave a general description and then his hand waved the cameraman further inside to a central position.

'A double bed, still complete with pillows, sheets and duvet, all blackened with mould and filth. Great quantities of old blowfly larva cases crunching underfoot.' The camera panned down to floor level and the screen filled with literally thousands of the small red half-inch long empty shells. 'I'm expecting the worst here,' Stodford's voice came through.

There was a slight jolt to the otherwise professionally stable video as Stodford's hand pulled back the rotting duvet. The blackened skull and other bones now on show were all completely devoid of flesh. The only hint of colour was the loop of blue nylon rope around its neck.

Stodford almost casually stated the obvious. 'We've got another.' He touched nothing and got back to the job in hand.

The two men met Forrest and Brenan at the front door ten minutes later. Arrangements were already being made for the full forensic search and the start of enquiries into the latest corpse.

It was no huge surprise to Brenan and Forrest that Quinn had added another to his tally and, whilst this was going to increase pressure even more, Poppy remained the priority.

Stodford assured them that the search had shown no signs of false walls or access to lower levels. 'No, nothing, boss. There's still a slight possibility of perhaps furniture or something hiding a hatchway or door, but it's unlikely. With all the filth in there I'd have spotted evidence of recent interference.' He pulled down his face mask and gave the garage a determined stare. 'That's got to be it.'

Stodford pointed Quinn's remote at the garage door and hovered a thumb over the button, ready to press, when an urgent voice shouted over from the pub car park. 'She's playing! Poppy! She's playing again!'

'Hold it there for a while, George,' Forrest said. He looked back at Brenan, tiredness showing easily through his darkening chin stubble. The pair set off across the garden to the pub car park and headed straight for the beer cellar door.

Phoebe Halton had been refreshed by a one-and-a-half-hour doze. She was sitting alongside Madeleine Scott, eyes closed, with her stethoscope firmly pressed against the sewerage pipe. A smile crept to her lips as her foot started to tap. She clearly knew she had company as there was no surprise on her face when she opened her eyes. 'Pop music now. My God, she's good. Dexterity doesn't even come into it. Wish I could hear properly. I know the tune – something from the eighties.'

'Yes, I know it too,' Scott said. Her hand had gone to her mouth as she struggled with her memory to grasp the song's title. She gave a frustrated shake of the head as she concluded that it was not going to come to her. 'Shall we try the hammer?' She looked up at Brenan.

It was agreed that now was the time to try to make contact.

Halton was a little slow to agree. 'Seems a shame to interrupt her but, yes, we must. Just wish I could pin down that tune.'

Brenan whacked the pipe a couple of times with the hammer. Halton and Scott both pressed their stethoscopes back against the pipe and searched for the right spot as though seeking a heartbeat. 'She's stopped,' Halton said.

'So she definitely heard then.' Brenan said.

The two solid, but distant-sounding taps that followed did not come from Brenan's hammer. No stethoscope was needed to hear them and only one second separated the first from the last. Each small resonance had the penetrating clatter of a pebble being dropped onto a stone floor. Halton, stethoscope still pressed to pipe, flinched against the sounds. 'My God, she's answered!'

No more comments were made, just silence as the two women searched with their stethoscope diaphragms against the pipe's painted metal surface. 'She's playing again,' Halton said. 'Same tune.' Her forehead wrinkled with concentration as she tried to wrench the song's name from her memory banks.

Scott raised a hand to hold the silent moment as it came to her. 'It's a *Moody Blues* number…' Her voice tailed off. The stethoscope fell away from the pipe to dangle against her stomach as she sat upright. A tear dripped from her chin as her breaking voice spoke the title: '*I Know You're Out There Somewhere.*'

Chapter 63

THE GARAGE DOOR commenced its rumbling climb. Stodford and his camera man stood alongside Forrest and Brenan, watching as sunlight flooded inside the double-car width for the first time in years. Brenan peered in, now able to put detail, perspective and colour to her previous visits. Stodford's survey and film record took less than ten minutes. Brenan and Forrest watched through the open door and Forrest made no objection as Madeleine Scott sidled in alongside. He was more than willing to accept that, without her, they would never have got this far. It was understandable that she wanted to be up close and personal with this part of the action.

Stodford stepped from garage concrete onto driveway tarmac. 'Can't be sure,' he said before any questions had been posed of him. 'If the access is in there somewhere, then it's well disguised.' He pointed back at the heavy workbench. 'That's covering some floor space, but no one could shift it alone.' He stared at the freezer. 'We know its drawing its power from elsewhere and, even from here, you can see some fairly recent looking marks on the floor in front of it. My best bet is that it's under there, but it'd be bloody heavy even empty.' He gave Brenan a stare. 'And we know it's not empty.'

Scott stared at the freezer thinking about its horrendous contents. This police case had been one hell of a wake-up call for her. She was beginning to feel hardened to some of her awful new experiences.

Forrest dropped to his knees and pressed a cheek against the dusty cold floor in the hope of a glimpse beneath. 'It's fitted onto a metal frame, heavy duty with rubber wheeled castors on the right-hand side.' He shuffled over to his left. 'Torch, George,' he requested, his left arm held out towards Stodford and eyes still fixed at ground level. The CSI manager duly switched on and handed over. 'Yes,' Forrest said, as he directed the beam. 'The freezer itself seems to be fitted onto a sturdy metal hinge post on this side. It swings outward. The marks in front are from the castors – several years-worth of use. It's a simple wheel brake to release it.

Stodford took a few shots of the freezer in place, dusted for prints, and then nodded the "okay" for Forrest to make his move. The DCI squeezed his hand under the right edge to locate the castor. He snapped the brake lever upwards, struggled back to his feet, took hold of the right-hand edge and pulled. He was expecting some resistance, but the industrial-sized appliance with its grisly contents trundled noiselessly and easily outwards. The quarter-circle route it took tracked the black wheel marks on the concrete. It came to rest with its rear panel a full ninety degrees from the wall.

The group looked down at the section of floor it had so neatly concealed. A three feet by four feet, heavy steel trap door lay flush with the surrounding stone slot into which it so perfectly fitted. A six-inch iron ring was fixed at one end, worn silvery smooth through years of daily use.

Forrest stood on the edge of the lip, took hold of the ring and pulled upwards. The vacuum effect created by its meticulous engineering resisted his initial attempt. There was a low inwards suck of air from below as the seal separated. It then effortlessly swung upward, aided by a cleverly fabricated counterbalance.

Out of the sun's reach, the square black void had all the foreboding of a bottomless mineshaft. Stodford's torch beam illuminated a full eighteen inches depth of masonry which had been sliced through the garage floor and the ceiling of the space below. 'Jesus,' he said. 'Look at the thickness! A metal light switch at the bottom edge of the cut came under the torch's light and along with it the suggestion of wooden steps leading down.

Forrest reached in, pressed the switch and settled on his haunches as a series of fluorescent light tubes flickered into life, bringing detail to the room beneath. The wooden steps were, in fact, a well-constructed heavy-duty staircase, complete with metal handrails. A grey painted hard-standing floor sat ten feet down.

There was an eagerness building between Forrest, Brenan and Scott to get down there and get on with it. Stodford shrugged and accepted that his CSI procedures had become a secondary issue. He followed the trio down the staircase.

They found themselves in a dusty room measuring some five metres by four metres. Smoothly plastered, yellow painted walls rose up to where the ancient-looking brick vaulted ceiling supported the weight of the garage above.

A door was fitted into the wall opposite. Complete with spyhole and serving hatch, its heavy steel construction immediately gave away its former life of cell door. They stepped over and a quick examination showed that the flap-down hatch had been welded shut, but the spyhole's sliding shutter still worked.

Brenan somehow shouldered her way in for a privileged first look and applied her eye to the spyhole. An immense and brightly lit corridor stretched away. Several open doors were fitted into the right-hand wall. The others took turns at their own peek before a short discussion ensued.

'We don't want to startle her,' Brenan said.

Scott's hand was clasped to her chin in a sort of worried, thinking gesture. 'I heard the tune she was playing. She's expecting us.'

'Let's go for it,' Forrest said. He looked over at Stodford, hoping the giant key on Quinn's bunch was the right one. 'Keys, George!'

The metallic, echoing clunk as the key slotted in perfectly is a sound unforgettable to any police officer and doubtless any prison warder. Forrest took a firm grasp, feeling the lock's heavy levers shift round as its mechanism drew back the deadbolt with a satisfying snap. He twisted the flat steel handle to release the latch bolt and watched as the door slowly swung inwards.

The little girl was five or, maybe, six and barefoot. She looked up, ringlets of dark curls covering her forehead, skin whiter than any skin they had ever seen before. She was wearing a Princess Pocahontas outfit, complete with headband and feather. She held a small bow and arrow in her right hand. She continued to look silently up for several seconds, her little chest rising and falling with each breath.

She turned her head to look down the corridor, her voice resonant and clear. 'The people are here, Mummy.'